I0831723

I've Never Danced

B.A. McRae

ISBN | 9780578944579

Cover Illustrations by Džana Serdarević

Table of Contents

Content & Trigger Warning

‖ severe anxiety ‖ ‖ toxic relationship ‖ ‖ grief ‖
‖ suicide ‖ ‖ self-harm ‖ overdose ‖ PTSD ‖

Within this story are sensitive topics that could potentially cause discomfort and or stress to some readers.

As an author who cares about their readers, I wanted to make these clear, and express that the topics mentioned above are not and should not be romanticized.

Humanity suffers and struggles with a multitude of hardships, let's always remember to be kind, because you never know what someone may be going through.

1. Coffee 

I loved my morning coffee.

I loved the smell of it.

I loved the simplicity of it.

I loved the sound it made when I dropped my sugar in.

I loved the taste that lingered in my mouth hours after I drank it.

My Grandpa gave me my first sip of coffee when I was four years old, and it's been true love ever since. Coffee is my comfort, my go-to when life sucks. So, as you can imagine, we're pretty close.

Love has and probably always will be my deepest agony. It's like that math problem on your homework you skip over, and hope makes more sense when you finish the rest of your work, but when you come back to it, it still makes absolutely no sense.

Besides the inevitable little crushes our hearts pump out in our early years, I've only been in one relationship. Only one within my nineteen aimless years on this crumpled-up-map-worthy of a place, and one was quite enough. I'm not talking about Earth, by the way; I've got nothing against it. I'm referring to what I suppose I would fill in on the dotted line next to home: Virginia Beach.

Regarding my relationship history and my feelings towards the thought of love, in the pie chart of relationships, it lands full speed in the small pie slice that reads ***The Absolute Worst.***

That was about a year ago, and granted, out of mainly peer pressure from my best friend, I've had a few dates and let my lips be kissed again. I haven't fallen in love. Really, I didn't feel a need to anymore, and I kinda had this vision in my

head I never would. And it wouldn't be so bad. All I really need for a start to a decent day was the sound of my coffee pot brewing, and I guess I just figure out the rest as I'm jiving along; the coffee really helps with that.
I worked at a nursing home a few blocks from my tiny apartment, and I'd bike there every morning and bike back hours later to another cup of coffee. As of right now, I don't have a lot of free time. But typically, I enjoy reading, watching TV shows and movies, letting my music carry me away, and spending time with my dramatic best friend. You know, the basic boxes you would click on under hobbies when making a profile. So, as you can so clearly tell, there just simply isn't any room for romantic notions in this oh-so-busy life of mine. Even if I wasn't sarcastic, and I happen to run into it, I don't know if I would budge.

Wait,

I apologize,

I take that back.

If you can be romantically captivated by a building, yes- love, you can walk right on in. For there is a small bookstore around the corner from my apartment building that gets me every time. I stop by whenever I have the chance, and I know the spines of practically every book there. In reality, I probably don't, but I go there at least once a day. I love the store's atmosphere and the smell of old and new adventures. And the clerk that works there is none other than the lovely character of a person I mentioned before, my best friend Carder.

So, I have that going for me to get through the days.
We've been best friends since middle school; our awkward souls were just meant to meet. He's a big flirt and just loves talking to people even though he hates most of them. I admire how outgoing he is, despite the fact it's gotten us in quite some trouble in the past with his big mouth.
But I could never stay mad at him; he's practically my other half.

2. Books & Such

I have today off, so what way to spend it then in the bookstore. My date with Netflix could wait a few hours or so, and it's always a joy to see Carder and all his sassy glory.

I loved the familiar and warm charm of the bell that rings when you open the door; I always have the biggest smile on my face.

"Well whoop-de-do, it's Lucy-Lou," Carder sarcastically greeted me, not even looking up from the computer at the counter.

"Oh, stop, you know you love me," Walking over to the counter and leaning in a little so I could sneak a peek at the screen.

"Okay, seriously, Lucy, you are going to get me fired; I can't have you looking at the merchandise list every time!"

I gave him a smirk because I knew he'd budge. He looked around carefully as if he actually cared whether the whole two customers in the store saw or not. Quickly we switched spots while I checked out what was coming in, and Carder started shelving some new books that must have come in this week. That's something I loved about this charming little place; it had a mixture of old donated books and brand-new books. The best of both literary worlds coming together; the intertwining of their attached aromas. Man, I love that book smell.

I was scrolling down the list when I overheard Carder say something about the front desk. My eyes slowly peeled away from the glossy screen as I turned my head. Classic Carder, sending *me* customers.

"Welcome to Books & Such. Can I help you find some books and such?" I chirped like an actual loyal employee.

Yes, your suspicions are correct; this has happened before.

I'm not going to lie. I didn't completely register (Ha, register, I'm standing at a register) the guy's appearance until he started talking.

"Umm yeah," he drew out just enough until he could find his following words, "Just looking for something to pass the time, I guess." The tone of his voice made me feel at ease, even though I wasn't feeling any anxiousness before. He's some kind of easing Wizard. You know, thank God no one can read my mind.
"He," kindly referring to Carder, "said to ask you because he '*doesn't know shit about books, just the stuff*?" His sentence ended with his eyes just a tad widened and a cute little crooked nervous smile.

I looked over where he was pointing, Carder with this ridiculous smile on his face. "Oh yea," I responded while glancing over at Carder to make sure he heard me. "We're most likely going to let him go soon." And like that, his stupid smile was gone.

Point for Lucy.

I walked from behind the desk and into the fiction aisle. "So, I'll agree to help uplift your request to pass the time if you help me out to what you enjoy reading." I proposed to him while slightly turning back to see who I was, attempting to flirt with. I'd probably get heckled by Carder when he leaves. When his eyes for a second caught mine, I turned forward again and continued walking through the aisle.

"Well, I enjoy a story with a good plot, you know? Something timeless yet unexpected." His voice almost sounded poetic. I silently laughed at myself for even thinking that.

"We have a lot of adventure books over behind this section-"
And in my moment of trying to be the cool, mysterious girl who works at a bookstore but doesn't actually work at a bookstore, I ran into the fricken poetry section and fell.

Am I shocked? No, not at all. This is a typical Lucy coordination malfunction.
Am I embarrassed? Entirely. Completely. I'd like to go into hiding, and oh look, some of the books fell with my clumsy ass; nice touch.

"Oh, geez!"

"It's fine! I'm sure the books will survive the fall. I mean, they are poetry books; they're probably both happy yet sad they crashed to the floor." Another attempt to be funny yet cute as I tried to gracefully stand up from my minor catastrophe. Key word tried.

"No, I mean," he kneeled by me and pointed to my forehead, "you're bleeding; I think one of the books cut your head a little bit."

Well, that's just great; I'll never see this boy again.
I felt my head where the now apparent throbbing was and looked at my fingertips. "Yepp, that is my blood coming' on out."
Goodness gracious, yea Carder is never going to let this one go.

"I'm sure your work offers some health care or something if it's worse than it looks."

"Oh, I don't work here," I blurted out. My eyes widened, and the guy's eyes mimicked. And this is why I am an awkward human being. I scrunched my face up and walked over to the front desk for the first aid. Passing Carder, I could hear him giggle as I lightly pushed him; I swear the situations he puts me in. I started rummaging below the desk for the first aid kit.

"Hey, I'm gonna take my break, bbbyyeeee" Carder said with a tap of his fingers on the desk and a chime of the bell as he left. I lifted my arm and flicked him off, a sweet sign of our affection, and then continued my search. He literally just left his place of work; what a diva. How does he still have this job?

"Well, let's find the cooperate of this crime." The customer called out to me while I was still searching.

I panicked and forgot I was under the counter. "Owe!" resulting in yet another head injury as I hit the bottom of it. "Ah, no, no, you don't have to clean that up!" Quickly I ditched the quest of finding band-aids and went over to the scene of the accident. As I approached, though, he was already propped against the shelf. With a book in his right hand and his left hand in his dark jean pocket, his thumb hanging out, catching a breeze from the window.

I was staring at him, like hardcore; oh geez, I really need to work on that.
His strawberry blonde hair wasn't messy, but it wasn't all gelled up and sticking out of his scalp like a cactus. And apparently, he was a fan of chucks; I like that in a complete stranger.
His eyes must have burned a hole in that book. Those grey-blue eyes probably caused my fall; they were so distracting.
Okay, I really need to stop looking.

After my overanalyzing, I realized he was holding the guilty book due to the tiny bit of now almost dry blood on the corner of the top spine. I opened my mouth to begin my apology for traumatizing him to ever walk into the store again when I was beaten to the punch.

"Her smile caught my eyes, like the way the sun searches through the leaves."

Oh my gosh, he's reading poetry.
No, no- he is reading the poetry to me.
The poetry that hit my head. The poetry that hit my head and caused my blood to flee my forehead.

"The feeling her smile gave me inside my chest was the warmest feeling I could receive. Her laugh would make you crack a smile, and her voice would melt you whole."

Holy goodness, yea, he was melting me whole; who was this guy? And why in the hell is he reading this out loud to me?

"I loved when I turned back to her and found she was already staring at me like she knew already we were matching souls. And even though we hadn't talked for quite some time, whenever we did, it was like we had never stopped. Though we both were moving along with our own separate lives, it was like our love for each other was on lock."

I thought he was joking when he started, but now he gently pushed himself off the shelf and continued reading it in his smooth voice. That transition right there was probably the geekiest badassness I'd ever seen.

"Like no matter who I was seeing, in the back of my mind, it was her I longed to be talking to. Somewhere in my messy mind, I had the crazy idea we were thinking the same thing, and someday we'd see it through."

I was lost in his words, I knew they weren't *his* words, but the way he was reading it was like he had ownership of the words. He didn't look up from the page, but he started to walk forward. My eyes widened, and I started freaking out inside; I let him pass me, and I just trailed behind him.

"We'd battle the broken hearts and smile through the pain. Because we knew one day, we'd see each other through the rain."

He was snaking through the aisles, and he turned once in a circle, smiled to me, and returned to walking and poetically reading.

"Somewhere inside me, I know, this most likely isn't true. But somewhere inside me was a feeling, a longing for her that was long overdue. In no way was she a perfect soul, but her soul fit perfectly with mine. Maybe someday again, we'll intertwine."

By the end of the last word, we had circled back to the counter, where we first met, and none of the embarrassment that just happened in the previous five minutes existed. He set the book on the counter, and I returned behind it. I was almost afraid to look him in the eyes after all that; what even was that?

He killed the silence with a small and simple smile. "Thank you." I could feel the confused expression on my face, and he answered before my lips even parted. "You helped me find something timeless and unexpected."
My immediate reaction was the stupid grin I know I make when something sappy happens on TV. In an instant, I felt that painfully familiar feeling of embarrassment that evilly warms my soul. He slid the book by my hand, and I gave him a small smile as I felt the material of the old binding touch my fingertips. Putting away the stupid grin, I started to ring up the book for him.
"So you don't work here, huh? You just came to visit your boyfriend or helping him out with the store?"

"Surprisingly, I don't work here, and Carder is not my boyfriend. I am not his type." I laughed, thinking about what a dangerously sassy relationship that would be.

"I don't know; I think I sensed some love in here." He replied with a bit of playfulness in his voice.

Just then, literally, saved by the bell.

"I got us coooffffeeeeee!" Carder sang, because if there is ever the tiniest moment in life where he can sing you damn well know he is going to take it with full force and grace. He pushed the door open with his back because his hands were full. Carder then turned around and discovered the customer was still there.
"Oh, fancy, embarrassment." Carder set my coffee down, winked at me, and headed to the backroom to do whatever. He's a troubling wingman but a good coffee man.

"Well, he seems like a nice guy," the poetry reading customer clucked a little.

"He has his moments." I smiled back while just finishing checking out his book for him. "That'll be four dollars even, please."

He pulled some singles out of his jean pocket where the loner thumb had been. I put his book in a small bag and handed it to him. Gently he took it and smiled at me. But it wasn't a quick smile and go. He hadn't turned or let alone moved a muscle; he was just smiling and looking at me with those kind eyes.

"I hope you find a band-aid without any further injury to your head" Once again, he broke the silence.
He's the silence destroyer.
That sounded a lot more violent than I intended.

"Oh yea, I actually forgot about that. Thanks again for helping me pick up the books and for the poetry session." I reminisced the spontaneous poetry reading; damn, he's like a badass combination of Michael Bublé and Shel Silverstein.

Smiling again and following it with a nod, he still didn't move; was he waiting for something?

"Aaaaanyting else I can help you with today?" I asked in a customer service-appropriate tone.

He looked at the ground and then back up at me, still with that smile. His eyes looked a little back and forth into mine; I could only imagine what he could find captivating in a pool of brown. And not even a cool brown at that, with a hint of green or something, just strict all-natural dark brown.
"I feel like, I'm going to fall for you, and you won't give me any reason not to."

Holy goodness.

What-

He said that so naturally.

And with that, he smiled at the bag, holding the book of poetry. The poetry that hit my head, and left with the ring of the bell that now haunted me.

I was still in the same position.

I was still trying to process what happened.

I was still not an employee here.

I was still bleeding.

A few moments after the bell rang, Carder came rushing in from the backroom, leaping onto the counter and sitting down right in front of me.
"What happened what happened what happened, I need details, come on!"

I turned to him with my forehead still bleeding, the top of my head still throbbing, and the confused expression back on my face.

What.

In the heck.

Just.

Happened.

3. Carder oh Carder 

It's been about three days since I ran into the odd but strangely attractive customer at Books & Such. Yesterday I had to work the 8am to 8pm shift; my coworkers and I lovingly call it *death's shift.*

After I was done at the nursing home, I biked back to my apartment and decided I would sleep until my next shift, which wasn't until 7:30am. I crawled into my twin-sized bed, decorated with homemade quilts passed down from my great grandma to my grandma, to my mom, and now to me. Sad to say, I'll be the one to stop this tradition; this lady ain't reproducing anytime in the future. And with that notion in my mind, of not procreating and leading a life of certain solitude, I began to drift off into the insanity of my corrupt dreams.

It's strange how you can't quite see the beginning of your dreams. I never really liked them; I always seem to have bad ones. And maybe that's because, after all this time, I assume they'll be uneasy, but either way, I wish I was one of those people who just don't dream.

The blackness of my dead-end thoughts faded into the image of a brown-haired boy whom I love with all my heart. Who knows my soul like it was written in his own imagination. Who has undoubtedly created their own little pocket on my heart, a pocket in which I can dip into thousands of moments and memories.

This boy is Colin, my brother.

Colin's a year younger than me, but it felt like we were only mere moments apart. My parents bragged quite often about how they had the best kids, and we never fought. Which was true. We rarely argued unless one of us brought up some smack about the other's favorite show, character, or superhero; then all hell would break loose. We took our interests very, very seriously.

Okay, we're dorks, we get it.

Most people from the outside looking in thought we were weird for being so close, but it's whatever. We're just two puzzle pieces that fit together. Best friends, in other words.

As my dream submerged past my brother's face, I saw the setting of the apparent show being put on for my brain tonight. I was in an apartment that appeared to be Colin's. We were wrapped up in our own blankets on a comfy couch, watching one of our favorite shows: *BBC Sherlock.*
The apartment was small, a little drafty, which would explain the blankets, but it was cozy. Colin had some posters hanging up; that was him all right. Maybe this would be a pleasant dream after all.

We were totally engaged in the show; I think we both forgot the other was there, or at least I may have. I hadn't even noticed that Colin had gotten up and made popcorn until he laughingly placed the bowl in front of me. Whatta gent I tell ya.

As we were reaching the peak of the episode, suddenly, the screen was frozen. For a second, I was pissed because I thought the Wi-Fi wasn't working or something, but I got that weird tingly feeling you get when someone is looking at you.
Turning my vision from the captivating screen to my side, I saw that Colin had the remote in his hand, and he was looking at me. His eyes looked so sad.

"Hey, whatcha think ya doin' huh?" I threw him my best Boston accent, which best is very generous because my accents are horrible. But doing random accents is an inside joke of ours, and I thought it would cheer him up.

"Lucy, do you think Mom and Dad hate me?" Colin desperately asked.

No accent back.

I guess it didn't work.

I wanted out of this dream already.
Somehow, my dreams usually come back to some variation of this question Colin asks. I hate these dreams.

"Colin stop, you and I both know our parents adore you. So stop!" My throat didn't want to claim the ownership of this tone and volume; I hated yelling. It sounded unnatural coming from me and especially towards him. But I can't handle this. I can't take this repeated question.

We sat there in silence as my words marinated the room, and our eyes were fixated on each other. I felt like I couldn't move, and my vocal cords had lit their closed sign. His eyes were so deep when you were looking closely at them. Really everyone's eyes are if you give them the attention.
There was something about this moment and his brown eyes staring at mine that was just a slightly different copy of mine, that made my body as frozen as the TV screen. When you focus on something for so long, your vision begins to get a little hazy. I'm not sure why this is, but my vision felt like it had just gotten off a merry-go-round and was trying to regain its balance.

Out
and in.
Out
and in.

And finally, my vision became crisp again.
As my eyes refocused on Colin's forever resting-concerned expression, his eyes were completely gone from his face. Black, disgustingly inhumane holes were where his brown eyes should be, and still, he stared.

I screamed,
I screamed at the top of my lungs as I looked at my brother in horror, and my heart wondered where his precious eyes had gone.

Then my surroundings became as black as the holes on his face, and I had woken up. I sat straight up; I was in a cold sweat. My face was wet. I felt my back, ugh gross; more sweat. But now, my disgusting back sweat and the terrible dream were the least of my worries as my ears perked to an unwarranted sound.
I heard my front door shut. I looked at my phone; it's 3:30am. Slowly, I got out of bed, trying not to make noise as I grabbed the aluminum bat I've had since I was a kid from under my bed.

"Come to murder me huh, why couldn't you come when I was on more than a few hours of sleep? Ya no morals bastard." I mumbled quietly, with some audacity within me.
I tiptoed out of my room and made my way down the hallway to the living room and front door. I could hear my mom now, oh man. She'd be crying to Heaven, why I couldn't have had some social skills so I would have a boyfriend or roommate to help *'protect me'* so I wouldn't have been murdered by an early bird psychopath.

My heart felt like it was going to leap out of my chest as I turned the corner to the living room. In one, surprisingly swift, motion I turned on the light and screamed, hoping it would alarm the intruder. Whelp, it alarmed the apartment building alright.

"Carder!" I exclaimed as I held the bat in one hand and slapped his arm with the other. "What the hell are you doing?!"

"Oh, like I can't stop by and see the only person I hold dear to me and kept connections with after high school. My best friend, my platonic soul mate, wow Lucy, thought we were better than this. And you know I bruise easily; I do not appreciate this." If I could compare him to someone right now, it would be *Miranda* from *The Devil Wears Prada*, my gosh, he is so dramatic.

I looked at his Louis Vuitton overnight bag, which he spent all his graduation money on, that was sitting by the door, and then looked back at him with a cocked eyebrow. He let out a giant sigh and made his way to the couch. To which I followed his dramatic parade, waiting for the floats of explanation to drive by and throw me candy. Ooo, now I want candy.

"Fricken Jason. I gave him two years of my life, and now they're gone." He let out as he plumped down on the old cushions.

I knew Jason was a total douche, but he made Carder happy, and hell, that was hard to do. Sitting down beside him, I gave his hand a squeeze; through our years of friendship, that was our little sign of reassurance.

"He cheated on me. He cheated on me and then broke up with me!" He started to get worked up; he rarely ever cried, he hated to cry, but this was one of those *'I could really care less'* moments.
"And you know who it was with? Huh? Sara. La puta Sara, with her fake ass breast implants and stupid blush. She looks like she's from a poorly supervised 50's cartoon. So, I guess Jason is bisexual. Just one of the many secrets he kept from me. And can we just take a moment to reflect on how of course, this would happen to me? That Jason would cheat on me with the woman who did our makeup for our one night of drag at the club. Of course. How did I not see this coming? The world hates a happy Carder. And my drag was damn good that night; he was mediocre at best-"

He was out of breath from venting and yelling and crying. He wasn't crying anymore, though. His processing is letting every spill out and burst at once, and then he pulls himself together. It was like a very abrupt firework show of feelings. But hey, whatever works. And I'll be here, no matter what.
We were holding hands in silence for a bit. Sitting in silence with Carder never felt quiet in a sense, though. We've always had a good connection of energy between us.

"I sincerely thought you lost the key I gave you a while ago, so it didn't even cross my mind that it could be you." I realized I was still holding onto the bat. Then my

uncoordinated clumsy self just decided to drop it, and then the sound of it hitting the wooden floor scared the life out of both of us. Our hands clasped tighter for a split second, then we looked at each other and laughed—a moment of comedic relief. Then our hearts returned to the reality that was at hand.
No pun intended. Slightly.

I glanced back at his bag by the door. "If you're moving in, I'm alarmingly surprised at the one bag." I saw the corner of his mouth turn a little; at least inside, I made him giggle just a tad.

"Yea, I'm sorry I didn't call, I figured you were almost dead from your last shift, so I tried to come in quietly. Jason and I were arguing all night, so I just packed some things and left." His fingers, which were wrapped around mine, fidgeted a little. "Honestly," His voice sounded quieter for a moment, "I don't even really miss him." He looked forward as I was looking at him and sidebar: he has a very exquisite jawline. "He was gone a long time ago." His voice was back to its Carder-self.

"He doesn't deserve you, Carder, and you can stay here as long as you need. You've already had a drawer of your own things in my bathroom since I moved here, so you're halfway there!" I tried to give him a smile that would reassure him everything would be fine, but I could tell it lacked some emotion from my lack of sleep.

His gaze came back to me as he gave me the best half-smile he could muster. We were both deprived of several things right now, but now the only thing we could control in fulfilling was rest. Carder doesn't really do emotions and sadness; he prefers life to be a mixture of a musical and a sitcom in his head. And so, he walked me to my bedroom, and I heard him set my alarm for 6am.

I sloppily collapsed in my bed like a person at the end of their 21st birthday.

"Scooch ya size two"

I scoffed at him. Yeah, right, size two- try size gazillion.
Don't judge me; I can't do numbers or comebacks right now.

I was so exhausted I let him slide me over as he then made no effort at all to be subtle while climbing into my bed.

"This is ridiculous; you need a bigger mattress," Carder grunted while trying to find a comfortable position.

"Would you stop moving" I sighed as my eyes were closed, and I could feel my body craving sleep. I winced suddenly to the reaction of coldness and Carder's mischievous little snicker. "Carder, I'm warning you right now I will literally break your legs if your cold feet touch my back one more time." Finally, he gave up after a few more rotations and hopeless sighs.

"Big spoon or little spoon," Carder said during a yawn.

"Well, I'm not rolling over."

"Gosh, you needy little woman."

We both laughed a little and then hushed ourselves into the quietness that occupied the room. I was way too tired to care about anything; I think we both were. And I think we both needed the feeling of being close to someone. I was terrified of falling into the same dream again.

4. Scappy 

Carder informed me that morning, via text, that he would gather his remaining things from the place he and Jason used to share when he was done with his short morning shift. When I came back from my shift, he was there. I could tell he was still heated by everything; I didn't blame him, so I just headed to take a trip to the rain room.

I cannot explain the amazingness that is a shower after a long day of work. Granted, I love my job, I do; it's just, some days take a toll on me.

"Sorry I didn't say anything when you walked in, Girly."

Honestly, I shouldn't even be surprised. I peered my head out of the shower to see Carder sitting there like this is a natural thing to do. We both laughed as I put my head back in. "It's fine; I know you're going through a rough time."

"Well, still. Oh, I did actually come in here to talk to you about something."

"Oh really," I poked my head out again, "I thought you were hitting on me" *'Seductively'* winking.

"Woman lay off- I just got dumped. No, it's about your lover from the bookstore. He came back in today!"

I turned off the shower,
popped my arm out of the curtain,
and Carder put a towel on it like it was a rack,
as I then wrapped it around me.
I stepped out of the shower and sat on the edge of the tub.

"Lucy, this guy likes you, like a lot; it's weird!"

"First off, thanks, and secondly, I'm sure he doesn't like like me."

"I know what's happening" He looked me dramatically in the eyes. "Lucy, we are in a Nicholas Sparks book."

"You need help. Go get it." We both joined in for a laugh, and I let him continue.

"But really, he came into the shop and looked over at the desk and realized you weren't there. I spared him the awkwardness of aimlessly walking around the store, called him over to the desk, and asked him if he needed help finding anything. Of course, I made it *super* obvious because that's my job as your best friend. So, he tells me that he and I should get coffee so we can talk. Next thing I know, I'm lost in those fricken eyes of his, Gurl those eyes are right on point. Like, damn. Anyway, my shift was done in like five minutes, so we walked to the coffee shop. He started telling me how you seem so beyond uniquely interesting, his words, and I said, '*yes, obviously she is the best person ever!*' Anyway, he keeps talking, and he saw that I was distracted, so he stopped and asked me what was wrong. I was so done with everything that just happened with Jason, I let it all out and told him fricken everything. He's an excellent listener. Then, he took a giant swig of his coffee, slammed it down, and said, *'Let's get your stuff back from that lying son of a gun.*"

I could tell from his mimicked reaction, he saw my eyes widen; and I can't lie, Carder is a great and dramatic storyteller.

"Oh my gosh, it was so awesome! Like, I couldn't believe it. We got in his Jeep, and I showed him where the apartment was, and I saw Jason's car parked there, so I was like *'Hey, you should probably stay in the car, things could get ugly,'* it was like a *John Wick* moment, ah! It was so cool, he whipped out two pairs of aviators and handed one to me, like who the hell is this guy!? We put them on all cool and headed up there. Immediately as we walked in, Jason tried to act all tough and protective over me. Like, who the hell does he think he is, and bookstore guy was like *'Carder, you can go get your stuff,'* so I went and next thing I know I'm

hearing yelling, so I hurried back to the living room with my hands full. Right when I got in, ***BAM!*** He punched Jason square in the face! I was like, holy crap! Then he grabbed Jason by his shirt while he was on the ground and got all in his face and said, *'You disappear, got it? You are no longer in Carder's life. You're gone.'* Then he looked down at Jason's shirt and pants and then back at his face and said, *'You have horrible taste in fashion.'* Then he let go of his shirt and escorted me out, and Lucy, it was so awesome! Like that kind of thing never happens in real life! It actually made me feel better about everything."
Carder had the biggest smile on his face as he kept rambling; I was zoned out imagining everything he just said. Damn, it was like badass action movie meets coming-of-age feel-good bro film.
"So, we gotta make you look hot; this wet hair isn't working for me."

I snapped out of it. "Wait, what're we attempting to look hot for? And you know I don't care for that word choice."

Rolling his eyes, he began to fill in the blanks. "I swear, what am I? A rerun episode of *Full House*, don't you ever listen to me?" Carder stood up and put the tips of his toes against my wet pruney ones and then cupped his hands around my face, moving it playfully back and forth with each word he said next.
"Yo. Lova'. Is. Seeing. You. TONIGHT!"

At that last word, he put my head back straight, looking right at him. I imagine the face I had was not the face he was hoping to see. I felt scared but happy at the same time. I was Scappy.

"Oh, don't give me that; you haven't gone on a real date since that Seth douche." I gave him a stern look. "Sorry. You haven't been on a date since *Voldemort*."

"That's better, and I don't even know this guy! I don't even know his name; what the heck is it anyway?"

Carder looked away for a second with this straining look on his face and turned back to me with bewilderment. "Sweet Mother of Joan Rivers, I don't even know his name. It never came up!"

"How does that not come up?!" I stood up in protest, my towel almost falling off.

"I don't know! We were in a flippin' action movie; there was no time!"

This was just fantastic.

Fan-Fricken-Tastic.

I had a date.

I had a date with a stranger.

I had a date with a stranger that walked into a bookstore that I was working at,
but I wasn't actually employed there,
and he read poetry to me
a girl he had never seen before.

Holy Buckets.

I am terrified.

5. Making it or Breaking it Moments 

Twenty-five minutes.

I had twenty-five minutes to achieve Carder's *'Date Perfection.'*

I had twenty-five minutes to make sure I smelled okay.

I had twenty-five minutes to find the right shoes.

I had twenty-five minutes to mentally prepare myself.

Carder, of course, took over on the outfit side of this abrupt change of plans.

Did I even want to go on a date?

I'm not ready for a date, am I?

Dramatically, Carder made me snap out of it by turning my head to face him while holding up different pieces of contestant clothing. I kind of just zoned out while he did his thing. I nodded when I heard his voice emphasize something. And that was probably his fashion-passive-aggressive way of saying, *'Sure, you could formulate your own fashion opinions, but this is the right one.'*
Eventually, we found the winning outfit as he stood me in front of him, and he stepped back.

"Honestly, why am I not on TLC or something? I'm a genius." Looking at me like I was a piece of art he had just spent months on.

"Wow, Mr. Humble, should I step out of the room so you and your ego can have some alone time?" He waved his hand, dismissing my comment as he was lost in his *'Fashion Masterpiece.'*

"I'm glad we went with this natural look; well, I know this is how you always look but let's just say it was my call." He spun his finger in a circle as he spoke to me, "Go ahead, look at what I've created, be proud of me."

I turned around to my reflection, and I gotta hand it to him; I was happy with the result. My hair had this loose, wavey look to it, I was wearing a plain white t-shirt with a bit of v in it, dark jeans, and Carder decided to be bold and put me in my red converse. Typically, I avoid seeing myself in the mirror, but he made me feel so, well, kind of confident. And that was mighty hard to accomplish.

Point for Carder.

"Carder, I'm so nervous; what if we have nothing in common? What if I don't even want to go, or I'm not ready?" I gasped loudly, turning around, and grabbing his shoulders. "What if he hates *Sherlock*?"

"You know, other women would be worried like, *'OMG what if he like doesn't think I'm hoottttt'* but not you, you've got your nerdy priorities right on top," He teasingly replied.
Releasing Carder from my grip, I sighed, drug myself to the living room, and plopped myself on the couch. He took a seat next to me and rubbed my back. "He'll probably be here in a few minutes." Patting soothing little circles on my anxiety-riddled back. I wrapped my arms around my stomach and focused on my shoes.
"Lucy, you're going to be just fine. And so what if it goes horribly wrong and the guy is a total weirdo, you know what you do?" I let go of the focus on my shoes and turned to Carder, looking him in the eyes. "You come back home, laugh it off, and keep living. And you can hit me in the arm again if you want."
This guy, he always knows how to put a stupid giddy smile on my face. It also made me smile that he called this place home. It really did feel like home with him here. There was a quiet knock on the door suddenly, and with much excitement, Carder tapped my knee with the rhythm of his words "Show Time!"

He got up like he was on his way down the wedding aisle, and I got up like I was on my way to the execution aisle. Carder graciously opened the door, revealing the darling face of the poetry guy. It wasn't until Carder opened the door all the way that I saw we were wearing almost identical outfits.

Oh my gosh,
there was an awkward silence,
already,
and we hadn't even walked out the door
let alone moved!

"We're twins!" He said in a cheery tone, still standing in the doorway.

"Yea, I need to go rekindle my confidence and watch some RuPaul or something" With that dramatic statement and an exchanged handshake, Carder went down the hall to his new bedroom. And then there were two of us.

I looked at the mystery man's outfit; he was wearing a white t-shirt with dark jeans and white all-star chucks; so close, but no cigar. We both gave each other a grin as he held the door for me, and we made our way outside.

"Is this your car?" Asking as I pointed to the clean white Jeep parked on the side of the street.

"Yepp, that's it!" He seemed so calm and easy-going, like he wasn't nervous at all. I hope I was giving off the same vibe. He opened the passenger door for me, then did a little jog around to the driver's side and smiled at me as we both were in our seats. "So, what would you like for music?" He asked, starting up the Jeep.

"Oh, it doesn't really matter to me" I could tell my voice was choppy, and I sounded nervous. Come on Lucy, let's pull it together.

"This could be the make it or break it moment; you can tell a lot about a person based on their music." Before pulling out into the street, he gave me another smile and focused back on the road, his head barely bobbing to the sound of the blinker. "Madam, could you please retrieve a cassette out of the glove box?" He said in this mild tone British accent.

Grinning a little at his dorkyness because it reminded me a bit of Colin, I accepted his request without a word. Upon opening his glove compartment, though, a flood of cassettes escaped out and fell at my feet. Startled, I was quick to apologize and pick them up. Well, as many as I could at a time, this glove compartment was packed full of cassettes.

"Oh my gosh, I'm so sorry! Please don't worry about it; I should really clean it out. My sincerest apologies. You can just pick a random one, whichever you'd like!"

How did his smile already feel reassuring in some way? And he's either really positive and smiley, or he smiles a lot when he's nervous. None of the tapes were really labeled, so I just picked one that was colored with yellow and blue strips and handed it to him. A smirk was painted on his face when he saw what tape I picked out.

"Well, I believe" He flicked the tape up with his fingers as it spun just a little out of his reach, and he caught it again. "Fate helped you pick this tape" he popped it into the radio.

He was trying to be all badass and cool,
damn it,
it was working.

The first song was fading into the speakers; I felt like I knew this song. I swear I know this song. It made the whole car seem so cheery, and like we had our own little party, I was getting lost in the crispness of the instrument's sound. The words started to come in; the guy singing had this raspy tenor voice, and it was really unique. And now I could hear my *'date'* singing along with the artist, and the first thing I learned about him, other than his talent to read poetry, is he is indeed not shy when it comes to singing in the car. He turned down the music for a moment. "Do you know this song? It's one of my favorites by Van Morrison."

I wanted to impress him, it was my turn to be the cool and mysterious one, but all in store for me was a bland response. "It sounds really familiar, but I'm not sure."

"That's fine! Hey, you can set your inner band-choir geek free; we all have one" He laughed and hushed it with a smile, turning up the radio again and continuing to put on his little show.

I looked over at him, singing his heart out; this guy was such a geek and so gosh darn proud of it! I felt crazy giving in, but I pretended to play the air guitar for him; he was thrilled to see that. He belted out the notes with pitchy confidence.

" *With you, my brown-eyed girl!*"

Oh my gosh, those really were the lyrics; there's no way he didn't plan this. He turned over to me, leaning in a little "You have to sing this next part with me" he leaned back to his seat and once again began to sing the little break-down of the song. I let him sing, and then I shrugged and thought, why the hell not and sang with him. I started laughing and caught my breath from singing loudly; he turned the radio down a little.

"So, how was that for make it or break it?" Turning for a second to ask me with this smile, I couldn't help but reflect; come on, it was too cute.

"Well, I'll give it to you, just because the song was catchy." There's lots of smiling today; my face actually hurts a little. He gave me a generous nod and kept his eyes on the road, still smiling.

It was quiet now, as the tape kept playing softly in the background; I think he forgot to turn the volume back up, or he wanted me to talk or spark up a conversation. Either way, it was starting to get awkward, so he was going to get one of his wishes.

"Soooooo, where are we heading?" I popped some whimsical curiosity in.

"Well," taking a deep breath, "It is a whopping 75 degrees, which is pretty nice for a late afternoon."

"Yea, it is a pretty nice night," Observing from out the window.

"I was thinking, if it's alright with you, we could walk along the boardwalk; does that sound okay?" He turned his head toward me to see my response.

I smiled and nodded. I don't know what's up with me, but my words are getting caught in my throat. I felt like a moron, but he just kept on smiling. As he parked the Jeep, it actually startled me a little how quickly he got out of the car, ran to my side, and opened my door. He was trying to catch his breath subtly. I unbuckled my seatbelt and hopped down as we then began our walk.

"Kinda looks like we planned this, huh?" He said, gesturing to our outfits.

I let out a little laugh "Yea, aren't we adorable," oh my gosh, why did I say that.

"I dare say we are. I especially like your shoe choice, nice touch."
Again, I just smiled and tried to look around at everything. I loved the boardwalk towards the end of the day, all lit up and full of sounds. I hadn't been out here for, well, actually a long time.
"So if you are up for it, I propose we play a game."

I thought about it for a second, amused by his peculiarity. "Okay, what game do you propose we play?"

"I call it the Question Game, creative I know; we just go back and forth asking each other questions, making conversation in between"

"Alright," I turned over to look at him. "You first" We made eye contact for a second and then turned away.

"Where were you born?" Turning over to me with that damn captivating smile.
I used both hands and, with my pointer fingers, pointed at the ground.
"No kidding? Born and raised here in Virginia Beach?"

I nodded with a sigh.

"Do you mind me asking why you never left?"

I thought on that one for a moment. "I guess I never found my opportunity to leave." Things were getting to sound serious, so I changed that mood fast. "Alright, Mr. Mysterious Man, what is your name?"

He laughed, and I joined him for a moment. "That's right; we never did exchange names, did we? How about ladies first." We stopped walking, now facing toward each other like we were meeting for the first time. "Hello Miss, you have adorable shoes" He put his hand out, "Might I ask your name?"

I couldn't help but laugh as our hands met for a classic shake. "Why hi, I'm Lucy MacArthur, and you are?" He shook my hand, then gently let it go and continued onward. My jaw dropped while still smiling as he kept walking, and then he turned back to me.

"Miss Lucy, come along now; we can't have you getting lost," Giving me this sassy playfulness in his voice.

I caught up to him, and then we continued our walk. "I believe you still owe me an answer." Giving him the sass right back.

"I kinda like this Mr. Mysterious character though, gives this timeless effect, don't ya think?"

I nudged him. "Oh, come on, what is it?"

"Hmmm, maybe by the end of the night" He flashed his smile at me and then pointed up at the giant lit-up Ferris Wheel the boardwalk was famous for. "Would you like to take a trip?"
I nodded, and we got in line. Surprisingly it didn't take very long to get on the ride. We got into the rocky seat. The machine started up again, halting every few moments to let the previous passengers off.
"Lucy, I believe it is your turn since I asked if you wanted to join me for a nice trip in here."

"Oh yes, hmm, let's see," I paused. "Well, where were you born and raised?"

He looked out to the boardwalk, embracing it all, and then answered my question while still enjoying the view. "I was actually born in England; my parents were on a trip for business, and I was a premature baby. They really should have postponed the trip, those crazy kids. But I was mostly raised in the big NYC."
I raised my eyebrows, turning my head toward him as the ride came to another rest. My mouth opened to talk, but I stopped. He was so lost in the sight of how the city looked from up here. And man was the one defiant side profile he had.

MMM- Oh, goodness, I think he can tell I was staring at him. Whelp, oh well.

"But anywho," Turning his attention back to me, though I was no match for the beautiful view. "Who is your favorite person in the whole world?"

I gave him a surprised look and bit the inside of my lip while thinking about that oddly quick question. "I'd say my brother, what about you?"

"Bob Ross, please do tell me more about your brother,"

"Bob Ross? Why Bob Ross? Oh no, we really don't have to."

"Because Bob Ross is the best, and I am terribly sorry, but the rest of the game is canceled until further notice, in place of family discussion." He turned his whole body, shaking the cart in the process, folding his hands in a praying position under his chin, waiting for me to speak.

Letting out a sigh, I gave in. "His name is Colin." Only because he was kind of adorkable.

"What a nice name; what's he like?"

"Total geek, like you" I smiled and looked out to the view "Big heart, loves TV and writing."

"He sounds like one heck of a character," Joining me with the view viewing, "Can you tell me a story about you two, please?"

I took a deep breath, shuffling through memories in my head; why was he so fascinated by this? And why is it so hard for me to talk about?

"Let's see, when Colin and I were kids, our parents gave us money to see one of the *Harry Potter* movies in theaters. This was a big deal because we had just recently become absolutely obsessed with *Harry Potter.* But long story short, we ended up getting kicked out of the theater because Colin and I kept chanting out spells and waving our homemade wands in the air. Now it's hilarious, but at the time, I was terrified because an usher came up with their flashlight, scolding us. Colin looked at me and saw I was scared, then he turned back to the usher, jumped right up, pointing his wand at them, and shouted a spell. Then he got on his hands and knees as I did the same, we crawled under the usher's legs, and we sprinted for the exit. I think we were too afraid to go to that theater for like a year" I giggled and sighed as I felt myself trailing off.

"That was a long time ago." We reached our time to get off the Ferris Wheel and returned to our walk. I didn't really want to talk about Colin anymore, though. "Mr. Mysterious, why did you move to the oh-so-grand land of Virginia Beach?"

"It's not as exciting as you may hope." I really liked listening to him talk. He was so poised and smooth. "My great aunt, whom I never knew, passed away a few weeks ago. To my surprise, I inherited her little house just outside the city. I asked everyone at the funeral why she would leave it to me, and all I got was, *'She always wanted to get to know you, but you lived so far away.'* I then found out she was actually my God Mother; I didn't even know I had one of those."

"I'm so sorry for your loss. And you never knew you had a God Mother? You are just full of surprises, aren't you?"

"I do believe that's my job, given my title" He smiled and gave me a little nudge as I nudged him back.

"Where's the farthest you've traveled, Miss. MacArthur?" Again, I used both hands and pointed to the ground. He stopped in his tracks and stared at me with bewilderment.

I smiled and kept walking, then I stopped when I was a little ahead and turned back to him, finding he was still staring at me. "Come along now; we don't want you getting lost, do we?" I turned back around and started walking. I tried to walk in a more intriguing feminine way, which resulted in me losing my balance a little and swiftly transitioning back to my default walk.
Or as Carder so caringly calls it, the *'virgin walk.'*

He ran up to me. "You mean to tell me you have NEVER left this town?"

"Never Never Never"

"That is insanity, your whole life just in these walls of Virginia Beach?"

"Yepp, I've just been roaming around here. Where's the farthest you've traveled?"

"Italy, with my mom. Hey!" He just lightly placed his hand around my arm and pointed up to the tall coaster ride to our right. I could feel it. I was giddy he was touching me. "Wanna ride it?"

I hadn't been on the Skyscraper ride before because I'm not psychotic and would like to live. But I couldn't stand to say no. And there he stood, still with his hand gently around my arm, getting all antsy. I finally let out a yes, and instantaneously he let go, and we booked it for the ride, which had no line—surprise surprise.

"I'll ask the guy about the ride," He reassured me with a smile. "Excuse me, sir? Could you please give my lovely company and me a little background on this ride you got here?"

The guy took a look at us and then looked at the ride and began to explain. Basically, you're strapped, safely, in a small box cage thing and then spun in a giant circle 165 feet in the air while going 65 miles per hour.
Safely, in this case, feels like a cruel oxymoron.

On the inside, I was freaking out.
I hate thrills. I get my thrills from not looking at the cast list of a movie before I watch it; that's enough for me. But he turned to me with that smile again, and I smiled back and nodded, giving him the okay.

Two guys came off the ride jumping around and hyping each other up with vocabulary like *'Bro, that was tight! Brroooo!'* Many high-fives followed. And here it was, my make it or break it moment. Or at least it felt like it. We walked up to the cage, the cage of death, and before we stepped on, he whispered to me,

"We don't have to go on if you don't want to; we can do anything you'd like."

I don't know what the hell got into me, but I just hopped into the cage and looked at the amazement in his eyes as he grinned and joined me. My stomach started to turn as the guy strapped us in and headed back to his control station. I closed my eyes and gripped my hands on the bar, praying to God that this ride wouldn't lose a screw or something. I felt him place his hands on the bar, too, as he cleared his throat.

"I have a confession to make. I have never been on a thriller-type ride before." And just then, the ride started up.

"What?!" I yelled while both our heads hit the back of the headrest as the ride zoomed up, and our grips got even tighter on the bar, and he let out a *masculine* scream.

"Well, I never got brave enough to ride one!" Screaming again after saying so.

I yelled as the ride spun in a circle and whipped back, "And you thought now is a good time?!" My hair was a total mess, thrashing around my face and probably in his too.

"I'm going to hold your hand now!" He yelled as we were now upside down.

His hand landed, and I let him wrap it around the back of mine, mostly because I'm pretty sure we were both terrified. The warmth of his hand radiated, and I could almost feel how big both our smiles were now that we were kinda sorta holding hands. After a few more death-defying spins, the ride came to a stop, and we stepped out, taking a few steps to regain our balance.

"Woah, now that is a ride!" He said, stumbling a little bit.

I tried casually fixing my hair; I could feel how tangled and messy it was. "Carder won't believe I road that; I still can't believe it!"

"Heck to the yes we did!"

Checking the time quickly, I gasped a little under my breath. "Oh geez, I'm sorry- is it okay if we head back? I have to work an early shift tomorrow, and I didn't realize what time it was." Politely asking with my troll hair; polite troll.

"Oh yea, yea, of course! I'm sorry! Where do you work if I may be so bold?"

Gahhhh him and his dorkyness. "Oh, don't sweat it, it's fine! I'm sorry I have to cut the evening short; I work at the Sandbar Nursing home."

"That sounds like a nice job, peaceful as the name sounds? And no worries, I completely understand."

"It has its moments," And at that we were pleasantly silent until we got to the car, embracing the last of the delightful sounds and lights of the boardwalk.

On the car ride back, we listened to some more of the yellow and blue striped cassette. And to my surprise, I knew the next song. Nat King Cole's *L-O-V-E.'* And not to be punny, but I absolutely love this song.

"King fan, huh?" He asked; I think he saw me smiling from ear to ear, and I could tell he liked talking about music.

"You know, if I could have any artist sing at my wedding, it would be Nat. I just love his voice." He turned to me with this cute little smirk and looked back at the road turning up the song. "Sorry, that was a little much" Who in the hell is operating my communication system right now, letting me talk about weddings? Whose idea was that?!

He laughed. "Oh no, not at all, what a fun idea! If I got to pick anyone to sing at my wedding, it would have to be Sir Paul McCartney." I perked up; thank God he liked The Beatles.

"Beatles fan, I presume?" Asking me as we continued to jam.

"Favorite band, actually," I wittily replied.

"Should have known by your name you were raised by Beatles parents."

I grinned, and just by the end of the next song on the tape, we made it to my apartment. He parked on the side of the street and once again, quickly walked to my door and opened it for me, this time offering his hand to help me down.

We walked to the door, and my heart started to race.

Would he try to kiss me?

No, not on the first date.

Was this being labeled as a date?

Oh my gosh, I haven't kissed someone in a long time; what if I mess up and we hit our teeth or something?

Eww gross.

Gross me, not gross him.

What if I think he's leaning in and I lean in too, and he's like:
'Chick, what da hell it's the first date.'

I snapped out of it when we reached my apartment door.

"So, I don't know if you'll be up for this, but could I please put my number in your phone?"

I was overly happy he asked me. I tried to act cool, pulling it out of my pocket and handing it to him. He smiled widely as he swiped my screen and started clicking in his name and stuff. "You like *BBC Sherlock* too, huh?" I totally forgot that was my home screen.

Holy goodness, I lost it. Yepp that's it, the inner fangirl was released. "No way, no fricken way!" I couldn't contain it.

"Binge watched it and became unhealthily hooked." He smiled with giddiness as well.

"It's the best! I don't even know how many times I've watched it!"

"I know, right! Every time I catch something or appreciate something I didn't see before!" He laughed and handed my phone back to me. "Thank you for giving me a timeless and yet unexpected night, Miss. Lucy."

My mind instantly raced and connected his last words to the first time he said that to me in the bookstore. And I think we both knew I was thinking of that moment as we both smiled and then went our separate ways. I didn't even mind or really notice that we didn't hug or anything as I walked inside my apartment, closed the door, and fell on my back onto the couch.

Carder came running in from his room and leaned his face above mine, overly ecstatic. "How'd it go?! What'd you do?! Did he kiss you? Was there any funny business? TELL!"

I sat up, and he sat practically on top of me. "We took a walk on the boardwalk, and it was actually really nice" I was lost in thought, replaying the night in my head, and unconsciously smiling.

"Aww, that's cute! Oh! What's his name? It's been killing me!"

I looked down at my hand where my phone was and unlocked it as my other hand then covered my silly smile that developed clear across my face as I saw what he put as his contact name: Sherlock.

Still looking at my phone, I moved my hand away from my mouth and answered Carder's question before he exploded from suspense.

"It, it never really came up, I guess" I was smiling like an idiot.

6. Colin 

I sunk into my bed, my pathetic twin-sized bed, and the memories from tonight sunk even deeper into me.

My hands have been touched by quite a few people. I've let them be touched by people I'd give the world for, and I've let them be touched by people who took part of the world from me. Regardless of my past, I felt like it didn't matter as much anymore. There was something about the feeling when, ugh, Sherlock's hand landed on mine. I let it play through my head, thinking what it would look like in slow motion. I'd imagine he had that Mona Lisa smile on and, as his adventurous hand landed, a purely surprised expression painted on mine.

Abruptly enough, though, I didn't want to feel this feeling. I didn't want to fall into something I knew for a fact I'd be broken if I wasn't caught. And though his arms look comforting, I'm still not sure if he can catch.

Goodness, okay, I need to stop conclusion jumping. How in the world could I even know that? I hardly know him- I don't even know his real name. Yea, this feeling will fade.

My alarm blared at 5:30am, and the only thing that motivated me was hearing the coffee machine begin its day as well. Slowly creeping out of bed, I filled my lungs with the scent of the brewing coffee grounds, aka the best smell in the universe of aromas. I made my way to the dresser to find a pair of matching scrubs when my eyes got fixed on a picture I've had framed for years.

Every year my family would pick one day to build a giant fort. This tradition started on my first day of kindergarten. Shortly after, my parents discovered I was prone to severe anxiety attacks. They've gotten better with age; I haven't experienced one in a long time. Growing up, though, they were awful. I'm not even sure how or why they started, maybe because I didn't want to be away from my family. Who knows why our brains get all messed up.

I was terrified to start school; my mom was staying home with Colin while my dad taught advanced painting classes at the Art Institute. I made it about halfway through the school day until I had an attack; my dad canceled his classes for the day and picked me up from school. I swear I'll never forget him walking into the nurse's office, and I'm sure the school nurse and staff still talk about it to this day. He wore khakis, a white dress shirt tucked in with a navy-blue jacket over it and top it off with a superhero cape. I ran to him as soon as my eyes reached his, and he knelt on one knee and embraced me. When he brought me home, Mom had all the fort supplies set out in the living room, and for the rest of the day, we worked on creating the most incredible and best fort that all four of us could fit in.

The picture was a Christmas gift a few years back. We were all lying on our backs inside the fort. Colin and I were in the middle, and our parents were on the outside. Dad held one of his arms out and Mom the other, both holding the camera so we could fit all of us in. We actually got the picture on the first try; Colin smiling so big with his two front teeth missing, I was in mid-laugh, and my parents were smiling at one another. Like a last-minute connection they felt. I always like to think this picture perfectly describes their love; I had never seen them argue with one another. I know they have their disagreements; they've just learned how to work through them so well it became a whole other language of their own. I really admire them.

I put the scrubs under my arms and forced myself away from the picture, continuing my morning routine. Just a quick shower, get dressed, and all that jazz, coffee, work.

Quick Shower.

Dressed and jazzed.

Coffee.

Work.
Shower.

Clean.

Memories.

Ready.

Coffee.

Work.

Quick.

Forts.

Jazzy.

Java.

Panic.

Colin.

Colin- I couldn't get the image of him out of my head now.

Hastily I went to the bathroom, and I turned on the shower, not even waiting for the water to heat up as I stepped in, hoping the cold would shake things up in my head. I wrapped my arms around myself and let the cold water caress my body; the image was still there. Goosebumps covered me so fast that it felt like individual pricks everywhere.

Too many thoughts.

Too many snapshots.

Too many mistakes.

Too many regrets.

Too many memories.

Colin.

In the time, all these things created themselves in my mind and rammed against my skull, my chest filled with intense sharp pain. I began to panic. I began to breathe too fast. Or was I even breathing at all? Why couldn't I pull away? Why can't I just stop thinking of this? I don't want this- get out!

This was it, the bitter reunion of the anxiety attack. I'd spoken too soon. I screamed. At the top of my lungs, the cold water still stinging as it hit my back, my hands were holding my chest; my knees felt like they were caving in. I could hear Carder racing to the bathroom and pushing the door open; thank God I didn't bother to lock it anymore.

My knees gave out as I listened to the doorknob hit the wall, falling on my ass and letting my back hit the tub. It's strange how we don't feel the pain in some moments of intensity, but I'm sure I'll feel the bruises later. I put my arm out from behind the shower curtain as the cold air took hold of it. Carder knew about my anxiety attacks; he just never saw it firsthand. I heard him sit down on the tiles, and he lightly grasped my wet, trembling hand and cupped it inside his nicely warmed palms, like a delicate snow globe.

My attacks prevent me from moving, any movement causes severe pain to the chest, and the nightmare starts all over. All I could do was try to breathe.

"I'm taking you in Lucy, I don't care if it's been forever since you've had one; this isn't okay."

I didn't say anything, really, I couldn't, but even if I could, I didn't have the words. I just squeezed his hand tighter.

Carder let one of his hands free as I heard him sniffle, and his voice became shaky. "Lucy, you-" He was silenced, momentarily, by a sudden gasp of trying to hold back his tears. This took me aback as he drew in a deep breath and reunited his other hand with mine. "You were screaming Colin's name."

7. Pistachios 

"No dance, huh?"

"Nope," sighing and taking a seat on the kitchen floor across from him, my sparkly dress drowning me as I cross my legs. "He ditched me last minute because of some stupid argument. I don't even remember how it started."

"Well, that's extremely immature and rude."

I nodded and stared at the wooden floor. "Why aren't you at the dance?"

"Because you aren't" He gave me a smile. But I gave him a doubtful look, along with a laugh he joined in on. "Alright, alright, I didn't ask anybody; dances are stupid."

"Colin, it's your Junior year, your Junior Prom; you shoulda asked somebody! What about that girl at our bus stop?"

"Cliché," He effortlessly said with a fake snobbish tone.

"Oh please, you think everything is cliché."

"Not *Star Wars*"

"Oh, so while we're on the subject of trying to figure out how on earth you are single."

He busted out laughing, slapping his knee with each breath of laughter that escaped him. "It's funny cause it's sad, and it's sad cause it's true!"

I only laughed a little. "Colin, I was obviously joking; *Star Wars* is amazing. Come on, you're gonna find that nerdy girl that'll rock your geeky world someday."

He swiftly got on his feet and helped me up. "Lucy, this is your last dance; this was supposed to be your night."

"It still is I'm just spending it here," I slugged his arm, "with you."

"You know what's even worse than that lie you just said? Mom and dad are out on a date, having a blast. My my my, how the tables have turned."

"Yea, we're lame."

"Completely. But! I'd rather be lame here than listen to whatever trash music they're probably playing at the dance." We exchanged approving nods and departed for a bit.

I needed some time alone to process everything. I locked my bedroom door and stood in front of my body-length mirror; my dress couldn't even fit in the frame. Dad spent a fortune on this dress, and its only audience is the mirror.

What did Seth not like about me? Was it my thick brown hair; he wanted thin blonde hair instead? Was it my brown eyes; did he want to look into an ocean rather than a dark puddle? Was it because I asked him too many questions; did he want to control something with no mind of its own?
I stretched my arm back and unzipped my dress, wondering if I could still return it, letting the heavy fabric fall to my feet. My body isn't anything special; I couldn't get a guy's attention if I was the only girl at Comic-Con. What made me think I was anything extraordinary? I kicked the dress aside; the little pieces of jewels sewn into the fabric scratching the top of my foot. I stared into the mirror and looked at myself. Welcoming the silent tears, I wrapped my arms around my bare stomach. Why on earth do people fall in love?

Ugh, my stomach hurt so bad; my chest felt like it would cave in any second. I really didn't care anymore. Lunging for the framed picture of Seth and me on my bedstand, I threw it at the wall. The sound of the glass shattering confirmed my heart was cracked. I really can't remember when I last screamed, and it felt good; it felt good to let all the emotion scrap through my throat and escape off my lips. I started throwing everything; everything that was from or reminded me of Seth.

Amid my generous pitching of objects, I heard Colin pounding on my door, commanding me to stop. Dropping the pressed flowers Seth gave me Sophomore year out of my clammy hand, I put my robe on and let Colin in. As he walked in, I embraced the fact that he would be calling me a psycho for the rest of my life. Instead, he handed me the TV remote and showed me to the door, shutting it behind me.

I watched reruns of *Monk* while he was cleaning my room. I wanted to go back up there and stop him, but something in me just wouldn't let me get up. Eventually, he joined me.

"We haven't watched this show in a while," he said as he sat down on the other end of the couch. We didn't look at each other.

"Colin, you didn't have to clean my room," Breaking the silence.

"*Monk* didn't have to spend pretty much his whole adult life trying to figure out who his wife's murderer was, yet here we are watching it on TV. You know, arguably, this is the greatest love story written in television history. It is wildly underrated and-"

Turning my body towards him, I hit the cushion. In reaction, he turned to me; he turned to me with a quick dead serious look in his eyes that made me feel so guilty inside. "Look, I'm sorry, Colin, I really am. I just don't know what to do with myself; I'm a mess. Everything Seth said about me was right; I just-"

Colin snapped, "Lucy, Seth is the biggest jackass in the history of jackasses that even the kingdom of Jackasses told him *'Beat it ya' jackass!'*"
I didn't think he'd get me to crack a smile, but lo and behold, he made me giggle. "Don't let him waste a moment more of your life, Lucy. I know this all sucks. It does because you don't deserve this pain at all, but this happened because you deserve better, and you'll find better. Preferably someone who actually knows how to read a book."

"Hey," I said with a whimsical and impressed tone in my voice, "Okay, *Sherlock Holmes*, I see you. Where'd my little brother go."

"Oh please," he playfully snapped as he gave me a hug and then once again swiftly got up on his feet, "I'm *The Doctor*!"

I felt a tender push on my shoulder, the light from my window started to peak through the cracks of my eyes. Carder was shaking me awake before he was heading to work. And I had been dreaming of memories yet again. Go figure. At least this one didn't turn into a nightmare. As for Carder, I am currently not speaking with him. I haven't for a few days. He knows why.

"Yea, yea, whatever, don't talk to me, but you're not dying of starvation on my watch, so get up." He walked out of the room as I slowly trailed behind him, only for the fact that I smelled pop-tarts in the toaster.

I rubbed my eyes and looked over to the corner of the counter where my coffee pot is. Was. It's gone. "You ignorant little dirtbag," I directed at him with gritted teeth.

"Love ya too, gotta go to work."

The nerve of him! Walking towards the door, thinking he's oh so clever. Not today, pal. I ran to him and leaped on his back; I'd imagine he was pretty startled as he caught his step while I tried to shake him off balance. "You put my baby back!" I protested while still trying to get him unbalanced.

"Never!"

I let out a battle cry and shifted all my weight to the right as we fell, and I pinned him down. "Carder George Elizondo, you put it back RIGHT NOW!"

"I am NOT putting it back until you do something with yourself! You've been wearing the same clothes for two days, you haven't watched anything besides *House*, and you ate all the Nutella! I bought that Nutella!" All at once, he pushed his arms on my shoulders and swiftly pinned me to the floor. It happened so fast I was slightly impressed but more so pissed.
"I will give you your coffee pot back when you go start living your life again. Now, I'm going to be late for work. Go do something today." Before lifting himself up off the ground, he gave me a kiss on the forehead.

The sound of the shutting wood echoed through the apartment while I laid on the floor, currently unmotivated. Not even pop-tarts could get me to move right now. The past few days have been, how do I put this- not grand. Carder took me to the hospital, even though he knew I didn't want to. Every time I went for this particular reason, I heard basically the same things. I wasn't sick; there's nothing wrong with me aside from the fact I will have to learn how to cope with these attacks and try to control my anxiety better. Medications, therapists, breathing techniques, all things I used to do and should try or at least consider again, but as of right now, I'm just, I don't know, not ready.

But my main reason for being so upset with him was beyond that. When I accepted my job at the nursing home, I also signed a release to notify my boss of my hospital visits for the resident's safety, and I had a small healthcare plan through my work. After informing them of my ER visit and a painfully awkward meeting with HR- ugh, long story short, I was let go. In their words, they couldn't risk me having an attack when I was in the presence of a resident or while I was taking care of a resident. Which I understood when I accepted the job; now it's just a harsh reality. Yes, deep down, I did appreciate the fact that Carder took me in after holding my hand through the shower for a good hour. I just wish it didn't cost me my job.

"And now I am far too lazy to get up off the floor," I said in all my dramatic glory to an audience of silence. Suddenly, I heard my phone vibrate off the bedstand in my room. I groaned as I sat up. "I swear if that's another call for my *'extended car warranty,'* I'm gonna be on the next episode of whatever true crime show is taking off right now." Fortunately, as I unlocked my phone, it was a pleasant surprise.

Sherlock:

Boardwalk. Come if convenient.

I put the phone down for a moment and turned away to softly laugh. Is he really referencing *Sherlock Holmes* right now? This is magnificent, oh my gosh- my geeking out was interrupted by another vibration.

Sherlock:

If inconvenient, come anyway. -SH

I was actually surprised with myself how quickly I got ready. Keeping Carder's fashion advice in mind, I dressed in something cute and flattering. Still, more importantly, maintaining my best interest in mind, I dressed comfy. I fashioned up my own fashion formula: Comfy + Cute = Content. It's called The CCC Method. Anywho, the boardwalk was a bit of a walk, but I appreciated a nice walk. I liked walking past life, moments, and memories already in the making while walking past it. It's like I'm an extra in their life movie, and they're an extra in mine. I always smile when I think of that; if everyone had this drilled in their media-filled heads, maybe everyone would feel important. Everyone should feel they are important.

Daydreaming had me reach my destination quite fast, as I then found Sherlock at the boardwalk. Of course, he looks great, just fantastic. He probably doesn't even try. He probably wakes up and says something like: *'Look out world, good lookin' comin' your way!'*. Oh my gosh, I could actually picture him saying that, but in a joking manner. He doesn't seem like the full-of-himself type. I didn't realize while this embarrassingly dorky unrealistic scenario was playing through my head that he had already seen me and started walking my way.
Oh goodness, I was feeling nervous already. You're fine; remain calm. He's just as weird as you, so it seems. Plus, you don't even like him like that, well I don't think-

"Lucy! I am happy to see you received my text!" His goony smile was contagious, as was his bright spirit.

"Yes, I did, Sher- okay, can I please know your name? People are going to look at us weird if I keep calling you Sherlock."

He gave me a mysterious smile, bending his right elbow and offering me his arm to hold. Silently giddy to take up on his offer, I checked out his shirt while we began to walk; it was a *Wham!* T-shirt. Gosh, he is such a dork. Oh my gosh, Lucy, stop, control your admiration.

"Now that we are done asking silly questions, Miss. Lucy, might I excite you with today's agenda?"

"I suppose you can burden me with this, news of yours," I snickered with a sarcastically playful tone.

"Oh, Madam, you are too gracious!" He touched my hand that was holding his arm with his free one for a moment. Not gonna lie, I was smiling like a dork, and there were some pretty solid seconds of eye contact going on. "I was hoping you would be up for a little kayaking; there's a small river lake thing by my house! Does that sound appealing to you?"

Oh, oh goodness, complete eye contact now. "Mr. *Holmes*, I would be delighted" This time, I got him to smile like a little kid who just received an animal cracker from their crush.

Point for Lucy.

Should I be going with him? Is this wise? Or will people scoff while watching a poorly budgeted documentary on how I died at the hands of a serial killer, mocking the TV saying, *'Whelp, she earned that one! Hoping in a car with a dude who won't even share his real name! Way to go, stupid!'*
Or is this a sign of what Carder wanted me to do? To start living my life and doing something new and different? At least I know Carder will write a pretty decent obituary and put one honorary pun in for me. Here goes nothing, I guess.

The car ride wouldn't take too long, I hoped, as he opened the door for me, and I hopped into his Jeep. When he fastened himself in, he smiled over to me before starting the car. "I just live a little outside of town, got a house nestled in some nice nature! So, what's new in the wonderful and mysterious world that is Lucy?"

Ugh, did he have to ask that? I mean, it's lovely he cares, but it's kind of a sore topic as of right now. Quite literally, I think that battle I had this morning gave me some new decorative bruises.
"Oh, not too much, let's move on to the world of Mister he who shall not be named"

"Firstly, I am happy to say I am not *Lord Voldemort*. Secondly, you do know my name, it's Sherlock! Lastly, no, no, no, you're holding out on me." Shockingly he is rather good at talking and driving simultaneously, all while seeming very interested in the conversation. I say shockingly because the only other person I really go with is Carder. On the long list of skills he wears in that fabulous tool belt of his, multitasking is not one of them.

"I don't really want to get into it, but I lost my job, so I've been a little down, I guess." Politely, I cut him off before things got pitifully awkward because of me. "But I'm fine, I'll miss the residents, but I'm fine. I'll find another job." Discreetly I looked at his face, a sad expression kind of consumed his joyful smile that covered it before.

Clearing his throat, I think he was trying to sound cheery. "So, how is Carder doing these days? Still sassy, I presume?"

"You know his back hurts a bit, not sure why," I laughed a little to myself. "But he is doing good, of course still very sassy. I'd be worried if he wasn't." That actually made me feel better; nice segue there, Sherlock.

"Yes, what would the world do without a sassy Carder" Taking a moment to give me a reassuring smile.

He's pretty smooth. I'll bet he's got quite a few romantic experiences under his belt. With that thought, I felt my guard coming back up again.

We came up to a cute little white house with deep red shutters on the windows and a matching front door. It was like a painting in a storybook. "Your Great Aunt had great taste in houses; it's adorable!" Geez, my voice cracked; that's not embarrassing.

"Oh yes, from the stories I heard, she was one hell of a woman. Are you comfortable with going inside?"

I nodded, avoiding another catastrophe of my vocal cords failing on me. Holding the front door open for me, I realized I walked into a complete dork's house. It's official now. He is the poster boy for dorks everywhere. The walls were evenly decorated with framed movie posters, *DC Comics* canvas art; I couldn't help but smile. I could feel my cheeks pinch a bit from smiling so much.

There was a small side table where he took off his shoes, sliding them underneath, and I followed his lead. On top of it was a little fishbowl full of pistachios. I giggled under my breath.

"Alright! Before we start our journey, would you like something to drink? Water, soda, coffee-" The muffled sound of a song from *Tarzan* came from his pocket as he pulled out his phone, and the sound of Phil Collins voice was now clear. "Oh shoot, it's my boss; I'm so sorry. Do you mind if I take this? I'm so sorry, please make yourself at home," He was rambling. "The TV remote is on the coffee table in the living room; I have *Netflix*, you can watch whatever you want and-"

"Oh my goodness, I'm okay go go go, " I laughed as I shooed him away and walked into the living room, vaguely hearing him professionally answer the phone. The living room was lit up with the natural light from the open windows. There I found the TV remote, right next to a tiny teacup filled with pistachios, this guy and his pistachios.
I clicked the button, and the comforting red screen I know and love all too much came forth. Featured on his continue watching list was: *The Office*, *The Help*, *Middleditch and Schwartz*, and *Avatar: The Last Airbender.*

And enter stage right "All is good, I requested today off, and he forgot, no worries though we're still on!" Sherlock paused and sat down on the sofa with me, sitting just close enough that we weren't touching as he looked at the screen. "Did something catch your eye?"

I knew he was talking about the shows and movies, but I couldn't help but smile like perhaps he meant something else. "I've actually always thought about watching *The Office*, but I never got around to it. Is it any good?"

Dead silence. He turned his head over to me with a look of astonishment grasping his facial muscles. "I just want to make sure I heard correctly,"

"Yes?"

"Never, you have never seen *The Office*?"

"Yes," I started laughing at his frazzled behavior. "That is correct" this was hilarious.

He pretended to be in distress, or at least I thought he was. "Kayaking must be postponed, I'm sorry, but this is a mercy call. You should probably text Carder as well because I don't know when you'll be back home. We have so much ground to cover."

"Oh, so you're kidnapping me, huh?"

"Yes, I suppose so," he paused while setting our apparent binge session up. "Hmm, maybe I should have thought this through. Should I ask for ransom, or should I play it casual?"
With my laughter, I guess I confirmed our change of plans. I can't even deny how witty and fun it is to banter with him though, it felt effortless.
"I'm assuming you think Benedict Cumberbatch is attractive, yes?" He was the star of the *BBC Sherlock* we both enjoyed watching, a good icebreaker on his part, but I'm going to have fun with this.

"Seeing he is my husband, yes, very much so."

He laughed and turned to me with raised eyebrows, "My regards to your husband for kidnapping his wife. You're going to love one of the main guys in this then, *Jim*. He's easy on the eyes, and he's like the *Sherlock Holmes* of pranks, if I may be so bold." He could feel the judgment as I looked at him with a grin. "Yes, I am a straight man and think a fictional male character is attractive. I stand by my statement." And with that and an escaped giggle from me, he pressed the play button.

Sometimes I feel uncomfortable and awkward sitting with people in silence. Still, something about him just felt so warm and light. I don't really know how else to describe it. We got two episodes in before I decided to break the silence; aside from laughter, of course, he was right; this is quite funny. "So, what's up with the random displays of pistachios, Sherlock?"

His eyes transferred their focus onto me, and he paused the show, shifting his body towards me and putting his arm over the top of the sofa. I turned my body to him as well. "Did you know that the Queen of Sheba loved pistachios?"

"You're doing this in the Queen's honor?" I teasingly replied.

"Heavens, no, I just really love pistachios and fun facts. I believe there are seven other pistachio stations around the house. Not sure, I lose count." While he was lost in thought, I tussled his hair and slipped the remote out of his hand. He looked surprised while his grin grew with satisfaction.

"You are quite the character" I pushed play and returned my posture back to the TV, leaning back comfortably. I felt pretty badass. From the corner of my eye, I saw he was still grinning at me for a moment before settling back as well.

We watched one episode after another, he had a lot of fun facts about the show, and of course, we'd join in for laughs. Besides that, we didn't talk so much. We just enjoyed the show and each other's company. He got up once to shut the curtains because there was a glare, and when he sat back down, he was just a tad bit closer to me than before. I decided to text Carder that I would be home late tonight with a smiley face because maybe I overacted about being upset with him for so long.

Okay, I overacted, I know.

But he took it to extreme measures by taking away my coffee pot.

We were probably well over halfway through the second season already; the room was only lit by the TV light, I loved it. I decided to break the silence again.

"Gotta hand it to you, Sherlock; I think you've got me hooked on this show." I turned over to him to see the reaction on his face- Oh my gosh.

Oh my gosh. He's asleep! Well, what the hell do I do?
How long has he been asleep?
Is it too soon for me to draw a sharpie mustache on him?
Okay focus-
I checked my phone to see the time; it was almost 8.
I guess I missed a text from Carder.

Carder:

Best not be losing your V-Card tonight

I shouldn't be surprised. How gross.

Me:

Mayday Mayday- He fell asleep!

Waiting for his response, I kept watching the show. I'm sure he's seen each episode like twice with all the commentary he was giving me, so I didn't feel too bad about continuing without him.

Vibration

Carder:

I bet you won't draw a mustache on him

I tried not to laugh out loud and texted him back immediately.

Me:

Oh would you stop

I don't know what to do!!!

I clicked the lock button on my phone, and for some reason, that little sound woke him up. He looked around confused for a moment and rubbed his eyes, then it clicked that I was still here, and the panic kicked in. "Oh dear, how long was I out? Oh my gosh, I'm so sorry, I had a killer shift yesterday at work, and that's why I thought if we went kayaking, it would wake me up, but I didn't know that you had never watched *The Office* before and, oh no, I didn't snore did I?"

I love how he rambles when he's nervous; it's the cutest thing. Wait, no, not cutest, just a thing. Ugh, no, it's pretty cute. Undeniable. "No, you're fine, you're fine; where do you work?" Trying to politely calm him down.

He took a little breath, still gathering his sleepy self. "I work at a small cranberry bog about thirty minutes out of town; actually, I'm surprised I got the job. I have no farming experience whatsoever. Hardly any work experience to call experience, to be honest. But a super nice older gentleman, Tom Wyatt, owns it. It's called Duck's Cranberries. Duck is a term of endearment in England, and his wife was from there. She passed away a few years ago, but he devoted his business to her. It's amazing, their love, even though she's not physically here, it's like in his mind she never left. Just from the stories, he tells me about her, I know she's in Heaven. Woah, look at me, waking up and then just going off about myself; I'm terribly sorry."

"No, I don't mind at all; keep going. What do you do exactly?"

He smiled and moved a little closer to me; one of his legs was bent at the knee and resting on the couch, just slightly touching my leg. His arm returned once again to the top of the cushion. I felt so warm and giddy suddenly. Smoothly I shifted towards him, bringing my legs up to my chest and my arms relaxingly wrapped around my legs, my feet touching his leg just a little bit.

"Tom is too fragile to work in the actual bog, so that's where I am most of the time and a few other guys. For some reason, Tom has really taken a liking to me and trusts me to kind of be his eyes out there. As for the bog aspect, it's like a clean swamp for cranberries. We pump the water in, so the cranberries get all washed up, and then we put our gear on so we don't get soaked while harvesting. Most of the time, though, I'm just tending to the water. We had quite a lot to do yesterday, so I was out there until around 1am. There are giant floodlight posts around the bog, so it felt very intense like I was in a movie or something. Tom felt pretty bad, but it all had to be done, so it's all good. I talk to Tom with respect, of course, but I caught on that he's the kind of older gent that doesn't want to be treated like he's an older gent." He paused and then mimicked me, pulling his legs up as our feet were touching now. "If you'd like, maybe next harvest, I can take you out there?"

"It's a date," I said with confidence, wiggling my toes a little to get a giggle out of him. Which was successful.

"Deal. But don't tell your husband." We both laughed, and he offered to take me home, explaining that he wishes we could spend all night watching the comedic greatness that is *The Office*, but he must be out at the bog at 6am.

We got in the Jeep, and as he shut the door, he shook his head. "I'm sorry, can you please get out a moment and shut the car door?" I looked at him, confused as he jumped out of the car, and I accepted his request. As I shut the door, he walked over to my side, smiled, and opened the car door, offering his hand to help me into the jeep. I laughed and got in. "I'm sorry I lost my manners for a second there." He said politely as we pulled out of the driveway.

"I'll tell you what; I can get in the car on my own now since you so kindly showed me how to on many occasions."

"Hmm, I think I would miss opening the door for you too much." I smiled and looked out the window; soon, the streetlights appeared and illuminated the inside of the car. And like a gentleman, again, he opened the car door and walked me to my apartment.
"Thank you for today. Though I was shocked to discover your marital status, I must admit, I enjoy your company very much."

I smiled at my feet and looked back up at him. "I have to agree; your company is lovely, even when you're asleep."

He rolled his eyes and gave me a smile. "Goodnight, Mrs. Cumberbatch"

AugghUgghhhh, his voice sounded like melting caramel. "Goodnight, Mr. *Holmes*" And with that, we parted ways.

I walked inside with the stupidest grin on my face. Carder rushed me in, catching me off guard. "Did you kiss yet?" He bombarded me.

"No, we didn't, Mr. Pushy-Nosey."

"Did you find out his name?"

"Nope"

"My gosh, please tell me you did not sleep with a man that you haven't kissed yet nor his true identity." He could barely get through his ridiculous sentence without laughing.

I laughed and hit his arm. "Carder, he's just so" I paused. "It seems too good to be true."

"Don't overthink it, okay? It's just hanging out, nothing to analyze. Now, can I please get a hug? I'm very deprived."
I wrapped my arms around him, and we gave each other a much-needed hug. Gently letting go, his smile was so bright. "Come on, there're new episodes of *RuPaul's Drag Race*." I smiled at Carder as he was going on about some customers that stopped in today; someone spilled their drink on the carpet.
I turned my head back to the kitchen, and a smile once again visited my face. Turning back to Carder and investing in the rest of his elaborate carpet stain story. The coffee pot was back.

8. Lucky Swing

"**M**y name is Aldo," Looking up with a bit of a smirk on my face.

"Don't read it out loud, goodness gracious, please just read it and tell me how it is,"

"Colin, you're an amazing writer, and you know it, now go to beeeddddd!"
I playfully threw the paper at him and wrapped my head under my blankets. Whenever he finished writing a chapter or wrote anything for that matter, the minute it escaped from his restless mind and onto paper, he came straight to me. Which I didn't mind at all; it's really an honor. I was just playfully teasing him. "Besides, it's like" taking a look from under the blanket at my phone for the time. "Yea, exactly what I thought, flippin' 3am. Colin, you need a healthy sleep schedule," Covering my exhausted face yet again; perhaps that was a tad dramatic.

"I haven't written anything in ages," I heard Colin sigh as he crumpled the paper in his hands.

Letting out a tiring exhale, I uncovered my head and faced him; he was cross-legged, looking at the floor, with the paper in his right fist. "You write practically every day."

He shook his head, not breaking his concentration. "No, I can't sleep, I need to write, but nothing comes out. Nothing that I want at least." He caught my attention now as the tone in his voice grew with concern. "I'm lacking inspiration Lucy, I'm a Junior in high school, I don't have much going for me; I'm running out of things to write about."

I felt my eyes widen, and I knew what was happening. It's happening again. The tears were starting to form in my eyes, I didn't want to let Colin see it, but his gaze reached my face before I could wipe the evidence away. He turned from my eyes for a moment and then returned them back to me, and I could just tell that it clicked in his mind what was going on. He tilted his head just slightly, still fixed on my eyes. "Lucy," he paused as the tears silently cascaded down my cheeks, "Why are you dreaming about me?"

"Hey, bum, up and at em!" Awakened by Carder jumping on my bed and landing on the back of my legs. Of course, he laughed and then hugged me close, making my quilt wrap around me like a cocoon.
"I don't have work today, and I took the liberty of making us some plans."

"Plans, huh" I respond with my face still buried in my pillow, trying to forget the eerie dream.

"Yes, pay attention; our plans start soon, so let's get movin'."

Groaning while Carder released me from his loving, grip "Oh Lucy, you look good without any makeup. You're an all-natural beauty" I pretended to talk in his voice.

"Yea, your *natural*self, when anybody wakes up, there ain't nothing in the natural order about how they look." I swear he thinks he is the Simon Cowell of hair and fashion. As Carder walked across the hall to his room, I could see he was already dressed and ready for the day he had planned.

I called out to him from across the hall. "Beyoncé?"

"Goddesses are obviously pardoned from that rule of nature." He called back. Laughing, I didn't answer back. I think that about did it for that debate. As much as it pains me: point for Carder.
I started opening my dresser for some shorts when Carder shouted to me after the sound of the drawer opening echoed to him.

"No no, no! I already picked out your outfit; it's in the bathroom!"

Ugh, of course. "I lose my job, and now I'm helpless," I mumble under my breath, making way to the bathroom to find my yellow and white striped sundress hanging on the back of the door. Peculiarly looking at it, I can only imagine what in the world Carder got us into today.
I slipped into the dress, and with its length, I didn't have to worry about how my legs looked. And it was rather comfy! I threw my messy brown hair in a bun and called it good enough. So, so many bobby pins.

"Meet me in the car, please; I don't want to be late!" Carder called as he walked out of the apartment.

I took one more look in the mirror to see how I looked; my skin was starting to clear up, thank God. I grabbed my wallet and keys and then hurried to the car. "Okay, so where are we going?" I asked as I shut the car door.

"I signed us up for a day class. You need some fun, and I need this new skill." I gave him a strange look that I could tell he caught from the corner of his eye. "Oh, don't give me that, it'll be great! And it's just a few hours, very relaxed."

After a few minutes of gazing out the window at the lovely sunny day we were having, I laughed in disbelief as we pulled into our destination. I can't believe he did this. "A dance studio? You signed us up for a dance class?"

"Swing dance, to be exact." He winked at me and then hopped out of the car.

"Are you kidding me?!" Slamming the door and pulling him back from the studio entrance.

"I'm sure you'll use this someday" He smirked at me in his sarcastic tone.

"When will swing dancing ever come in handy, huh? You know I don't have a rhythmic bone in my body; why do you want to learn anyway?"

"Honey, it is swing night at the club, and I am looking to swing into a charming fella." I let go of his arm and swallowed whatever future embarrassment I was going to inevitably obtain. He really deserved a fun night out after all the horridness of Jason.

"Well, well well, let us not be late for our dance class then." Holding the door open for him with a smile and meeting our small class for the day.

After we checked in, I saw about five other '*couples*' aside from us, all ranging in the retirement years. Taking a good look at Carder as our instructor explained what our short class would consist of, I hadn't even noticed we were cutely matching. His yellow striped bowtie was a classy touch.
Caught off guard, everyone unanimously turned to their partner and giggled.

Carder leaned in and whispered, "You're lucky I pay attention," as he placed my hands and his where they needed to be for our first position.

The instructor then continued her lesson. "This is your starting position. Always come back to this position; kapeesh?" We all nodded, and Carder smiled at me with an excited, giddy sparkle in his eyes.
"Now, gentlemen, you're going to lead, and you are starting with the left. Ladies, you will always be starting with your right. Remember everyone that the lady is always right" She giggled, and as did the rest of us women in the room. I nudged Carder and chuckled as he jokingly rolled his eyes.

Over the next hour, we learned how to jive with our partner and finally got some swinging in. The room was filled with the crisp sound of the bass strings thumping, and the trumpets and trombones never missed a beat. It was like the band was in the room with us. Miraculously Carder and I caught on fast; really, it wasn't all that hard once you let loose and stopped caring if you looked ridiculous or not. I felt Carder's smile radiate on me while I looked at the darling faces around us. I swear the elderly couples looked like they were 21 again the way they were smiling and dancing. I loved how my dress twirled with my body when Carder spun me in a circle; it was like the fabric was chasing my legs throughout the dance. And seeing Carder smile and laugh so much erased the agony of the past few days. He was right; we both needed this little break from the stress that is reality.

When the instructor informed us that we were all officially swing dancers and our class was concluded, we all groaned in an *aww,* and one of the elderly men in the back shouted-

"Group hug ya bunch of bastards! Even you young slicks!"

I'm guessing a retirement home arranged this, or they were all once traveling swing dancers. But before we knew it, we were being shuffled into a soft group hug. The woman I ended up right next to in the group hug had the most beautiful eyes, crystal, ocean blue. She turned to me with a genuine smile and whispered to me.

"This will be our last class; we're getting too old for this gig." She cut it off with a relaxed sigh. "I'm glad you and that nice boy could see us young, just one last time."
Smiling as she joined back in the noise of laughter and old memories, I turned over to Carder, who was already waiting for my attention. We gave each other a weak smile; though the room's tone was young and cheerful, you couldn't help but feel almost guilty for our youth. After the class was done, we headed back to the apartment so Carder could freshen up.

Plopping myself on the couch, I talked to him while he got ready in the bathroom down the hall. "Looking forward to dancing the night away?"

"You bet your little uncoordinated ass I am."

"Hey, I actually did pretty decent thank you very much!"

I could hear him laughing and then thrashing his clothes around, trying to find the right outfit. I loved seeing him try to perfect every detail of his hair and every wrinkle in his clothes. It was pretty entertaining.

"Crisis! CRISIS!" Carder hollered.

Sighing, because I had to actually move, I hurried to tend to the drama queen's urgency. "What is it, your highness?" I asked in a mocking medieval tone.

His back was faced away from me, and looking into the mirror, he turned around so fast it nearly knocked me over. "No, no jokes, this is awful. A catastrophe. Look at this!" He yelled, pointing to his chin. I looked at his chin. Then back to his eyes. Back to his chin. Back to the eyes. Chin. Eyes. Chin. Eyes. "Stubble Lucy! I have fricken Stubble!"

I took a closer look, good thing we are best friends. "Well, looky there, you're a scruffy man!" He gave me a death glare as I tried to hide my laughter. Carder didn't mind facial hair on guys, but he never liked it on himself, and for a while, it seemed like his hair got the gist and just stopped growing there! But of course, today of all days, they decided they'd like to come out and play. "Okay, it isn't bad if that's what you're worried about."

"I need to do my hair, and I'm going to be late meeting some regulars at a cafe before the club. Can you shave my face? Thanks, babe" He chopped off his sentence and put the razor in my hand as he put a blob of some product in his hand and began rubbing it in his hair.

I put a towel around his neck and draped it on his shoulders a little while I got the razor wet. "I hope you know I've never shaved a face before. Unless you count the time, I shaved my upper lip in middle school." While wetting his face, we both started laughing.

"Never thought from the first day I saw you that'd we'd end up here," Carder chuckled as he started working with his stubborn hair.

I grabbed the shaving cream and rubbed a thin layer onto his stubbled face. We both looked at each other, so concentrated with suspense, just as I took the first stroke along his chin. I lowered the razor as I looked at the hairless patch and then up to his anticipation-filled eyes.
And like he could read my mind, we both lifted our arms in the air and cheered "***SUCCESS***!" as he laughed off his nervousness, and I quickly but carefully finished.

We both ran to the door, and I checked over him once more to be sure he looked perfect for the remainder of his day.

"Okay, may not be back till the AM, so don't wait up for me if you get tired. Gonna get my swing on!" And with that, Carder kissed my forehead and then sprinted out the door. Didn't even get a word in. I pulled my phone out of my back pocket to check the time, and, well, hello there, I had a text message from about an hour ago.

Sherlock:

Hello Mrs. Cumberbatch, might I interest you in a Concert tonight?

Gosh, I hadn't been to a concert in a long time. I started getting a little nervous just imagining it. But I thought about how proud Carder would be that I was getting out and doing stuff. A new memory with the mystery Sherlock sounded quite tempting, to say the least.

Me:

What time shall we depart, Mr. *Holmes*?

9. Café of Blues

According to Sherlock, the concert was later tonight at a cafe I'd never heard of. So, I decided to be a brave little Lucy and invited him to hang out before we went. And bravery paid off, as he agreed and, in his words, was '*delighted to come over after he was done at the cranberry marsh*'.

In the meantime, I decided to pour myself some coffee and indulge in a guilty pleasure of mine. No, I'm sure, to your surprise, it isn't something wild and crazy. As anticlimactic as the reveal may be, it is reading. Alas, not just any reading, though; this is none other than fanfiction.

I set my laptop on the table and began reading a story that features *BBC's Sherlock* and *BBC's Doctor Who*. This story is super awesome and entertaining because *Sherlock* meets *The Doctor*. They solve cases together in all sorts of different timelines and places. I could feel myself smiling like an idiot; gosh, how I love escaping into words, there's nothing like it.

Just as I was reaching the end of chapter 5, a knock came from the door. I smiled and leaped from the kitchen chair but then calmly approached the door; I didn't want to seem *too* eager. I opened the door to reveal the dorky boy who's been running all over my mind for the past few hours; his strawberry blonde hair was a little messy but in a cute sort of way. He was wearing a striped crewneck with warm colors, accompanied by dark skinny jeans. Not that it's entirely essential to note, but it made me smile pretty big, so why not take a mental picture of it.

Oh goodness- his smile; man, he's got a great smile.
It made me forget about my present troubles.
It made me feel at ease.
It made me forget about my past.

It made me think way too much about my future.

"Thank you for inviting me over, Miss. Lucy" His voice chimed into my daydreaming thoughts as I snapped out of it.

"Oh yea, yea of course!" I rambled as I opened the door wider, offering him inside the small apartment.

Stepping in, he took a quick glance around as he slipped off his shoes; Converse, of course. "This is quite a lovely apartment you have here!"

I laughed a little, "Oh yes, I only settle for the finest of things, you know," Giving him a smirk of sarcasm, which lightly drizzled in my voice as well.

"Explains Mr. Cumberbatch," He wittily replied. I turned to him at the exact moment he faced to look at me; I smirked again. Oh, he's good.
"It is a charm though" He gave me a slight, quick wink and changed the subject. "What would you like to do, Madam?"

"Well, I would love to hear more about this concert we're going to tonight," I responded with interest.

He glanced over to the open laptop on the table and gestured to it, in which I gave him a gracious nod of approval. He began walking over to the table; he was about to touch the mouse pad when I realized I have just made an enormous mistake. Goodness gracious. My fanfiction was still up. I jolted my head toward him just as a smile came across his face.

Picking up the laptop, he began to ***READ IT OUTLOUD***. "*The Doctor* curiously looked at *Sherlock*, which immensely irritated him. *Sherlock*-"

Quickly, I reached for the laptop in which now he was holding above his head and reading with his neck titled up. Walking in the opposite way of me around the table. I could feel my cheeks turning red with embarrassment. A thousand different thoughts of rejection flew into my brain. They then ricocheted off one scenario, multiplying into another, ultimately leading to frustration.

"Come on!" I tried to catch him at the other end of the table, but he slickly spun on his heels and began walking the other way. This slightly reminded me of when we first met, and he started reading aloud with sly movements. My spurt of frustration has kind of turned into amusement; if I had a reason to be embarrassed, he probably would have found an excuse to leave already. And I like my fanfiction. I have nothing to be mortified about.

"But I like this story; it has my name in it!" He teasingly pleaded, still marching with the laptop above his head as if he was expecting rain.

"It's not your name Sherlock; it's the *real Sherlock*. You're the imposter!" I jokingly said in a '*serious*' voice as I tried to catch him again.

Dramatically, he gasped and turned his head to me with his jaw dropped. He spoke in an absurd and wispy voice that made me crack from my undercover seriousness. "Why I am offended beyond reconciliation, how could you-" He began to '*choke up*' "How could you say such things?!" I broke out into laughter as he gave me a little chuckle in return, putting the laptop on the table and pulling a chair out for me and then one for himself. "You know I've seen little snippets of fanfiction before on *Tumblr*, just never dared to explore it."

"Yeeaaa," I drug out as my laugh dissolved into a pause, "I wouldn't recommend it if you enjoy the current free time or sanity you have left. It will take it without mercy." I smiled at him while he was already smiling at me. Before this turned into a *Hallmark* moment, I turned my laptop towards me and went to *Google*. "All a righty then, what are we going to be jamming out to tonight?"
He leaned a little into the laptop and typed the answer quickly into the search engine, and after he excitingly pushed enter, I read it out loud. "The Reggae Moms?" Turning to him in awe and laughter.

"Oh yes, what could be better? Some middle-aged hippies jiving to some good reggae vibes" as he then started tapping his heart out on his imaginary portable bongos. I couldn't help but laugh. He's the definition of a dorky boy.

We had some time to kill before the concert started, and before I could even suggest something for us to do like watch TV or something, Sherlock chimed in with an idea. He wouldn't tell me what it was until we were all set up, as he emphasized. The next thing I know, we are back-to-back in the middle of my living room; both of us have headphones in but not plugged into anything yet.

"So, we're going to plug our headphones into the opposite phone, and then! Then, at the same time, we are going to play a song. Any song we like!" He was so enthusiastic; it was hard to match even though I was really giddy about this.

"So, we're essentially swapping music?" Asking him while we were still back-to-back, holding our headphones, ready for the music exchange.

He turned his head as far as it would turn and lightly leaned it on my right shoulder. "Precisely," returning his head back straight and handing the end of his headphones to me as I exchanged mine to him. I'm glad he couldn't see my face; my cheekbones are getting a workout.

On three, we were going to push the play button on whatever song we had chosen within the music library on our phones; no YouTube, that was apparently cheating. I scrolled down my artist list to *Edward Sharpe & The Magnetic Zeros*. I'm going to play him the song '*Man on Fire*'; for some reason, it kind of reminds me of him. Man, I love this band; I had a feeling he might too.

Okay, on three.
One.
Two.
Three.

As I clicked on the song, my ears flooded with this mesmerizing sound that faded into a steady drumbeat and magical sounding *oooOooOoooOoooos*. Then a man's voice, calm and elegant sounding, began to sing. I was captivated just by the first set of lyrics. That's when you know a song is soul-touching when it hasn't even hit the chorus yet, and you're sucked in. Unconsciously I was smiling and shut my eyes. I could feel the tiny bit of heat radiating from Sherlock's back onto mine, and I gotta say I liked the feeling of being close to him.

My head wasn't leaned against his; I thought that might be awkward or something. But obviously, he wasn't too concerned about that. I felt myself convulse just a tad in reaction to him laying his head delicately on my shoulder. I didn't open my eyes, but I could just picture what he looked like right now. His eyes gently closed, not a facial muscle in distress. And his smile, his smile as precious and fragile as a snow globe in a child's hands. I didn't want to move at all. I never wanted this song to end. I honestly didn't even know what I was thinking anymore. I was literally back-to-back with a dude I still didn't know the name of. And what did he even think about me? Better yet, what was I exactly even thinking about him. I don't know what I want, and I don't know what this is. I guess, as of right now, it's too unique to categorize.

He broke the movement barrier as he moved just a little bit to reach for his phone and pick a new song for me. I hadn't even notice mine had ended, being too preoccupied in my compulsive worries. He placed his head back into the same place as before. I chose a new song for him as well. I loved the warm feeling of his head against my shoulder. It was-

Vibration

Vibration

I tried not to shift a lot; I didn't want to make him move. Almost like, when you have the honor of a dog or cat choosing to snuggle up next to you, and they fall asleep, you don't want to move because they look so cute and peaceful. Oh my gosh, yea, thank goodness he can't read my mind; I just compared him to a house pet.

Sherlock:

That was '*Paradise*' by the wonderous *Coldplay*

My shoulder is cold

I giggled on the inside, gosh this dork. Carefully I leaned my head back on his shoulder; to my surprise, it was relatively comfortable! Back and forth, we played each other songs, slowly becoming more comfortable with one another. Just as the last song he had chosen ended, I felt his head lift from my shoulder, and I lifted mine up as well, taking my headphones out. He stood up from the ground and put his hand out to help me up, which of course, I accepted.

"Miss. Lucy, are you ready for some groovy fresh rhymes?" I laughed and opened my mouth to respond. "Yea, I wouldn't know how to answer back to that painfully embarrassing word choice either; off we go!" And like the switch of the lights, I hit on the way out, we were in the car and on our way to the venue.

There was a modest number of cars at The Café of Blues; it must be a new place in town. Walking in, we were immediately taken into the world that is the chillness of reggae. It was neat because you could just sit at a table and listen to them, still have a cup of coffee, and have a chat with someone. I've never had an experience like this before, and the experience itself had hardly even begun!

The hostess sat us at a table for two in the back corner; we could still hear the band well, though. Both of us ordered a cup of coffee which the waitress brought to us right away.
"And can I get you, folks, anything else?" The cheery waitress's voice made me smile.

"Oh yes, yes, please. Could I have an order of pretzels, please? Like the little pretzel sticks? I think I saw that on the menu as I walked in." He's so polite and goofy. If I received a cup of coffee for every please he let out, I'd be an even happier Lucy.

"Believe you did, sir. I'll be back with those for ya!"

I gave him a funny look as she came back and placed a small cup of pretzels on the table, and quickly went to tend to other customers.

"Would you like some?" He offered while picking up a pretzel stick.

Snickering a little, I shook my head as he gave me a shrug and began to stir his coffee with his pretzel and then eat it. Then once again, he picked up a pretzel, dipped it in his coffee for a few moments, and then ate it.

"I suppose at this point I shouldn't be surprised by your surprises anymore, huh?" I liked to poke a little fun at him in a friendly way; I think he took a liking to it.

I also loved how we could talk without saying anything. Most of the time, it was a laugh or a smile that answered our questions or began a conversation that only consisted of silence, yet it was still equally profound. Oddly, you can have a silent conversation. I suppose you may not even exactly understand the concept of it until you're in one.

Looking around, I noticed something about the wallpaper I had never seen at a cafe before. The wallpaper base was a crummy vintage-looking white plaster, but it was decorated with poems, song lyrics, and words, all in different colors of ink and a variety of penmanship; it was breathtakingly cool. The waitress must have noticed me admiring it when she swung by again to check on us.

"Our rule is you can write whatever inspiring words you want, but you can't overlap other people's words and no foul language. Otherwise, it gets painted over." With that, we each received a smile, and she was off.

"We'll have to come again sometime with pens and write some words of our own, huh?" Grinning at me, still enjoying his pretzels.

Smiling back, I nodded. "It is a definite yes," I spoke with such confidence. Who is this confident Lucy? Nice to meet ya, ma'am.

I loved the feeling of the guitar's bass beating in my chest. At the same time, Sherlock and I sipped on our coffee and admired the music while the many conversations that floated about the restaurant mixed in with the sounds from the band. It was like a mash-up. I was looking around the place, taking in the atmosphere, when I got that feeling you get when someone is staring at you. And I was right. Someone was staring at me—the dork across the table.
Looking at him, his expression didn't change a bit; he was still smiling while he looked at me with curiosity and a speck of wonder in his eyes.

"Alrighty then, what is it?" I asked him with a forceful smile of embarrassment on my face.

His smile got more detailed as his eyes strained just a little deeper into mine. I nudged him with my foot which broke his concentration.

Ha, point for Lucy.

"I was just thinking of something."

"And what would that be, Mr. *Holmes*?"

He put his elbows on the table and propped one arm up with his chin resting in his palm and the other arm holding onto the crook of his elbow for support. "May I please hear more about your brother, Colin?" I could feel my smile slowly escaping my face as there was a pause. "He just seems like a fascinating person, and I was thinking about that nice story you told me on the Ferris Wheel, but by all means, if you don't want to that-"

"No, no," I cut him off. I didn't want this night to be spoiled; I really liked how tonight was going. "I guess I can share another story," I decided hastily in my head which memory I was going to tell him. It was the story of my family and I moving into our family home.

Colin and I were young when my parents had saved up enough money to buy a house. It was a modest older house that belonged to a very kind family before us. It had been in their family for over a hundred years. But alas, they, unfortunately, had to let it go. Around the time when Colin was eleven, and I was twelve, we found a note hidden in a creaky floorboard in the hallway of the living room. On the top left corner of the paper, it was dated back twenty-five years ago, and in the top right corner, it read *'Note Four out of Six.'* The notes described the old memories the children before us had in the house. What games they would play, secret hiding places for stashes of candy, and most importantly, the author of the notes would always reference *Sherlock Holmes*. That's when Colin and I first got interested in the famous detective that would, in good time, end up being the obsession of my life.

The discovering of all six notes lasted until my Junior year and Colin's Sophomore year of high school. For a while, we couldn't believe it was over. It felt odd for it to be complete. We had always hoped to find just one more surprise note, but we never did.

When I finished, I grinned so big at the look of astonishment on his face.

"Now that's a heck of a story! Do you still have those notes?"

Nodding, I answered, "Yea actually, I think I do! Well, all except one, Colin has one of them." My weak smile hung on while my memories played back in my head. I glanced down at my phone for the time. "Oh my gosh, I can't believe it's already past ten o clock; where did the time go?!" I lifted my head up to him as his cheekbones lifted with his smile.

All in all, we really didn't care. I had nowhere to be, and as far as I could tell, neither did he. So, there we sat, talking the night away about moments and endless refills of our coffee.

"Okay, okay, so now your turn. What was your childhood like mysterious *Sherlock Holmes*?" It's hilarious you can tell how much he loves being called Sherlock.

"Hmm, you really care to know?" Dragging out his mysteriousness, I really didn't know what to expect. He played the part well. I mimicked his sophisticated look, complete with hand and arms placement as he gave me earlier when asking about Colin. He playfully sighed and took a deep breath.

"Well, my father is the founder of a company that works with a lot of worldwide trading and networking. So, my family's home is in New York City, a nice apartment in the heart of the big apple, but we traveled so frequently you could barely call it home. My father liked to conduct business in person; he's pretty old school and charismatic. He also liked having us all travel together as a family, so off we went. My mother didn't have to work because of my father's income. Still, she had a full-time job on her hands, raising and homeschooling me and my sister Julia practically on her own. My sister and I are two years apart, but like you and Colin, we're pretty close. Mostly because we didn't really encounter kids that much. And when we did, we couldn't really become close friends because we were always up in the air or sleeping on a train to the next destination."

I didn't expect to hear anything like that come from him.

"My Father wanted me to take over his business. Finally, one day I told him I had no interest in taking it over, and our relationship kind of broke. Luckily and thankfully, my sister has always wanted to walk in our father's footsteps and take over the company for him. So, I wasn't forced into the trade, but I can tell he's still disappointed in me to this day. My parents aren't very good at showing affection anyway. Their love language towards us is like, paying for stuff. I'm glad Julia and

I are close, though, and we've become nonmaterialistic people despite our upbringing. I just think there's more to life than expensive things, you know?"

Though he told me quite a lot about his life, he still felt like a mystery. I cleared my throat softly. "Do you mind me asking what you want to do then? If you didn't want to take over your dad's job?"

He quietly giggled and looked down at the floor to his feet. "You'll laugh at me," the words just barely lifting off his lips. I tapped my fingertips gently on the table to get his attention as he looked back up to me to see a reassuring smile. "A Train Conductor," His bright smile returned, "I've always wanted to be the man behind the train. Trains are pretty fascinating to me."

Something inside me just awakened with butterflies; could he get much cuter? "You could still become one, you know?" Trying to be inspiring in this happy moment.

There was a slight pause. "Nah, I think I'm going to be taking over Duck's Cranberries. Which sounds quite ambitious and perhaps a little cocky, in which case I most certainly am not trying to be" Oh Sherlock and his nervous rambling "It's just from what it sounds like. Tom talks about it a lot. And I'd be honored to carry out his work. He's a good honest man."

Before I could respond, he swiftly stood out of his chair and announced to me that it was almost midnight and he sadly had to work tomorrow, so he should probably drop me off. Without a thought, I blurted out that he could crash at my place if he'd like, on the couch, though, of course.

"Mr. Cumberbatch won't mind?" He teased as he opened his car door for me and helped me in as he then got into the driver's side.

"At the expense of a gracious gentleman, I'm sure he'll let it slide." I wanted to wink at him, but I didn't know how; and if I tried, I probably would have ended up looking like a girl shy of a straitjacket.

10. Sticky Note

Just as we stepped foot in the apartment and the door quietly closed, something must have clicked in his mind. "Aw, Luuuccyyyyy" There I go again, weak at the knees with that voice of his. I raised my eyebrows as I felt the sides of my lips curl just a tad. I blame this on the immense giddiness I get when he drags my name out like that.

"How I am so gracious of your far too generous offer. For what I'd imagine would be nothing less than a miraculous sleepover; I must, with a heavy heart, decline."

Why did I feel like my smile was drooping? I shouldn't feel affected by this; I hardly know him. I should be relieved my spontaneous offer is sliding by! But here my mind is, feeling sort of disappointed.

"I feel like a complete dirtbag. It's just, I didn't bring a change of clothes, I don't have my toothbrush which in the morning leads to bad breath, which leads to people avoiding you when you talk to them, which leads to rejection which leads to insecurities which leads to feeling sad which leads to watching sappy low budget romance movies which lead to ice cream-"

He was rambling again.

"-Which ultimately leads to me being an old forever alone man with like a dozen turtles. Yes, turtles, if I'm going to be a lonely old man, I'm going to be original about it."

I held onto my smile and tried to open my mouth to respond, but I couldn't part my lips. I didn't want him to leave; time really flies by with him, and maybe just maybe, I selfishly wanted a tad bit more.

How could I get him to stay a bit longer?

A romantic jester?

No, obviously out of the question.

Food?

Everyone loves food, and free food at that.

Well, the only thing I've seen the man eat is pretzels and pistachios.
Oh, hey, those both start with a P, how strange. I wonder if his name starts with a P.
Oh my gosh, I still don't know his name.
Focus, Focus, Focus.
Okay, I need to think fast; he was still searching through my eyes for my response to his trailing explanation of why he couldn't stay over.
Maybe it was too soon anyway.
Well, it's not like he was going to sleep in my bed, for goodness sake.
Wow, both of us on my twin-sized mattress.
How pathetic.
Nope, stop thinking of that, pop the thought.
Come on, Lucy, where are those creative problem-solving skills you so graciously wrote on your resume.
My weak smile grew strength as my lips parted just slightly.
There she is, there's the lightbulb.

"Okay, Mr. *Holmes*, I'll accept your apology under one circumstance." His eyes still searched through mine, this time with some curiosity. "An episode of *The Office*." I cunningly proposed. He couldn't hide the grin that crept upon his face. I think he was somewhat surprised by it as well; he nodded a few times as if he was negotiating it with himself in his head. With all the etiquette of a true gentleman, he shook my hand and excitingly closed our deal.

While setting up *Netflix* and figuring out what episode we left off, both of us sat comfortably on the couch. Well, after I set my phone on the end table, it was stabbing my hip.

"Oh, my goodness, I hadn't even noticed Carder wasn't here. I miss my bro" The word bro came off weird; it's sort of funny when you can tell there's a word someone doesn't use often. I loved his vocabulary though, he's so interesting to me.
But back to our reality, great, a bromance was forming.

I answered the question I knew was soon to follow his deduction. "He is currently swing dancing his heart out; I've always been convinced that there's never a normal night out for Carder."

"That should be a surprising sentence to receive, but I can actually see him doing that, and rather well too, good for him!"

"Believe it or not, we actually took a swing dancing class together; I even sort of got the hang of it." Looking at him, this would have been another perfect opportunity to have the ability to wink as he looked at me with slight astonishment.

Finally, I got to the approximate episode we were on. I was intrigued the first five minutes, but it was like I was hit by a train—a train of drained tiredness. Fight the urge. Keep those eyes open. It's really not that long of an episode if you think about it. This was your idea too! Don't be rude! Oh no, I could feel it happening. My eyes were manipulated by my sleep-deprived brain that they were merely blinking for a moment when in reality, I could feel my mind lift to the strange land of dreams.

Once, comfortingly, again, it was Colin and me.

Dreams are often dismissed by people. Sometimes you can make no sense of them, but I've found, in my case, my dreams like to take me to memories. And then sometimes they put their own twist on said memory. I would rather do without it, but sadly I am not in the business of lucid dreaming.

I looked around at my surroundings; we were in the backyard of our family home. In this backyard is the most perfect climbing tree. Like, this was the prized tree that would put all the other trees to shame. The two of us raced up the tree to our usual spots; I was typically always on a branch lower than he was. He's quite the daredevil with trees. It felt nice outside; the sun wasn't being obnoxious. It was friendly. I leaned my back against the trunk. My legs were extended and crossed on top of one another on the relatively stable branch. My arms were crossed over my stomach while my eyes danced along the painted sky, twirling into all sorts of troubling daydreams. Every couple of seconds, Colin's bare feet would come into the framed picture in my mind. He always swung his feet over the branch.

"Lucy, am I a good writer?"

"Colin, am I a majestic cactus?" I loved making him laugh when he was trying to be hopelessly serious.

"Oh, why do I even bother,"

"Well, I don't understand why you ask me that question; yes, of course, you have a gift."

"Can I come down on your branch?"

I knocked once on the bark; that means yes. A tree language we had developed from our many hours spent in it. Gracefully Colin swung down and balanced himself out on the branch, sitting with one leg hanging off each side.
"Life is kind of a pain, huh?" he sighed, and I nodded. "The only thing I can somewhat do with certainty is writing. But everyone can write, so it isn't special."

"No, no one writes like you; your writing is different."

"Biased," He blurted while looking off. I scoffed as he directed his attention back to me. "You know it's true," he said it so plainly, that it actually hurt.
I knocked twice; that means no. Colin rolled his eyes and flatly disclosed, "Writing is my fuel for life, my only sense of sanity. If I can't write, I'll lose my mind. And if I lose my mind, well, you've seen me when my mind has gone on a trip."

We sat in stillness for a few moments. But those moments drug out. Those moments each felt like an embrace of decades worth of memories that corresponded with each chirp I heard from the birds flying overhead.

"I'm not normal, Lucy."

"What in the hell is normal, Colin" I asserted, and shortly after, we both turned to each other and softly smiled.

"Lucy," I hated when his voice got small like that. "Knock for an answer, please, okay?" He's so much more than he'll ever realize. I gave him a nod and awaited his question. "Am I a bad person?"

Two Knocks.

Like I had an eternal alarm, I sat straight up. Wait- straight up? I looked around; I was in my room. I was in my bed, tucked in with my quilts. My phone was resting on the nightstand, and my eyes widened; what in the hell happened last night? Throwing the heavy quilts off, I grabbed my phone; it was 10:30 am.

Walking out of my bedroom, I quickly peeked in Carder's room; he was sound asleep. I tiptoed into the living room and kitchen area, scanning the premises when I heard some faint, sleepy breathing. Curiously and cautiously, I walked over to the couch and leaned over to find the one and only- Sherlock. I giggled at the sight of him. He was wrapped in one of Carder's comforters, lying on his back, with a yellow sticky note on his forehead. I gently took it off.

Do I have a story for you! Please wake me when you're up! –SH

Giggling in a hush to myself, I softly shook his shoulder, and he startled me as his eyes shot open; apparently, he's a light sleeper. His sleepy smile made my face break out into an instant blush and wide grin, though, slightly turning my head to one side and poking his shoulder.

"Good morning Mrs. Cumberbatch" his sleepy voice sang as he sat up and folded his hands in his lap.

"Good morning Mr. *Holmes*, I believe this" I waved the sticky note like a flag of surrender. "Is yours"

"Oh yes, yes yes, my goodness, where are my manners!" He pulled his legs up to his chest and patted the now unoccupied couch cushion. I sat down on the opposite end and kicked back, and relaxed. I could only imagine the kind of story he must have in store for me.

"Now I do have an explanation for why I slept here, which I must thank you again. You're a gracious host even if you are perhaps a little sleepy," Giving me a playful wink as I gave him a playful nudge. "So, about halfway through the episode, I noticed you had fallen asleep. And then, shortly after that realization, I heard your phone that was chillin' out on the side table go off like five times. I turned to you each time it went off, but you didn't wake up. So, okay, I felt terrible, but I looked at your screen, and it was Carder, sending these SOS panic texts. Carder said he really needed you, and he wasn't okay and- let me tell ya, Miss, you are not an easy person to wake up. I wanted to be a good friend to both of you, and just knowing he was in a bad situation made me feel anxious because I wanted to help. So, I carefully carried you to your bed and went back to your phone. Once again, I just want to say I am truly sorry; by no means did I mean to seem like a snoop or creepy or something along those lines. I was sort of panicking. I guess we were in a bit of luck that you don't have a passcode on your phone,"

Jokingly I gave him a small round of applause and laughed. He still seemed unsteady and had guilt in his voice, though.

"I got Carder's number from your phone and then placed your phone on your nightstand. And, and I'm rambling, aren't I?" I smiled and shook my head as he gave me a weak smile back and continued his story while fishing in his pocket.

"Long story short, Carder had a mishap at the club and needed a designated driver to bring him home." He pulled his phone out of his pocket, and I'm assuming he checked the time. "And long story short, I may be late for work," he nervously laughed.
I got up without hesitation to help him out of the cozy couch and then gave him a pat on the back of his shoulder. What the hell? A pat on the shoulder? Really- what are you, his fourth-grade football coach?
I could see the worry in his eyes; he didn't want me to see it, I could tell.

"You could maybe give Tom a call while you're on your way to kind of explain what happened? I'm sure everything will be okay." I was trying my best to sound reassuring.

He flashed me that damn smile and began rambling again while scrolling to Tom's contact. "Brilliant idea! Geez, I'm so sorry; gosh, I feel like an idiot. I hope Tom isn't too upset. I don't want to disappoint him. By the way, your couch is lovely; my neck isn't stiff or anything! And please thank Carder for letting me use his blanket; well, he yells at me when I say blanket because I guess it's a comforter"
While he kept going on about everything that ran through his worried mind, I turned him towards the door with my hands on his shoulders and guided him. He slipped his shoes on without tying the laces as I opened the door.
"I'm so so sorry, I'll make it up to you, I'll-" He turned to me while slowly lifting the phone to his ear, speaking in a whisper.

I chuckled and shook my head. "You're fine, you're fine. I hope everything turns out to be okay. Now go go go."

The smile on his face was slightly different this time as he answered the phone and began to speedily race down the stairs. His smile was radiant, as always, but it was like it had a chip in it. Like a crystal vase soaking in the sun, it was captivating, even if it existed with a small crack in it. The colors from the sun's rays would still illuminate from it, just in a different way.

Shortly after Sherlock's departure, Carder had woken up and made his way to the couch, plopping down and snuggling the comforter. He then went on to tell me about how the night started out great, but then how people got a little too rowdy and tipsy and crappy. You could see Carder's eyes were swollen from crying so much last night.

"Those handsy swing dancing sons of bitches, I thought I was going to run into more gentlemen than animals. Ugh, so, by the end of the night, my night knight in shining armor was '*Sherlock*' as he says you call him. He was very patient and nice; I probably talked his ear off and ran in nonsense-conversational circles. There were also most likely a lot of pop culture references mixed with rants in broken Spanish; I really wish I could see a playback of that car ride home."

We both busted out laughing and agreed we needed some Carder Lucy TV Time.

A little bit of *Say Yes to The Dress*.
Some *Community* always hits the spot.
Maybe I could even sneak in some *BBC Sherlock*.
Probably not, but you never know.

Carder obnoxiously cleared his throat. "So, did anything happen last night?"

"No, we're just friends, nosy."

"Bull a crap" he always liked being dramatic; throwing an '*a*' between words somehow did the trick. I gave him a little shove and laughed.
"Well, he's a million times better than Seth, I'll tell ya that."

"Okay, do we have to bring him up? He's gone, no more, done, out of sight, out of mind." I could feel the annoyance in my voice, and I honestly hated that.

"Yeeaaaaa word in the *Facebook* world is, he's back heerrrreeeee."

My face became flushed, and my heart felt like it was in a faulty elevator shaft that's cord just snapped.

Seth and I had dated off and on in middle school and were together through high school. Carder and Colin were the only ones who knew the behind-the-scenes of what he really was. We were that adorable couple that had been together forever and will be high school sweethearts to everyone else. He was sweet in ways that made your stomach churn when you realized what he was up to.
Seth was over-possessive, to the point of abuse, manipulative, and became very aggressive towards the end of our relationship.
My parents didn't know. His mom probably didn't know. I didn't even realize it until I fell into his grasp too tight. My muddled mind was to the point of begging to wiggle out but also terrified of being out of the grip, for we had learned we were nothing outside of it. Least, that's what he told me for so long. Even now, we've been apart for almost a year, and I still feel like he's looking over my shoulder. Like he's in the back of my mind.

I snapped out of it, "I don't care." Maybe if I act like it doesn't bother me, eventually it won't, and I'll be fine.

"Lucy, just promise me you won't talk to him, please?"

I excused myself and went to my bedroom and shut the door. Carder would find something to do; I just needed to be alone right now. This all felt overwhelming. As I climbed into bed and wrapped myself in my quilts, the haunting memories flashed like lightning in my mind. One haunted me, in particular, the turning point of his aggression. Carder found out through Colin, and Colin found out by mistake.

We had been dating for about four years at this point in time. My parents weren't home, and Colin was a tutor after school, so Seth and I had a study date at my house. We sat in the living room; he played music on the speaker while I studied for my Geometry exam. Geometry is the worst.

The headbanging music was so loud; I dropped my pencil and looked up at him, laughing. "Yea, this is great study music there, buddy," I sarcastically said, loud enough for him to hear.

He smiled and slipped his hands in mine, standing me up in front of him. "Well, Mac, I think you are smart enough, you don't need to study" He leaned in to kiss me, but I teasingly dodged his attempt of affection.

"Seth, I really need to study for this." Again, he tried to kiss me. And once again, I moved before he could.

The thing about Seth was he took any frustration he had in the back of his mind and twisted and molded it to become your fault- my fault. After years of repetition of this mind game he would play on me, I crumbled down each time it was my turn. When you are told something repeatedly, it begins to melt in, making a thick coat around your mind. To this day, I'm still chipping away.

He screamed at me that I was mocking him; he was behind in math, so I was ridiculing him for not being smart in his eyes. Simply I was just trying to study. I could have cared less if he knew how to solve a stupid math equation or not; I loved him for him. But he was stubborn and blinded by anger rooted so deep inside him that I don't think he even understood it. He felt betrayal; I felt a sharp sting on my cheek.
This was when Colin chimed in. As I was on the living room floor holding the side of my face, Seth grabbed his things and walked out the door, shoulder checking Colin on the way out. Colin was in shock. He ran to my side and examined my face, helping me to the bathroom so I could gather myself.

"Leave him, Lucy. I'm not kidding. I'm gonna kill him for hurting you." I would not cry in front of him. Seth's words played on repeat in my mind, refusing to leave.

Lucy, I'm going to show you and give you everything you want in this world.

You deserve this world.

You are my world.

Lucy, what would I do without you?

Lucy, what would we do without each other?

Lucy don't be silly, of course, we will always be together.

Besides, what would you do without me?

It's not like you could make it,

out there in the world alone.

That's why I'm here, to show it to you.

I get scared when you think about the future,

that's my job.

I'm the one who loves you.

Say you love me more.

You might as well.

Because no one else does.

"Colin, this was a mistake, an accident; this was my fault."

"Lucy, no!" I didn't dare look at him, I kept my eyes on the mirror, but I could see he was looking at me through the reflection. "Lucy, you did nothing to deserve to be hit. He's just abusive and horrible and a psychopath"

My eyes drifted to his, his angry and concerned eyes, and I broke. He gently moved me to the floor of the bathroom while we sat up against the bathroom wall, and he held me in his arms. I cried into his boney shoulder, gasping for clarity in each sob. This went on for several minutes until he gently grabbed my shoulders and looked me in the eyes.

"It's you and me, Lucy; we have to stick together. You're my best friend." He returned me back to his comforting embrace as I wrapped my arms around his frail body. Colin rubbed my back and softly hummed '*Hey Jude*' by The Beatles, a nostalgic song of our childhood, courtesy of our Beatles fanatic dad.

Shaking my head away from those thoughts, I tried to fall asleep, to escape for a while. I heard the door shut; Carder must have gone out. In a sense, I felt guilty, but I knew he would be okay. I knew he understood why I needed to be alone.

Vibration

I reached for my phone and pulled it out from under the blanket. A small smile came to my face.

Sherlock:

I ended up being Tom's wake-up call, so we both got off the hook for sleeping in today!

I was relieved; I think it would have broken my heart to see him break down from his boss's disappointment. I admired how much he cared about Tom; he was like a grandfather to him.

Sherlock:

But enough about me and my silly mistakes, let's talk about YOU

I made a puzzling face at the screen.

Me:

I can reassure you there is not much to talk about on the subject

I felt rather witty with the wording of that one.

Sherlock:

Hmm, seems false

Alas, I shall supply the questions

He was determined. I'll give him that.

Me:

Very well then

Shoot

I didn't enjoy talking about myself; something was unsettling about it. It felt wrong. But I couldn't help my curiosity-

Vibration

Holy buckets, he was quick.

Sherlock:

Perhaps sometime you and I could swing by your house, your family house? I'd love to see where you found all the hidden notes

I let out a deep sigh, not knowing how to respond.

Sherlock:

I'm sorry; too soon, too soon, pretend I didn't say that. The story was just super cool

Me:

Ha, no, it's fine, I would show you, but my parents don't live there anymore, they moved to New Orleans about a year ago

I did miss the old house. I missed the smell of it. I missed watching Dad make bread. I missed Mom having to climb up on the counter to reach a bowl from the cabinet's top-shelf.

Sherlock:

Awww, I'm sorry, Miss Lucy

Do you miss them?

Me:

Yea I do

Usually, we talk on the phone quite a bit, but these past few weeks have been pretty busy

But they always loved the sound of New Orleans, so they moved, which I'm happy they did. They deserve everything and more

Wow, that was very mushy.

Sherlock:

It sounds like you have a nice relationship with them. I'll bet they're wonderful

Me:

My dad would like talking with you, he always has something to talk about. And my mom would appreciate what a gentleman you are

I don't know how many times I retyped and deleted a smiley face at the end of that text. I wanted to put a smiley face, but I didn't want to be the first person to put the smiley face into the conversation. What if he wasn't an emoji kind of person?

Sherlock:

:) They sound entirely lovely

Well, what do you know, there's my answer.

Sherlock:

I feel like you and my sister Julia would hit it off, she's awesome

Do you think Colin and I would get along?

Well, that was nice of him to say about his sister. If she's anything like him, I'm sure she is fantastic. But my eyes closed; how was I supposed to answer that text? I hated to think about it. It's been close to a year since we last spoke.

Sherlock:

Lucy?

I must have blanked for a while; he was typing again.

Sherlock:

I don't mean to pry; I'm sorry, I sort of got a sense that your relationship with him might be a little rocky

Me:

What?

What makes you say that?

Now the response time was almost back-to-back.

Sherlock:

Carder and I touched on it just a little bit

Me:

What did he say?

Sherlock:

I just mentioned to him that you talked about your brother with me, and he was pretty surprised, and I wondered why and he told me he couldn't tell me, and if I wanted to know, I'd have to ask you.

I’m sorry if I overstepped my boundaries; I’d never want to be disrespectful to you

I couldn't believe Carder; he shouldn’t have said anything about it. He should have just left it alone.

Me:

You can't meet him

It was a few minutes until he responded.

Sherlock:

I understand, I’m really sorry, Lucy

I hated myself right now; I never wanted to be mean to him.

Vibration

Quickly I looked at my phone, hoping it would be another text from him, so I could recover from my stubbornness.

757-555-7823:

Hey, it's been a while

Me:

Sorry, wrong number

They texted back quickly.

757-555-7823:

Haha I see you deleted my number

I wasn't in the mood for this

Me:

Who is this?

Vibration

757-555-7823:

Come on Mac, it's me

11. Broken Daisies 

I felt a pit in my stomach that I hadn't felt in a long time, but now it didn't feel like long enough. I didn't want to deal with Seth. I didn't want to deal with this; I wanted out of this moment, out of this time. Maybe, I could find myself somewhere else with all my juvenile whimsicalness if I close my eyes hard enough. Even if for just a moment.

I thought about Mom and Dad. I imagined waking up to the sound of Dad playing his records while he and Colin lay on their backs in the middle of the living room floor, taking in the rhythms and discussing each song.
I imagined Mom making waffles as she patted a spot on the counter to jump up and sit on so I could help whisk the batter. I thought about how beautiful Mom is. She's the most beautiful woman I'll ever see.
I thought about how Dad and Mom met. Dad would always beg to tell the story when it came up; he knew every detail. He would go on about the washed-out jeans she was wearing and how her Bob Marley shirt made him instantly think: *'Oh my gosh, I have to speak to this woman.'*
Then he would ramble on about how he remembered it was a Tuesday afternoon and partly cloudy and- and mom and Dad met at a bookstore-

"Lucy?" I heard Carder come into the apartment; I was no longer in my nostalgic daydream thoughts as I felt my cheeks get warm.

I'm not really one to get easily upset or angry, but this and with the combination of Seth, I felt myself getting wound up. Rounding the corner of my bedroom to confront Carder, apparently, he was on his way to me. We ran into each other, resulting in me dropping my phone. Clumsy Lucy strikes again.

"Are you alright?" Carder asked while gathering himself, as was I.

“No, actually, I’m not alright. Why are you telling Sherlock about Colin? You know that’s not right; why would you do that?”

With his hands up in a surrendering pose, sassy surrender, I may add, he began to defend himself. “Okay, I am sorry if I spoke out of line or something; I would never mean to intentionally disrespect you. But I was speaking out of hurt feelings. I was shocked when Sherlock, a person we hardly even know, brought up Colin.” As I brought myself up off the floor, I didn’t pick up my phone, a generous Carder did, but as he picked it up it vibrated. "Whose number is this?"

"What're you, my boyfriend now? Give it here," I snapped at him as I reached for my phone.

"No, I'm the crazy-ass girlfriend who is going to go buck wild if you don't answer my question."

Quickly while he was caught up with his dramatic anger, I snatched my phone and read the text as another one came in.

757-555-7823:

I'm just not doing too well, and I need someone to talk to

I miss u

"It's no one," I answered him while looking down at the screen. The room was quiet.

"It's Seth, right? Of course, it would be, ooofffff cooooeuurrseee" He drug out his words in an annoying voice like he knew everything; his voice cracked a little at the end. I didn't speak, I didn't know what to say to him, and I had nothing to say to him right now.

Me:

I don't want to talk. Leave me alone.

I pocketed my phone and looked straight up to find Carder staring at me with bewilderment in his eyes. "Are you kidding me right now?"

"Oh, Carder, stop, please just stop" I had to turn away from his eyes when I talked to him; I couldn't look at him.

"No. No look at me" His voice shook with anger, a tone I wasn't familiar with from him. "Look. At. Me." Each word he pushed out with force and assertiveness. I looked up to find in this time, we only had one thing in common; both our eyes were wet.
"I have been there with you, holding your hand, wiping your tears through everything, Lucy. Everything. And you know what, most of those cases when you were crying were because of Seth. That egotistic jerk who doesn't give a damn about anybody but himself! Ever since you met him, he's been controlling you in some way or another; it makes me sick, and I'm done with that-"

"Carder, it's not like we're getting back together, okay?!" I snapped back as I felt a sting of embarrassment from the things he said. "You don't even know how I feel or what I said to him, and what if he's having dark thoughts and he does something bad, and it's on my conscious because I didn't reply; we both know how he gets when he sounds like this-"

"That's my point! We both KNOW how he is! He just wants to drag you back in and-" Abruptly, he stopped and looked at the floor and shook his head, looking back up at me. "Whatever, do what you want. I'm getting out of here." His voice was still a soundboard of anger, irritation, annoyance, and I sense a bit of disappointment and sadness. But right now, I was just hurt and upset; and for some reason, I was even more hurt that he was leaving and stomping to the door.

"Fine, whatever! You know, I never stopped you when you went back to Jason!" I yelled out as I stood in the hallway watching him go to the door, and right after I yelled, I felt disgusted with my words.

Carder froze in his steps just as he was about to walk out, his back faced away from me. He turned his head just slightly in my view. "You're right" his eyes still looked wet, "I wish you would have."

I could feel the vibration of the door slamming travel through the floorboards and to the bottom of my feet. My face felt warm; I could hear Carder walking out, and then I could hear his car start. I could feel the tears staining my face. My knees felt like they were buckling up. The beat of my heart couldn't have been faster. I'm so not used to feeling upset, the emotion of anger, so when it comes on, usually anxiety is skipping right along beside it.

Vibrate

Sherlock:

Lucy? Could we please talk?

I broke. All at once, I felt my chest collapse as a tearful gasp escaped my throat, and my fingers shook while I touched the screen. Am I just an eternal mess? Do I look lovely and pleasant from the outside but in reality, I'm a poisonous flower that taints the hands I touch? Why did I have that stupid fight with Carder, I know that he's right, and he's my best friend. I was just upset, and now Sherlock- this is all too overwhelming. Too much. Too much hurt. I couldn't hurt him. I couldn't let him hurt me. I wasn't meant to be with someone. I was meant to be alone, that's just- it's easier. I was done with people making me feel special and then watching them walk out the door. They all walk out the door. And maybe I can't blame them for leaving the unconsciously poisonous flower.

Me:

I'm sorry, I just can't talk anymore, I can't

Please don't message back

I held back the tears in my eyes as I pushed send, walking over to my bed and flopping onto my back. Blankly I stared at the ceiling, talking myself into believing I had done the right thing for myself. I just feel overwhelmed. I have too much going on right now in my head. He doesn't need someone like that in his life; he seems too nice for that.

Vibrate
Vibrate
Vibrate

I glanced at my phone, oh what perfect timing. I answered on the fourth vibrate.

"Hello, Lucy? Come in, Lucy," the soft and cheery voice on the other end sang.

It almost felt wrong to smile at this time. Quickly I cleared my throat and wiped the tears from my eyes as if she'd be able to see them. "Lucy in, Roger that. Mother come in, Mother."
She giggled. "I'm sorry dad and I haven't called in a while; it's been a bit hectic! Oh, and Honey, don't worry, dad and I will help you out with finances until you get back on your feet. We know you can do it! How are you feeling, by the way? Oh! Wait! Wait! Let me put it on speaker!"
I could hear her fumbling on the phone, trying to find the right button as she yelled in the background for my dad to come over. After a few seconds of them debating over which button it was, they were back on.
"Okay, we're back! So how have you been feeling?"

I took a deep breath "Yea, I'm fine, thank you for asking. It's just something I have to gain control over, that's all, and I'll find another job soon, I promise."
It was best to put mom's worried thoughts to rest as soon as you could; poor mom can get anxious pretty quickly. But I did feel a sense of warmth from just hearing her voice; I needed that.

"Take it at your own pace, Traveler," Dad's voice chimed in. I missed the sound of his reassuring voice; it made me smile.

"Oh! Dad and I saw on the *Facebook* that Carder moved in with you! Finally, I was wondering when that was *going* to happen! Isn't that right, Dear?"

I rolled my eyes. "Mom, he's not interested in me like that. He likes guys. We're just friends. We've been over this." My parents were mumbling in the background to themselves. I could hear mom telling my dad that Carder *obviously* has *always* had *some* feelings for me. In response, I heard dad laugh.
"Anyways, mom, dad, what have you guys been occupying yourselves with these days?"

Dad cleared his throat. "I've been long term subbing for one of the Art Professors at the University, your mom and I have been taking a pottery class, and she's

joined the church choir!" I could just imagine them both sitting at their kitchen table with the phone sitting in the middle of them as they hold hands; they're so cute.
"Look at you two! That's great to hear!" I honestly was happy for them, they always knew how to make the best out of life, and I admired that so much.

"Dearest, I wish you would come here, there's a lot of neat things to do, you'd love the culture and-"

"Mom"

"Tucker, say something," Mom spat out impatiently.

"Em, you know she doesn't-"

"Mom, come on, please-"

"We'll drive to her and visit Em,"

"She needs to get out of that town!"

"Oh, here we go again," I muttered.

"What, what, oh I see I see!" She was getting flustered, another thing she did kind of quickly, but with grace, I must say. "I'm crazy, right? Go ahead, say it!"

"Mom, calm down" Geez, this conversation flipped fast. Good distraction, though, I guess. It was comical, I can't lie.

"No, really I insist, say it! Go ahead, Tucker, say it! Say I'm crazy!"

"Yepp, you're crazy," he said in a playful yet flat-out tone; gosh, she hated that. Of course, he didn't mean it, though. I had to hold back my laughter; I hadn't heard classic mom and dad banter in a while.

"Oh, yea?! Well, I'm, I'm done here- I'm going to throw out all of your stupid records!" Hearing her get up from where she was sitting and stomp away.

"Please leave The Beatles!"

"They're going first!" I could hear her distant, upset voice.

Dad chuckled as I heard him click a button, and he cleared his throat; he must have taken it off speakerphone. "I adore that woman; it's never a dull moment, be sure to find someone like that."

"Dad, you're a brave soul, you know that?" We both began to laugh as I imagined he recalled old memories while he let out a soft sigh.

"That's the love of my life, Traveler. But hey listen, your mom is worried about you. And I agree with her, I know you don't want to, but you really should get out of town for a while."

The line was only engaged by our breaths until I found the words to say. "You know I can't Dad," And they just barely wandered out of my mouth.

He sighed. "I know Lucy, I know," pausing for a moment, "Mom will come around, and we'll get to you soon. How's that sound?"

"Sounds really nice, Dad" I tried to keep it short. I didn't want him to hear my voice crack.

"Your mom sends her love- I should go before she breaks my *Abbey Road* album; I love you, kiddo."

"I love you too, Dad." I was about to hang up when I heard him say something, and I pulled the phone back up to my ear.

"Lucy," The phone was up against the side of my face again, "Don't go changing on me" I swear I could hear his smile.

I set my phone on my bed stand and closed my eyes. I could feel my whole body begin to ease, surprisingly. Like my bones were heavy against the quilts, I felt my body begin to sink. It seeped through each thread and square of fabric, each filled with such memories and generations of hands.
I slipped down each string like I was being unraveled.

Down down I went.
Cascade from each and every argument.
Down down I go.
Ditch reality far below.

Falling asleep felt like I was falling through each fiber of fabric that laid with me in bed. I had dropped onto the grass, looking down at my hands, and then to the rest of my body. I was seven years old. I was seven years old again.

"Lucy!" I heard a cry from behind me, turning around to see a six-year-old Colin jump off the swing and run to my side; I must have jumped off the swing as well.

"I'm okay, Colin!" I smiled as he helped me up, and we ran to the teeter-totter and climbed on. It was strange to hear a younger version of my voice.

He went up. "Lucy, let's play the answer machine game!"

"Don't you get tired of this game?" I pushed off the ground.

The answer machine game was when I pretended to be a machine that knew every answer, and Colin would ask all the questions he most desired to know.

"No! You know everything! Please, please, please!" His smile covered his face as he looked up at me and pushed his feet.
I went down. "Okay, Okay," Giggling at how excited he was, "Go on."

He pondered a bit, "How do the leaves let all the other leaves know it's time to fall?"

"Hmmm," I hummed as I lightly pushed off. "That is decided by the Leaf Council, of course!"

Colin smiled as he looked at the trees in the distance. "Aren't they afraid to fall?" His feet crashing into the Earth beneath him. He went up.

"They go through a course when they are just little seedlings, so they are experts at falling."

"That makes sense" His feet dangled in the air; he looked lost in thought.

I shook my handle a little to get his attention. "Next question," I said in a robot voice that made him chuckle. But not for long.

"Why don't I have friends?" Colin's voice was so small and innocent.

"You do," Pushing off, "I'm your friend."

He went down. "Kids at school are really mean."

"It's because they're stupid." I went up.

"Should I call them stupid?"

I smiled a little "No, don't call them stupid" I went down. "Wanna pick some flowers for mom?"

He smiled and nodded, like the question before never crossed his mind. We raced out into the small field by the playground; the area was covered with daisies. I let Colin pick out the flowers; he would hand the individual ones to me while I held onto them, slowly creating a small bouquet.

"Will we always be friends?" Colin chimed as he handed me a daisy.

"Not always" He looked up to me in mid-motion of picking another flower. "Forever," I smiled at him as he reflected me, "Not always, forever, Colin."

With a fist full of daisies, Colin helped me find one with a long stem, and we broke the daisy off from the top. Colin hated that part. He always felt guilty. We used the stalk as a makeshift string to tie around the bouquet. Then we started to run back home together-

Vibrate

Damn it. Hello, reality.
My eyes opened to my phone; I had quite a few text messages and one missed call. Sitting up, I heard a small creek from the other side of my room where my desk resides. I must have been asleep for a while; the light no longer flooded the room from my window. I clicked my lamp on while swinging my feet to the side of the bed, expecting to see Carder sitting in the chair. Expecting.

"Didn't mean to startle you. I was just worried when you didn't answer my texts."

Calm, keep calm, “Seth,” keep your heart rate down. “How did you even get in here? Are you insane?"

His eyes caught the light from the lamp. They looked so desperate for comfort. "The door was open, I thought," He gulped, "I thought something had happened to you; you were responding so quickly and then nothing."

Carder must have left the door unlocked when he left the apartment, and the only reason why Seth knew where I lived was that he helped me move in. Shortly after he did, I explained that we weren't going to be moving in together. Then he left for California to go to college.

"You have no right to be here; I'm calling the cops" I hadn't seen his face in so long, and it looked slimmer than the last time I saw him. "Why are you even back in town?"

"My Mom is sick; I'm taking off school to help her around the house and be with her. Please just give me a minute, don't call the cops." He responded slowly.

"Sorry to hear that," Hesitating a little, I didn't want to lead him on a train of thought that what he's doing right now is okay, and his mom was always very kind to me. "I'll pray for her."

"Everything is changing; I just, I can't handle it, Mac."

"Don't call me Mac" I looked him dead in the eyes. I was surprised with myself how quickly that came out. "I agreed to talk to you for a minute, so don't do anything stupid."

"Why? Because you think I'm stupid?"

"No," Letting out a frustrated groan, "Stop, Seth just, don’t.”

He placed his hands on his knees and steadily stood up while his eyes pierced into mine. "You do. You think I'm stupid. Sorry, stupid Seth."
All the haunting familiar feelings of panic and paranoia rushed into my veins and petrified me. The words smashed against my skull. Screaming to be heard.

You did this to yourself, Lucy.

Happily, ever after.

Just me and you.

You have missed this, don't lie.

He stepped closer to my bed; each step felt like it pounded into my chest, and my heart felt like it was beating up into my throat. I was looking at Seth's eyes. They once looked full of the promise of love and security, and now they're consumed with anger and violence. Or had they always been, and I was just blinded. But this is no longer our story. It's no longer his turn. This was my story. And I was going to be my own hero, damn it.
I stood up with my chin held high, and any sign of fear fled as my feet met the wooden floor. I stood right in front of him, looking straight into his eyes. His fists were closed, as his jaw was clenched tight.

"I am not in high school anymore, Seth." From the corner of my eye, I could see his right fist closing tighter. I stood my ground, taking a small step forward forcing him to step back.
"Now get" I stepped forward again, he stepped back. "Out," Now I walked until I forcefully guided him back to the front door; he was standing against it. I got in his face "Of my" and looked deep into his eyes "Life."

His face was blank as I finished my sentence. To my amazement, a slight chuckle came from him. "Who do you think you are? Who is going to love a messy girl like you?"

I gave him a stone-cold look. "Me."
"You won't be able to stay away Mac, you never have been." He pushed off the door as I stepped back, and he turned the knob, "I'll see you soon." finally, he was gone. I don't even know where he begins to think that I'll come crawling back to him. He's delusional.

I felt so badass about what I just did, though. Carder would be- oh, yea, we're currently fighting.

Vibrate

Speak of the devil; it's like he knows when I'm thinking about him.

Carder:

What in the hell did you do to this poor guy?

What was he talking about- Oh, oh my gosh, I completely forgot.

Vibrate
Vibrate
Vibrate
Vibrate

Great, now he's calling. "Carder, let me explain before you start yelling" Wherever the heck he was, it was loud, I couldn't make out the music, but it was loud.

"Hold on, let me get to the bathroom where it's quiet" I was put on hold while I heard the music fade "Alright, now what did you say to him?!"

I had to pull my phone back from my ear; when Carder yells, he yells loud. "You're at Sherlock's right now? Look, I was overwhelmed, and hurt, and confused at the time; I didn't mean what I said, I don't know,"

"Yeah, well, he texted me, and it sounded weird, and I had nothing better to do, so I asked if I could come over. I pull up to his house, and I can literally HEAR the music's bass from outside. I tried knocking, but obviously, he can't hear me, so I walk in, and he has terribly sad Glee Cast music blasting throughout the entire house. Sad Glee music, Lucy! How could you make a human being stoop so low, have you no compassion!"
Okay, now he must be monologuing; sometimes he gets carried away, and either doesn't notice or can't help himself. Either way, it's pretty Carder.
"I hadn't listened to this music since I was in middle school when I was trying to pull off fedora hats. You know the dark ages, you think I want to be reminded of the dark ages, Lucy! You know how many somber cover songs I've heard since I've been here, huh?"

"Goodness gracious"

"Yea, you're telling me, my ears and subconscious weren't ready for this Glee reunion. What if this awakens something in me, geez we aren't ready for that. And I don't mean to be rude, but why? Out of all the music he could pick-"

"No, I mean, I feel awful, Carder," I started trailing off, thinking of the effect of my words. I really didn't know it would hurt him that much; I'd never meant to hurt him. I didn't really want him entirely out of my life either- Geez, I need to apologize. I really messed up.

"Look, you guys need to work this out, I know we got in a fight, and we'll talk about that later, but you need to talk to him. Like damn, Lucy, he must really like you or something. I'm going to pick you up."

"Carder, I need to tell you something-"
"Okay, just get ready. I'll be there soon; run outside when I honk the horn." And with the click of an ending call, I was sent out on my orders from General Sass.

Throwing on a plain blue crewneck and some jeans, I waited to hear him pull in. I let my hair down; it was kind of wavy, sort of straight, kind of whatever. Fits the mood. After a bit of time, I heard him honk the horn as I switched off the light and locked the door before I ran down the stairs and hopped into the car. It was uncomfortably silent.

"You can talk to me, you know, I'm not mad at you anymore" Carder broke the silence; thank God.

"Okay, well, some stuff happened while you were gone. My parents called; my mom is still on the idea you're secretly in love with me, by the way, so you're up to date on her conspiracies. And while I was asleep after the phone call, guess who broke in? Technically it wasn't a break-in because *you* didn't lock the door."

He glanced over to me for just a second and looked back at the road. "No fricken way, he did not" He saw me nod out of the corner of his eye. "What a fricken psycho! Did he hurt you?! I'm so sorry I forgot to lock the door, oh my gosh- I'm pulling over,"

"No, no, keep driving; he didn't hurt me. I actually" I stopped for a moment, taking pride in myself. "I told him off. Straight up told him to get out of my life."

Carder smiled. "That's my girl" While taking a turn, he leaned over and quickly kissed the side of my head, almost costing us our lives in the process as a car honked at us, but of course, Carder's road rage took care of that.

When we pulled into Sherlock's driveway, the music wasn't playing like Carder described. He was probably Gleeked out. It was pretty dark, but I saw lights on in the backyard. We both got out of the car and quietly shut the doors.
"You go talk to him; I'll be in the house. This just needs to be the two of you. Carder out." He went inside the house with two exaggerated peace signs while I made my way to the backyard.

This guy, I tell ya, he's so creative. It was like a picture off *Pinterest*; he had strings of lights hanging from the trees, illuminating the backyard. I felt myself smiling. For a second, I forgot why I was here, then I remembered as my smile dissolved. I saw him in a hammock with the lights above delicately shinned around him while his face was in a book. Cautiously I walked up to him; I could tell he saw me. I felt so nervous like we were meeting for the first time again.

"Whatcha reading?" I managed to squeak out. The hammock was decorated with comfy pillows, seeing he was leaned against a few, and his feet were under a pillow as well.

"Due to the absence of my other beloved books, as I'm waiting for my sister to ship them to me, I'm preoccupying myself with this one."
He didn't look up at me as his eyes danced about the page he was on, like a sad waltz.
"I would think you would recognize it." Now he sounded like *Sherlock Holmes*. It took me a moment to register what book he was reading, and then it clicked when I saw the tiny red stain on the corner of the spine. The poetry book that hit me in the head, the day we met.
"You can sit if you want," He offered as he tried to keep as straight of a face he could when scooting in the now swaying hammock, still not looking at me. I gave him an odd look; he wants me to sit in the same hammock as him?

I tried to gracefully sit down on the opposite end of the hammock; surprisingly, neither of us fell out as I landed in. My feet rested by his shoulder as his feet rested by mine. I thought it would be less awkward if I pretended it wasn't uncomfortable, so I leaned back and looked up at the lights above. It was still a little awkward. Awkward but with a lovely atmosphere.

I looked over to him; his face was blocked by the book still. Just as I was about to look away, he let the book fall out of his hands, revealing his face. I can't lie; the bookworm in me quivered for a moment that he didn't even save the page he was on. Course, I guess he could have memorized it; he is Sherlock.

"It's actually a good book, I made it sound like it's a punishment reading it, but it's a good book."

I gave him a weak smile, I felt so guilty still for what I said, and I could see his eyes were still recovering from his *Glee* session. "I didn't mean what I said," I looked down at my hands that were in my lap. "At the time, I was just overwhelmed, and I had a lot on my mind. I'm" My eyes found their way back to his face. "I'm sorry. That's not fair to you. I really can't even begin to express how sorry I truly am-"

"Miss Lucy," That damn smile, "all is forgiven," it's back.

"I'm just scared," I blurted out, wishing I could take it back right as I said it.

He sat up as much as he could and gave me a confused look. "Am I really that scary?"

He made me laugh a little. "I'm scared of whatever," I let out a troubling sigh "this is." I was afraid to look up at him, but when I did, he still had his lovely smile on his face, like he was somehow amused.

"Lucy-" I cut him off; I had to explain more before I heard what he had to say.

"You know how when your house is a mess, you don't want to invite people over? Well, that's me. I'm a mess, I can't, I can't let people get close to me. The only reason why Carder is, is due to the fact he crafted his own key to get in. I'm just not who you think I am. My life isn't what you think it is. I don't want you to see that, to tell you the truth; I liked that you didn't know much about me. It was like I was someone else for a while." I paused to let him respond if he even felt like he could. He gave my words some thought, and he looked at me with no fear in his eyes and no hesitation in his voice. "I never wanted you to pretend, Lucy. I knew there were things I didn't know about you, and there are things you don't know about me." He smiled just slightly as the glow in his eyes softened.

"Lucy, I have been in every continent, well except for Antarctica, no offense to Antarctica, but I will probably never go there. And I have met so many amazing people in my travels with my family. I have met men who volunteer every day despite barely feeding themselves and their families. I've met brilliant women who give up all they have just to put their kids through school. And I've met kids that are happy with just simply playing outside. I have met so many people. But I've met no one like you. Nobody who makes me smile the way you make me smile and laugh the way we laugh." I looked up at him; I couldn't believe what he was saying. I could feel my eyes swell up a little.

"That first day I met you, and I saw you, I was just, lost. Lost in giddy daydreams, in possible joy, and wide smiles. I was only planning on fixing up my God Mother's house, selling it, and then heading back to New York, but something about you just made me want to stay. And I just wanted to get to know you. You have such a kind smile; did you know that? After the first day I met you, I called my sister and told her about my change in plans and what happened, and she didn't believe me; she said it sounded like something out of a quirky indie movie." He was sporting his wide smile now.

"Lucy, I'm not all cleaned up as you may think; I don't have everything together, and as far as I know, I have no idea what I'm doing with my future. I don't know everything about your past, and I am deeply sorry I crossed the line when trying to find out so. I guess I was just eager to have a friend that I could actually continue to get to know. I know you may be scared, but I just want you to know that I just want you to be happy. That's the one thing about my future I do know, that you should be happy. You deserve to show the world your smile every day. And I'll be damned the world is deprived of that."

I was smiling and crying softly at the same time. I sniffed and looked at my hands as I folded them together. My heart felt like it was being stitched back together, slowly but surely. I'd never been told something so beautiful, sweet, and raw.
"I don't even feel like I deserve those kind words, Sherlock." I softly let out, still looking at my hands. I closed my eyes for just a second as a tear fell. I expected the tear to drop on my hand, but as I opened my eyes, it had landed on his hands that were wrapped around mine. He had moved closer to me with his legs crisscrossed, looking at me with the most comforting smile. I looked into his eyes, sniffling, trying to control my emotions.

"Lucy, you are more deserving of those words than you will ever know." His smile sparked a sense of hope in me. "I can't tell the future, but I can tell you that it would be a privilege to make you laugh, to make silly faces at you, to plan adventures for the three of us, and to help you with whatever you need." His hands embraced mine, an embrace that I didn't know I had been longing to feel.

"I'm just such a-" I couldn't hold it in anymore; my vocal cords cracked as a sob filled with sorrow broke off, and I pushed as hard as I could to make the words come out through my crying breaths. "I'm such a mess" The tears felt like they would never stop; I didn't know what to do, I felt my body tense up. I didn't want to look like this in front of him. I'm an ugly crier. My thoughts are just so mixed up and overwhelmed right now; I can't help it. My mind felt like it couldn't even comprehend why he wasn't running away right now, dealing with this absurdness. We sat in silence until my crying had turned into quiet sniffles once again. And then, I heard him humming. Humming? I looked at him.
"Whatcha humming there?" My voice was still wispy.

Turning his gaze to me, he began to sing.
Great, of course, he can sing.
And it was good.

Gosh darn it, it was good.
His voice was so light, so peaceful.
He was singing a verse from 'Hey Jude.'

I just, I couldn't even believe it. How is any of this even real? And though his voice was delicate, and I wanted him to keep singing, I felt a sharpness run through me when he eventually gradually stopped.
I felt the pit of my stomach ache. I had to tell him. I wanted him to stay in my life, be the presence he has been, and if I wish that, I need to be honest. As much as I tried to pretend it wasn't a part of my reality, Carder was right; I had to tell him. Because I'm obviously still working on processing, and if he's going to be in my life, he should know.

"I have to tell you something" Sitting up a little, now we were at equal eye level. He gave me a nod, still looking at me with such a sincere radiance in his eyes. "You can't meet Colin" My heart was racing; he could tell. The corners of his lips were turning down as he anxiously bit the inside of his lip. I felt my bottom lip quiver; I needed to be strong. I needed to hold my tears back and ignore the lump growing in my throat. This is it.
"You can't meet Colin because," I looked into his eyes, soft and reassuring as I took a settled breath. "He died about a year ago."

12. Headlamp Dorks 

Right as my last word cut off, I saw the spark in his eyes dim and the desperate look for clarity fade in. I wasn't expecting anything less; I did just drop a massive bomb on him. What could I even expect him to say back? Especially not even knowing Colin. But selfishly, I wish he would say something. Something so monumental that it would strip the pain away from the reality that just settled in. Goodness, I can't stand having these invasive-impulse-selfish thoughts.

"I uh," his voice trembled while he took a pause, "I thought you said he had one of the notes you found in, in your old house?" I hated that I made his voice shift to this, this tone that I wasn't familiar with.

I felt my chest rise, harshly trying to hold the tears back; I was so over crying tonight. "He does" I looked down at my hands that were resting on my lap. "At his funeral, I put it in his jacket pocket." My eyes were glued to my hands; I felt the crying would start over again if I looked up. I regretted this so much. But I guess it did need to come out if we were really going to be friends. And holding it in was only hurting me.

"Lucy" He lightly cleared his throat. "Thank you for telling me and for trusting me with something so fragile. I just want you to know that you don't have to talk about this if you don't want to. Or if you want to at another time, it doesn't have to be right now." He paused for a moment. "I can't even imagine." His words drifted off softly. I kept looking at my own hands as his hand came into my view, and he gently tapped his finger on the crease of my thumb and pointer finger; he got me to look up at him. "Does that sound okay?"

I wanted to give him a sweet, simple smile back, but I just couldn't muster it right now. I settled for a nod. "I think I just need to do something to get this off my mind; I don't want it to get too comfortable in my thoughts, you know?"

Carefully, without rocking the hammock too much, he pulled his phone out of his pocket and checked the time. "By our luck, the night is still young; any ideas?" How does he have this miraculous talent of not letting things get awkward? It's like a superpower. Shrugging, I thought on it for a moment while my eyes got lost amongst the hanging lights in the process.
"Well," the tad bit of suspense he lingered forced me to look at him yet again, "We never did take that kayaking trip."

I raised my eyebrow to him, in a sassy way, I may add, and let out a chuckle. "Kayaking? Now? In the dark?"

"Miss Lucy, you really are silly, no, of course not in the dark." Swiftly he jumped out of a hammock and then stood in a *Superman* pose. "I have headlamps!"
With all the confidence in the world, he held out his hand and helped me out of the hammock. He really is a dork; I love it.

Giggling as my feet hit the grass, I think it instantaneously hit us both as our heads turned to each other. An expression of panic mixed with hilarity pierced in our eyes, and the word blurted out of our mouths simultaneously: "Carder!"

I broke out laughing as I hushed myself. "Oh gosh, I completely forgot; Carder went in the house when we first got here."

Quietly we both snuck into the house, tiptoeing into the living room as I saw flashes of light from the TV while I watched my sneaky ninja feet.
Yes, I was impressed with myself.
Point for Lucy.

"Never thought I would be sneaking into my own house," Sherlock whispered from behind as my feet just met the living room floor. And there we saw him, the majestic Carder, deeply asleep on the couch with some reality show rambling away in the background. We both spoke in a whisper so we wouldn't wake him. "So, up for kayaking?" The whisper conversation continued; I must try to

remember later to compliment him on his whispering skills. My smile crept up on me as I nodded to him and started to make my way out of the room when I was quickly stopped by his soft plea.
"Wait, wait, wait, please, please, please" Turning around to him to see he held his phone out. "Can you take a picture quick?" This guy has some nerve.

Accepting the request, I stood in front of the TV to get some lighting without the flash. At the same time, Sherlock cautiously posed himself next to Carder, a huge goony smile on his face and both thumbs up. I will have to enjoy this night with him. Because once Carder sees this picture-
The world will be short of one consulting detective.

Like school kids, we hushed our laughter as we snuck out of the house as quickly as possible. It was like we were runaway teens, and Carder was our overprotective mother. Scary the amount of truth that sentence has. We both caught our breath as Sherlock let out a sigh of relief.

"At least we don't have to whisper anymore. I gotta hand it to the ninjas; that is some serious cardio." We walked to the edge of the yard near the hammock when he came to a stop. "So, this little path right here," pulling out his phone as I did the same so we could utilize the flashlight feature, "Leads down to a small creek? River? Stream?" He pondered for a moment, "Small mass of water." and he was satisfied with that. "By that small mass of water, there is a shed with the kayaks and headlamps in it."
We turned to each other and nodded, like a signal that we were ready to begin our mission. The woods we were walking through looked straight from a *Stephen King* novel and triple dipped in *Steven Moffat's* tea, frightening yet strangely beautiful at the same time. Course, I didn't mind so much, walking with him and being in his company was not the worst way to pass the time.
"Sorry for the creepy effect; I swear I'm not a murderer." Sherlock prompted as we continued to walk the eerie path.

"Hmm, I was about to compliment your murderous scenery choice." I heard him giggle just a little, and then I felt his finger tap my wrist.

"We have reached the wonderful kayak shed! I must say I do love the color of this shed. My Godmother had a keen eye for color. A nice bright yellow, she seemed like a spunky woman. I mean, how can you not smile at yellow. Yellow is like that friend that kind of gets on your nerves because they're always so gosh darn happy. Still, then you take a pause and smile and think, *'Well, no wonder they're happy, it's a Fan-Fricken-Tastical life'* that it is! Yellow is just- " He paused, turning his attention to me. "Rambling- got it. I'll drag out the kayaks and all the supplies we'll need. Let's see- we'll need two headlamps, oh we'll probably need the pegs too, Mrs. Cumberbatch, would you be so kind as to please hold my mobile device while I get our equipment?"

I smirked at his word choice and held onto his phone while he went inside the shed. "Do you need some help?" I called out to him.

"No! No, no, I got it! If you'd like, I'd love to set that lovely picture you took of Carder and me as his caller ID!"

Laughing in response, I pocketed my phone and worked on the task. Alright, let's see, contacts:

Angelo.D
John. W
Julia Sista'
Mom
Sir
Sassy Carder
Tom Wyatt

I heard him beginning to drag out our stuff, so I scrolled to what I was assuming was Carder's contact, cleverly named 'Sassy Carder', and changed his picture. I guess before, it was a goony picture of the two of them in Aviators. What a bromance. But where was my name on his phone? It's not like I could ask him because then I'd sound like an obsessive weirdo. And then he would leave me to fend for myself in the woods. And there very well isn't any coffee in the woods, so we can't have that.

Sherlock set the kayaks down and walked over to me with a headlamp already on his head, the second one in his hand waiting for me. His feet stood at the tips of mine as he worked on adjusting the headlamp to fit my head. I admired the messy adorableness of his hair, little strawberry blonde hairs poking out from under the straps. He gently placed and tightened it as needed, then while turning the light on, he smiled down at me while also squinting from the light—us headlamp dorks. I told him I knew how to kayak, but I would trail behind him to follow his lead to wherever we were going.

"Look at you, always on top of it!" He turned to me while I squinted at the light from his lamp, which made him laugh. "Sorry about that! Oh! Phones! There's a compartment on top of the front of the kayak we can put them in there- you know what, water gets in there sometimes." He looked down and rubbed his neck while thinking. Then again, my eyes took a surprise attack from his light. "Sorry again for the light; I have an idea!" Awaiting his response, he turned away from me and started- Woah, there goes his sweater. Yepp, that's the bare back of an attractive gentleman.

"So, I can wrap our phones in my sweater and place it in the compartment, which should be enough security." He held his hand out while holding his phone and sweater in the other. I tried to play it off with a smile as I handed him my phone, but he could tell I was totally checking him out. That's just great.

While he wrapped our phones up in the sweater and placed it in his compartment, I drug my kayak by the edge of the water as he soon followed me. We used the paddles to push off the grass and into the water. At first, I was uneasy about all the noise we were making by the splashing paddles and the restless ripples. But that faded reasonably fast when I realized I was amid a memory in

the making, and I should just be in it. And this time, I didn't bother to ask where we were going; Sherlock is a man of many surprises. I did notice something, though, while I was a bit behind him. We were paddling on in blissful silence when I saw something on his back. My eyes strained forward while trying to concentrate on not bumping his kayak. I couldn't make out exactly what it was, but for sure, it looked like a tattoo on his right shoulder blade.
Alright, that's pretty cool.

A few strokes through the water later, he turned his head over his tatted shoulder. "See that small island thingy up ahead? That's our stop!" He smiled wide with his teeth and turned his head back forward. Now paddling like a maniac.

I shook my head in laughter as I tried to match his pace, which was unsuccessful, but we both floated onto the small shore. As my kayak hit the sand, he had already gotten out of his and offered me his generous assistance—Whatta gent. Gazing around as he helped me out, I gathered that this wasn't really a big island. It was just a lost patch of mounded grass, with its only inhabitance being a single tree. It was a large tree, though; this was the loveliest tiny island.
During my observative inner monologue, Sherlock had pegged down our kayaks. His gentlemanly acts continue.

"The first night I settled into Virginia Beach, I found the shed and decided to go for a kayak trip, and that's when I came across this place. I spent hours here just thinking. Just sitting on the grass, thinking the day away. But then I got pretty hungry, so I left." He walked over to the tree while taking off his headlamp and hung it on one of the lower branches.
"Care to sit with me?" Smiling as he sat down and leaned against the tree. The lamp's light acted as a spotlight; I hung mine beside his and took a seat next to him while fixing my hair. "Lucy," Lightly pulling my hand away from my hair. "Your hair looks great, as always." Geez, I was smitten.

"Aren't you cold?" I asked while trying not to cringe at myself for not fixing my hair. But I suppose I'll take his word for it that it looks okay.

We both looked out to the water; it was calm and decorated with a few shining sparkles from the stars overhead, they kind of reminded me of his backyard lights. "Surprisingly no, it's actually rather quaint. Are you cold?"

"Oh no," I answered far too quickly. "No, I'm comfortable." Seeing him smile from the corner of my eye, I gave him a nudge. "So, you have a tattoo on your back, huh?"

Turning to him, he mischievously looked behind his back and faced me with a childlike gaze in his eyes. "Have I?" He teased.

"Oh, stop," I protested with a pretty heavy amount of sass. "Might I ask what it is?"

He titled his head a bit down and gave me a look of wonder. "I can't see my back; how would I know?" My jaw dropped as I smiled, and a soft giggle came out.
"My my my, how your silliness never ceases to amaze me. Now that we are done joking around, is there anything else on your mind?"
Not even gonna fight this one. I'll see it sooner or later. He can hide his name, but he can't- oh my gosh—his name.

"In fact, yes there is; when am I going to know your name?"

He groaned a little. "Names are so old-fashioned; I'm past it, never looking back!" Shouting with excitement riddled in his voice and hands in the air like he was showing me the universe.

"Aw, no, come on, you've kept it a secret long enough; it's literally killing me!" I shifted, so I was facing him, but he didn't move. He was still looking forward, now with his legs crossed over one another and his hands resting on his thighs.

He just barely shook his head, his voice not any louder than a whisper. "I don't think I can bring myself to it just quite yet." I think my confusion found its way

into his thoughts; there we go again, talking without talking. "As you told me before, how you liked who you were before I knew what you didn't want me to know, I like" His silence was almost painful to endure for this quiet second.
"I like this. Being 'Sherlock.' Because I'm afraid if I tell you everything about me, then you'll get bored. You'll gradually get less interested in spending time with me, and I've really come to like your company." His voice cut out; his gaze still didn't reach mine.

"I can almost guarantee that you will always find a way to surprise me." Clearing my throat, he finally circled his eyes to mine. "But just like you told me when you're ready, I'll be here listening," I swear it wasn't the light from the headlamps that brightened those dazzling eyes of his; it was pure delight.
"Besides, I kinda like Sherlock." His smile made me lose my focus for a second.

Now he copied me as he shifted himself as well; this reminded me of the night we were sitting on his couch. "The water just reminded me of my grandpa," He smiled at me, then got lost in his own nostalgia back at the water until his gaze returned.
"This is a bit random, but could I maybe please tell you about him, now that it's kind of on my mind?" I could faintly hear him trying to cover up his soft sniffles. "I haven't talked about him in a long time, and to be honest, I like sharing things with you." With his smile still a bit weak, I nodded to him with a modest grin as he perked up. I felt honored he asked me.
"This tradition started when I was around five years old, and Julia was seven. My parents would let us stay at my grandpa's house the whole summer while they took some alone time to themselves. Despite my father's cold-heartedness towards me, I will always admire how he loves my mom; the way they love each other. Miles, time zones away, and they still talked about one another like they were just one room over." I smiled at him as he discreetly scooted a bit closer to me; I hadn't noticed until he started talking again.
"She's a witty woman. But back to me and Julia's summers at my grandpa's! His house, which is my father's childhood home, is in Rhode Island. It was a road trip to drive from our New York home to grandpas. Still, the excitement I felt

whenever we did take that long car ride, that feeling always pushed me through the months until summer finally strolled along. My mom's parents passed away before Julia and I were born. My father's mom passed away when Julia was a baby, so it's always been just grandpa for us. Which, I wish I could meet my other grandparents, but my grandpa was such an extraordinary man, it made up for it. Grandpa had a dream beach home, about thirty minutes from the big city and built right off a private beach. A big set of stairs from the back went down to the beach, and then there was the lighthouse on the shore. That lighthouse was the only reason why grandpa stayed there. Back in the day, his father built that lighthouse, and it was the only one Sailors would trust. Though it wasn't used for its original purpose in I don't know how long, grandpa just gave random tours sometimes for tourists. He didn't like charging for tours; sharing the lighthouse was a joy of his. He didn't need a whole lot of money anyhow, seeing as he mostly lived off coffee. Hey!" He caught me off guard as he poked me in the shoulder. "Sounds an awful lot like this girl I know!"

"Oh, does it really?" Intriguingly I replied as I returned the poke back to him.

"Oh yes, most definitely, perhaps you know her! She's married to that Cumberbatch fella! Oh, what's his name, Benjamin? Bartholomew? Barrington?"

Letting out an exaggerated sigh, I laughed and playfully pushed him just enough for him to slightly fall over. As he sat back up, he was now sitting closer; like, our arms were touching.
Play it cool.
Hide your dorky giddiness.

"While Julia swam and played on the beach, Grandpa and I would climb up the lighthouse stairs and watch for the boats. I can remember racing Julia up the stairs, the both of us laughing as we tried to push past one another in the narrow stairway that twirled up, our laughter echoing. But most of the time, it was just grandpa and me up there; Julia got bored fast, for me though I couldn't get enough of it. I loved being up there. Grandpa had endless stories, and he never repeated one. Stories, though, and pictures, I guess, are the only things I have to remember him by. I suppose that's with most anyone we miss, though. But they're stories I'll never forget; I know I'm sorry I keep bringing up these sad, awkward memories. I'm sorry, I don't know why I-"

I shot him a look that stopped his rambling. I'm sure he could tell by the gaze in my eyes that there was no need for him to apologize, and I wanted him to keep going; and that he did.

"Well, there is a memory that comes to mind, and it kind of weighs on me because I've never really opened up about it much before." His eyes floated off me for a moment, almost in contemplation.

"Can I share it with you, please?" I shared something tough with him tonight; maybe he felt he could do the same. I gave him a gentle, reassuring nod.

"It was the 4th of July; I was twelve years old, and Julia was a teenager now, so she went with her friends she made over that summer to the city to watch fireworks. It was the most beautiful view from the lighthouse to watch the fireworks Lucy, breathtaking. It was my favorite night of every summer I spent there. Grandpa and I would throw on some warm clothes because it got chilly up there at night, and once we got up there, we would set our chairs up on the small observation deck and watch the fireworks all night. Since it was such a great view, we caught lots of shows off in the distance. There wasn't one year we didn't end up just sleeping up there. But that particular 4th of July, grandpa and I got on our comfy warm clothes and headed out to the lighthouse when it was dark. The fireworks were bound to set off any minute; we were running a bit slow that day. I remember grandpa hadn't been feeling the best that whole week and more so that day, but he insisted we stick with our little holiday tradition. We got down to the beach, and just as grandpa unlocked the door to the lighthouse, the first fireworks started to go off. He told me to go on and run up there before I missed the good ones and that he would be right behind me. I started running, my chest was filled with anxiousness, but my smile was wide and open. I could see the flashes of color plaster every few seconds against the walls inside while I ran up the spiral stairs. I almost reached the top when I heard another loud sound break off a previous bang, but no color reflected onto the wall. That's when I heard grandpa, and my smile disappeared. I just about tripped myself with how fast I was running down the steps, each stair my foot slammed on, I felt my heart pound while the loud bangs from the sky kept making me flinch, and the colors kept coming and going on the walls. He had fallen; he must have tripped trying to keep up with me. Grandpa didn't really live long after those injuries; it's harder for older people to recover, and he had some other underlining stuff going on." Sherlock's eyes looked out to the water and then to his hands before his attention was brought back to his story.

"So, the 4th of July is a bit different now, but I still think of him when the time comes around. I think you would have enjoyed his company, you two drinking coffee and watching the boats come in and sail out."

At the end of this story, he didn't seem as sad as I thought he would. He just continued to look out to the water in front of him with a mindless smile; I think he felt like his grandpa for a moment.

"My Dad was an only child, so he sold the house. Someone lives there now." He leaned himself back with ease against the tree and looked up to the headlamps hanging above us with a more pleasant smile on his face as he turned to me. "Looks like we've got our own little lighthouse, huh?"

I smiled at him as my eyes searched through his, trying to fathom how he could keep such an incredible spark alive, how he copes with so much. I didn't mean to, but I glanced down at his lips and back up.

And oh,

dear holy buckets,

he caught that.

Our faces weren't that close together.

Oh, but our arms are still touching.

He looked down to my lips.

Do I have nice lips?

What even is a nice mouth?

Mouths are kinda weird now that I think about it.

Like a hole in your face.

Speaking of faces, his was moving closer to mine.
Panic-***Panicking***!
What do I do?
Close my eyes?
I don't even know if I want to kiss him!
What the hell am I saying?
Better yet, what the hell am I doing-
Wait, what, what is that?

"Mosquito!" I abruptly altered as the only inhabitants on this tiny island.

"What? Where? On me?! Get it!"

Annndddd I palmed him.
I palmed him.
I palmed him on the forehead.
I palmed him on the forehead without hesitation.
The bug has squashed above his brow.
He whipped it off while I just now felt the complete horrific expression on my face as he started laughing.

"Good lookout Lucy!" He looked at his fingers after wiping his head. "Got him right in the act, thank you! I like my forehead blood, and I intend to keep it."
He gave me a little nudge and seemed to forget the fact that he was, at least I think he was, leaning in to kiss me, and I hit him in the face.

Smooth, Lucy, *smooth*.

His laugh softly faded as he moved away from the tree and laid on his back, patting the open grass next to him. The stars looked so close to us; I wonder what we looked like to them. We weren't touching this time as we laid and gazed at the sky, but I could still feel the heat from his body greeting my skin.

"Lucy, we should name this place; what-do-ya think?"

A thought fluttered and raced through my chest and my stomach. "I have an idea." I smiled while we still observed the night sky.
A quiet hush surrounded us. The water was at rest. The wind flew off to another destination. It was like the Earth was taking a pause just for us. One star caught my eye when we first laid down, and I hadn't taken my sight off it since. I couldn't help but think that maybe, it could be Colin.
"Let's call it Lighthouse Island."

13. The Great Book War 

My gosh, the way he looked me in the eyes made me feel weak with emotion, an emotion I didn't want in fear of rejection, but a feeling I felt oddly drawn to. Ugh, what is this-
oh gosh, *feeeeeelings.*
I thought maybe he would move closer to me, but I heard my phone ringing within his sweater in the kayak. Breaking the mid-motion awkwardness, I smiled and went to retrieve my phone. Unraveling it and tossing his phone to him, my eyes grew with fear at the sight of mine.

"Oh, boy," Not taking my eyes off the phone.

"What? What's wrong?"

I gulped, "It's Carder."

He stood up quickly and rushed to my side. "Oh my gosh! What's wrong?! Is he alright?!"
Taking a deep breath, I showed him my screen.
"Oh no, it's worse than I thought."

I nodded. "It's not going to stop."

"We have to do this."

With much anxiousness, I slid my finger across the screen, answering Carder's FaceTime call. With that, Sherlock quickly ducked down and crouched by my feet, so he wasn't seen. I couldn't help but laugh when Carder's face popped up, and he was not happy about that.

"You giggling bastard, I go outside after waking up from a glorious, unexpected nap to find an empty hammock. What the hell am I supposed to think about that?!" I opened my mouth to answer, but as I expected, I was promptly cut off. "Oh no, you shut that pretty mouth; I ain't done." From the looks of it, he was still at Sherlock's house, and he must have noticed my wandering eyes as he continued his dramatics.
"Where is he, by the way, huh? He kidnaps you, doesn't leave a note, and doesn't have any fricken food in this house! Where is he?!" Believe me, I tried to hold it back as much as I could. I felt my lip quivering from trying so hard not to laugh. Alas, I failed. A small giggle escaped off my vocal cords from the small crack between my lips. He went from Carder to *Regina George* in a split second.
"Oh, I see," he said in a deeply concerning and frankly frightening tone. "I'll just have to do some investigating on my own, LIKE *SHERLOCK* FRICKEN *HOLMES*!"
While Carder was looking around the house, I smirked at Sherlock at the sight of him huddled down in a fetal position with a reflected smile on his face. He mouthed, asking me to ask Carder what he was doing; I returned my attention back to the screen and cleared my throat.

"Carder, Hooonnneeeyyyy" I was *really* pushing it now; he hated when I used pet names with him when he was angry. "What're you doing?"

"I will give you five seconds to tell me where you are and both of your faces on camera. Or I swear I'll find every piece of blackmail material I can find in this house starting with your real name, Sherlock!"
Like crisp toast flying out of a toaster, Sherlock popped up, almost knocking me over by his spontaneous bounce. We both smiled obnoxiously at the screen while Carder death glared at us.
"Where." Carder blankly said.

Sherlock cleared his throat. "We huh, we went on a kayak trip to Lighthouse Island."

"A kayak trip. At night. Yea, is that why your shirt is off? You know what- I don't even care, get yo asses kayaked back over here. I have work in the morning. And I'm taking your *Nutella*, it's mine now."

Click

We looked at each other; "I'm really gonna miss that *Nutella*." He is such a dork, a cute dork.

While he grabbed the headlamps, I took the initiative to wrap our phones up in his sweater and placed them back in the compartment. He tossed one of the headlamps to me, and like we had read each other's minds, we worked on adjusting the headlamps on one another's heads. I had to tiptoe. He had to bend his knees a little. But we both had matching smiles.

The whole way back, we kayaked side by side, occasionally bumping into each other. The few times I glanced over, he was lost looking up at the stars. And I couldn't blame him; the sky was magnificent tonight. All the stars put on their best this fine evening.

After putting the supplies away, we raced up the path back to the house. In our panting, we were stopped in our tracks at the sight of Carder. His arms were crossed, and the jar of *Nutella* was tucked in the crook of his arm.

"To think, I was going to give you Jason's old work boots that I didn't accidentally take when I got my stuff back, but I'm most certainly not going to return to him." Carder traded his deathly glace to me.
"You, car, now." Returning his eyes back to Sherlock. I nudged him, about to say goodbye- "Ah, no no, no touching."

I laughed as I started to make my way to the front of the house, faintly hearing Carder lecture Sherlock, but quickly that turned into a bromantic apology.
I'll never understand how guys work.

I knew Carder wasn't seriously mad at me; he loves adding as much drama to any situation as possible. If life were a musical, the world had it coming when it was time for Carder's solo. The car ride back, he kept pounding me with questions. "Did he tell you his name?"

"No, but he has a tattoo."

"That's a tad bit sexy; what is it?"

"Well, it's on the back of his shoulder; I couldn't make it out. It looks like a word, though."

"Maybe it's his name."

"Yea, Carder, because people just get their names tattooed on their shoulders."

He looked over to me with the light of the passing streetlamps illuminating the inside of the car. "Are you shocked by anything at this point?" There was a glisten in his eye as he drove us to our apartment building.

Walking down the hallway where both our rooms were, he walked past his door and followed me to mine. I turned to him with an amused and confused look on my face. Before I could ask, he scooped me up and carried me to my bed, tucking me in like a child. He sat on the edge of my bed as my laughing from his 'motherliness' came to ease.

"You're my best friend, you know that?"

"Oh, Carder, don't get all soft on me now."

"Come on, let me have this." Teasingly I rolled my eyes and gave him my attention.

"You know I've never had many close friends because, let's face it, I'm too real for these two-faced bitches." He scooted closer to my side and traced the outlines of the fabric squares. For the first time in the history of Carderness, he seemed nervous to say what was on his mind.
"Lucy, you have been there for me. Through every rumor, every stupid guy, racist, low lives with tacky insults, when my parents kicked me out because they couldn't handle my fabulousness- everything. And I want to let you know, if it wasn't apparent when I moved in, that I'm not going anywhere. I will always be here for you." Looking up from his fidgeting, his eyes looked glossy; gently, I grasped his hand and gave it a little squeeze of reassurance.

"Carder, you're like the glue of my life." I sat up and wrapped my arms around him. "You can't get rid of me either." He embraced me tightly and laughed.

"Dammit, Lucy, this was supposed to be my Oscar-winning moment; stop stealing it." Releasing his grip and moving me, so we were now looking at each other. "If Sherlock doesn't put a ring on that finger someday, you can bet your ass I will."

"Well, if that wasn't the most romantic-forceful proposal I've ever heard, I don't know what is," I responded while giving him a playful smile.

He's joked about that before, but he's going to find that special guy someday, though. A guy that will throw his sass right back at him, admire his clothes, challenge him, make him dinner, and spin him around the kitchen at night. That guy was out there, wondering when his Carder would twirl into his life. And I couldn't wait to see my best friend truly and deeply happy.

I woke up around nine-thirty in the morning and decided to treat myself to a fancier drink at the coffee house today. And after I have my coffee, I'll surprise Carder with a drink while he's at work. Yepp sounds like a heavenly morning.
I got my backpack all packed up with my essentials and made my trek to the coffee house I went to way too often. Gotta love that regular status.

I got my little boujiee order and set up camp at a side table. Geez, it was packed today. Pulling out my book and placing my phone on the table, I was happy I finally got some reading time. I didn't mind the noise of small talk and shouted coffee orders; I was pretty good at reading among noise as long as I had my coffee.

I felt my phone vibrate.
How he manages to make me smile without even being in the room, I do not know.

Sherlock:

You're not grounded, are you?

Me:

Ha, thankfully Mamma C showed mercy

Setting my phone down, people probably thought I was insane by how much I was smiling at it. As I was about to continue my reading session, he quickly responded; I might as well wait until we're done talking to start reading.

Sherlock:

Phew! I was hoping that wasn't our last goodbye, would have made a crumby one at that

Me:

Next time I see you, I expect an answer about that tattoo mister

I contemplated whether to slap a winky face at the end, but I think my sassy remark did enough justice.

Sherlock:

Hmmm, I don't think so, Mrs. Cumberbatch

I smiled wide and typed quickly.

Me:

Come on, you must get tired of hiding all these secrets. Spill your story, Mr. *Holmes*!

Sherlock:

If people didn't have secrets, where would be the fun in reading their stories?

Why must he always have the wittiest responses; somehow, this sparked a random question out of me.

Me:

Okay fine, but out of curiosity you must answer this
Biggest Fear

I doubted he'd answer that, a doubt which grew with his belated response.

Sherlock:

I will satisfy you with this
Bees
Bees?

Huh, that's inter-

Vibrate

Sherlock:

I am sorry for my abrupt departure; I promised my sista a Facetime date with her fiancé Angelo. I'm serving as a third opinion for flower arrangements for their wedding.
Wish me luck!

Ah, so that's Angelo, thinking back to the contacts in his phone.

Me:

Go get 'em!

After responding, I pondered what made bees his biggest fear. Maybe he was allergic? Perhaps he just really hates yellow. No, he loves yellow. Oh, whatever, he's afraid of bees, moving on with life.

With that, I reunited with my book as an undeniable smirk greeted my face, and I felt the binding crease in my fingers. I believe reading will always be one of the purest joys of my life, I'd say coffee, but it's not as pure. Coffee punishes me with caffeine headaches if I don't have it every day. Reading just patiently waits for you to return.

After getting lost in the words and pages for a while, I was caught off guard by an unexpected guest.

"I thought I recognized you when I walked in; it's pretty busy today, huh?" I felt a bundle of sudden stress in my stomach.

"Remember when I used to take you here all the time? I still remember your order." He tried to smile at me, but I looked right through him.

"Looks like you decided to treat yourself today. That's good, you should."

"What do you want, Seth. I realize this is a public place, but I told you to leave me alone." Discreetly I placed my hand over my stomach, trying to hush the discomfort.

"I was just grabbing some coffee for my mom, I wanted to surprise her, and then I saw you."

"I see," I breathed in deeply as a sharp pain emerged into the pit of my abdomen. "Look, can you watch my stuff for a second? I need to use the restroom." I didn't want to ask him, but holy goodness, this was an emergency.

"Yea, no problem, of course," He smiled at me; I just gave him a nod and swiftly made my way to the bathroom.

I felt lightheaded as I shut the door. My head felt warm. My hands were clammy. Oh great, and my face was hella washed-out. Wow, my face is surprisingly clear. Focus- feeling sick. I haven't eaten today, and I could probably use some water.
You're fine, calm down.
Go to the bathroom.
Wash your hands.
Tell Seth to get a life.
Finnish your coffee.
Get Carder's coffee.
Surprise him.
Call it a day.
As I came back to the table, Seth was on his phone, looking up just as I sat down.

"It was nice seeing you, Mac, but something just came up. I gotta jet."

I hated him calling me Mac like he thought everything was how it used to be. I just sent him off with a nod, finishing my coffee and packing my book away. Just gotta shake that interaction off; why would he even approach me after I told him off last time I saw him? Maybe I should have been more assertive this time. But at least he didn't stay; he left on his own.

Carder always got the same order: a medium iced caramel macchiato with a double shot of espresso. The shop was about two blocks away, and as I approached, I heard bickering screams from inside. Quickly I opened the door with my free hand, and just as I did so, a book flew and hit the wall right by my head.

"Awww! Is that for me?!" I could tell it was Carder's voice but couldn't see where he was.

"Umm yeah, what's going on?"

"***DISTRACTION***!" I heard some raspy rugged voice yell from across the store as a figure that I *swear* looked like a human Sasquatch blindsided me and took me, hostage. "***SURRENDER!***"

"Carder!" I yelled to him. What in the literal hell was going on-

"Alan! I will not hesitate to throw another atlas at you!"

"Do it, and you're fired!"

"Ta hell I will be!" And out launched a heavy atlas from behind the bookcase where I could now see Carder hiding. Thank goodness he has terrible aim. "Sorry, Lucy! This is war!"

"Aren't you two worried that you know, a customer will come in the middle of this 'war'- "

"*Oh*, you're Lucy!" My abductor spoke gleefully. "Carder never shuts up about you!"

"I feel I'd appreciate that more if I wasn't being held captive."

I felt him shrug. "Carder, admit you're wrong, and I'll let her go!"

I heard Carder's dumb stubborn laugh. "Ha! Yea, after you admit that beard is fake, and you don't live in the woods!"

"I live off the land!"

How does anything get done around here, ever?

"I know you live in the suburbs, you homely poser! I've got the entire *Harry Potter* series at the tips of my fingers, ready for fire! Let her and the drink go!"

"For the sake of J.K. Rowling, why are you guys arguing?!" Simultaneously and suddenly, our heads turned to the sound of the desk phone ringing.

"Well, you better answer the phone; that's your job." The hostage guy directed to Carder.

"You answer it, Alan, you're the fricken owner."

"You know I'm not leaving my post until you admit you are wrong!"

"What if it's a loyal customer Alan, huh? Huh?!"

Suddenly I felt this Alan guy tilt me, so I was faced with his scruffy face, which indeed I could tell was a fake beard like Carder had accused.
"You require a job, right? I know you come here a lot, you probably know the stock better than him, and you guys have a good existing dynamic; go answer that phone, and you've got a job."

Without hesitation, he released me, and instantly I ducked as '*The Sorcerer's Stone*' flew across the store. I raced behind the desk, just catching the phone. I plugged one ear so I could hear clearly while the war of unknown reason continued. The caller just wanted the store hours for tomorrow. Well, that was the strangest and easiest job interview of my life.

Alan hopped the desk and shook my hand. "Welcome aboard the Books & Such family. This was strangely convenient!"

As we released hands, I gave him a grateful nod. "Yes, thank you very much for hiring me; I love this store! Now, as an employee, perhaps I could please receive some clarity on what's going on?"
"Oh, why yes, yes, of course." He obnoxiously cleared his throat. "Carder's an asshole."

Laughing at his response, Carder came out from behind the bookcase and approached the desk.
"Hold it there, you sorry excuse of a caveman." He leaned against the counter. "I may be an asshole, but I am correct."

I interrupted before he could answer, and it would turn into another battle of book-throwing nonsense. "Answer the question, please; what are you guys arguing about?"

Carder rolled his eyes. "He keeps insisting that Phil Colin's version of *'You Can't Hurry Love'* is better than The Supremes, and it's complete ludicrously!" Immediately after explaining, they started bickering again as I slid Carder his drink, but Alan snatched it from my hand and held it over his head.
"Put. The. Drink. ***DOWN***." Carder's eyes were scary, serious.

"Not until you admit it!"

"I would rather take a verbal beating from Joan Rivers ghost." Carder spat, and Alan pretended to drop the delicious drink but caught it. "Stop! You monster! Please!"

Surprisingly I've kept my composer; this is absolutely ridiculous.

"I will sleep just fine knowing this five-dollar drink fell to its death and splattered across the floor. Without ever knowing the touch and appreciation of a human's need for such expensive liquid."

I turned to Carder.

He groaned. "Honestly, you are a heartless person; I'm disturbed by your lack of compassion."

I turned to Alan.

"Time's ticking"

I returned to Carder.

"Fine, fine, Phil wins, you were right. Give me my drink." Alan was quite happy with himself as he handed over the beverage. When it was in Carder's hand, he pulled the other from behind his back, reviling his crossed fingers.
"Ha! You fool!" He took a big swig and started to pick up the books, leaving Alan speechless.

"You think you know a guy. Whelp, I'm heading out anywho." He pulled out a scrap piece of paper and started writing stuff down. "Here's your work hours and a number where you can reach me if you have questions." He handed the paper to me and once again jumped over the counter and shouted before he left. "And for your information, I do *not* live in the suburbs!"

Pocketing the paper, I laughed and started helping Carder clean up.

"We're closing early anyway; wow, would ya look at that! Getting hired on the spot, congratulations!" Giving me a sweet smile, I couldn't help but feel a tiny bit proud of myself, even though I literally just answered a phone.
"I have to run those boots out to Sherlock's place; did you want to come with me?" He shelved the last of the fallen book soldiers. "Oh! And thank you for the drink, Deary." Giving me a wink.

"No problem, I figured it was the least I could do after giving you such a scare last night." Giving me a playful glare, I continued. "And no, I think I'm going to go home; I'm not feeling the best today." I debated telling him about the encounter with Seth, but I didn't really want to get into it now. And nothing really happened anyway; I didn't want him to get worked up.

We hooked our arms after locking the place up and walked to his car. "I will be sure to give him your Hellos that I know you're just *dying* to tell him." And with that, we departed for our two-minute cruise to the apartment where he dropped me off.

I slipped into some sweats, threw on a cozy sweatshirt, and crawled into bed with my phone. I laid there for a while until I decided I'd call mom and dad about the news of landing a job.

"Traveler!" Dad happily exclaimed.

I giggled at his comforting voice. "Hi dad, is it just you at the house right now?"

"Yepp, your mom went out for a lemon bar run. That woman and her lemon bars." I could hear his *Abbey Road* record cranked in the background. "As you may hear, I am properly taking advantage of this time."

Imagining Dad jamming out to his favorite album and being on alert made me laugh as I turned on my side. "I've got news you can pass along to mom."

"Did you give up coffee?"

"Dad, no, that's craziness."

"Good, just making sure this is the real Lucy." We shared a silly laugh.

"I got a job at the bookstore Carder works at! So now we live together and work together-"

"Oh wow"
"Yea, I didn't really think of that until just now; holy buckets, that's a lot of Carder."

"I meant I'm going to get an overload of conspiracy theories from your mother."

I couldn't help but laugh again. "Mom's still on that, huh?"

"Lucy, no, I don't think you understand. I don't know how she does it; they get crazier each time. She is very convinced you two are going to get married someday." I laughed as he joined me for a few seconds. "Oh, kiddo, I'm happy for you though, I love you, and I'll tell her the good news."

"I love you, dad."

"I love you, Traveler."

Gosh, I missed them so much. I hope they're coming to visit soon. Sometimes I wondered what they thought about when Colin came across their minds. I'm sure a day doesn't go by when they don't think of him. A day doesn't go by where he doesn't cross mine.
His witty remarks. The collection of sweaters he had; literally all he wore were crew necks no matter the weather. His fantastic writing; notebooks and notebooks worth. How you could tell, it was his footsteps in the hallway.
I remember when he was in middle school, he saved up enough money to buy this sound system he had been raving about for months. It was like an intercom, but you could hook your iPod to it. He put the speakers all around the house, and he would play music over the intercom to wake everyone up. We all wanted to strangle him some mornings.
One time, it was Saturday morning, and he played '*Come on Eileen*' by Dexys Midnight Runners at seven-thirty. I was so tired, and who the heck wakes up that

early on a Saturday? I threw my blankets off and ran to his room to yell at him, but he wasn't there. Running out of the room and gliding down the stairs, ready to throw it down, I ran into the kitchen where mom and dad were swinging and twirling about. They were laughing and singing off-key. Colin grabbed my hand and spun me in a circle before I could even get a word out. But as I went in a full circle and united my other hand with his, I forgot I was mad. This moment with my family, all of us overtired, singing along to an 80s classic and dancing around the kitchen, this moment with my family I'll never forget. I'll never let Colin slip away.

Vibrate

Carder:

Hospital. 5 min

His text scared the hell out of me as my fingers felt numb, quickly texting him back.

Me:

What's going on???

Anxiously awaiting his response, I jumped out of my warm bed and ran to the front door slipping on my chucks as my phone vibrated again.

Carder:

14. Yellow Jackets, Blue Skies

Though Carder's words weren't spoken out loud, they echoed through me. Aching and echoing with every step I took. I left the apartment. I just started to run. My feet slammed on the pavement as I felt my thighs harshly brushing past each other and the bottoms of my sweatpants tangling around my ankles. Each time my sole met the concrete, the words plastered across my mind. *It's Sherlock.* I could feel the sharp stabbing pain begin to grow in my side, but I ignored it. The scenarios that were playing through my mind got worse the closer I got to the hospital. I could feel past memories try to flood in, but now was not a time for the past. On the contrary, I was petrified by the present and in fear of the future under the circumstances.

I ran into the ER entrance, where Carder quickly rushed to me from the waiting room while catching my breath.

"Oh my gosh, did you run here?"

Nodding while still panting, Carder took me over to his seat in the small waiting room. "Car-" Catch your breath, breathe slowly. "Carder, what happened to him?"

A tint of sorrow mixed with anger lingered in his eyes as he cleared his throat softly. "I went to his house to run the boots to him, and when I pulled in, he was just getting out of the house. I'm not sure where he was going, but I got out of the car with the boots in my arm. We talked for a bit about how he just got done talking with his sister Julia who is getting married. He was helping her and her fiancé with flower arrangements. So, we talked for a good ten minutes, and he said he sadly had to go or something like that, so I gave him the boots, and we said our goodbyes. We each got in our own cars, and when I started my car, the radio was already turned up. As I glanced over to his car before pulling out, Lucy he-" Abruptly Carder grabbed my hand. "Right as he shut the car door this swarm, I swear, a swarm of bees or wasps I don't know, just attacked him! I panicked; gosh, I feel so stupid I completely froze! He screamed for me to stay in the car while he quickly ran out of his. He fell on the ground; he was getting stung like crazy. I'd never seen anything like it. Oh my gosh, I didn't care what he said; I got out and dragged him into the back seat of my car. I got stung just a few times." Looking down at his bare arms, I could see a few band-aids where he must have been stung.

"Lucy, I was so scared; I whipped out of his driveway and slammed on the gas trying to get to the hospital. I looked back at him, and I'm not exaggerating; he had to be stung well over a hundred times. I was freaking out; I didn't want him to go unconscious or something, I don't know what that many bee stings can do to a person, so I kept talking to him. He handed me his phone, and I could barely make out what he was saying, but he told me to call his sister when we got to the hospital. I pulled into the ER parking lot; I didn't even turn off the car. I just jumped out and carried him in and explained, well, I was screaming to the nurses what had happened. They took him back, but they wouldn't let me go back with him because I *'wasn't family,'* I was so fricken pissed. Now that I'm thinking of it, I should have said he was my boyfriend or something. But on some kind of a bright note, the nurse I was arguing with went home, and thank God, those scrubs were not doing this facility any favors."

His hands grasped mine tighter as he looked away from me. "I called his sister; she's flying out right now from their dad's private plane. Who in the *hell* has a private plane? I had no idea Sherlock came from a rich family. Hot damn. But anyway, she should be here in about two hours. Lucy, someone must have planted that hive in his car. There's just no other possible explanation. Probably some punk-ass teenagers. I hate people."

I let everything sink in.

I couldn't even imagine the pain.

How scared he must have been.
How scared they must have both been.
I couldn't imagine someone's intentions of doing such a thing.
Over one hundred bee stings-
I pray to God he'll be alright.
"Oh," Carder squeezed my hand, pulling me away from my questioning thoughts. "When I unlocked his phone to call his sister, he had an unread text. Though I'm no '*Sherlock Holmes*,' I could tell it was from you. It's pretty cute. I gotta hand it to him, your name in his phone." A guilty smile came across my face waiting for the answer. "It's *John Watson*, that's his friend, right? In the *Sherlock Holmes* books?"
I couldn't help my growing smile as I nodded. That's why I couldn't find my name in his contacts. I wasn't Lucy. I was his *John Watson*.

Carder and I sat in silence while waiting on news from the doctor, for Julia to arrive, really for anything. He still had his hand around mine; I assume he was lost in his own thoughts while I was preoccupied with my own. I was fighting to keep my eyes open. I felt so exhausted and worn out. My eyes started to feel heavy; I could feel my head tipping down slowly as it would jerk up when I noticed what I was doing. Finally, I gave in; it was comforting to know Carder's hand was holding mine.

I didn't want to dream; I just wanted to sleep. Nightmares disguised as dreams. But really, sometimes, they were memories mistaken for nightmares. And away I slipped, as I fell in and took a look around to the familiarity of my old house.
As I walked around, I didn't see mom or dad, and looking out the window, it appears their cars were absent too, so they must be at work. Colin should be here, though. Probably in his room, writing away. He never disappointed with his writing; he was truly wonderful. But he never seemed satisfied, and that lead to him never doing anything else in his free time other than writing and-
I could hear footsteps from what sounded like the bathroom. Easing down the hallway, I saw the light from the bathroom under the closed but unlocked door;

there was a shadow occupying the light ever so quietly. It probably should have occurred to me before opening the door that someone may actually be using the bathroom, but of course, that thought came too late as my hand slowly turned the golden knob. Pushing the closed door, I wish I had never opened. This is the nightmare, a play-by-play of the old memories, every detail of the past flooding in.

Colin stood by the sink, one hand holding up his John Lennon t-shirt and the other gliding a small razor across his pale and boney hip. The sound of me releasing the doorknob resulted in Colin dropping the razor out of surprise.

He was the surprised one?

I didn't even know what to say as I watched his cut turn into a slow dotted line of deep red, and he watched my eyes in fear of disappointment.

"Lucy," He gasped while grabbing a piece of paper towel and holding it to the cut. "Let me explain-" He winced a little in applying pressure. I couldn't gather a single word or expression. "Please" His soft frantic voice reached out to me. "Lucy, please don't get angry with me."

I looked at my little brother, my deeply pained brother. How did I not see he was this distraught, that he felt this much agony to go to such lengths, my little brother.

Inside I wanted to be angry; I felt hurt and upset that he would do such a thing to himself. But my actions spoke otherwise as my arms gently reached to fill him in an embrace, I knew he needed. Gosh, who knows how long he's needed it, my poor baby brother. He started pulling down his shirt when something caught my eye. I lunged for the hand he was using to adjust his shirt, pushed it away, and reviled what I was afraid to see. The both of us just stood there for a moment.

Scars.

Hashed-

Deep-

Shallow-

Long-

Small-
Jagged-
Scars.

Some of the cuts were already healing; some had already started to scab over. Releasing the fabric, it fell back into place as I stared at the bathroom tile. The small razor was resting at our feet, decorated with just a tiny line of blood.

"Please don't tell mom and dad."

Sharply I looked up at him. I could see the tears settling into his eyes. "I don't even know what you're thinking anymore; I don't even know what to think-" and I could feel a wave of anger pushing itself out through the glaze of sadness in my eyes. "Don't you see this isn't okay? Do you even realize what you're doing?!" Colin and I hardly ever yelled, but this was hardly like any other conversation.

"What do you want from me, Lucy?! I'm not like you. I'm not like anyone! Every single second I wish I could be happy; do you think I enjoy this? You think I like looking in the mirror after I've just hurt myself? I would kill to feel anything, to feel at all. I can't even feel this-"

With the sound of a quiet cry released from him, I looked up. This is my little brother. The only other person in the world who knew precisely what face to make at what time at the dinner table to make me do a spit take. I wouldn't let anyone else outside of a café make my cup of coffee, but he always made mine perfectly. No one else knew where I hid my stash of candy when we were kids. The only person who would stay up with me until 3am on a school night just to watch *Doctor Who* or *Sherlock*. The only one who could sing every word and note of '*Bohemian Rhapsody*' while completely catching every emotion of the instrumentalist in the process. No one else could tell me everything was going to be okay like he could.

He wasn't just my little brother; he was my best friend.

His glossy eyes searched through mine, trying to find clarity in the destructiveness he had become. Placing my hands on his boney shoulders, he sniffled and tried his best to keep himself together, as did I.
"I'm not going to tell mom and dad because this never happened and will never happen again, okay?" I was hoping I was saying the right things. I had no idea what to say. You don't learn about these things; you can't possibly be prepared for something like this. A big part of me wanted to tell mom and dad, but I also didn't want Colin to feel like he couldn't trust me or for him to get in trouble. I just wanted my best friend to be okay again.

His voice was breathy as it shook to get the words out. "Lucy, I'm so scared about the future."

I pushed through my unshed tears and gave him a small smile. "That's why I'm here; you're not going through this alone. You will always have mom, dad, Carder, and me. I don't want you to forget that." Giving his shoulders a little squeeze, I could tell from the look in his eyes the confusion was gone; he knew everything. He knew this was a dream. Still, I held his shoulders. If I moved, I feared it would all go away, and he needed me right now.

"Do mom and dad hate me?" It felt like he was trying to ask questions about reality before I inevitably went back to it.

"No, no, Colin, of course not, they could never hate you" I pulled him into my arms as his delicate body sunk into mine; it almost felt like he wasn't even there.

"Lucy, can you sing the song" His silent tears seeping into my shirt. "Please?"

Growing up, Colin had frequent nightmares. As much as mom tried to reassure him or dad wanted to tell him a music legend story, he could never calm down enough to fall back asleep. The only thing that got him to was a song I made up for him. He felt me nod as I softly sang while running my hands through his soft hair.

"Blue skies
comin' your way
Bluebirds,
singing your name
They sing
Colin
You're doin' just fine.
Blue skies
stayin' your way
Bluebirds
flyin' away
They sing
Colin
You're doin' just fine
They sing
Colin
You'll be just fine."

My hand moved with his head as he looked at me. His eyes weren't as wet anymore. I ran my hand through his hair one more time. "Colin, are you afraid I won't keep holding on to you?"

To my surprise, he gave me a small smile as he wiggled out of my hold and walked towards the door. "No, quite the opposite actually," turning to me, his face a moment ago was smooth and healthy-looking, now it appeared to be sunken in and frail. "I'm afraid you'll never let go."

I felt a nudge on my shoulder as I jolted awake, and Colin dissolved through my racing memories. As my eyes adjusted to the obnoxiously bright light in the waiting room, I saw who woke me.

"Sorry to wake you, you must be Lucy, right?" Her smile was bright and kind, with eyes just like her brother's.
"Yes, sorry, and you must be Julia?" I sat up and shook her hand, giving her the best sleepy smile, I could pull off.

"It's nice to finally meet you, the famous Lucy. My parents are out of the country right now; otherwise, they would have been delighted to meet you too." The smile that came clear across my face woke me straight up.
"Oh! I met your friend Carder; he is quite the guy." She chuckled a little as she sat down; where in the heck did he go anyway?
"He answered a call from my brother's boss; he said he was going to go over there and explain what's going on and help him out." And with her report of Carder's mission, I let out a small laugh in which she joined in.
"Yea, I didn't really peg him for an outdoorsy guy, but he also seems like a man of surprises!"

"I would say he's more of an indoor person, but surprising indeed." We both giggled.

"I know it's strange, but my brother has told me so much about you; I feel like I know you already." She gave me a smile and then rolled her eyes along with her following sentence. "And as far as I know, he still hasn't told you his actual name?"

I let out a sigh and sat more comfortably. "Nope, I'm afraid he hasn't."

"Gosh, he's so weird. I would tell you, believe me, I am dyyiinnggg to, but I am sworn under sibling secrecy." She, too, then sat more comfortably.
"The nurse described the swelling his poor face and body had when he first came in, and it's gone down a lot, but they gave him some sleeping medication and

morphine to put him out of pain for a while." She trailed off for a moment. "I called the police because someone obviously put the hive in his car; whether it was coincidence or not, I'm not resting until I see something done about this." I felt a confused expression captivate my grin as she noticed.
"I'm sorry, the mother side of me is coming out. I took care of him a lot growing up, and, well, you know, he's my little brother."
I nodded slowly; I knew all too well about feeling protective over a little brother. "You said whether it was a coincidence or not; what did you mean coincidence?"

"Oh," She waved the thought away. "I just automatically connected it with this giant fear he has of bees. There just doesn't seem to be another logical explanation, but it could be just a coincidence." There was a pause for a moment, then she smiled at me.
"I don't know what it is, but you flipped a switch in him. I've never seen him this happy and involved in life, and I love it. Ever since we were kids, he's been kind of sheltered to himself. We've both endured a lot of loss, but the poor guy just always seemed to be on the front lines." I could tell by the look on her face, the old memories were playing through her head like a slideshow; she put it on pause. "Can we keep all this between us, like a heart to heart? I don't really have that many girls in my life to talk to, and, from what I've heard, you sound pretty awesome."

I laughed while nodding in agreement that we could keep our chat between us. "I don't have other girls to talk to either, so this is nice."
Julia's smile was so genuine and kind; she was gorgeous beyond belief as well. Her brunette hair, with just a tint of red, fell in perfect waves past her shoulders. Her grey-blue eyes were the spitting image of Sherlock's. Cheekbones I would kill to have. Basically, she was the type of girl who could pull off red lipstick.

"Well, I'm glad we got past the awkward stage; just a heads up, I'm a pretty straightforward gal. I blame my dad for that. But thank you for letting me get this stuff off my chest; I haven't really been able to talk to anyone about this stuff." She

let out a sigh and pulled herself back together. Just from that, I could tell she was the kind of person who would pretend to be strong for everyone else's sake.
"I feel like my brother is a book I've already read, and you're currently reading, and I'm trying to be careful with which parts I tell because I don't know if you've got that far." She giggled as I was amused by her analogy. I like this girl already. "Has he told you about his tattoo?"

"Kind of, he wouldn't tell me what it meant." I playfully rolled my eyes while Julia did the same.

"I apologize for his oddness." A more sentimental expression covered her face. "It's a word, on his shoulder blade, it's the word Finley." She looked down at her hands on her lap. "In Irish, it means fair hero or something, but to me and" She let out an irritating sigh, still staring at her fidgeting hands. "Sherlock, it wasn't just a word." Her eyes met mine as her hands folded together. "It was big brother."

I could feel my eyes dilate. An older brother? How could he avoid the subject of an older brother entirely- well, alright, I can't really be the one to talk.

"I kinda figured that he didn't say anything about it. He never talks about him." There was a strain in her voice like it was painful for his name to slip off her tongue.
"Everyone adored him. Every girl wanted to have her arm around him, and every guy wanted to be his best friend. He was two years older than me and four years older than Sherlock. Finley went to this top-notch school in New York for extremely talented kids. Like if you got accepted into this school, on the back of that acceptance letter was pretty much a stapled acceptance letter into Juilliard. He could sing, he played cello and piano, but his deepest passion was dancing." Her eyes swayed forward as if he was dancing in front of her. "He could do anything: tap, jazz, hip-hop, swing, waltz, ballroom, and ballet- anything and everything. He loved the adrenaline from moving his feet to the music." Excited by a sudden thought, she turned her body towards mine as one of her legs rested in the chair and the other hung down; she liked to talk with her hands.

"I remember one time he planned this little sock hop for me, Sherlock, grandpa, and our parents the first night of the summer at grandpa's house in Rhode Island. We were in the living room, mom put on grandpa's old Frank Sinatra records, and it was the happiest we had ever been. All of us except for Sherlock were dancing; he was about eight, and like I said before, he's always been really to himself. He watched everyone else dance, and Finley went over to him and asked if he wanted to dance. Sherlock said no, because he didn't know how to dance, and he didn't want to look foolish in front of everyone. I can remember Finley promising to teach him how to dance someday when he felt ready, and everyone would be amazed at how great he was. For now, he said Sherlock could pick the music. He always loved looking at all of grandpa's records."

Her eyes got lost, looking past me as I tried to meet her gaze. "Julia, if this is too hard to talk about, by all means, we don't have to?"

Discreetly shaking her head, she gave me a strong smile of reassurance. "No, no, I'm sorry I got lost in thought. If you don't mind, I think I'd feel better if I just let all of this weight off." I nodded and repositioned myself the same way as her.
"That summer, the one I was just talking about, was the summer Sherlock became deathly afraid of bees. Mom and dad went off on some business trips, and the three of us stayed with grandpa. I usually played on the beach or tried on grandma's clothes, and grandpa would tell me how much I looked like her. Finley and Sherlock always went on 'Adventures,' as they called them, around some trees by the house. One day they went out for their walk while grandpa and I were building a sandcastle on the beach. I remember we were almost done when we heard this faint screaming; grandpa shot up and accidentally stepped on the castle we had worked so hard on, and he told me to go into the house and lock the doors while he ran off to find the screaming. I did as he said and waited for any sign of my grandpa and brothers. To cut it short, we had to make a run to the ER because they got themselves into a beehive, stupid boys. They got stung so many times; Sherlock was traumatized. But if they hadn't gotten themselves almost stung to death, we wouldn't have found out about Finley as soon as we did." She paused, looking like she was gathering her thoughts together.

"The doctor noticed something and recommended an MRI; again, in short, we found out he had DIPG, Diffuse Intrinsic Pontine Glioma. A stupid fricken tumor disease. My parents were called; Finley was hospitalized until they returned a day or so after they got the news. It's an aggressive brain tumor that attacks the brainstem area that controls things like your breathing and your heart rate, very vital things. It can't be surgically removed; it's too risky because it's at the base of the brain. No one would have ever guessed or noticed. The doctor told us bluntly that Finley wasn't going to be able to fight this for long. They would start Radiation and or Chemotherapy but would only slow down the tumor growth to buy us more time with him. And the therapy had a reputation of increasing the pain of the symptoms."

Her breaths were becoming sharper, trying to hold back her tears that I could see developing in the corner of her eyes. I was fighting them back myself.

"The symptoms kicked in a few weeks after the bee accident. Finley was moved to a more comfortable and advanced research hospital in New York. Our parents put a fortune into making sure he was as comfortable as he could be. And everything in the doctor's power was done to try to stop this hideous disease. It was horrible to see him like that. Eventually, he couldn't chew anything without almost suffocating on his food, trying to swallow it. Slowly, he just started to lose control of everything. He lost his coordination; he didn't know the last time he got to stand on his feet alone was the last time his feet would ever touch the ground. To take away a dancer's ability to dance is one of the cruelest things to see. Every time we saw him, you could see in his eyes that he was so exhausted, but he just kept on trying. My parents, Sherlock, and I were there every day; he was never alone. Sherlock was always on the bed with him; I don't think he completely understood at the time what was going on." A tear fell from her eye as it hit the edge of her cheekbone. And at its release, she soldiered on.

"You know how I said Sherlock and me, we endured the same loss, but he was on the front lines? This is the moment I was referring to, the moment he told me he can never get out of his head." A part of me was kind of wondering if she should be telling me this stuff. It almost felt kind of wrong, but I didn't want to be rude. Especially when she said she just felt like she needed to get this off her chest and tell someone.

"It had been close to five months after Finley's diagnosis, and the doctor told us, unfortunately, there wasn't anything more he could do. After a lot of deliberation, the doctor, our parents, and Finley decided to stop the therapy because it was just hurting him. Shortly after the therapy was stopped, he lost control of his speech. I don't know how doctors do it, but outside of the room, he told us that it would most likely be Finley's last within the next few days, and we should say everything we wish to tell him, just in case. Sherlock didn't understand; I mean, he was only eight. Even though we knew Finley wouldn't be able to say anything back, we each told him everything we wanted to. Each of us individually. My mom sat in a rocking chair by his bed while my dad stood beside her, holding her hand. I sat at the end of the bed by his feet, and Sherlock laid next to him while holding his fragile hand. We were all waiting for Sherlock to say his last words, but he was quiet for the longest time. After a few hours, we saw Finley's eyes start to close, my dad's eyes were glued to his heart monitor, and my mom's sniffling was getting harder to bear. Sherlock shook Finley just as his heart monitor released the agonizingly long beep. And- his words echo my mind almost every day,"
She drew out a long breath. "Sherlock panicked and started yelling, *'Wait! Wait!'* and he held Finley's hand to his face and cried, just barely being able to get his words out that Finley never got to hear. He said, *'I'm ready to learn how to dance now'*".

I felt an ache in my chest. All those times I saw something hidden behind that gaze in his eyes, this was it. This was what he was hiding behind those grey-blue eyes. Gosh, I felt so horrible; seeing her cry made me want to cry, and she didn't need to see that hot mess.

"To this day, I swear, besides maybe seeing him move just a little in his seat or in the car while listening to music, I have never seen him dance. Ever. He refuses. He doesn't talk about him at all. It was so traumatizing it just stuck to his mind and never left. I think that's why he keeps to himself a lot; besides me, he didn't really tell anyone anything. When he turned eighteen, he told me he was getting a tattoo in Finley's honor in Finley's handwriting, on the back of his shoulder. Because he needed to put it behind him, but never forget. So, after the ink met his skin, he never talked about him again for some reason that was easier for him. That's why he's afraid of bees; it triggers that memory. He has the idea drilled in his head that if they had never gotten into that beehive, Finley would still be here."

She wiped her damp eyes with her sleeve; damn, she didn't even look bad when she cried.

"He's never perused a romantic relationship either. For the longest time, I thought maybe he was asexual. I still think he might be, and that's perfectly fine; there's nothing wrong with that, obviously. It's not really my business either. Other than me, our parents, and grandpa, he just doesn't have attachments to people. After so much loss, I guess he started to avoid emotional attachments." Now we were both looking at one another, as Julia smiled through her tears.

"Until you. You got him to open up. And I applaud you for that. That night after he first met you, he told me that he had never been so intrigued by someone. That you were like an entirely different world, he wanted to have the honor of exploring. His exact words, by the way. Oh my gosh, he'd kill me right now if he heard any of this." We were all giddy by that last statement.

"He talks about you a lot too; he loves you so much." Trying to cheer her up, I felt so grateful she felt comfortable enough to confide in me.

"I love him so much. Gosh, I'm sorry for dropping all of that on you. I feel a lot better having it off my chest. Thank you, Lucy."

We decided we ought to get some snacks from the vending machine while we are waiting. As we sat back down, my phone vibrated.

Carder:

How's our boy doing?

Me:

He's on some medicine now, asleep, his sister is super nice

As I sent the text, I looked over to Julia, who was also on her phone.

Vibrate

Carder:

She's super pretty, but not as pretty as you

I titled my screen closer to me, so Julia didn't accidentally see that; Carder was so blunt. And incorrect.

Vibrate

Carder:

Keep me posted!

Vibrate

Carder:

Gotta go
Breaks over

Vibrate

Carder:

I don't know how this old man did it, but I am covered in mud and harvesting cranberries
Sherlock owes me.
BIG TIME.
Peace Out.

I laughed as I locked my phone and slipped it in my sweatpants pocket. "Apparently, Carder is doing your brother's job right now." We started laughing as we shared a bag of pretzels.
"I would die at the sight of Carder trying not to get wet, at a cranberry marsh." I really never had a friend that was a girl; everything felt so natural talking with Julia. I was glad the mood lightened a little, given the circumstances.
"So, if you don't mind me asking, Sherlock mentioned you were engaged; can I see a picture of the lucky guy?"

"Totally! I don't mind at all; I love showing him off." She pulled up a picture on her phone, and I indeed could tell why she enjoyed showing him off.
It was like he was ripped out of a magazine. He had soft-looking, tan skin. A fair amount of facial hair, but not like Alan's '*beard*.' A chiseled face, but not too chiseled to the point where he looked like he never ate. Obviously, he worked out a bit. He had light brown hair—deep brown eyes. Aw, man, they seemed so happy together.

"You guys are too cute! What's his name?"

She looked at the picture before putting her phone away; she probably missed him already. Who wouldn't, let's be honest.
"Angelo D'Amore" She let out a sigh. "I know, he looks and sounds like a dream. I'm honestly too lucky. But he always tells me he's the lucky one. Cheesy, I know, but he makes so so happy."

I let out an audible *Awww!* "How did you guys meet, if you don't mind me asking?"

"Not at all! All the wedding planning makes me want to talk about it even more. Okay so, we've known each other for four years. I was with my dad learning the ropes of the business, and we were on a business trip in Italy. I wasn't allowed in this particular meeting, so I took that time to just walk about the city. I turned the corner, and I wasn't paying attention, and then I ran into him. Embarrassingly enough, we hit heads, and when we looked at each other, we just started laughing. He quickly apologized which I told him not to because it was my fault. But he insisted on making it up to me by being my personal tour guide of the city. So, we walked down the sidewalks as he told me stories that came with the different sights we passed by. Before I knew it, it was way past the time the meeting had ended, and my dad was probably worried sick. We exchanged names after I told him I had to go, and unfortunately, this was the last day I would be in Italy. When I asked him if we could exchange numbers, he was embarrassed to tell me he didn't have a phone. He was an architect student on a scholarship and couldn't afford a phone. With my dad's quick permission, via text, I gave Angelo the company address in New York so we could write to each other. I wasn't, at least at first, going to give a stranger my home address; Angelo understood that." She smiled so big; it was contagious.

"We wrote back and forth; he would talk about how school was going, and I would talk to him about New York City. He always wrote about how badly he wanted to see it someday. It was strange, in a sense, we never straight forward said it, but it was like it was in the background of our conversations, we knew we only had eyes for each other. Or, as Angelo later put it, *words* for each other. We wrote letters for two years; I still have all of them. One day I got a letter from him that he was accepted to be transferred into an architect program in New York. I swear it was the work of God; we were just meant to be together." The both of us were smiling so big, it didn't feel like we were in a waiting room anymore. It felt like we were on a couch having a sleepover and talking about boys like high schoolers.

For just a few minutes, I forgot about everything.

I forgot how worried I was about Sherlock.

I forgot about the fact that I didn't even know his real name.

I forgot about the thought of Carder doing dirty, heavy labor.

I forgot about how I probably looked homeless.

For just a few minutes, I forgot about everything in the world that hurt.

Everything except for Col-

"Miss. Johnson," Julia and I looked up to a doctor standing in front of us. He was obviously addressing Julia, so now I knew Sherlock's last name. "Your brother has woken up."

15. Pistachio Moments 

Julia and I exchanged numbers as she reassured me she'd talk the doctor into letting me and Carder see Sherlock. I wasn't too worried. That woman could talk Joan Rivers into buying a pink camouflage jumpsuit. With that, I decided it would probably be best if I made my way home and cleaned up a bit, though I think I pull off the homely look ravishingly.

On my way, though, I decided I'd take a walk on the boardwalk, regardless of my attire. There was a shop that sold pistachios there. It would be the perfect get well soon gift.

Vibrate

Text message?

Vibrate
Vibrate

Ah, phone call.

As I walked into the small shop in search of the pistachios, I pulled out my phone. Dad? Why?
"Dad? Everything alright?"

"Traveler! Yes, of course; where would you happen to be at this hour?"
I could hear my mom ranting in the background about, well, who knows what.

"Well, I just stopped to pick up something at the boardwalk, kind of by the spot where we used to skip rocks. Why do you ask?"

Hmmm, let's see: cashews, peanuts, roasted peanuts, honey peanuts, where in the hell- Oh!

I balanced the phone between my face and shoulder as I grabbed two small bags of pistachios and politely set them on the checkout counter. The cashier looked about, ready to die of boredom while he scanned the snacks.
"Your total comes to $11.65, ma'am." He drug out his words like he was pulling me into the pain of his job, and goodness, I felt it- Holy buckets! $11.65?!
Kindly, I paid the unenthused dude, grabbed my bag, and headed out of the store as I heard dad clear his throat.

"Well, Luc-"

Suddenly there was a ruffling sound on the other end, and, yep, that was the sound of bickering.

"Lucy, it's mom; we decided to surprise you!" Mom wasn't very good at speaking through the phone; I could hear her in the background trying to whisper to my dad to say it at the same time- "SURPRISE!"

The one time they decide to spontaneously visit, and my friend has been attacked by bees. And I still don't know his name.
"Oh wow!" I managed to get out. "That's so great-"

"Your dad and I are so excited to see you! You're on the boardwalk? We'll be there in a flash! Love you, Lucy!"

"Mom, I can-"

Click

Ugh, Mother. Why. Why must you be so- I don't even know what adjective she is sometimes.

While waiting for my parent's arrival, I decided to park it on a bench I spotted by the shop. I've probably sat on this bench before, but I wouldn't remember. I can't even imagine how many times my feet have run across this boardwalk.

Growing up, we had a tradition of going to the beach every Sunday. Mom and Colin usually built sandcastles and ran in the water. Dad and I typically just spent the whole-time skipping rocks and talking about whatever was on our minds. Sometimes we wouldn't talk at all, and we hardly noticed. But towards the end of our time there, just as the sunset started easing in, mom and dad would go on a walk. Colin and I would sit at the end of the pier with our feet dangling over the edge. I think my favorite Sunday memory was when we spontaneously decided to jump into the water, hand in hand.

It was my junior year, his sophomore year, and Seth and I had gotten into a fight earlier that day; go figure. I hadn't spoken a word about it. But that was the thing with Colin and me; neither of us had to say anything. We could always tell what the other was thinking.

We sat in silence for a while, just watching the reflection of our feet swinging back and forth over the waves that crashed against the wood. Eventually, he got it out of me that I was upset, and we talked about Seth. Then we just started venting back and forth. Then, again, it got quiet. But out of nowhere, absolutely nowhere, Colin jumped up on his feet and started singing '*Welcome to the Black Parade*' by My Chemical Romance at the top of his lungs. I laughed so hard, trying to pull him down and cover his mouth; everyone and their mother was staring at us. I'm pretty sure our parents knew it was us and decided to completely ignore and deny all signs that we were their offspring.

Finally, when I got him to shut up, we laughed so hard, harder than I remember ever laughing. Amid our laughter, he blurted out that we should just jump off the pier because, why the hell not! We inherited lingering colds.

Vibrate

Carder:

Remind me to never live on a farm or wetland of any sort

Vibrate

Carder:

I'm at the apartment, are you still at the hospital?

Me:
We have a situation
Sherlock's sister is working on letting us see him
Pistachio Prices
My parents are in town

Just as I clicked send, I heard a car door shut; looking up in reaction to the sound, my thoughts were correct. Here comes Mr. & Mrs. MacArthur!

My Mom is about my height, sandy blonde hair that ended at her shoulders; she's a petite woman, a little too small since, well, everything that's happened over the past year. But I swear I've never seen a day she was anything less than flawless.
Dad is a tall, slim fella. From what I've gathered when looking through old pictures of him growing up, he's always had a soft-looking face. He has dark brown hair. And brown eyes, a trait my parents shared. My Dad was a hipster before the word was even being tossed around.
I gotta give it to him.
Point for Dad.

I just barely got up from the bench when my mom ran to me and nearly knocked me down from hugging me so hard. She wrapped her arms around me super tight, to which dad couldn't stop laughing as I looked back at him while hugging mom. After her embrace, she insisted dad, and I go do our thing, skipping rocks, and she would go walk the beach and roll the bottoms of her pants up and walk through the water like she used to do with Colin. Dad gave mom a smile and kiss as we departed and slipped into old memories.

My high score was six skips.
Dad's was eight.
After a few skips in silence, dad broke it. "I'm worried, Lucy," He softly spoke as he threw another rock.
Only three skips.

I followed his up, "I kind of got that vibe from you, shall we talk about it?" barely two skips.

He nodded, beginning to search the sand for skipping rocks. "It's your mother. I'm worried about her." His voice was starting to shake at the end of his sentence.
Turning to him as our eyes met, I could see the concern glaze over his eyes. "How's mom handling everything?"

Letting out a short sigh, he gave me a weak half-smile. "The best she can Traveler, the best she can." As he cut off his sentence, I couldn't tell if he had more to say. Before I could even process responding, he chucked the rocks he found into the open water. We watched the ripples for a moment in the silence of the pier before he continued.
"I've been working at the University more so she doesn't have to work, and I've been saving money so we can go on a proper trip. The honeymoon she always deserved." He kept looking at the water like he didn't want me to see his eyes. "I can see how sad she is and how much she tries to hide it." We both glanced over to where mom was; her back was to us; she was ankle-deep in the water a little ways away. "She's starting to lose interest in the things she used to enjoy. I'm

worried-" He paused and drew a deep breath in. "I'm afraid someday she's going to lose interest in me."
He continued to look out to her; the corners of his lips were turned down, but his eyes looked like they were admiring fireworks. I had never heard my dad talk about the possibility of losing my mom. No, it wasn't possible; they were made for one another.

"Maybe if you told her about the trip, she would have something to look forward to? To help keep her mind from the bad things?"

Rotating towards me, he gave me a slight smile. "When I come home from work, sometimes, she doesn't hear me come in. Sometimes, either she's doing the dishes or laundry, but she'll be talking to Colin, and it's almost always about you."

I felt my head perk up a little.

"She'll say things like '*You and your sister are simply remarkable and the best* or '*I miss your sister an awful lot.* There are times I wait a minute or so before knocking on the door or wall near me just so I can feel and picture them actually talking again." Over the clatter of the restless waves, we turned to the sound of my mom calling and waving us down. Dad put one arm over my shoulder and kissed the top of my head as we walked over to mom. "I sure did miss our rock skipping chats."

I guess mom got impatient because she ran to us. Mother never runs.
"You guys" She stopped as she was huffing and catching her breath. "You guys are incredibly slow; Carder called me on my cell phone."

"Oh! I must have missed a text from him or something; what did he say?" I asked her while she was currently bent over.

"He," Still catching her breath. "He said dad and I should go visit him at the apartment, and you need to go see Sherlock at the hospital." She straightened out her back, looking at me. "Who's, who's Sherlock?"

I am personally going to tie Carder to a chair and burn every piece of clothing he loves right in front of him. He just *had* to bring him up.

Dad gave me a nudge. "So, who's this Sherlock fella? Does he wear a funny hat?" I was picturing him in the famous *Holmes* hat. Dressed in a long dark coat with the collar flipped up. Dad nudged me again and laughed.

"No, no, he's no one, just a friend. He's in the hospital."

"Yea, no, you guys aren't just friends, I can tell. Why is he-"

Mom cut dad off. "No, she doesn't like him; what about Carder."

Why do I even bother anymore?

"My Love, though I admire your persistence, I believe they will always be just friends."

"What's that thing you say, Lucy? Sailboat it? I sailboat you and Carder."

Oh, dear Lord mother, no. No. It's physically painful.

"Hun" Dad was trying so hard not to laugh. "It's '*Ship*,' not '*Sailboat*.'" Mom shot him a death glare which resulted in dad completely losing it and busting out in laughter. He pulled her into his arms before she could start getting flustered.
"Oh, you're too cute, I tell ya."

I love how Dad knew exactly what to say all the time.

Just as we stepped foot into the apartment, Carder ran out of his room and attacked my parents with a massive embrace of affection and giddy squeals from him and mom. Dad looked at me while I shut the door, the look of pain mixed with annoyance in his eyes; it was my turn to laugh.
Carder offered his room to my parents since he had a queen-sized mattress and said he would camp out on the couch for however long they were planning on staying. While they were discussing, I grabbed a small mason jar from the cabinet. I filled it with the hella expensive pistachios.

"Alright, so I'll help get your luggage up and get you guys all comfy, and Lucy, you go to the hospital."

"Oh, Lucy," Dad said as he noticed the jar. "Why is Mr. *Holmes* in the hospital?"

Naturally, Carder cut in. "He was attacked by bees, right in front of my eyes, captain. Damn, that was some scary-ass sh-."

"Carder George Elizondo, you watch that sailor mouth of yours!" Mom scolded him, and I discreetly giggled.

"I apologize," Clearing his throat sarcastically. "I meant; My holy goodness that was quite frightening if I do say so myself!"
Dad got a kick out of that.
So did Carder; a kick right to the leg.
Mom is a feisty woman.

Carder sent me out before I could say another word. Although, thankfully, I was at least able to change my clothes. I wanted to ask why he wasn't going but trying to reason with Carder is like trying to understand math; it just doesn't happen.
My parents offered to drive me there, but I didn't mind walking again—just me and a mason jar full of pistachios.

Once I arrived at the hospital and found his room, I gently knocked on the door. Julia opened it and gave me a quick hug; as she released me, I saw Sherlock with that flippin' smile again. Even in a hospital gown and an IV in his arm, he could display such a smile.

"I hope I wasn't intruding or interrupting," I spoke softly while shutting the door.

"Miss Lucy, of course not; welcome to my humble abode" I saw that little sparkle in his eye that I didn't realize I missed until it caught my attention once again. As I sat down in a chair at the end of his bed, Julia cleared her throat.

"I don't mind if you hear this, Lucy," Julia smiled at me and then returned her attention to Sherlock. "You know mom and dad moved out of the family home, right? This new house is huge, lemme tell ya; it's still in the city, though. Private neighborhood."

I glanced over to Sherlock, who had a blank expression on his face. "Wait, they what? When?" He looked somewhat surprised, both in his facial expressions and the sound of his voice.

"About two weeks ago, mom sent you pictures of the options they were looking at so you could cast in your vote, didn't she?"

"Well, yea, but I thought she was joking,"

"Why would she- "

"I didn't even pick the one I liked."

Turning to Julia, she facepalmed herself and looked at me. "Thank God he has you; this child needs some voice of logic in his life." Oh goodness, she was getting flustered. "I mean, look! Look at this! He made me tape paper over the nurse's whiteboard so you wouldn't see his name! I need some fricken chocolate; you drive me crazy." And with that, Julia had left the room in search of her much-needed chocolate.

The both of us turned to each other at the sound of the door shutting and laughed. "You really know how to get under her skin, huh?"

"Oh, Mrs. Cumberbatch, I dearly love my sister's company, but I must admit I have missed yours a tiny bit more."
He also knew how to make me blush like an idiot.
Politely, he gestured to the chair where Julia was sitting, right next to his head. As I then presented him the mason jar of expensive pistachios while I took a seat. His eyes looked like they were mesmerized.
"Lucy," Looking up at me from the jar. "You didn't have to go out and buy this?"

"I didn't have to, Sherlock; I wanted to." I liked giving him sass; he always gave me a smirk after I delivered it.

"Thank you so very much, Lucy" It seemed he paused to think for a moment. "Before this whole incident happened, I had something planned for you, actually, for tomorrow." His words lingered around my ears and made me smile.

I tilted my head just a little and pretended to give his response some thought. "Is that so, Mr. *Holmes*? You've caught my attention."

And then it was my turn to make him smile, and what a lovely smile it is. Though it almost seems misplaced in this setting. I saw the band-aids and medicine on his arms and spots on his face from the bee stings.

"I'm being released later tonight, and after I'm settled in, Julia is returning home to continue the final decisions for the wedding. I would really love to treat you to a wonderful surprise day tomorrow if that fancies you?"

The way he spoke,
no one talks like that.
No one is like him,
and it drives me crazy.

"I dare say I would fancy that only my parents are in town right now. They're actually with Carder at our apartment." Gosh, that felt so weird to say, our apartment. "But I'm sure something could be arranged." His strawberry blonde hair was cute even when it was in bed head formation; the jar of pistachios rested in his lap.
"Sherlock, do you have any ideas of who would have done this to you?"

"What's the first word you said to me?"

Exchanging him a strange look, I proceeded to answer, "Um, Sherlock?"

He nodded and smiled. "Exactly." I playfully nudged him, and he chuckled. "I think I have a clue, but it is nothing we are going to trifle over."

"Wait, no, no, what happened is not okay at all. Who would have done this?"

Swiftly he popped open the mason jar. "It is nothing for you to worry about; I'll solve it, okeydokey?" With that, he started eating some pistachios. The expression of delight on his face said it all how much he loves them as he handed one to me.

Smiling while shaking my head at his response, I accepted his offering. "You know what I can't wrap my head around?" Starting to crack open the shell, he tilted his head like a cute little puppy. "How can you be so, I don't even know what words to use; how can you be so *you* after everything that just happened?"

He giggled at my question while cracking another pistachio open and clinking it to mine like a glass of champagne. "Miss Lucy, I'm an open book with a missing title." He raised his pistachio to me as I did to him.

16. Caught through the Reflection

I have a date tomorrow.
He didn't necessarily *say* it was a date.
Assuming it is, though, which I'm pretty sure it is,
this would be our second date.
Unless we counted the kayaking.
No, that wasn't much of a date,
I smacked him in the face.
Yea, let's not count that.

Julia gave me a ride to the apartment, which was incredibly kind of her. As I walked up to my door, I heard yelling. Yelling?
I expected, well, at least my parents, to be sleeping; it's kind of late. But upon opening the door, I was mistaken.

"Am I a man or a woman? Just answer the damn question!" Carder shouted with a piece of paper taped to his forehead.

Ha, dad pulled out this classic game. dad, mom, Carder, and someone who has their back to me, were in a circle on the living room floor, playing dad's favorite game. We used to play it as a family after dinner; everyone writes a celebrity on a slip of paper. You pass it to someone and then stick it on your forehead and ask yes or no questions to find out who you are.

As I shut the door, everyone turned to greet me with a smile, including the mystery person, revealed to be Alan. "Hi there, Alan? Pleasantly surprised to see you."

Alan was about to speak, but we all know how much Carder loves speaking for people. "Yea, we needed another player, Alan answer my question!"

"What question are you referring to?" Alan asked while stroking his 'beard.'

I loved seeing Carder get all flustered but push him too far, and it's the scariest thing in the world.

"AM I A MAN OR A WOMAN?!"

Alan scoffed. "Quite obviously you're a man, Carder."

"Alan, you had better pray to God you are talking about the fricken piece of paper on my forehead."

"Well, you aren't a man or a woman. You're a girl."

"Okay, fine, whatever" Carder flashed me his dazzling smile while patting the floor next to him. "Lucy, come sit by mmeeeee."
I giggled at Carder's request and sat next to him in the circle; it was pretty hysterical how serious they were all taking the game.

Carder was *Dora the Explorer.*
Alan was Simon Cowell.
Mom was Leonardo DiCaprio.
And dad was Beyoncé.

I wonder who put that in there.

It was mom's turn. "Alright, so I know I'm an actor, oh! Have I ever won anything?"

Dad started laughing uncontrollably. He has definitely hit the wall of overtiredness. "Well, I'll tell you what, it took FOREVER for you to receive your well-deserved Oscar!" On continued the over-excessive laughter.

"Am I Jack? From the ship movie?"

"Leonardo DiCaprio Darling, yes, well done" Dad gently pulled the slip of taped paper off her head and kissed where it had been. "Okay! So, I am a woman, am I of royalty?"

"Hells yes!" Carder fist-pumped after scaring mom half to death from his sudden outburst. I elbowed him in the side. "Well, not technically."

Alan cleared his throat; I'm still in shock he's even here, to be honest. "I am Simon Cowell." All of us stared at him in bewilderment.

"No way in hell you didn't cheat," huffed Carder; he was getting heated.

Alan gave off this cunning smile. "Oh, but how could I? I was sitting here the whole time."

"Oh shut up, you cheated, I know it. Get outta here."

Standing up, Alan shook everyone's hand, well, except for Carder's. "Shops closed for tomorrow, guys; I'll send you your work hours via pigeon when I've updated it." Alan disappeared into the night, and I looked to Carder with a confused and amused expression.

"Just ignore him. Can we call it quits for this game? I'm tired" Aww, Carder was getting cranky.

"Yes, I was going to suggest that as well," Dad responded as he and Carder took their slips off. "Beyoncé," Dad snapped his fingers in defeat, "I should have known."

"*Dora* the fricken *Explorer*, how was I supposed to guess this?!"
It was nice to genuinely laugh with the people I loved most in this world. I don't know how I'd get through the day without hearing mom or dad's voice of reason in my head whenever I was uneasy or afraid. I don't know how I would keep going if I didn't have Carder; I don't ever want to see that.

Carder made do on the couch while mom and dad slept in his room; I was utterly exhausted. Right as I slid under my quilts, I felt myself crash.
This didn't feel like a recalling memory, though- It didn't feel familiar at all. For the first time in forever, I think I'm actually dreaming.

"I wouldn't count on it."
That voice was all too familiar, and it was right.
This wasn't a dream.
"It's quite dark in here, isn't it?"
This was a nightmare.

I was in a chair, and amidst the darkness, a little click chimed. The voice was kind enough to provide some light. A blinding light that illuminated the white room I was apparently in. But this voice was not kind.

"Seth?" I squinted, adjusting my eyes to the brightness. "What is this?" His smirk was nauseating as he snapped his fingers, my wrists felt heavier as I looked down; they were tightly tied to the armrests. "Nice touch," I sarcastically commented. I scoped out the room, trying to find some indication of where the hell I was, but it was just a white room.

"Think so?" The sound of his voice was equally sickening as he walked behind the chair elegantly. "I always was one for a dramatic," I could feel the heat of his breath on the back of my neck. His voice disgustingly caressed through my eardrums. "touch" His fingertips traced my right shoulder as he walked a few steps in front of the chair, then turned to face me.

Concealing my anger, I looked at him straight on; I can't let him think he has the upper hand. "I don't understand what's going on, Seth."

"I don't understand why you *insistently* continue to break my heart, Mac." His contemptuous grin dissolved into a flattened line, with his jaw clenched; his eyes didn't have a soul behind them as they stared through me. I wasn't afraid. I'm not afraid. "I've seen the way you look at him and how he looks at you."

"Seth, you and I-"

"Did I sound like I was finished?!" His voice roared, and my thoughts were still as he mockingly chuckled under his breath. "Look, look what you made me do, Lucy, you know I hate raising my voice."

I knew this game; I just have to let him talk.

"Gooooooood," He praised. "You're *finally* getting the hang of this. It took you long enough." His deviating smile recoiled; his eyes still fixed on me. "You broke your promise Mac, but like everything else in your life, I'll take the liberty of fixing it. I'm just," He strained his neck slightly while turning his head. "disappointed in you." His eyes gazed off me for a moment.

I just needed to deescalate things. I don't want to panic. I don't want to have an attack. I can't let my voice shake, not this time, this time, I need to be strong. "Everything is okay now, Seth. It's okay."

His pupils dilated as its emptiness met me once again. "Oh, oh yes," Smoothly, taking a few steps closer to the chair, "Of course it's okay!" the tone of his voice was solely scraped from insanity.

He was only a few steps away.
"I mean"
Five steps.
"if you shoot somebody in the heart and put a band-aid on it, it's okay,"
Two steps.
"right?"
His hands clutched each armrest as his face was inches from mine.
"No, it's not okay."
The hairs on my arms were standing straight. I felt like I wasn't breathing.
"It won't be okay until the day I see you with the bullet wound through your chest"
My eyes looked to the half-smile he had displaced.
"and I'm holding the band-aid."
He pushed off the chair as he walked away once again and turned on his heels, facing me.
"Oh, it will be a marvelous day, I'll tell you that; perhaps I'll have spaghetti."

I could feel my left eye twitch in anger; I couldn't play this game anymore. "Why Seth" Trying to hide my rage.

"Well, I love spaghetti."

Rolling my eyes, I spoke once again in a monotone voice, "Why are you doing this to me."

"Oh!" He clapped his hands together. "Because Lucy,"
His hands parted as one grasped hold of a string coming from the lightbulb up above. "We belong together."

Click

Gasping, I sat straight up; I was breathing fast. Calm down; it's over—just a nightmare. I reached for my phone; it was 9am.

Well, there's no way I'm going to be able to get back to sleep. And I feel disgusting—rainroom time.

Quietly exiting my room, I made way for the bathroom and turned on the shower while I got undressed. My hair was going to be hell to run my fingers through. Standing underneath the showerhead, I closed my eyes as I felt the relaxing ease of hot water run over my overly stressed body.
Ah, this was great.
I felt completely relaxed- with my eyes still closed, I slightly turned my head down, straining to hear. Did I hear something?
With the warning of the shower curtain opening on the other end, Carder, in boxers, stepped inside excitingly and shut the curtain. I proceeded to appropriately yell at him.

"Carder!" I grabbed the inside layer of the curtain and covered my body. "What the hell! Get out!"

"I have to talk to you! This, this isn't okay?"

"No, it's not okay!"
Stepping out of the shower, I rolled my eyes and let go of the curtain. But once again, he barged in seconds after.
My hand shot up to my eyes to cover them.
Yepp, he was naked.
"Carder. That is not what I meant."

"It isn't?"

"No! Get out!"

"Well, I'm already in here, might as well take a shower too."

"Carder."

"This is actually a great money saver."

"One, I am very self-conscious, and two, if my parents find out, they'll flip. Well, my mom will probably flip for joy, but still, that's not the point."

"One, I'm only looking at your face, and two, your parents went out for breakfast early this morning and are going to some art museum thingy; I bought the tickets."

"Best friends don't see each other naked."

"This is one hell of a friendship then, huh?" He laughed, but I was not laughing.

"Wait, you bought my parent's tickets to an art thingy, for what?"

"Sherlock texted me from Julia's phone; I still have his phone, by the way, I gotta give that to you to give to him. He asked me to distract your parents for a while. Look, are you going to shower or not because I'm getting cold over here"

Groaning in annoyance, I traded places with Carder as I kept my back to him, putting shampoo in my hair. "Carder, this is beyond weird. This isn't okay; I feel so violated."

"If it makes you feel better, you've got a cute ass!"

"Oh my gosh, don't look at it!" He laughed as I heard him exit the rainroom. I peeked out the curtain and saw he was wrapped in a towel now. "I do not forgive you for that, I hope you know," Although, with the geeky smile on my face, I guess subconsciously I had already forgiven him. It is a bit funny, now.

"Oh please," He sarcastically responded while giving me a wink as I then flicked water at him. He ran out of the bathroom, and he shouted, "Your date starts in an hour; I've got your outfit picked out!"

An hour. Are you kidding me? I frantically got under the water again and scrubbed my scalp clean. Why are these date-arrangement-hangouts always so rushed?

As quickly as one can rinse shampoo and conditioner out of their hair and dry themselves off, I ran to my room to find one of my old dresses lying on my bed next to my white flats. It was my favorite dress; I hadn't worn it in forever—Mint green, topped with a white bow around the waist. I couldn't help the smile on my face. Then it hit me that I don't have much time to get ready, so I quickly slipped into the comfortable outfit and put on my shoes. Standing in front of the mirror, I shouted out to Carder, "What am I going to do with my hair?!"

Carder walked in and marveled at my reflection with a gentle knock on the door; I smirked at him through the mirror.

"My goodness, why don't I have my own reality show? You look gorgeous."

"Yea, don't congratulate yourself yet; we still have to do something with this mop on my head."

"Leave that to me; I have the perfect idea in mind, just" He fished in his pocket and pulled out a few hair ties and a hand full of bobby pins. "hold these, please."

It still amazes me how terrible I am at hair, but how marvelous he was at, you know what, he's just great at everything. All except personal boundaries and telling me how he is really feeling. As he stood behind me while trying to make something of the mess atop my head, I could see something in his eyes that's never there when I look at him.

He did a loose French braid across the right side of my head and pulled the rest of my hair into a neat bun. I caught his eyes through the mirror when he put the last bobby pin in my hair. Wrapping his arms around my waist, he rested his chin on my shoulder as I then placed my hands over his. It was strange, looking at ourselves in the mirror, but I didn't mind at all his embrace.

"Carder," he perked up a little bit, still resting his chin, "are you alright?"
He presented me an odd look and gently began to sway, his smile trying to cover up the look I could still see in his eyes.
"You've been acting kind of off lately." I tried to keep a straight face but couldn't help giggling a little at our tipsiness. Continuing to sway, he closed his eyes and smiled at the sudden sound of a knock coming from the front door; his eyes opened as he spun me around.

"Madam," he leaned in, just a tad, "we mustn't keep him waiting." He could tell I was flustered with him as he shuffled me to the door and opened it all proper and keen.

Sherlock's hair was brushed to the side; he wore a light grey shirt, dark jeans, a mint green bow tie with white polka dots to match my dress, and but of course, white converse. Carder must have told him, through Julia, what I'd be wearing. His smile was so goony as he offered me his arm. "Shall we?" Goony and proper as always.

I turned to Carder and gave him a kiss on the cheek and then returned to Sherlock. "Why yes, we shall." We began to walk out the door; I turned my head over my shoulder as I saw Carder's head leaned against the door frame. One hand on the doorknob, and his smile brittle and small.
Sherlock's hand slipped into mine; turning to him in reaction, I gave him a smile. Turning my attention back over my shoulder to Carder, but instead, I saw the closed door.

17. Surprise Surprise 

As I turned my head back around, I was met with what appeared to be our transportation of the day. "Is that a tandem bike?"

He let out a gentle sigh. "Isn't it beautiful?"

I laughed while I slightly shook my head.
I'm wearing a dress.
And we're supposed to go biking.
No, *tandem* biking.
This isn't going to end well.

While he helped me onto the back of the odd bike, I couldn't help but look at his clothed shoulder hiding the tattoo. I wanted to see it again, this time in the natural light, not headlamp light. I also noticed a backpack hanging by one strap on the front handle that he swung onto his back as he then climbed on. He turned his head slightly over his shoulder to me.

"Ever ride one of these bad boys?" Smilingly I shook my head while I admired the youthful twinkle in his eyes. His mouth opened just a little, showing off his cheesy smile. "Me neither"

I felt my jaw open while the corners of my lips were still turned up as I then jolted for the handlebar while he kicked the kickstand and pushed us off. Looking down at the pedals, they were spinning fast; I pulled my feet up, so they weren't amputated. He was biking like a mad man in a marathon-A very nicely dressed man in a marathon.
I think he thought I was pedaling too, and though I felt a little guilty not putting in an effort, I was not going to try and catch my feet on those blades of plastic.

This will make a funny story someday.

Hey, remember that time we went tandem biking?
Yea, I wasn't pedaling.
That was all, you man.
Nicely done.
And then, with my awkward instincts, I'd probably give him a pat on the back.

Once again, I didn't ask where we were going. I'm actually surprised how well we were keeping balance, but it appeared we were slowing down. Sherlock steadily brought the bike to a halt by the beach, to which we got off and utilized the odd bike's kickstand.

"What a lovely surprise, Mr. *Holmes*" I gave him a smile, taking in the ocean air.

"Oh no, this actually isn't a part of the surprise; it's more of a spontaneous thing. We don't admire the ocean as much as we should, and I admire to admire things; how about you, Mrs. Cumberbatch?" He really has a talent for making me grin. I gave him a nod in exchange.
My, my the beach had quite the audience today. Well, I suppose most days it's a full house.
We started our admiring process, taking in the view, the scents, the people. There was a group out in the distance all wearing the same T-shirts; it looked like a church group, maybe. Church group + water = baptism event? Well, it is a pretty sunny day if that is the case.
Families were creating moments, kids were forming moats and sandcastles, everything seemed to be in its rightful place for a day at the beach. And yet, something in me felt like the beach deserved a little more originality.

I think Sherlock noticed I was lost in a thought or several. "Might I be bold enough to ask what's occupying your mind? Or am I intruding?"

I found myself smiling at his question; it was nice to be recognized and noticed for something I didn't even say out loud. Or perhaps I have loud facial expressions. "I don't know; it's kind of a weird thought, I guess."

"Oh, I'm sure I'll appreciate that," He bantered with a grin.

I nodded in approval to proceed with my peculiar thought. "Well, I was just looking around, people watching, I guess. And everything is lovely, of course, but I was just thinking how predictable all of this is. Yea, this is the setting that, sunbathing and kissing under an umbrella is supposed to happen, but I don't know. Something about the beach just seems like more interesting things should be happening." Feeling hesitant about my unfiltered thought, I attached a self-conscious buffer. "I don't know; maybe that sounded more put together in my head." I didn't turn to him right away until I heard him begin to respond.

"You know what" Sherlock looked around, taking in our surroundings with my perspective in mind. "I believe you're right, without a doubt" He looked to me, replying with 100% agreeance, not patronizing. "Lucy, we must do something about this, immediately!"

I felt a sudden surge of duty within me like I had just called a meeting for the spontaneous counsel. "Yes, we must!" It felt so fun and refreshing to be excitable about something kind of imaginary like a child. "This beach deserves impromptu justice! What shall we do?"

Sherlock looked around, searching for peeks of inspiration. He looked down at his clothes, then to mine, and an inventive smirk visited his face. "I've got it." Sherlock's eyes wandered straight out to the ocean, almost in confirmation of his thoughts, until his gaze circled back to my patient eyes.
"Follow me if you wish to break this beachy normativity." In an instant, this guy-dressed like he's about to attend a cocktail hour or apply for a loan, began to sprint towards the ocean.

I was in amused shock; I felt like I was watching my favorite scene from a movie, and I wanted to wait to react until it was done. He ran straight into the water, no hesitation holding him back. He was firm in his decision that this is what would shake the cliches that rested on the hot sand. Once he was knee-deep in the water, he turned to me. My hands were shot up to my mouth; I was laughing and smiling.

Because my mind finally caught up with my muscles.

Goodness gracious, I was going to follow that mystery into the ocean.

I grabbed a bit of fabric from my dress to run without restriction and into the cold water awaiting me with nothing but silly, impulsive intentions. And there waiting for me was the Captain of Silliness himself, waist-deep now in the freezing water that greeted my bare legs.

I shrieked a little from the shock. "Oh my gosh," I looked to my now wet dress and back up to him, smiling, "We did it!"

His smile was wide and ludicrous. "We have broken the mold of beach expectations!"

It felt like we had taken charge of the daily moments we're given. We didn't move with the motions; we created something of our own. And I felt like I was doing that more and more in his company, and I really enjoyed that.

After we soaked in the spontaneity, we said our goodbyes to the ocean. We made our way, soaking wet, to the tandem bike. The people walking on the sidewalk or driving past would probably assume we just biked straight out of the ocean.

"Mrs. Cumberbatch, how you manage to look flawless even in soaked apparel is and always will be beyond me." With my open-mouthed smile, I shook my head in disapproval of his compliment, but he continued on without my insight.

"Now, off to the surprise! It's actually right at the dock down the street; we can just walk alongside the bike if you'd like?"

Nodding to him while we began to walk, I looked around on what street we were on; we headed for the dock where all the big fancy boats live. And indeed, we walked up to an incredibly impressive Yacht with its stairs out and resting on the pier. A woman dressed up and looking all business-like came up to us. What in the world has he got up his sleeve?

"Mr. Johnson, you're soaking wet!" The fancy business lady exclaimed in horror.

"Why yes, yes we are," he said in polite confidence. I couldn't help but smirk a little at his response. He was so nonchalant about it; I'd probably laugh even harder at what she's thinking.

"Oh, but you and Mrs. Johnson look adorable even in, wet, attire." She gave us a fake smile and was apparently leading us onto the boat. Mr. and Mrs. Johnson?
"I'm so glad you could make it, your secretary Julia was very kind, please give her my regards. I hope you enjoy the luxury Island House Tour. If you have any questions, let us know, your bike will be put below deck, and you have the upper deck to yourselves as our schedule was cleared for your convenience."
With that mouth full, she gave us a quick, once again fake, smile and left to speak with the captain.

I turned to Sherlock and lightly backhanded him in the arm as he turned to me with a gleeful smile. "Mr. and Mrs. Johnson?"

"My Father's name *literally* opens doors, and boats apparently!"

"You mean to tell me we are posing as your parents right now?"

"I can't take all the credit; Julia did a swell job." He gave me a little nudge. "Surprise!" His smile couldn't have been brighter. "We get to just sit back and enjoy the ride and look at all these expensive houses. The tour is only available to '*rich people*,' so my parent's identities came in handy with that."

We both made our way to the patio chairs set out for us; I still couldn't believe we were on this extremely high-class boat, and we were dripping wet. And the fact that he *knew* we were going to be present on this fancy boat, he still insisted we literally visit in the ocean. He's a character; I'll give him that. At least the sun will help us dry off.

"So what's my name right now?" I asked as we both took a seat.

He chuckled a little before answering my question, which I never thought I would be asking him of all people. "Pippa Johnson, and I am Walden Johnson. It's delightful to meet you." Extending his arm out to me, we shook our wet hands.

"Hmm, I like our names; they're quite unique."

"And what might your parent's names be, Madam?" He had his arms raised over his head with his fingers spread out. I think this was his attempt to dry off faster. Of course, he talked to me like he was sitting formally and not as an excited kid in a classroom.
"Emmylou and Tucker MacArthur" I chuckled a little, still from the sight of him in his nice, drenched dress shirt with his arms raised.

"I dare say those are very unique names as well" He gave me a cute smile and looked out to the view as the boat began to sail.

For a while, it was quiet between us, a pleasant quiet. We listened to the sounds of the waves fearlessly crashing and then gently retreating back into the ocean. We listened to the somewhat rude-fancy-business-lady on the intercom talk about each house we passed. I couldn't imagine what some of these people do for a living to have such a giant house; they were like fairytale houses. As I turned to see Sherlock's reaction, it almost looked like he was looking out past the houses; he didn't seem fazed at all. I think it was the sky he was getting lost in; it looked like a watercolor painting decorated with a few stretched-out cotton balls.

I saw Sherlock break out of his gaze and turn his attention to me. "I'm actually almost dry! How about you?"

Checking the dampness of my dress, it was still a bit wet but, for the most part, dry "I'm almost there!"

He giggled at my dampness-progress report. "Are you ready for the next surprise?"

I felt my eyes widen just a little "Another surprise? No, no, no, that's too many surprises."

"Oh yes, yes yes, Miss Lucy, it's quite alright. You can never have *too* many surprises!" I gave him a teasing frown as he opened his mouth to speak again. "Switching gears here a little, if I may be so bold as to ask, are you spiritual?"

I will admit I was a little caught off guard, but it wasn't a question I was uncomfortable with answering. "I used to attend church pretty often, but I haven't really been going over the past year. Carder offers to take me, but I don't know; it's just been kind of hard to bring myself to over this past year." I looked down at my hands that were folded in themselves, too embarrassed to look back up at him now from my flimsy answer. I have the social skills of a mime.

I heard him clear his throat quietly. "It's pretty nice that Carder is supportive of that area of your life, that you guys can share that. I also think anyone's spirituality is valid outside of the walls of a building."
I gotta say I didn't mind so much when he tried to cheer me up. It wasn't uncomfortable, like when other people try to transition into a different conversation to avoid awkwardness.

"Yea," Smiling as I joined his comforting eyes again. "Carder is a pretty spiritual person. His parents don't understand that. They kicked him out when he came out to them, so he moved in with his awesome-hippy Aunt Figgy, and then we became friends. He's originally from Delaware." As my sentence cut off, it hit me just how far Carder and I had come; we had enough memories for a low-budget sitcom.

I felt the boat slowing down and noticed that we were harboring into a different dock than before. As I turned to Sherlock, he gave me a playful raise of his eyebrows and stood up swiftly, offering me his arm. He guided me down the steps as I let out a discreet sigh of relief to see his Jeep parked on the sidewalk. Thank God, no more tandem bike riding. Goodness, wow, he really has this day planned out.

One of the men who had brought the bike onto the boat was now loading it into Sherlock's- well, Mr. Johnson's car while the well-dressed woman came to thank us for the 'pleasure' of meeting us.

Sherlock gave the woman and two crewmen a handshake and a tip. With that, he opened the door for me, and off we were to our next destination.

"I suppose you're wondering where we are off to next," Sherlock playfully initiated.

"It has crossed my mind, but from experience, I think it's more fun to just let it happen." I wasn't looking at him, but I could feel him smiling at me in an astonished kinda way as he turned his view back to the road, still with that giddy smirk.

We drove for a while in smiling silence until I saw the familiar sign of our lovely place, The Café of Blues.

"I did say I was going to take you back here, remember?"

For the life of me, I couldn't control how much I was smiling. I didn't even answer; I just nodded like I had forgotten how to talk altogether. The mime social skills are kicking in again.

Before I could reach my hand to the door handle, Sherlock was already rushing to my side and calmly opening the car door, like the gentlemen he is. "Madam," He was trying out a French accent, "Our reservation awaits."

Though my hair was frizzy and messed up, and my dress didn't look pressed and crisp anymore, I didn't feel like I was stepping down from a Jeep. I felt like I was stepping down from a carriage, and he just happened to maybe, quite possibly, be my prince. I had my hand around the crook of his arm, and the cheery hostess greeted us as we walked inside.

"Welcome, fancy couple!" She smiled at each of us, ready to take on any task we were to request, it seemed.

"Why hello! I have a reservation for two under *Holmes*, please."

As she looked down at the paper on her podium, her eyes lit up even more than they had been, which was surprising. She turned to what I'm assuming was supposed to be our seating and nervously turned back to us, speaking in a hushed tone.

"Mr. *Holmes*, I'm awfully sorry for this inconvenience. We weren't expecting you for another thirty minutes, and we have someone at your requested table. I am terribly sorry. It looks like they're almost done. Could I interest you in another table, or you can eat at the counter until the table is available?"

I turned to see his reaction, to which I wasn't surprised; he still had that darling smile on display. "We'll wait for the table at the counter; no apologies needed. What would you like, Miss Lucy?"

Caught off guard, I was shocked how long it took me to think of what I wanted. It should be an impulse at this point. "Um, coffee, coffee, please." I smiled at the hostesses as she smiled back and turned to Sherlock for his request.

"Please make that two coffees and a side of pretzels, thank you." With that, she showed us to the lunch counter. A soft hum of music was sweeping the room, just loud enough to block out the conversations around but soft enough to hear the one you were holding. Gosh, I loved this place.

"When we were on the bike earlier, I hardly recognized the street we were on. I actually don't think I've ever been on that side of the sidewalk before, isn't that crazy?" After it came off my lips, it felt like that was a stupid thing to say, but it was the first thing that popped into my head.

"Isn't it strange how something can look so different when you ride on the other side of the street?" He smiled and gestured with his head that our coffee and pretzels were arriving. We thanked the waitress as she placed our mugs down and then our little bowl of pretzel sticks.

"Couldn't resist the pretzels, huh?" I teased as I stirred in some sugar with my coffee and then passed it to him.

"You gotta admit it's good, don't deny yourself," He '*lectured*' me, waving the pretzel in-between his fingers.

"Okay, okay," Taking a sip of my prepared coffee. "This is our last surprise, right?"

Before answering, he dipped the pretzel in his coffee and ate it. "Incorrect, we have one here, and then one more elsewhere." I gave him a glare. These were too many surprises; I felt guilty inside.
"Lucy, this is a special day; it would be unfitting to *not* have this many surprises."

Damnit, he made me lose my glare and break into a grin. Damn his swift moves.
"So to kill time, I do recall telling you about my grandpa. May I hear about yours?"

We both ate a few more coffee-dipped pretzels before I could gather my thoughts on his question.
"Well, the only grandparent I got to really know and grow up with was my dad's dad, which would be my grandpa MacArthur. He designed hot air balloons, his creations were amazing, he was always traveling. For most of the year, he would be attending events, shows, conventions with his balloons. There were a few times grandpa had local showings for his balloons, sometimes he'd even do rides."
I looked to the reflection of my coffee as the memories began to play like an old fashion reel in my mind.
"He used to tell me about the feeling he would get, riding up in the sky by yourself. I always liked the thought of that. He would spend all the time he could up there just thinking and riding along in the sky. Imagining what the people below think of his design and imagining little kids pointing in excitement. He passed away my senior year of high school. But he was tough and humble until the very end. I think one of his balloons was invited, so to speak, to a huge event in Turkey that was a big deal. But yea, he was a pretty awesome guy."

"I would say so, wow- not many people can brag about that. If I may," Gently he lifted his cup, "a toast, to your grandfather, who is without a doubt incredibly proud of his extraordinary granddaughter."

Pleasantly surprised, I joined my cup with his. "To grandpa Mac" With a slight clink and sip to go after it, our contagiously gleeful hostess came back to inform us our table was now available.
Sherlock grabbed his mug and the bowl of pretzels as I held my mug, and we transferred ourselves to our designated table. Sitting down, this seemed somewhat familiar. And looking at Sherlock, his smile was wider than usual.
"Sherlock," I questioned with a hint of curiosity in my voice as he smiled. "Is this the same table we sat at last time?"

As he stirred his coffee with another pretzel, he nodded. "Why yes, excellent deduction, but it's not entirely the same; there is one thing different about it."

Well, now I was extremely curious, "Is it the surprise?"
All he gave me was another nod and a theatrical performance of him pretending to lock his mouth shut and dropping the key into his coffee. He folded his hands under his chin and watched me with an entertained expression as I tried to figure it out. For a moment, we were having a staring contest until I blinked by accident.
Okay, focus. Where- well, more importantly, what, could he hide at the table?
I slid my chair a little back and tilted my head just a tad to peer under the table: nothing.
After scooting my chair back up, I felt under the table to see if something was tapped down: still nothing. I doubt he would tape something under the chair. Where in the hell, and what in the hell could it be.
"I give up. Can I at least get a hint, please?"

He held up a finger as if to tell me to hold on and then proceeded to stick his hand in his coffee to '*retrieve the key*,' took out a napkin, '*dried it off*', and then '*unlocked his mouth*.'
He was the biggest dork in Virginia Beach. Impeccable acting skills, though, I gotta say.
Pretending to stretch out his jaw like it had been stuck forever, he returned his hands in their folded position and proceeded to answer my question.
"Mrs. Cumberbatch, you must look between the lines."

Sassily I rolled my eyes and pondered on it.
Look between the lines?
Lines Lines Lines.
What lines could he-
Oh!
The wall!
The restaurant walls had writings and lines all over them!
I think he saw in my expression that it finally clicked. I opened my mouth to tell him that I figured it out when he pointed to a passage on the wall just above the napkin holder.

The handwriting was neat, small, and in black ink. And it, it was addressed to, me? Turning to Sherlock, he nodded to the passage, so I began to read.

Lucy May (<--Carder told me) MacArthur, it is with great pleasure to have the privilege to ask you this question. Growing up, I didn't have many friends, and the ones I had made I never got to keep in touch with. I have always been distant from others and have never been confident in myself. But becoming friends with you and Carder has been the best thing that has happened to me in quite some time. I may have traveled all over the world, but Virginia Beach has become my favorite place. I believe everything happens for a reason, and with that reason comes destiny and and I messed up. I can't erase it because I'm writing with a pen. I don't want to scribble it out because I wanted this to look neat. Now I'm going to have to start writing smaller, and now I'm rambling on paper, well, a wall, please don't look at me I'm already embarrassed for myself. I'm gu-

I paused and smiled at him as he probably knew what place in his passage I was in; he shook his head with a cute little grin of embarrassment as I picked up where I left off.

I'm guessing you looked at me anyway. You are a daring one. But onto my question, I would be honored if you and Carder would accompany me to Julia's wedding. She would be delighted to have you and insists you come. It is in two weeks and will be held in New York, please please please take your time to think about it. Thank you for bearing with me through this day, I'm not sure at this point in time if it went all according to plan, but if you're reading this, I must have done something right. Thank you, Miss Lucy.
Sincerely,
Jude Keats Johnson

As soon as I read his name in my mind, I instantly thought of Colin. Our song, '*Hey Jude*' that was our song.
I blinked blankly at the wall.
I couldn't come to speak.
I didn't know what to say.
Did he just finally tell me his name?

"Like I said, please don't rush into answering. I know traveling isn't something you're most comfortable with, and I think you should talk to Carder about it."
I was kind of afraid if I looked at him now, maybe I would see him differently.
I know that sounds silly, and I was dying to find out his name, but I had gotten so used to calling him Sherlock, it almost seemed like I was meeting someone new.
Turning my head to him, I could tell by the tone of his voice and the look in his eyes he was nervous. But putting the face to the name now, now he just seemed even more him. He was Jude Keats Johnson, and he just happened to maybe, quite possibly, be my Sherlock.
"I had a very nice day with you" his voice cracked a little, still nervous, as he smiled, trying to play it off.

Reaching my arm across the table, his smile grew bigger as we shook hands.
"Our second introduction today; it is very nice to meet you, Jude."
We released hands as he got up from his seat and offered me his arm again.

"Madam, shall we go to our next surprise?" Engaging his French accent once more.

I don't know what more of a surprise I could get or really need, but with a nod, I took his arm, and after we paid for our small meal, we were off in the glorious Jeep to our last stop of the day.
His mystery was unraveling little by little, but I had a feeling it wasn't nearly solved. He had too much of a mysterious background.

I hadn't even noticed by this point I was completely dry. I also hadn't noticed we were on my block and now parked outside my apartment building.
The Jeep came to a stop as he always jumped out and helped me out of the car.

"This is quite the surprise, Sir."

"I sense a hint of sarcasm in your tone, Ma'am."

"Maybe just a tad," I giggled and nudged him. "But really, what're we doing here?" And as he mimicked my grin, he held the door to the building open as we then walked to my apartment door. "The last surprise is you're taking me home?" I could feel the strain in my voice. I was kind of sad; I didn't want the surprises to end now.

Without having to knock on the door, it swung open with a short yell of '***Surprise!***' And indeed, I was.

It appeared Carder and mom made a big meal for all of us. Dad was there; also, an older gentleman, I'm assuming, was Tom, and of course, Alan was here. All in our tiny apartment, but I was so happy to see them.
Carder shuffled us in and shut the door as my parents came up to the both of us. I could feel how wide my smile was.

"Mom, dad, this is Jude Keats Johnson"

18. Coffee & Confetti

As dad shook Jude's hand, mom announced that we were having breakfast for lunch, and it was now up for grabs. It was like a little buffet! There were waffles, scrambled eggs, a bowl of fresh fruit; goodness gracious, I haven't eaten like this since, well, since I lived with my parents. Dad loves his breakfast for dinner, and mom loves seeing dad's goofy smile over morning aesthetic foods.
And apparently, Jude and my dad really hit it off as they made their way to Carder's room while everyone else was serving themselves. Alan, mom, and Carder dished up and sat in the living room to discuss the business of Books & Such. Tom sat at the tiny dining room table for three with his plate. After I poured myself a cup of coffee and grabbed a waffle, I took the seat across from him and smiled as he looked up to find he had company.

His smile seemed so fragile, and I began to wonder how many times he had smiled in his lifetime.
How many of those smiles were genuine.
How many of the smiles were faked.
How many of the smiles appeared spontaneously because of the butterflies he would get from his wife.
How many of those smiles appeared at this exact time on a different afternoon such as this.

"You must be the famous Lucy" His voice lingered a bit in my thoughts before I noticed my smile had grown.

Politely we shook hands as I nodded while still smiling. "Yes, sir, and you must be the famous Tom Wyatt, owner of Duck's Cranberries." What a nicely done adult introduction, no stutters or anything; wow.

Point for Lucy.

He chuckled a little as we released hands and sat back more relaxed. "Oh, I wouldn't quite say famous. You, on the other hand," His eyes wandered a bit as he then focused back on me. "He never stopped talking about you."
Again, he laughed a little as I put together, he was probably looking for Jude. Still feels a bit weird to actually know his name now. I could now feel my cheeks begin to blush at the thought of him talking about me.
"The whole time he's workin' when he came to fill in for JudieBoy, I tell ya, he just went on and on about you."
JudieBoy- that's adorable. But- he wasn't talking about him, talking about me. Tom was talking about Carder filling in for Jude when he was still Sherlock when he was in the hospital, talking about me. Tom's eyes were looking at Carder in the living room, not searching for Jude.
"He's nice company and all, the guy is funny as hell, but he ain't much of a farmer." Tom sure liked to laugh.

Just as I was about to speak, dad and Jude came down the hallway. Dad was holding his travel battery-operated turntable, which looked like a clunky briefcase, on top of his head, with but of course, his favorite album playing. *Abbey Road*, by The Beatles. I can't tell you how big of goons they looked like as the first track, 'Come Together,' played while they strutted down the hallway and to the living room.

"Tucker! How did you smuggle that here?! I swear I checked every inch of that suitcase!" Mom's protest made everyone giggly. I love that woman, but her frustration was hilarious sometimes.

Dad set his turntable down and slipped his hand in mom's as he lifted her off the couch. "Oh, I've gotten more clever at hiding my records, don't deny yourself the beautiful music, let it" And as smooth as one could, he dipped mom down. "Sweep you off your feet." I think that line right there made everyone blush; damn, dad had the moves. He gently kissed her nose and lifted her back up as they danced, and he twirled her around. My parent's marriage would always be the most beautiful thing I have ever witnessed.

I glanced over at Tom as I saw his eyes dancing along with my parents. I wonder if his thoughts became preoccupied with memories of him and his wife dancing. Within my wonder, I turned my attention to Alan as he and Carder walked up to the table.

"We were just talking about you" I smiled at Tom and then Carder as he and Alan took a seat.

"Well," Alan cleared his throat and turned to Tom, "I don't believe we know one another, but nonetheless, I am flattered" Alan and Tom shook hands and began their small talk.

After a few moments, Carder motioned me to accompany him in the living room. Sher- Ugh, Jude, this will take some getting used to; he was sitting by himself on the couch. Carder jumped the couch like a fence and landed roughly.

Yea, mom, was not having that. She stopped dancing and went straight into mom mode. "Young man, I do not care if this is your apartment now too. You respect the furniture!"

Jude was sitting in the middle of the couch, so I sat on the other side of him as we quietly giggled at Carder being scolded. Carder lifted his hands up in a sassy surrender. "Okay, okay, Momma M, I apologize for my outrageous behavior."

"Don't make me swear at you, Gosh Dammit,"

"Gosh Dammit, Emmy, come on, we can do better than that," Dad said as he laughed and twirled mom around.

And like the twirling made her forget, she was smiling and laughing in my dad's arms again as the second song of the album, 'Something,' began to spin and play with them. The three of us admired them for a few moments until Carder reached over Jude to poke my knee and get my attention.

“Guess what we get to do from noon to nine tomorrow” Carder dug in his pocket and retrieved Jude’s phone, returning and balancing it on his knee. “Oh, here’s your phone, by the way.”
Jude gave him a gratitude-filled smile and pocketed his phone as they then both turned to me to see my response.

“Hmm, let me guess, working at the best place in the world?”

“Yea, Lucy Alan already gave you the job.”

Jude softly cleared his throat. “This may not be the best timing, but I was wondering if you two would like to accompany me to church tomorrow, there’s a service that starts at ten, and it would end right in time for you guys to go to work!”

Turning to see my parents still gigging and twirling around like they were at their last high school dance, I whispered to Jude, asking if they could join us, which of course, he nodded in agreement.
“Hey, you reckless teens and your British rock music,” I called out to my parents as they both stopped with a smile, hand in hand. “Would you guys like to join us three for church tomorrow?”

Mom turned to dad with a slightly disappointed look as she wrapped her arm comforting around his, and Dad returned me the same expression.
“I’m awfully sorry, your mom and I have to leave tonight, so I can make it work. My sub bailed out on me, I’m sorry, Traveler” Giving them the best smile I could pull off, I lifted myself up off the couch and wrapped my arms around them. “We’ll be back soon, Traveler, don’t you worry” Mom kissed me on the forehead; I didn’t realize how much I had and would truly miss them until we broke off from our hug.

As the afternoon continued, I couldn’t stop thinking about Jude’s big question among everyone else’s laughter and small talk.

To leave Virginia Beach for the first time in my life to travel to New York City. I don't think I can do it. I don't even know if I *want* to do it. Would we fly? Goodness gracious, that sounds terrifying. Perhaps we would drive.

The night was filled with old stories from everyone. Even Alan, to my surprise, had some funny things to comment on! And as things started to wind down, it hit me that mom and dad were saying their goodbyes and leaving for New Orleans.

They were never big fans of dramatic goodbyes or tearful departures. There was a silent understanding between us whenever we said our goodbyes that we would see one another soon. And I loved that. It was just the most brutal to wave goodbye to mom, especially after dad confided in me during our rock skipping. I know he always takes the best care of her; this past year has been an extremely tough trial for them both, with moving and healing from everything. I'm just afraid to see how much further she'll possibly drift away, like the waves she used to watch with Colin.

Once everyone left, Carder and I began cleaning up the apartment and putting away the leftovers, which was nice to have for a change.

"So, church tomorrow, huh?" Carder called to me from his room while I just finished loading up the dishwasher.

"It would be nice to go; it feels like forever. Are you looking forward to it?"

Carder peeked around the hallway corner. "Are you kidding me?" and now he came marching in the kitchen, energetically clapping his hands. "Ooooo, yes! I'm gonna get my praise on!" After barely pressing the start button on the dishwasher, Carder grabbed both my hands and began spinning and jumping in a circle with me. We laughed and spun as I watched the passing and blurring surroundings behind Carder as his face became more in focus, as he became the only clear thing in my view. His mouth was moving, but I was too concentrated on my footing to actually hear what he was saying. "Heellooooo, Earth to Lucy?"

"I'm sorry, what did you say?"

"I said" in one swift movement, Carder picked me up, and before I even realized it, I was over his shoulder as he started to march down the hallway. "Time for bed, Lucy-Lou!" Now he was galloping, which was not a pleasant feeling on my ribcage.

"Carder, put me down!" I couldn't help but laugh while I tried to be forceful, hitting his back while he purposely made me bounce.

"As you wish," Carder sassily replied, just in time to toss me onto my bed. "You know this would be the part I jump on there with you if you didn't have such a small bed."

"I don't know if I should be mad or surprised at the fact you can carry me on your shoulder."

"Considering you're a human paperweight, let's just go with mad" I gave him a smile with a shake of my head. "I think I'm going to ask Sher-" he caught himself. "Damnit! Jude! I'm going to ask him if he can pick us up in the morning. I have no idea where this church is."
Carder walked over to me and kissed my forehead quickly as he shut off my bedroom light and then began to walk out of the room. "And don't touch your closet; I'm picking out your outfit!" He called out as I heard his bedroom door shut.

Crawling under my quilt, I laid on my back as a huge smile came across my face; so giddy and wide I was embarrassed by myself.
What in the hell just happened today?
It was actually a really productive day.

I went into the ocean.
I went for a bike ride- I'm so counting that as exercise even though I didn't really help with peddling.
I got to ride on a boat that was probably bigger than my apartment.
I impersonated a woman whom I've never met, but I like her name.
I had my coffee.
I finally know the name of the mysterious guy I can't seem to get out of my head.
I had breakfast for dinner and spent time with lovely people.
I got a free ride to bed.
And Carder kis-

Vibrate

Sherlock:

Goodnight Miss Lucy, see you in the morning!

I smiled and set the alarm; gosh, I need sleep, like actual sleep. I don't think I've had a good night's rest in over a year. I feel like I'm caught between trying to create a positive life for myself and this emptiness that I can't even explain for myself-
It's like that feeling you get when you're dreaming, and you fall or slip, and it scares you so much you jolt awake, and you feel like you can't breathe for a second, that's it.
That's how I feel.
I'm continually finding myself lost in that moment where I'm trying to collect myself again, just trying to breathe.

I closed my eyes anyway and hoped tonight is different, but of course, the minute I feel like I'm finally drifting off, my alarm goes off instead. Groaning, I pushed through my sleepiness; I don't want to make Carder and Jude wait for me to get ready.

Let's be honest here if we are waiting for anyone, it's going to be Carder.
Speaking of him, he must have been up before me. At the foot of my bed was a cute outfit that was appropriate for church and comfortable enough to work in afterward. It was a short-sleeved shirt to match my red chucks and comfy skinny jeans.
As I got out of bed, I didn't realize I never changed out of my clothes from last night. Surprisingly that dress was comfortable to sleep in, though I was exhausted, so I wouldn't have really cared if I had fallen asleep in a clown costume.
Not sure why I would be wearing one.
But I wouldn't have cared.

After changing, I made my way to the bathroom in hopes that I had beat Carder to it; alas, I was defeated. He smiled at me through the bathroom mirror as I walked in, still in his nighttime apparel. He was messing with his hair as I reached for my toothbrush.

"You're looking ravishing this morning," Carder complimented me as I applied the toothpaste to my brush. Gah, I always put too much on. "Did you like the clothes I put out for you? I'm like your publicist; I love it."

Oh, I hate this- I hate when he does this. He purposely begins talking to me while I'm brushing my teeth. He thinks it's funny, seeing me trying to speak with a mouth full of toothpaste—especially this time since I went overboard.
While brushing, I mumbled out that it was a nice outfit, in which, but of course, he laughed and turned to look right at me. I just embraced the fact that he's going to poke fun at me and turned to look right at him, still in the process of brush my teeth.

"Now that," he smiled, not looking at my rabies-looking mouth but at my sleepy eyes. At the same time, he grabbed the lightly damp towel that was resting on the sink. "Is the most adorable face," and gently, he wiped a spot by my mouth that was decorated in lovely toothpaste residue. "I've ever seen."

Not what I was expecting.
Not, at all, what I was expecting.
What the hell-

"Jude's probably going to be here soon" He set the towel back in its place and made his way out of the bathroom. By the time I got done with my teeth and brushing through my knotted hair Carder returned to the bathroom in his church/work attire. Now I was smiling at him through the mirror. He stood behind me and looked at the both of us in our reflection.
"Ready for some praising?"

I giggled and nodded as I turned around, and we walked out towards the door, grabbing my purse on the way. "Did Jude text you that he was here?"

"He said he was on our block; when we get to the car, you take shot-gun."
Bless him for planning ahead of time and avoiding that awkward moment where the driver is the only one who knows where to sit.
We timed it pretty well. When Carder walked out onto the sidewalk, Jude pulled up in his Jeep; he had the top down today. It looked like he was about to step out, so I lunged for the door and beat him to his gentlemanly impulse. He gave me a defeated pouty grin as Carder climbed in the back.
Jude's hair was neatly combed; he looked like an adorable dork on his way to a book convention, in which case I would gladly accompany him. He pulled out onto the street and began our smooth drive; the weather was perfect to have the top down. After taking a few roads through town, Jude made a turn that would take us through the back roads; I guess the church wasn't in town.

"Miss Lucy, would you like to pick out a cassette for us to jam to?" I was cautious when opening the compartment door this time, quickly catching the tapes that fell as one with a light green label caught my eye, and I picked it up.
"Ah yes, I'm sorry, I still need to organize those. Is that the tape you're going with?"

"This is the winner" I smiled and popped it into the cassette player and turned to see Jude's face. He looked so ready for whatever was about to come through the speakers. And I was equally amazed as I was giddy that he had the tapes memorized, so it seemed, by their quirky colors.
Immediately, everyone in the jeep went from happy-go-lucky churchgoers to overly excited rock groupies. The crisp and extraordinary momentarily acapella voice boomed through the speakers. 'Carry on Wayward Son' by Kansas. My jaw was dropped, I hadn't heard this song in forever; Carder was literally freaking out.

He grabbed onto the back of Jude's seat and protested, "Turn this up!" I turned my head back to see the expression on his face as he was taking off his seat belt. "Permission to stand up?" Carder loudly requested Jude over the music as I turned to him, and Jude looked at Carder through the review mirror.

"Yes, but no dying!" He yelled back as he turned up the stereo, and Carder stood up like he was in a cliché movie with his arms in the air and letting the wind carry away his troubling thoughts.
He is so dramatic.

I laughed as we all began belting out the notes and singing our hearts out. Carder automatically took the role of lead singer, so I took the guitar. Because Jude was driving, he took whatever background sound he happened to pick up and hear while concentrating on the road. Granted, we were on back roads, but it would be a pretty lame obituary. I can't argue with the song we would die to though, that wouldn't be too shabby.

Just as the timeless song was fading out, Jude turned down the music and began to slow down.
"Hey, Kansas," He called back to Carder, who was still lost in his own little music video world. "Would you mind joining us, please? We're going to be pulling up

to the church here in a second" He gave Carder a slight smirk in the review mirror as Carder tried to play it off that he totally wasn't jamming out.
I gave him a teasing grin as we pulled into the parking lot. It was a nice size, a humble-looking church with a white cross on the roof. As I was admiring the view, Jude had hopped out of the Jeep and hustled to the other side. Before I realized what he was doing, he opened the door.

"Lady and Gent, welcome to Grace Church; I call it Grace Central though" He gave me a cute smile while helping me out of the car, and jokingly he did the same to Carder. Which he took full advantage of and took the opportunity to act like the Queen of England. Jude then led us to the main doors, where a lovely couple was there to greet us. They were probably in their late fifties.

It looked like the service was about to begin as we got further down the lobby hallway. People began to file into the sanctuary. There was a laid-back feeling in the congregation, a very diverse congregation at that, and it was nice I didn't feel like an outsider. I felt pretty welcomed. We sat down in the middle section towards the front. It took a few minutes for everyone to settle into their seats; Carder sat between Jude and me.

A podium was upfront on a small stage, and in the back, a piano and microphones were set up with a projector on the back wall. A man, I gathered was the Pastor, walked up to the podium; he had a friendly smile.

"Ladies and Gentlemen, thank you for joining us at Grace Church on this beautiful morning. It's beautiful out today, isn't it?" Everyone was pretty vocal on their opinions of the weather; there was a pretty good reaction.
"This morning, we are going to do things a little differently. There's been a lot of suffering over the past week throughout the community. We've had a lot of prayer requests, so this morning we are going to praise and wipe all that sorrow away!" The Pastor smiled, and a few voices within the congregation cheered *Amen.*

I turned to Carder, and it was like his little church dreams were coming true; to be among people that shout out their joy that cannot be contained.
"The worship song lyrics will be on the screen, and our prayer team members will be scattered along in front of the stage. If you feel you need someone to pray with about your strife, whether you're a regular or if it's your first time here, we are here for you, and we're going to help you through this hardship. Our prayer team will stay as late as you need; our piano man can't stay past our service today, but that's okay. He's not that good anyway." Everyone chuckled, it was unexpected to have a little comedy relief, but I liked the Pastor's sense of humor.
"Nah, I'm just kidding; we love ya, son. If the prayer team and worship team could find their way to the front, I will also be joining the prayer team today. God Bless, and let's leave our troubles here in the pews this morning."
The Pastor stepped down from the stage and stood with a welcoming smile as others joined him and spread out.

A few younger guys and girls stood up and made their way to the microphones; I turned to Carder and-
Jude stood up and began to walk up to the front. My eyes confusingly followed him as I felt Carder doing the same; without a word to us, Jude walked up on the stage and sat on the piano bench. Then, with the most mischievous smile, he glanced back to us and then fixed his eyes on the keys and began to play while the words came on the screen and the soft voices faded in. Honestly, should we be surprised at this point? I mean, come on, the guy is like something out of a *Hallmark* movie.

The congregation slowly began to stand up as a few people went up to the different individuals who were a part of the prayer team. The rest of the church was singing along with the worship team.
It was pleasant; no one in the church could hear your prayers with the singing, so it was just you and whoever you were praying with to listen to you. It was also great to have the words on the screen.
Glancing at Carder, he was lost in the singing and something wandering in his thoughts, I could tell. I moved a little closer to him; our hands were resting on the

pew in front of us, it was bold, but I placed my hand over his. Holding Carder's hand and just barely hearing him sing, I felt an ease of grace over me at this beautiful Grace Church. Or Grace Central in Jude's eyes. At that thought, my eyes drifted to Jude as he was lost in the surrounding sound of his playing. Though everything seemed to be okay in this still moment, there was something I couldn't get to stray away from my mind.

I'm not sure what came over me, but I gave Carder's hand a squeeze and let go as I made my way up to the front. I wasn't paying any attention if people had their eyes on me or not, and soon I was engulfed by the music as it got louder the closer I got to the front of the stage. The Pastor gave me a welcoming smile.

"Good morning" He smiled and shook my hand. I was surprised by how clearly I could hear him. "I'm Pastor Robinson. I'm glad you could make it this morning. Is this your first time being here?"

I nodded. I was trying to think of what I wanted to pray about exactly, what even drew me up here. "Yea, it is my first time actually, my name is Lucy, it's nice to meet you. This church is beautiful."

"My grandfather built this place when I was a kid. It was my dream to become a Pastor just like him." His eyes were so kind. "What's your dream, Lucy?"

His question caught me off guard; I felt like I hadn't opened my mouth to respond for hours.

I hesitated and took another moment to gather my thoughts. "I just want to feel okay, I guess. To feel happier." I gave him a smile, trying to return one similar to what he gave me, but I could feel it was a bit weak.

"I would love to help you get to that dream Lucy; what do you think we can pray about today to begin that path?"

When I woke up this morning, I didn't think I was going to cry in front of a man I had just met, a man whose only thought at this moment in time was to selflessly provide me a listening ear, and I couldn't help but cry. It was an overwhelming feeling; all this pain I've pushed aside for so long flooded into this moment. I gathered myself together, trying to swallow my tears down.

"I'd like to pray for my brother, my brother Colin." I was a train wreck. I could feel it, I felt so ugly and a mess looking down at my chucks. Pastor Robinson gently gave my shoulder a squeeze as I looked up to his gaze. He gave me a reassuring smile, and I think he could tell I wasn't in the best shape to talk anymore, so he took the reins and began the prayer as we bowed our heads and closed our eyes.

"Lord, thank you for bringing Lucy here today on this beautiful Sunday morning. Though Lucy and I just met, I can see she is a bright and resilient person, and she is struggling in this season of life with her brother Colin. Wherever he may be, Lord, please let him feel your loving embrace and let him know you are there."

Holy buckets.

I lost it.

The tears were falling faster than the notes were flowing out of the piano. I felt like I couldn't move; I didn't really want to look at him with my face looking like this. Pastor Robinson kept praying, and I kept trying to hold it together. I had my eyes closed for quite a while, but now they finally started to dry.

"Are you going to be alright?" he kindly asked me with a soft smile. I gave him a slight nod. "Thank you for opening up to me; I hope to see you and your friend again next Sunday. I just realized you came here with Jude; he's a good guy. He just started playing here a few weeks ago. Sadly, our long-time lovely piano woman passed away from Breast Cancer. But now she's rejoicing in Heaven on the grand piano she's always wanted, but I could sadly never afford."

He glanced down for a moment before he met my confused look. "We actually met in this church, we were married for thirty-four years, but she would have enjoyed Jude's playing. He is gifted."

I was in awe. He seemed so put together; I would've never guessed he just suffered such a huge loss. I'm not very good at deciphering people, but I could already tell he was one of the strongest people I'd ever met.
"I'm very sorry for your loss," Trying to sound as reassuring as I could. "Thank you so much; I haven't really prayed in a long time."

"Lucy, please try to remember that praying is just simply talking to God. Just talk to him, like you were talking to me or talking to your parents or Colin. Let him know what's on your mind; he just wants to have a relationship with you. The real you." He sounded so comforting.
It also felt good to just say Colin's name and talk about him as though he was still here. I shook Pastor Robinson's hand before wiping my eyes and walking back to join Carder. Instead of being pounded with questions, like I thought I would be when I returned, he wrapped his arm around me and drew me to his side.
Just as Pastor Robinson said, the prayer team stayed as the worship team said a closing prayer, and the service came to an end. Carder and I waited for Jude to come down off the stage to join us in walking out to the car.

Carder immediately gave him a small punch to the arm. "Hey, thanks for the heads-up, Stevie Wonder."

I gave Carder a nudge of disapproval. "He means you did a great job playing, and we were amazed."

"Yea, no, that's not what I meant, but good job."

Gosh, he's like a sassy little man child.

Jude got quite a few compliments on his playing as we made our way out of the lobby and to the Jeep. Of course, he couldn't help but open the door for Carder and me as we all then got in, buckled up, and then headed for work. The ride back seemed quicker than the ride there, though, probably because this time I knew where we were going.

"Thank you for picking us up and welcoming us into your church today; I really enjoyed it, and thank you for bringing us to work." I smiled at Jude as he took his eyes off the road for a moment to smile back.

Approaching the store, he pulled off to the side of the road and put the Jeep in park. Quickly I signaled him that he didn't need to get out; I knew he had to be getting to work too. I hopped out, and as did Carder as he thanked Jude and went to open the store.

I grabbed my purse and tapped on Jude's door. "Thank you again, piano man." Hehe, I made him blush.

"It was my pleasure, Mrs. Cumberbatch. You enjoy the rest of your Sunday." With a smile and a wave goodbye, he was off to work as well.
I could feel the giddy smile still on my face as I walked into the store; Carder was reading a note on the counter.

"Well, apparently, our only pressing task for the day is redoing our stock count because I messed up. Go figure." I hated when he beat himself up like that. I'm sure it was something we could fix.

"Can I help you with it?"

He looked up from the note. "No, no, it was my mistake; it's okay, I'll get it done. You can hold the fort down at the desk. When there aren't customers in the store, you can just chill out at the desk or straighten out the books." He then disappeared in the back with a disappointed look in his eyes. I felt a sense of guilt; it just makes me sad when he's hard on himself like that.

Starting up the desk computer I looked at the time, it was twelve o clock now, and we had to be here until nine. And as there are no customers right now, I decided to take a stroll around the small store and fix any books I saw out of place that caught my eye. All these book titles glimpsed through the corner of my eye as I walked down. All the different combinations of words just waiting to be flipped and read and understood. I loved books so much.

After I had done a few laps around the store and pushed all the books in and scanned almost every single one to be sure they were in their proper place, I sat back down at the desk; barely an hour had passed. This shift may be a bit longer to get through than I had expected.

I decided I'd kill some time by reading some more of my beloved fanfiction. *The Doctor* and *Sherlock Holmes*, solving crimes and saving the universe side by side. I wasn't even ashamed anymore by how happy fanfiction stories made me. After reading a few pages, I realized I would probably have more than enough time to finish this story. This made me happy and sad; I wanted to finish this one to start reading a new story, but I became so attached to this one.

I always caught myself thinking of Colin and me while reading this. Like Colin was *the Doctor*, and I was *Sherlock Holmes*. I can't even count how many times he would talk and act like he was secretly *the Doctor* when we were kids. If we weren't pretending to be casting spells in the hallways of our old house, we were running around outside. I was the companion, the sidekick, and he was *the Doctor*. I'm really blessed to have such beautiful memories from my childhood. It's a touchy subject for Carder, he was an only child, and his parents never showed him the love he deserved. He doesn't like talking about that part of his life.

Reaching the last chapter of my story, Carder popped out of the backroom and tapped on the desk to get my attention. I looked at the clock before looking at him; it was four-thirty now.

"Hey champ, how's it going?" Carder seemed a bit more like himself and less upset.

"I organized to the last possible detail, and I'm almost done with my fanfic. I'm bored out of my mind" I laughed and followed it with a sigh; Carder sighed too, like a confirmation of agreement.
"Yea, I'm almost done back there, then I can join you up here; maybe we can help hang one another. How does that sound?" Tapping the desk again as he made his way back to the room.

"Doesn't that sound delightful" I sarcastically called back to him.

"Never change Lucy, never change," he responded back to me in a joking tone before he shut the door.

I don't know what I'm going to do next after I finish this story. I can feel my eyes starting to strain from looking at the screen too long. Maybe I'll find a book to read in the store when I'm done. Oh, but I really don't want this story to end. I just want to keep reading until the end of my life, then I'll be content. But of course, it did end, and naturally, it would agonize and thrill me all at once that it ended wide open for a sequel, but the story was last updated two years ago. So, the hopes of having a sequel were about as slim as having *BBC Sherlock* return for another season.

I rubbed my eyes and tried to think of something I could do to pass the time. And then it hit me. It hit me so hard I was ashamed I hadn't thought of it before.

Netflix.
Thank God for Netflix.

Logging in and having the glowing red screen reflect my eyes, I decided to dedicate the rest of my time to an *Office* binge, so Jude and I could talk about it. And I've really grown to like this show!
I only had to pause a few times when some customers came in. It was actually pretty slow today, but the episodes flew by. And I started to feel it, that undeniable feeling you get when you know you've been sucked into a show, and there's no

turning back. You're stuck. You're going to be referencing lines forever; there's no escaping.

"You know you have a serious problem" I felt myself jump from being surprised. I didn't even see Carder come out of the stock room. And looking at the front window, I noticed it was dark outside. I couldn't deny it now; I had a problem.

I laughed and started shutting down the computer. "Yea, I know, I know, don't judge me" turning off the monitor, I turned around to him, "I thought you would be done sooner?"

"Oh, I was. I fell asleep back there. I woke up like ten minutes ago and was just standing here waiting until you noticed, but natural death just doesn't seem fitting for this occasion, so I spoke up."

I rolled my eyes at him as I grabbed my purse, and we both walked to the door. "Your sass is going to kill me one of these days," I laughed as we walked out of the shop, and the little bell rang, and I flipped the Open sign to Closed. Carder locked up, and we took our short walk around the corner to our apartment.
I liked the ring of that; our apartment.

As soon as I unlocked the door, Carder kicked off his shoes. "I probably won't fall asleep right away, but I'm going to just hit the mattress. I am so fricken tired, I hate counting, with a burning passion."

"I'm going to take a shower and then head to bed myself" slipping off my shoes, I quickly went up behind Carder and hugged him from behind.
"Thank you for a lovely Sunday." I hummed into his back as his hands found their way to mine, and he gave them a soft squeeze.

"No, thank *you* for making work more bearable now" he loosened out of my grip and spun around to look at me. "You have a knack for doing that," like always, he kissed my forehead and walked his sleepy self to his room. While I was going to mine, I heard him slam onto his bed; he's even dramatic when he's by himself.

Changing my clothes and tossing them in my hamper, I slipped on my robe and went to the bathroom. Setting my robe aside on the sink edge, I turned the shower on. I liked the water pretty hot; Carder calls it's blistering, but I call it comfortable. While running my fingers through my tangled and now damp hair, I reflected on today.

It was a pleasant Sunday.

Rocking out to a classic, timeless song.

Getting to know another one of Jude's hidden talents.

Attending church again.

Having my first day at Books & Such,

I thought about-

Colin.

I just, I didn't comprehend until now how much I had thought about him today.

I started to replay what happened at the church. Meeting Pastor Robinson and just opening up about that.

And talking about that.

And crying about that.

And saying everything like he was still here, like he never left.

Was I wrong? This was wrong-

How could I talk about him like he had never drifted away out of my reach? Was that like lying? To the Pastor, and even to myself? It was just uplifting, for once, to even pretend for a moment he was still here.

And Jude's question.

To leave Virginia Beach,

without Colin.

The water began to make my back throb from the heat; I reached my arm back quickly-it must have been too quick.

I was starting to feel it again, the feeling of not being able to find my breath. Unknowingly and out of my control, I was slipping into another panic attack. The sharp alarming pain traveled from my left arm, which had reached back, to my chest and slowly spread as I tried to stay as still as possible. Even the slightest movement triggered such a stabbing pain.

My shoulders slowly turned inwards as my chest felt like it was caving in, and the pain echoed and ricocheted every nerve in my body. My breath was lost in the deafeningly excruciating shots of pain that surged through my body; I whispered in my mind before I screamed for Carder that I was sorry. And as I felt my knees dizzily circling and slipping from their stance, I whispered it again in my mind; *I'm sorry, Carder.*

Closing my eyes as the stinging hot water pelted at me still, I yelled again. As loud as I could without trying to trigger more pain, which was inevitable. I felt so useless, so vulnerable. Well, at least he's already seen me naked.

I heard Carder barge the door open and reach his hand in the shower to turn off the water. "Owch! Ugh, you and your hell water showers-" after departing from the inside of the shower for a moment, I heard the shower curtain open. My head was faced away; I didn't want to open my eyes.

"It's okay, Lucy, it's okay" I felt Carder drape my robe on me as he stepped into the tub. "I'm going to lift you up on three, okay?" I gave him a slight nod, tightening my shut eyes, ready to embrace the pain.

"1, 2, okay 3" As smoothly as he could, he slipped my arms in the robe's sleeves, sat me up just enough so he could sit down beside me, and then gently rested me down, so I was laying against his side with his arm around me.

"I've got you; it's alright."

I kept my eyes closed. One of my hands was resting on Carder's chest; when the pain started to sharpen again, I would grasp onto the fabric of his shirt. I felt so horrible, so rotten inside; I couldn't imagine how exhausted and scared he must feel. The worst part is, I don't think I would even want to know. Carder rubbed my head; after about another ten minutes, the pain began to subside.

"I'm sorry, Carder" Softly, just barely, I let out. The pain still lingering a little, but it was almost done with its visit.

"No apologies needed; you didn't do anything wrong, Lucy-Lou."

Jude's question echoed through my mind again as Carder was still rubbing my head. "Carder, I can't go." He stopped for a second. "You know why" Gosh, I was trying to hold back from crying so badly.

"I know" he slowly rubbed my head again a few more strokes and then stopped. From him stopping, I got this course of energy to sit up and look at him.

"Carder," I questioned as I searched through his glossy and worrisome eyes, "I never even-" He gave me a confused look as he readjusted himself to face me more. "You never left after high school."

His facial expression went flat "Stop, Lucy-"

"You got accepted into your dream Culinary school in San Francisco,"

"Lucy"

"And you didn't go."

"Lucy come on, it's late."

"Why?" He just looked at me sternly. "Why didn't you go?"

His expression loosened. "Remember the old gang? Me, you, and Colin? All the stupid stuff we did and the things we found absolutely hilarious that no one would get?" It felt painful to smile at the reflecting memories that flashed through my mind that I missed so dearly.
"I wasn't- I couldn't leave you like that after all of that happened. No Culinary Arts school was worth it." I couldn't help but feel a disgusting pit of guilt dig itself into my stomach.

"But listen, that was my choice, okay? You weren't going to stop me from making that choice, and I would be paying off that tuition until the day I die, so there's a plus side to it. And you're my best friend, one of the only reasons I seriously considered following through with going was because I'd have you there. I'd rather be here, with you." He turned to look me in the eyes, but I couldn't look at him without feeling guilty. "Lucy, you-"

"I know, I have to tell him," I broke off from my gaze and looked at Carder. "I have to really tell Jude about Colin. It's just festering inside of me and turning into these episodes. I don't want to feel this pain anymore,"

Carder looked down for a moment before opening his mouth and looking back at me. "It's harsh, it's harsh. I know, Lucy, but I'm afraid if you don't properly go through this trauma and process through it, this is going to keep happening. This, this right here, this moment, and we are never going to leave this moment. And I want you to experience things. I want you to go make memories outside this Godforsaken town. Hell, Lucy, you more than deserve it. You keep literally beating yourself down from the inside out about everything."
It was quiet for a moment like we were waiting for Carder's words to dissolve into the droplets of water that were still left on the shower walls.

"You wanted to be a baker; that was your dream" Carder sighed and sat back a little, still holding me. His arm was probably falling asleep.
"You know when you look up at the sun, and when you close your eyes, and you see a black circle for a moment afterward?"
I felt Carder nod as he was following along with what I was saying. "That's what it's like. I'll close my eyes, and I'll see him." I swallowed my breath, inhale, Lucy, inhale and exhale.
"I see Colin. And I'm afraid if I let go, I won't see him anymore and" come on, push the words out. "and eventually, he'll just disappear."
Carder pulled me closer to him as his other arm wrapped around me. We both unintentionally slid down, turned towards one another. My head under his chin with my arms huddled against his chest. His chin rested on my head, and his arms

held my body when it felt more like he was holding every piece of me together. We laid in silence as my words floated about the misty air of the shower.
"Carder," I mumbled into his chest.
"Yes?" Feeling his jaw move on my head as he talked.

Anything, literally anything, just say something; don't lay here in weird silence. "When I die, at my funeral during the burial service when my casket is lowered into the ground, would you pour a pot of coffee down with me?"
What the literal hell was I thinking.

I felt Carder move his head and place it in my view, our foreheads lightly pressed together. "You are going to outlive us all, silly, but that's a damn good idea, yes." He gave me a small smile and returned his head in the oddly comfortable place it was before. "Hell, you better chuck handfuls of confetti down with mine."

19. Under Pressure

It was summer. I'm finally done. Yea, whatever, I'm told this is the easiest part of my life, but I'm happy it's over.

No more stupid bells.

No more status quo.

No more dances.

No more unwanted attention from the creep in gym class.

No more gym class.

No more math equations.

No more fricken high school.

I'm going to enjoy the rest of this summer because after this summer, I'm gone. I'm going to travel, I'm going to go far away, and hopefully, I'll find myself. I needed to find myself.

It's so strange to hear everyone's plans; what their first step is to the rest of their lives. I wasn't too concerned. Seth and I got accepted into San Francisco State University, and Carder got accepted into this fancy Culinary School in San Fran. I didn't tell Seth my reasoning behind wanting to go there; the truth was I just couldn't part from Carder.

Naturally, my parents were thrilled, even though I didn't have a major declared. I knew they'd always be there for me. It was nice to know I wasn't alone, and there was someone to catch me when I fall. Most of the time, it's an abrupt trust fall.

The only person who I was worried about was Colin. When I got my acceptance letter, he seemed happy for me, but it was more of a forced kind of happy. Not in a mean way; I think he just didn't want to tell me how he really felt. But with one year of high school left and his excellent grades, I reassured him that he would get into SFSU for sure. Which seemed to cheer him up, but I could tell as soon as he turned away from me his smile was only left in my memory. I talked to dad about it, he said that I was Colin's best friend; it's like if Carder was leaving and I

had to wait a year to go be with him. I hadn't even thought about it like that. I guess I just saw it as more of an adventure for myself.
We'll video chat like all the time, though, we'll send each other things in the mail, this year will fly by; then we'll both be rockin' the California life together. I'm just breaking it in for him, that's all.
I wasn't even sure why Colin wanted to go to the same college as me, then again what dad said-

Seth nudged me-
Oh! Geez, all this time getting lost in thought, and I'm still standing in line to get my coffee; nothing like totally spacing out in public.

"I'll pay; what do you want?" his voice struck me as a bit annoyed as we were next in line. Giving him a slight smile, I requested my usual, and I received an eye roll. And that's love, folks.
When our orders got called, we quickly grabbed our drinks and claimed a table for two.
"Good thing we got here when we did, huh?"

Giggling, I nodded. "Yea, it's usually not this packed, but then again, it's the middle of July."

"This is true," joining my short-lived laughter as we clinked our cups. "So your parents are out of town?"

"Yea, one of my dad's students got their piece into this fancy exhibit, so they both got tickets." His eyebrows rose as he gave me an eager look.
"Yesss, I told Colin I was going to be out for the rest of the night." And with much pride, he raised his arm in the air with his fist clenched, reenacting the iconic end of *The Breakfast Club*. After doing so, he leaned across the table to give me a quick kiss. I couldn't help but blush.
"So whatcha wanna do?"

Shrugging, he took another sip before answering. "I could kick your ass at some *Super Smash Bros*," giving me a mischievous smile while looking over his cup as he drank.

I pretended to give it some thought and glanced back at him. "I mean, if you *really* want to cry, I'm all for it" he almost did a spit take, trying to keep a straight face at my sassy remark.

Vibrate
Vibrate
Vibrate

A phone call?
Reaching for my phone, it was Colin. I gave Seth the 'Hold up' hand gesture and answered the phone.
"Hey! Everything alright?" I couldn't make out what I heard; it sounded like fumbling or something. "Hello?" Still nothing. "Colin?"
Just more muffled sounds: he must have called accidentally. After hanging up, Seth and I slammed the last of our tasty coffee and headed back to his house.

Seth's home was small but cozy. It was just him and his mom. Mrs. Clark works any shift she can get, so it's rare she's at home when I'm visiting. I do miss talking to her; she has a contagious laugh.

"I'll fire up the old *GameCube*."

And with that, we both grabbed a controller and sat crisscross on the floor. We could, and did, spend hours playing this game.
I would love it if sometime Colin, Carder, Seth, and I could play altogether, but Carder and Seth always fight, and Seth picks on Colin sometimes. It's always playful; he doesn't mean it. But still, it never turns out the best.
The last time we all hung out, Carder almost punched Seth in the face for calling Colin some stupid name. I yelled at Seth, and Colin pulled Carder away before he

would have broken his hand. From there on out, the crew was me, Colin, and Carder. It was better that way.

I snapped out of it after the repetitive clicking sound coming from Seth's controller chimed in, looking up to the screen to see I've lost.

"Awwwwww noooooo!" he chuckled. "The mighty and powerful Mac has fallen!"

"Psh, I just let you win," giving him a wink.

Vibrate
Vibrate
Vibrate

Seth was about to click on the start button.

"Wait, wait for a second, please; I'm getting a call."

Setting his controller in his lap, he leaned back on his hands. "Well, aren't you popular today,"

Taking my phone out, it was about ten-thirty. "Oh my gosh, I didn't even realize how long we've been playing; it's almost eleven!" Seth laughed and then readjusted to lie on his back.

"Colin is calling, again," giving Seth a confused look, I answered. "Colin? Are you okay?"

I could hear music now, still couldn't hear exactly what the sound behind it was, and the fumbling was back yet again. Plugging my opposite ear, I tried calling out to him again, still no answer. I hung up.

"This doesn't seem right, two weird calls today, and he hasn't texted me otherwise," I trailed off into thought.

"I'm sure he's alright. He's probably keeping busy," I shook my head slightly, still trailed off. "What're you leaving?"

"Yea, I think I should go back. This just seems off; I'm worried." As I began to stand up, Seth caught me by the wrist and pulled me down next to him as he sat up.

"Mac, you said you were staying?"

Letting out a sigh, I looked away from his eyes. "I know, I know Seth, but I need to go check on Colin" Looking back to his eyes, hoping to find support, I found frustration.

"You lie. You always lie. Is this what it's going to be for the rest of our lives? You ditching me to go rescue your little brother?" Trying to yank my wrist out of his hand, I immediately realized my mistake. He stared at me in disbelief. Looking at my imprisoned wrist and back up to my frightened eyes.
"Is this how you see me?" I wasn't sure if he was looking for a response or leading into another question, "Is this how you see me?!" giving my wrist a shake as I quickly shook my head no. His eyes pierced through mine; the silence scared me more than the tone of his voice. Releasing my wrist, he scoffed.
"Whatever, just go" looking away from my wrist, not meeting my eyes that focused on his, he picked up his controller and exited the two-player mode.

I was hesitant to stand up, but when I did, I stood there for a moment. Debating whether to ask him for a ride or not, but he was completely blocking me out. I suppose the walk isn't *that* bad. I just need to walk quickly; I knew it was going to rain tonight.

Thank God he lived in the city; the streetlights made the walk less sketchy. I tried to get a hold of Colin, phone call after phone call. The first few there was a ring; each one gave me hope. Soon after, about the fifth time I tried calling, it started to go straight to voice mail. Leaving a voice message would slow me down.

I kept calling.
I tried texting him.
Nothing, still nothing.
I gave Carder a call.
Of course, the one person who picks up.

"Carder, have you heard from Colin today?"

"No, I've been with Jason all day" I sighed as my throat began to feel tight. "Why, what's up?"

"I've been at Seth's house pretty much all day too, and Colin isn't answering his phone. He's pocket dialed me twice."

"Damn, he really needs to upgrade his phone. A pocket dial, how is that a relevant issue,"

"He hates change. Carder, I'm freaking out!"

"Okay, okay, calm down- Colin is just fine, stop worrying. You always worry too much."

"I'm walking up to the house right now. I'll call you later."

"What did you-" I heard him pull his phone away and say *hell nah* to Jason. "Did you seriously walk from Seth's house to yours? That douchebag couldn't have even given you a ride; it's fricken late!"

"It's a long story-"

"He's gonna have a damn long obituary once I get to him."

I laughed a little, but it faded as fast as it came out of my mouth. "Forget about it, it's fine I'll call you later, tell Jason I say Hi."

Ending the call, I pocketed my phone and turned the doorknob. It wouldn't budge. Well, at least Colin locks the door when he's home alone. Retrieving the house key, I opened the door as my ears were reunited with the music I had heard over the phone. It was blasted and coming from upstairs, Colin's room, I'm assuming.

I tried yelling his name again; it hit me that obviously, he wouldn't be able to hear me. Stepping onto the staircase, I made my way up, each step leading to the echoing lyrics I could make out now.

Freddie Mercury and David Bowie, singing back and forth. I hadn't heard this song in forever. Given the circumstances, I wasn't too delighted to listen to it now. I had no idea what to expect when I reached the landing. I felt this almost out-of-body feeling as I walked like I wasn't even processing that I was walking down the hallway.

The lyrics were getting louder and crisper as I stepped forward, finally reaching the door. I took a deep breath, hoping to God he was just lip-syncing like a bored dork. As I exhaled, a small quiet request escaped my lips before opening the door. "Please, Colin, be alright" Opening the door, the evidence was shown that my plea had only been heard by me.

His stereo was turned up all the way, playing the same song over and over; '*Under Pressure*'.

The floor was covered in ripped up paper,

broken pencils,

a shirt,

a pair of pants,

and-

I spotted a small empty orange bottle.

My eyes peeled off the sight to see Colin hunched over his garbage can.

My gosh, his, his body-
He only had boxers on.
He didn't even know I was in the room.
Gosh, he was so small.
Hurriedly I went to his side as he must have seen my feet in the corner of his eye; he was startled. He, was the startled one?
He moved as though he would look up to me, but he began dry heaving over the bin on repulse. I placed my hand on his back to comfort him, his spine creased inside my palm as the tips of my fingers distinctly felt the back of his ribcage.
Colin, what have you done?

He was shaking; his body felt cold to the touch. Looking over my shoulder at the clothes, I'm guessing he threw them off. He must have a fever or something?
Abruptly he looked up to me, and I was shocked at the both of us for not speaking a word. The music was deafening as Colin looked at me as if I had a gun to him. I looked to the stereo as I then felt Colin's freezing hand gently grab my arm.

He shook his head. "Leave it" it almost seemed like he was out of breath.
"I thought you weren't coming home tonight" It was hard to hear his voice over the earsplitting volume.

I leaned in to talk, "You kept pocket dialing me, I got worried" now I felt like I was screaming, well I was, "Are you sick? What's going on?"
I had never seen him so distraught as he opened his mouth to speak, letting nothing out, his jaw bobbed, trying to search for the right words.
"I'm going to call mom and dad" as soon as my phone was in sight, Colin grabbed it and threw it against the wall. The cracking sound couldn't be heard over the music. Looking to the littered floor to see my shattered, broken phone had joined the messy party.
I could feel how big my eyes grew, with anger, with confusion "Colin!" turning away from the destroyed phone and to my little brother.

My little brother, whose collar bone was practically jumping out of his skin.

Whose ribs looked like they were trying to escape his body.
Whose thigh could be easily grasped by a single hand.
Whose eyes were turning red.
My little brother, who was shaking while barely being able to stand on his feet, looking away from my bewildered gaze.

The music danced about our motionless bodies, petrified by our silence and the lyric's odd empowerment. I could feel my throat getting tighter as I stepped towards him.
"Colin, you're scaring me" he looked at me. His eyes didn't even look like they belonged to him.

"You weren't supposed to be here" his voice was so soft, yet it cut through the music, "You said you wouldn't be here."
My heart was racing.
I didn't understand.
I couldn't understand what was happening.
"I came because I was worried, Colin, you're scaring me, are you sick? Just tell me, please just tell me!"
I didn't mean for my voice to be raised, but I couldn't help it.

He just kept shaking his head and saying no, repeatedly, not looking me in the eyes. He didn't sound like he was crying. But the tears on his face looked like a windshield during a thunderstorm. Placing his hand on his stomach in his own discomfort, I looked around his room, trying to find answers. Answers to a question I hadn't even figured out.
I had forgotten about the empty bottle I saw when I walked in, or I didn't think much of it, but it felt like something much heavier once I found another one. Snatching it up, I held it in his view.

"Colin, look at me" Instantly, he broke out into an eased cry, not daring to face me. "Colin!"

"What?!" his face was wet as it faced me; he winced at his own shouting. He fell onto the ground, holding his stomach with his eyes tightly shut.
I got on my knees and tried to be as calm as I could, our knees touching each other. His eyes shot open at the sensation. I didn't even know what to say; I couldn't process anything.
"I planned-" the tears consuming his words as he pushed to get them out, "You weren't supposed to be her- here," gasping as he moaned and the crying continued.

I didn't want to piece it together.
Because this couldn't be real.
I didn't want to understand it.
Because it all made sense.

I looked at the bottle; it was his sleeping medication he had gotten a few months ago. The doctor had hoped it would help with his depression. Looking over my shoulder to the other bottle, it was his depression medication he had gotten a few months before his sleeping medicine. The doctor had hoped it would help him sleep at night instead of being haunted by his thoughts.
Now I was shaking.
I was being swallowed by fear.
By doubt- this can't be; this is a mistake.
I was crying.
I wonder how long I had been.
This music was so loud; I didn't take my eyes off Colin.
The music is so loud.
The lyrics plastered in my thoughts.
And I remembered it now,
this is the last part of the song;
the song is ending.

I looked at our touching knees, how small they were compared to mine. I saw how even hunched over his thighs didn't and couldn't touch together. His

stomach made me cringe at the pain I could only imagine he was in. His hair wasn't combed like it usually was. His chest was heaving. I didn't want him to look up; I didn't know if I could handle seeing it. His face was flushed and desperate for something, looking in my eyes.
He was desperate for life.
I think Colin was dying.

The music began to fade. With the stereo in reach, not breaking my stare, I turned it off. My ears ringing from the absent noise I had briefly adapted to.
Now, I could hear both of our snifflings.
I was in a panic; I didn't know what to do.
I needed to call someone, which is probably why Colin broke my phone, and why his was dead.
I needed to stand up; as I did, Colin gasped to speak.

"Please, please," his voice was agonizing, screeching to be heard beyond his pain. "Pp- please, I don't want to be alone now."

My jaw was left down, I couldn't deny him, and I couldn't help but sob at the sight of my brother's frail arms reaching for me.
Like a child.
Weakly trying to grasp for me.
The bones in his arms were peeking out, so defined.
I have never cried like this.
I couldn't believe I could pick him up; his bones pierced into my side as I held him in my embrace on the floor.
My tears fell into his hair; his tears fell and stained onto my shirt.
Drawing him as close as I could, somewhere inside me hoped my strength would soak into him as I gently placed my head on his.
I repeated the words why, again and again. After some time, the word had lost meaning. I didn't even want a response; I wanted a restart for the both of us.
I knew he was sad.
I knew sometimes he skipped lunch.

I knew sometimes he couldn't sleep.
I didn't know he was capable of this.

"I was scared, Lu-" his grip on my arm tightened. "I'm scared" he moved his head as I moved mine, he looked at me. "I wasn't made for this"
I couldn't help my tears from falling. I couldn't help asking questions I knew the answers to but hoped to hear something else.

Be strong, Lucy. "How long ago did you take your medicine, hh-" Stop it, stop. "How many did you take, Colin" He was trying so hard not to cry. I could see it in his eyes; I could hear it in his gasps of air in-between. "Colin, please"
I remembered mom had his medicine filled the other day as Colin was shaking his head and trembling. His watery eyes hadn't blinked since he looked at me.

"I just-" trying to slow his breathing, he exhaled, "I just wanted to go to sleep," blinking, as a single tear fell down and ran into another upon his cheek. "I wasn't made- I can't do the future."
For a second, his eyes drifted to his bed stand, then back to me. I didn't look at that when I first walked in.

There was a bottle of Tylenol,
what looked like quite a few enclosed envelopes,
and a small rectangular wooden box with a letter on top.

His fingers moved on my arm to bring back my attention; successfully, I looked back to him, shaking my head in denial. Colin lifted his arm with shuddering hands, ever so gently attempting to wipe my tears the best of his ability.
"This isn't," his thumb caressing my face, "your fault" the words, painful for him to speak and painful for me to hear.

I shook my head. "No," my breath cutting in and out harshly. "No, no," I tightened my grip around his frail body and pushed up off the floor, holding him closely. "This isn't how this ends, no." Walking over the mess on the floor, I

frantically grabbed his robe hanging off the back of his door, hastily wrapping him in it and picking him up once again.
He was too weak, too exhausted to fight back.
Which scared me even more.
Cautiously I went down the stairs and outside. I needed to get help; I needed to do something. This isn't it for him; there's so much more.
There must be more.

Opening the door, I saw the rain, down pouring. "Damnit!" I screamed in frustration and fear. I looked down at Colin; he was looking at me so innocently and like he felt sorry for me. I tried to shield him from the rain as best as I could. The hospital wasn't that far; we can make it.
We're going to make it.

I speedily walked while bouncing Colin back up when he began to slip; he kept saying my name, trying to get me to stop. I wasn't going to stop. His arms were tucked under the robe, his thin legs were exposed.

I saw a blue sign with an H on it;
I was close,
we're close!

An expression of hope covered my face looking down to see the pain on his. I needed to be faster. Holding him up closer and more securely, I started to run, my adrenaline and fear powering through my veins. The soles of my feet ached at the slamming on the wet pavement as the shooting pain echoed throughout my legs with each stride I took.
Take a turn,
turn her-
my right foot overlapped the path of my left leg.
Colin fell from my arms.
Both of us now getting even more drenched from the rain.

I ignored the throbbing pain in my knees from falling and began to pick Colin back up. Only, he pushed, to stay on the pavement.

"Lucy," he spoke clearly now. Faint "stop." but clearly. He could see it in my eyes; I was the scared one. Colin began to cough harshly; I kneeled to him, holding him once again like before.
"Please-" his cough was ruthless. "Sing me the-" it seized for a moment so he could finish his sentence, "the song, please."

"Colin-"

"Please" his single word made me so weak.
I cried again; I couldn't tell the difference between the rain and my tears hitting his face.
My little brother.
I cleared my throat and sang.

"Blue skies, comin' your way"
At the sound of my shaky singing voice, somehow, he found comfort.
"Bluebirds"
With all the strength it appeared he had left,
"Singing your name"
the corners of his lips slightly turned up.
"They sing"
The rain began to sting as it hit my back.
"Cc- Colin"
The words barely scraped out of my throat. Getting caught in the pain in my legs and the pain happening right in front of me.
"You're doin' just fiinee."
Gently I pulled him closer to me, moving his wet hair away from his eyes.
"Blue skies"
His perfect,
"Stayin' your way"

beautiful,
"Bluebirds"
brown eyes.
"Flyin' awaayy"
My voice cracked at the end of each word.
"They sing"
I didn't want to believe this was the last time I would sing this to him.
"Colin"
I didn't want to believe anything right now. I couldn't process anything. Everything was happening so fast.
"You're doin' just fine"
I just wanted to hold him forever as my hand gently held his head up to me.
"They sing-"
To my surprise, Colin cut me off as his eyes looked heavier and his small wispy voice sang to me.

"Lucy"
His head felt heavier in my hand as his hand slipped into my free one.
"you'll be just fine."
His eyes closed.

I was waiting.
I was waiting for him to say something.
To move.
To speak.
To say I love you.
I shook him a little, hoping he would shine his bright eyes again, and this was just a joke.
Just a joke.
This wasn't funny.
I lifted him up closer to me; his body was limp.

"Colin?" no response. "Colin, tell me everything is going to be okay" he didn't move. "Say it- tell me!" not even a muscle. I wrapped my arms around his frail body, burying my face into his boney shoulder.
"Please tell me it's going to be okay, I'll never leave you, it's going to be okay, I won't move, I'll never leave you."

We were both drenched in the rain.
But I was left there.
How could it still be raining?
How could I still be breathing?
How could the whole world have the audacity to keep spinning and continue on- when the world had just lost the only angel, it knew.

I gasped loudly, sitting straight up, finding arms around me.
They weren't Colin's;
they were Carder's.
He jolted awake, looking at me with concerned sleepy eyes.
We had fallen asleep in the bathtub.

20. Hit & Sunk

"Oof, we're gonna be sore in the morning," Carder shifted, as much as you can comfortably move in a bathtub containing two people. I wonder if anyone else has ever encountered this problem-
wait,
never mind.
Never mind, I don't want to know that.

His arm was still around me, probably asleep. With his assumingly numb hand, he gently stroked my head. I hadn't moved at all.

I almost didn't recognize my voice as I spoke, "I haven't dreamed of that memory since last year, Carder," staring off at my still pruned feet.
"I never wanted to relive that again" his hand stopped in mid-motion. I could just barely feel the hesitant hovering of his fingertips. His hand again went down my knotted, still damp, hair like he was on a pause for a moment. Then, we seemed to both be on pause. Just lying there, I wondered if this was going to be the last time his hand would stroke down and come back up. Or if maybe he would do it a few more times. He did it a few more times before he cleared his throat.

"Come on, let's get out," gently pulling his arm out from behind me. "Plus, I can't feel most of my body." The transition out of the tub was less awkward than I thought it was going to be. Of course, if the shower incident hadn't happened, I'd imagine it would have been very uncomfortable. Then again, it's Carder, so perhaps not.

While I was following Captain Carder's orders to stay in the bathroom while he went and got me some dry clothes, I turned my head to the misty mirror. I slid my hand across, wiping away the fogginess only to reveal a foggier image. A hazy layer I can't wipe away.
Carder appeared in the mirror; it wasn't foggy anymore.

Slipping off the wet robe and dressing into the PJs Carder grabbed me while he was turned around, for once. I looked at the mirror once more before we both left for my room.
Still foggy.

I practically collapsed in my bed, inhaling the scent of the quilts that would never go away no matter how many times they tumbled in the wash. It smelled like grandpa's house, which was close to grandma, which had to be close to some part of me. There had to be something in me that was like her.
As I was getting comfy, looking over to the door, Carder turned off the lights and was about to depart to his room. I always felt this unstitched feeling when he walked away. In a way, we were a lot like the quilt.
He was a tossed piece of fabric who found his way to another lost piece of lingering fabric. Which was attached to another piece of fabric that didn't want to be fabric anymore. Or anything for that matter.
Maybe that's why it hurts so much when someone leaves. Not only are they taking away the new colors you grew fond of, but when they came to you, they sewed themselves into the small spaces of you that hadn't yet been used. When they pull away, sometimes strands from you go with them.

"Wait, Carder! Carder?" I saw his silhouette from the hallway rhythmically step back into the doorway. I swear there is always a show tune playing somewhere in the back of his mind. With his neatly trimmed eyebrows raised in question, and his arms in a still motion, like he was a marathon-running robot who was stopped in the middle of its command. The use for such a robot, I have no idea, but it exists, and he was mimicking it. "Can you sleep in here? With me, just for tonight?"

"Because sleeping in my queen bed would be too easy, right?" Sarcastically mocking me, but still, he made his way over and was not shy about jumping on the bed. And just like times before, surprisingly, we both always manage to fit. Both of us lying on our backs, staring at the ceiling while breathing in the quilt's aroma. Our arms were touching, and Carder kept pushing my leg off the bed with his feet out of boredom.

"Carder?"

"Speaking"

Silently I giggled and gave him a nudge in the ribs. "How am I going to tell Jude? I feel like if I don't tell him, these nightmares are going to keep happening. Maybe it would be a relief to just get this just off my chest and not have it hanging over me" a sigh escaped my mouth as I felt like I was sinking further into the bed.
"I just don't know how."

While I was fixed on the ceiling, I heard Carder yawn before he leaned over and gave me his classic forehead kiss. "Don't worry, Lucy-Lou," rolling over on his side, putting his back to me and taking a tad more of the quilt than he needed, "We'll get through this together."

I grasped his words tight and let them dissolve into my worrisome thoughts.
I couldn't remember falling asleep.
I couldn't remember if I had rolled over or not.
I couldn't remember if Carder had snored or talked in his sleep.
I couldn't remember if either of us held each other for a moment or more.
I remember waking up to hear the most beautiful sound in the world accompanied by the most fantastically fantastic smell in the history of all smells.
Brewed coffee.
Your argument is invalid.
Snaps, just laying next to Carder, you get his sassiness.

Slipping out of bed, the apartment was quiet among the sound of the coffeepot. That little pot works wonders getting me out of bed. I could just feel the knots in my hair; it made me cringe with the thought I would have to comb through it. And taking a look in the mirror, I sadly was correct.

No points for Lucy.

Nah, not today. That's going in a bun. Attempting to get my ratted hair into a nest on top of my head while walking down the hallway to the kitchen, I heard a noise from Carder's room.

Quietly I crouched down on my knees to take a listen under the small crack of the door. I don't think I've done this since I was a kid.

I remember Colin and I taking turns, trying to peek under the door of our parent's room to see what we were getting for Christmas while they wrapped our presents. I remember my favorite Christmas; I think I was about eight, and Colin was seven. Mom, dad, grandpa, Colin, and I were all sitting in the living room at our old house. It would be our last Christmas altogether for a while because grandpa was going off on a Hot Air Balloon tour in Europe. Some balloon festival or something of that floating nature; it was an honor to get invited, so we understood he couldn't pass it up.

It was a typical Christmas day. Jumping on mom and dad's bed in the morning begging them to get up, and as soon as they peeked their eyes open, Colin and I would race to the tree sitting crisscross. Patiently waiting for our sleepy parents to give us the 'OK' to open our gifts. Grandpa was already up and sitting on the recliner, smiling at both of us.

Once we exchanged our gifts and overly thanked one another, we ate breakfast. After that, we would all get in our fancy-special Christmas church attire and attend the service. The Christmas service was always my favorite; towards the end, everyone in the sanctuary would get a candle with a Dixie cup poked through it to catch the wax. After the candles were lit, the lights were turned off, and we would sing '*Silent Night*. It was always so beautiful; I didn't go this past year.

After church and after eating the huge dinner my mom and dad tag teamed on preparing, we all sat in the living room. The only light was coming from our Christmas tree. I don't mean to brag, but Colin and I worked our asses off every year on that tree, and it was always top-notch.

After grandpa told us a few stories and what balloons were in the show, we sat in silence for a while. I think, at least for me, it was settling in that grandpa was leaving. We could hear the cars whizzing by outside that were filled with eager adults on their way to a party or kids piled up in the backseat exhausted from visiting distant relatives, perhaps even a couple that today marked their very first Christmas with one another. Still, inside the living room, it was hushed with silence.

Grandpa was sitting on the armrest of the recliner. Dad was standing in the doorway of the living room with his shoulder leaning against the frame. Mom was sitting at the end of the couch by the doorway. And Colin sat a little back from the tree, looking at it. I was sitting in the middle of the living room, diagonally from Colin.

My eyes were about to well up with tears thinking up scenarios on how the rest of the year would unfold. But before they could make their grand escape, Colin's soft, determined voice began to sing. All our heads perked up to Colin as his gaze was locked on the tree; I could see the lights reflecting in his glossy eyes. He was singing '*The Rainbow Connection*' from '*The Muppets Movie*'; grandpa and dad watched it when dad was growing up; mom watched it off and on as a kid. They showed it to Colin and me, not expecting us to fall head over heels for it.

As soon as *The Muppets* came on the screen, Colin would shout while lunging to the TV screen and pointing to *Kermit*. "I call being *Kermit*! That's me!" at first, I wanted to be *Kermit*, but I never told him that. I liked being *Gonzo*.

It's kind of strange how I can't remember facts or math equations if my life depended on it, but start playing a song I probably haven't listened to in ten years, and I'll sing every word loud and proud.

Colin, still looking at the tree, sang by himself until the chorus; then, all of us sang together until the end of the song. When we all started to sing, Colin turned around with a fragile smile.

He scooted next to me, grandpa, mom, and dad followed, and we all sat together. All of us looking at the same tree, singing the same song, but most likely having different things running through our minds.

At the last chorus, Colin and I looked at one another, smiling. Still, the Christmas lights found their way into our eyes.

Dad pulled me into his lap,
mom pulled Colin into hers,
and grandpa sat in-between.
I'm not sure where everyone else was looking, but Colin and I still looked at each other like we were singing a duet.
I'll never forget the lyrics of that song.

Lifting myself off the ground and turning the doorknob in curiosity, I shook the memory away. However, it was nice to imagine that again.
I opened the door to Carder, apparently trying on his entire wardrobe. There were clothes everywhere. Luckily there was some on him.

"Goooood Moooooorning," I sang in my best *Mary Poppins* voice. "I see you've decided to put on a fashion show. Why did I not get a ticket?"

"Because I need honest opinions, and you're too good to me to tell me this shirt does not do me justice anymore." He gave me a smirk as he took the shirt off and threw it to the side of the room that I'm assuming is the get rid of pile. He made me laugh; I decided I'd try to get a laugh out of him as I lunged and tussled his hair. Which made him laugh out of frustrated amusement.
"I made you coffee, damn it, go drink it." With a playful wink, he kicked me out, which wasn't too much of a punishment, considering I would be greeted by the most delightful thing ever.

While I was fixing up my coffee, Carder dramatically announced we had work in about 30 minutes, as if that wasn't enough time for me to get ready. I laughed a little to myself as I finished making myself a cup of coffee. Promptly after, Carder caught me off guard, snatched my coffee, and ran off to his room, slamming the door as I heard the click of his lock.
I've been coffee robbed, and what's worse is it didn't even faze me.

After making myself another cup of coffee, I started getting ready while enjoying its awesomeness. Carder and I made ourselves presentable for the bookworm strangers of Virginia Beach, and then we were out the door and on our way to Books & Such.
Fast-paced morning.

"Hopefully, today isn't as painfully dull as last night, otherwise-" Carder breathily broke our silence amongst our speed walking; we probably looked ridiculous. Still looking to Carder to finish his sentence, I followed his eyes to where he was looking and now understood his sudden cut-off. The shop lights were on.
Without a word, I followed Carder into the shop to see that today would be an interesting one.

On top of the counter stood a small girl, her back faced toward us. She had cute curly hair that was in tiny pigtails. She was wearing a light blue sweater that looked too big for her, bright orange skinny jeans, and to top it off, yellow rain boots. She was a character; whoever she was, I'll give her that.
With the sound of the bell ringing from the door, she spun around to face us. Her face had delicate features, deep brown adorable eyes, and long eyelashes, but she did not have a smile on her face. A rather serious one, actually. In her hands, she held a clipboard; now tucking the pen she was using behind her ear, she looked down at us. This well may be the most oddly uncomfortable introduction I have ever experienced. And just the fact that she was still standing on the counter, staring down at us. It was silent for about fifteen seconds.

Just as I suspected and hoped, Carder spoke up, clearing his throat "Um, hello there, quirkily dressed girl. What're you doing in a bookstore on a counter that is almost taller than you?" Damn it, Carder, now is not the time to have sassy banter with a clipboard holding little girl.

She raised her right eyebrow to him and gracefully jumped down from the counter, successfully landing on both feet. She never broke her eye contact with

Carder the whole time as she boldly stood in front of him. Holy buckets, we've got a little badass on our hands.

She pulled the clipboard to her chest. "From your lack of respect for authority and your mannerisms, you must be Carder," turning her eyes to me, she was a bit kinder. "That leaves you to be Lucy," giving me a quick smile before she returned to her stone-cold glare to Carder. I was both confused and astounded at the same time. Carder might just have met his match.
We were both silent, and to that, she rolled her eyes and pulled the pen from behind her ear, and wrote something down on her clipboard.
"I'm Maybelle Owens" She certainly knew how to speak her mind.

I stuck out my hand to her as I could feel the look of betrayal Carder gave me, gladly she shook my hand. "It's great to meet you, Maybelle. That's a pretty name. Might I ask what you're doing at the store today?"

After releasing my hand, which she actually had a firm grip, she answered. "My dad owns the shop. He's at an important meeting with his banker right now. My job is to start drawing up ideas of how I'd like the shop to look and make sure you guys don't cause trouble."
After stating her presence, she climbed back on top of the counter. Now I could see she indeed was drawing sketches of the store. Yet again, we were speechless.
A daughter?
Alan's daughter?
Is that even possible?
"Go ahead and ask me," she stated, not looking at us but continuing her drawing. "Ask me if I'm adopted."

"Okay," Carder was a bit calmer now. "Are you adopted?"

"No," Abruptly answering the question as soon as Carder's words cut off. "My mom is Black, and my dad is White. Get with the times."

Well, goodness gracious, I felt like we were getting a lecture; I looked to Carder as we both shrugged our shoulders.

"Sorry, yea, of course, that's awesome. We just didn't know Alan- your dad, was married" He let out his words slowly and clearly. Maybelle intimidating looked down at us again.

"Was, they're divorced. Mom said it's because she needs a man who can grow facial hair and wears designer clothing. But dad says she only stayed with him for so long because of the money gramps gave him when he died. Dad says it's okay, though, because he has the shop and me and that's all the hell that matters." Before we could get a word in, she intervened, "Dad says I can say hell, so you can't get me in trouble."

At least now it makes sense why Alan wears his '*facial hair*' all the time, kind of sad, actually. But I would not have put a guess down that he was previously married, has an adorable daughter, and is wealthy or at least well off. But again, I guess that makes sense; I mean, it's a small shop. It doesn't get that busy, and we still get paid well.

"Mr. Owens will be back any minute now. It was an early meeting; you guys can straighten the books."

I would pay to be able to hear the thoughts in Carder's mind right now. I don't even think I could handle it; I'd die of laughter. Making our way to the back Nonfiction aisle, I was on one side of the bookshelf as he was on the other, whispering quietly to each other through the books.

"Lucy, what the literal hell."

"You're asking me; he was your boss first. How could you not know he had a kid?"

"As if I would ever bring that up, he says one thing about his personal life, and I throw books at him; it's how our relationship works."

I switched a few books around that were out of order and then resumed scanning. "I wonder how old she is."

"I wonder if she can hear us."

"I'm eight, and I can hear you, no swearing!" I felt like she was a prison guard in her tiny prison guard tower.

Quietly I laughed at Carder, looking at each other through the small space above the books. Jokingly he rolled his eyes as we quickly got back to work before the '*warden*' could yell at us again.

We got about halfway through the Nonfiction section when we heard the bell ring. The both of us peeked from behind the bookshelf we were on to find Alan bending down on one knee as Maybelle jumped off the counter and ran to him. This was so bizarre. It was almost unnatural, like rare deleted footage from a *National Geographic* special.

And tonight, we show the secret life of your not-so-average bookstore owner.

Alan had his daughter that I could now see had similar features to him, balanced on his hip; this was so fricken weird. Yet unbelievably sweet.

"Carder, Lucy, I believe you have met Maybelle."

The both of us nodded; I think Alan was more shocked at Carder's silence than my wide-eyed bewilderment. Alan set his daughter down and sent her along to her break in the stock room, where she was free to go color.

"I suppose you two have questions."

We waited for the stock room door to close; once Carder heard the click, he darted his eyes at Alan. "You were married, you have a kid, and you're rich; explain."

The three of us gathered around the counter; Alan drew a deep breath before speaking. "My father owned a rather good oil company back in his day; he sold it to a rather wealthy man who gave us a rather big sum of money. Needless to say, I don't have to worry about finances. I was at the bank to discuss my plans on redesigning the store and how to attract more customers."

"Alright, and now the ex-wife" Carder knew no boundaries, and one day I swear it's going to get his ass kicked.

"Yes, well, we met before my father passed away, married before my father passed away, had Maybelle before my father passed away-"

"Damn it, Alan, stop stalling!" Pinching the back of Carder's arm, Alan continued on.

"She had an affair, which I knew about for five years. I just could never find a way to bring it up. So, one day at the dining room table, I got the courage and simply asked, '*How is Gary doing these days?*' He was a mutual friend, and in fact, I did want to know how he was doing; we hadn't talked in ages. And after we cleaned up the mess from her spitting her wine out all over the table and sending Maybelle to bed, we began to plan our separation."

Like it was a furtive habit, Alan stroked his fake beard.

"Now I have Maybelle every other week. Though my ex-wife fancies Gary and his fancy wardrobe and obnoxiously thick mustache she couldn't deny that I am a great dad."

Carder spoke up, "You do seem like a great dad" unconsciously, I looked at Carder in surprise. "It makes sense; I just don't get why you hired me and hired Lucy when we rarely have any customers and don't really do anything at the shop."

"You and Lucy are good people and good workers. And I like company."

"So, you're paying us to keep you company while you're in your own store." Goodness gracious, Carder, just let it go.

"Simply yes, I suppose, though I didn't think it through that I would get bruises from *Harry Potter* books on my forearms. Regardless, you both need a job, and I need someone over the age of seven I can interact with."

I don't think I have ever seen Alan really, genuinely smile, but through the ratted artificial hair fibers, I saw a grin.

"I did promise Maybelle today that we would privately discuss her future aspirations, and she could finalize the floor plans. Last night she informed me she wants to be a Mini-Golf-Course designer, and there wasn't a force on Earth to stop her. I guess I should have seen this coming, seeing her bedroom flooring is the artificial grass they use on courses."

The three of us laughed for a moment; Alan then dismissed us, getting Maybelle from the stock room as they both waved goodbye to us as we exited the store with the chime of the Books & Such bell.

I couldn't help but feel bad for Alan, all these things he kept tucked away, never even showing in his expressions and dealing with Carder's sassiness. I suppose it's a pretty prime example to see that not everyone truly shows how they feel; everyone is guilty of their own mask.

Seeing we both just had our plans for the day canceled, we made our way back to our apartment, letting out a sigh as we entered. Carder laid on his stomach, planting his face in the couch cushion and leaving no room for me. I laid lazily on the floor next to the couch. I discovered something underneath it that would keep us occupied until we found something else to do.

Battleship.

I hadn't played it in years; I didn't even know I still had it. Carder agreed to play; we set up the game on the table and sat across from one another. I was determined to win.

"Okay, ready?" Eagerly I asked, putting my last ship in place.

"Yyyeeepppppppppp," Popping his mouth to cut off the p.

"Your enthusiasm is overwhelming, Carder" His eyes pierced me over our boards. "You go first, Grumps."

"I hate when you call me that, you know it" after his childish groan, he finally gave out a command, "J-10."

Looking down at my grid, I was surprised. "Wha- How did you get that so quickly? You don't even like this game."

"I know you pretty well, your turn, Skipper."

Okay, alright, now it was serious "C-5."

"No, J-"

"You're supposed to say miss."

Another groan "Fail. J-9"

"Hit. Damn it." I grabbed a small handful of red pegs, embracing the fact he has captured my Cargo Ship. "G-9."

"Unsuccessful. J-8."

"Hit. This isn't as fun as I thought it was going to be."

After fifteen minutes of synonyms, three sunken ships, and many white pegs, I had not hit anything on Carder's grid.

"Are we almost done; this game is boring."

"No, it's not; I haven't even gotten one of your ships. This is ridiculous!"

"Hey, you should text Jude; I-1"

"Maybe we'll find something to do before we kill each other, Hit." Pulling out my phone while I planned my next attack, "A-10."

Me:

No work today for Carder and me.
Would you like to meet up?

Pocketing my phone to await his response.

"Target not found. I-2"

"Ha! Miss! It's a miss! Heck yes, take that!" Out of my over celebration, I threw a white peg at Carder's face. He didn't react, then I felt foolish. "Okay, um, F-8."

I saw his eyes scan his grid "Nope. H-1."

I didn't say anything; he knew, I put down a stupid red peg.

Vibrate

It was Jude; thank God I was about to lose it. Jude's name in my phone was now Jude's name; now that I know his real name. That sentence was far more complicated than I anticipated it to be.

Jude:

Why Mrs. Cumberbatch, I just got on my lunch break! Tom and I would love to see both of you down at the Marsh, I sent the address to Carder; see you guys soon!

"Carder, did you get a-"

"Yepp, shall we call it quits? I want to change my shirt before we go."

I hated losing, not in general, just to him. "Fine, but we are going to have a rematch."

As Carder got up, giving me a mischievous smile making his way to change, I scrambled out of my seat to see how on Earth he set up his grid. That little jerk. He came back with a light-yellow t-shirt on, twirled his keys on his finger, and smiled at me as if nothing had happened.

"You're an asshole."

"Hey now," he continued to twirl his keys, "That's no way to speak to your Captain."

"You didn't even put any ship pieces on the grid!"

"Now it's easier to clean up! No need to thank me; let's get going." Ugh, I should've known. What a sassy man.

Carder took me by the arm and escorted me to the car; he's lucky I can't stay mad at him.

Though we almost died twice, due to Carder's excessive road rage, we made it to Duck's Cranberries. It was lovely out here; Tom sure had a decent piece of land. After Carder parked the car and we both hopped out, we were greeted by sweet Tom and Mr. Johnson himself. I was still trying to get used to his name.

"JudieBoy just got done with the harvester in the bog" it took him a moment to gather his words. "We had to a, we had to flood it out last night so we could pick 'em today, our buyer is coming tonight for a, a pickup" Tom was the most adorable little gentlemen in the world. "Carder, I washed your gear from last time; it's hanging, hanging in the mudroom." I could see the look of surprise hidden in Carder's eyes as he patiently smiled at Tom while Tom had an even brighter grin on his face. "I pinned a cranberry brooch to your suspenders. It was Duck's. I couldn't pull it off but, but I know you will."

Carder looked like he was going to cry as they shook hands in the way of saying thanks as we all walked up to Tom's house.

Entering the mudroom on our way in, I caught a glimpse of the brooch. A few silver vines were decorated with five faded dark-toned magenta cranberries; Carder would love it. He and Jude grabbed their gear while I followed Tom to the kitchen, where it appeared he was baking.

"Wow, Tom, I didn't know I was talking to a professional baker" I liked to kid with him; he chuckled and waved it off.

"You know why consumers want Duck's Cranberries? Why it's, it's because we carefully handpick each cranberry, and every time the pick-up guys come, I send them with a batch of Duck's cranberry cookies. The best damn cookies in Virginia Beach." The kitchen island helped support him as his hand glided across until he reached the stove. Shakily but determined, he put his red and worn oven mitts on and pulled out a pan of the famous cookies.

Hot damn, they smelled absolutely fantastic; a close 2nd in the smells of smells, but coffee will always be the champ.

"While the boys are out finishing stuff up, I'd love a baking partner," requesting as he turned to me after placing the pan on the stove and tossing his mitts on the counter.

"I would love that, Tom" I really was excited; I hadn't baked in a while. And I enjoyed listening to Tom. In a way, it reminded me of my talks with Grandpa.

The table where I could see he was making the cookies was next to a huge square window that perfectly overlooked the cranberry bog. I get to make cookies *and* quite possibly see Carder fall into the water; honestly, it doesn't get better. But then it did; Tom brought us both coffee.

I mixed the ingredients in a large metal bowl while Tom prepared the cookie sheet; we were a good team.
"Alright, Sir, the dough is ready to be rolled" I pulled one of the chairs out for him and placed the bowl between us. He brought over two pans; look at us pros.
"So, how does the whole cranberry harvesting work exactly?"

Tom looked intrigued to tell me, and happy I asked. I had a feeling he would. "In the bog, the berries are attached to a stem and vines, when, when they're ready for harvesting the day before ya gotta flood the bog, that's what JudieBoy did yesterday. Then ya go in with the harvester machine, that's what JudieBoy did today, and that, that pulls the cranberries off the vines, cranberries have a tiny pocket of air in 'em, so they float. Then ya round 'em up with the net and pick the berries by hand. That's what those boys are doin' now. That's what Carder did last time; he doesn't so much care for the cold water in the bog."

Tom's smile and little chuckles in between sentences made my cheeks almost hurt from grinning so much.
We didn't so much look at each other while we talked; we were more focused on rolling the small dough balls and then looking out at Carder and Jude.
I've counted four times now that-
Oh man, Tom and I have been laughing for the past two minutes.
That's five times now that Carder has fallen on his ass.

"Ohhh, it's good to laugh," Tom said between his giggles. "I miss laughing; Duck and I use to laugh so much. I miss the wrinkles that would appear around her eyes and mouth when she laughed."
I looked over at him. He didn't exactly look sad as he continued to roll the dough in his hands; he just looked exhausted. Emotionally, exhausted. He would wince

quietly from scooping the dough from the bowl. He was shaking quite a bit while trying to perform tasks. I pretended I didn't notice though, I didn't want to, but I didn't want to embarrass him either.

It was around noon when we arrived at the marsh. I was having so much fun talking with Tom that I didn't even think to check my phone; Carder and Jude are pretty much the only people I talk to. And to my amazement, it was already seven o'clock.

Holy buckets, did we make a ton of cookies! We made so much Tom insisted I take two dozen home; with his stubborn persistence, I accepted.

After practically running out of ingredients, I put the last of the cookies on a plate with saran wrap over the top; this would be for the pick-up guy. I put the remainder of the cookies away in containers for Tom while he wiped off the table. When both our tasks were done, we regrouped at the table to see Jude turned the floodlights on. We both sat in comfortable silence for a while, sipping on our now cold but still delicious coffee.

"I don't so much like this gettin' old business without my Duck" discreetly I turned my head to Tom, who was holding his mug in both hands and lifting it to his mouth for a satisfying swig, he tried to set the cup down gently, but it landed roughly on the wood table.

"I never thought of it cause I didn't think I'd be doin' it alone." A few drops of coffee scattered around his mug. For a second, we were both looking at the tiny puddles, then at one another.

"I don't wanna worry JudieBoy; I don't want ya to tell anyone, okay?" I opened my mouth to ask what I was swearing secrecy to, but he beat me to it. "I can tell, I can tell I'm gonna be checkin' out soon. I had to tell someone; I can't tell JudieBoy."

To be honest, I was at a loss for words. My mouth was still open, but I couldn't find any words; instead, I reached my hand and placed it on top of his resting on the table. "It's our secret" Giving him a weak smile, he flashed one back to me as I kindly pulled my hand away, hearing the door open.

"Holy smokes, Tom, we had quite the time picking those berries out, looks like you guys were also hard at work; it smells fantastic in here!"
Though I'm always happy to see Jude's smiley face, I was more eager to see drenched Carder. And there he came, walking in with a dirty face and very wet clothes. Tom and I exchanged giggly looks as we looked back at them.

"Oh, not a word from either of you," Carder jokingly objected.

Carder threw his clothes in the dryer and borrowed one of Tom's nightgowns for the meantime. It was wonderful. While waiting for his clothes, the four of us sat at the table and played a few games of Kings Corner; it was a fun and simple card game.
Tom was looking through his cards, searching for the right one to put down when Carder bluntly and without consulting me requested that Jude would come over tomorrow. We learned five minutes ago that Jude had off because they finished harvesting today.
I kicked Carder's exposed leg under the table; he silently cringed and still dared to invite him over. Of course, he accepted because he's a gentleman, and no one wants to see the results of telling Carder no.
So, it was set. Jude was coming over tomorrow for the day; tomorrow was the day I would tell him everything about Colin. Well, only if it felt right, I'm not going to force it. Although I think I'll feel some weight lifted off my shoulders if I do open up about it.

Carder and I gave both Tom and Jude a hug goodbye once his clothes finally dried. While hugging Tom, he whispered thank you to me; I had to wipe the tear from my eye before he could see.

It had been a long, spontaneous day; when we stepped foot in the apartment, it was already ten. At least now we have some awesome cookies to snack on.

"I am taking a long-ass shower and then embracing a long-ass night of sleep. The stores closed tomorrow, but Alan wants us to brainstorm ideas for bringing more customers in. I may just pull a Lucy and sleep in the tub. I'm so tired." I glared at him with a tense smirk. "Huh, too soon?"

After slugging him in the arm, we both laughed, leaving me with a kiss just between my forehead and my hairline and departing for the rainroom.
With a giddy smile on my face, I walked across the hall to my room; my shades were open and had the city lights pouring in. One of the things I really liked about living here was the city lights at night. My gaze drifted from the dark sky to the buildings across the street, to the sidewalk down below, to- to the familiar car parked outside the apartment complex.
My stomach twisted at sight, the familiar feeling I hadn't felt in a long time. Carder would be in the bathroom for a while, he wouldn't hear me leave, and I needed to handle this myself.

Pulling a hoodie on, I made my way down and out to the loitering car; I crossed my arms, holding them close to my body. It felt like if my arms weren't there, everything inside would fall out.
The windows were tinted as the passenger one rolled down. My arm muscles clenched tighter.

"You weren't home most of the day; it was a pretty nice day to be out of the house, though." I didn't say anything; I just stared at the interior I had memorized in my head. I knew where the CDs were. I knew the glove compartment wouldn't open unless you gave it a kick. I knew there was, or used to be, a stash of gum in the middle compartment between the seats.
"Mac, can we talk?"

I still didn't say anything, and looking up over my head as if his words had been a queue, it started to rain. Fricken wonderful.

"I just want to go for a drive and talk, like we used to, just a short spin. I just, to be honest, I really need someone to talk to."

By courtesy of the rain that was now downpouring, reluctantly, I climbed into the car. I had my phone on me, and it was going to be quick; I'd be fine. I just felt something inside me worry when he said he really needed someone to talk to. Not that he deserves it, I guess.

I didn't like how he recklessly pulled off, as I was putting my seatbelt on like he used to do; nothing has changed. The windshield wipers were on high as Seth weaved between the cars in traffic.
Grabbing onto the door to keep me from flying all over, I needed to remember:
We weren't in a relationship.
He's not in charge of me.
I am not afraid of him.

"Where are we going?" throwing politeness out the window along with the basic rules of driving that he obviously threw out too.

"I told you, just a spin."

"Yea, well, can you recall a few things from your high school driver's ed class? You're going to get us in an accident."

He laughed, a laugh that used to be contagious to me. Now it made me feel sick. "I miss how funny you are; I'm sorry I'll slow down."

Ignoring his compliment, "So what do you want to talk about?" cutting it straight forward.

"I just needed to vent to someone, I guess, what better someone than you" I could feel his eyes on me. "It's about the past, certain things I can't get over."

You don't say.

He took a sharp turn I didn't see coming, quickly I grabbed the door again as we headed down a back road. I didn't want to look at him; I kept my eyes forward. It was best two people were watching the road anyway with how hard the rain was coming down.

"I know I made a lot of mistakes, and while I've been a part from you, I thought through each one so thoroughly, I started setting goals for myself to be a better person and get my act together. And you know why I did it? You know what kept me going through?"

Please let it stop. "I don't know."

I heard him release a sigh. I remembered, from experience, he made to keep himself calm, "It was you." And there it was, it was going to go downhill from here. I could feel it. "I realized how much I screwed things up for us. I should have stayed by you after I helped you move into your apartment-"

"I told you I wasn't going to San Francisco because I couldn't; you couldn't accept that. I didn't want you in my apartment, so you left."

"But Mac, that's it, we can still go, we can go to San Francisco, and you can get a degree in whatever you want!"

"First of all, you heard me say, and you damn well know that I can't leave. Second of all, you have to get it through your head that we aren't together anymore, that's done, and it isn't coming back. You need to let this go."
I wanted to yell this, I wanted to scream this in his face, but I kept my cool. I stole a quick glance at him, he was quiet, and that was strange; his jaw was clenched tight. He saw me look at him; the speedometer went from sixty-five to eighty-nine faster than I could react to grab onto something.
"Seth! Stop!"

Eighty-nine to ninety-four.

"We're going to hydroplane! Please stop!"

This was a mistake- a stupid mistake.
I should have seen, known, this was coming.
I could hear it in my head, his words pounding against my skull and making their way into my mind.

It's aalllllll your fault Lucy.
Can't you see you can't escape this?
Why you stayed so long before, how could you expect me to leave so easily?
Like pieces of fabric from a quilt, huh Lucy?
Like matching pieces of a quilt.

"Promises! Huh, Mac? Tell me, what's a promise?"
He was looking back and forth between the road and to me; I couldn't hide it now.
My anxiety felt like it was lodged in my throat, blocking off the airway and restricting me from getting a word out.
"Something you can just throw out the window, right?!"
Suddenly, a burst of wind mixed with pellets of rain gusted into my side of the car. I got my eyes open for a moment; he rolled down my window, locking it from his side so I couldn't roll it up.
"Forget all about it, right? Because it's just a promise, it doesn't *mean* anything!"
The wind and rain were achingly cold as they were hitting my face. I had my hands on top of my head while my arms shielded the rain from my face the best I could. It was hard to process this was even happening. Why did I do this? Why did I think this was going to turn out somewhat okay?

Get loud, Lucy. "Take. Me. HOME!" Scream it until you're heard "***NOW!***"

He whipped the car around, which was terrifying, and rolled up my window. Still speeding, but at least then, I would get home faster.
My hands were shaking; I couldn't feel my face. It stung to the touch. This was a mistake. I recognized the road now; we weren't far from the apartments.

Ninety to forty-five.
I felt sick to my stomach; it couldn't be far now.
Less than five blocks.

"You need to let this go, Lucy."

I swear I almost threw up at the sound of him saying my name. "I need to let this go? I do? Are you fricken crazy?!"

He turned to me for a moment. His expression was stone cold. "I'm not talking about *this*, your broken promises, I'm talking about- you know what I'm talking about."
I swear, oh I swear if he says it-
Slamming his fist against the steering wheel, his voice grew louder.
"Colin, Lucy, you-"

"You don't get to say his name, don't you say his name. Don't say another word, Seth, don't say another damn word, and let me out of this car."

"You know what, no; no, you need to hear this" My heart was racing, two blocks, just two blocks.
"He's not here anymore, and there's nothing you can do, so you need to move on. You're letting everyone around you get infected by this ugly overdrawn grief you have festering inside of you."
My heart felt like it stopped, and when the beat tried to come back, it had to speed to catch up to the rest of my body.
"You're gonna drive everyone away from you with this. Eventually, people are gonna be sick of being around you. Because you won't let this go. But I'm not going to leave. I'm not going anywhere."

Here, we're here, he unlocked my door. It was still pouring, Carder was standing outside of the apartment doors in his robe, and I almost tripped hurrying out.

I slammed the door and looked him directly in the eye, trying to control my shaky voice. "I do know what a promise is, and I promise you this is the last time you will ever see me."
He looked past me, then to the road, and drove away. He was looking at Carder, who ran to my side. Damn right, he had better be afraid of him.

Carder pulled me into a worrisome hug, squeezing me tight. "You didn't answer your phone, you didn't answer, and I didn't know what happened to you," I was preparing myself for an angry tone to come from him, but he sounded "Lucy, don't do that again" scared.

"I'm sorry," my wispy voice let out. I wrapped my arms tightly around him, my head buried into his damp cotton robe. "I'm sorry, Carder."

21. Allons-y 

The sky was so much more beautiful from when I last looked at it. In fact, it didn't look like it had rained at all. It was again that lovely Virginia Beach night sky that I never grew tired of staring up at.

Interrupting my gaze was the noise of a door quietly shutting behind me. In reaction, I turned around; interrupting my reality was the person who made me love the midnight sky in the first place.

"This may be the most groundbreaking badass thing we will have ever done," he quietly spoke with an intensity hidden in his voice. He was wearing black jeans and a baggy black crewneck.

"I highly approve of your idea to wear all black, very affective, makes me feel like we're in a movie," or maybe it wouldn't be so big on him if he ate a little more than Pop-Tarts. Still, I remembered this. I remembered it all.

I recall his giddy smirk with creased laugh lines that hid countless memories and his messy hair, shy of a trim. There were the tiny cracks of excitement in his voice that intersected between his words unexpectedly; man, just his voice in general. I remember, this was the summer before Colin's senior year.

The school year just ended; we had agreed that we would do more spontaneous things to pack the impact of five summers into one. I know what you're thinking, me and Colin- badass? Well, you best believe it now because we are damn it.

We weren't bad kids, obviously. If anything, we were the poster children for goody-two-shoes behavior. But then again, that made it the perfect distraction that we would never do *anything* wrong. Not that this was entirely bad, but it would probably be frowned upon.

"Lucy!" Colin yelled quietly under his breath, "The flight takes off in forty-five minutes; we gotta get pedaling!" After his well-timed command, he swiftly hopped on his bike, which followed with a mischievous smirk. I settled on my

bike and followed his lead, biking off with the moon as our spotlight and the stars lighting our runway.
Colin had a friend in school whose dad was a private pilot at the airport. When he brought this to my attention, I gave him the '*And how is this relevant?*' look. And with his response, I thought Colin was joking. But no, this boy was just as crazy as he was determined. With me behind the attire organizing, and Colin planning our schedule for tonight, we were about to break the law; with nothing but good intentions.

After about ten minutes of biking, we hid our bikes behind some trees about a block away and sneakily made our way to the back fence of the landing field. Colin slid his hand in the deep pockets of his pants and checked the time on his phone. "We've got a little less than fifteen minutes" it looked like he was about ready to climb into a bouncy house with how jumpy and excited he was "ready for this?"

I couldn't help playing along with his secretive mission-impossible-manner. "You bet your ass; did you bring the supplies?" I also couldn't help but ask the cliché action movie question to my partner in crime.

It was actually impressive how deep those pockets of his were. He pulled out a pair of black gloves and Dad's pliers. "Oh, you bet your ass" there again, his geeky smile appeared as he slipped his gloves on and awkwardly handled the pliers, which neither of us had experience with. "Alright, so I'll cut a line down so we can push it open a little; hence the black gloves, so there are no fingerprints." And so, he started cutting the fence while I kept a lookout.

"So, your friend told you about the flight tonight?"

While still heavily concentrated on the fence, he chuckled under his breath, "Yes, I overheard him talking to someone else on the last day of school in math class; no, he's not my friend."

He was about halfway done. "I thought you had a few friends in math?" As he finished, he pocketed the pliers. He gave me a sympathetic look as if I was a naive child just about to have the '*Santa doesn't really come down the chimney every year*' talk.

"The only '*friendship*' I have with anyone at school is just painfully awkward small talk. So they don't feel bad copying my homework or asking me what the reading assignment was about."
It didn't faze him; he shrugged it off and attempted to push the fence, so it had a narrow opening. It was still processing for me.
With both our efforts, we created a makeshift gateway for us to push ourselves through and onto the field. "Besides," he exhaled while struggling to smoothly pass through the sharp gap. "I've got my two best friends already. I'm not gonna get greedy and take more. I mean, come on, I already took the best," just barely, he missed a jagged piece of the fence on his sweater as he gave me a small smile.
This guy, I tell ya'.

Again, we checked the time; ten minutes, we were right on schedule.
We hastily ducked down each time the revolving light from the control tower would shine toward us. We just needed to reach the middle of the field, right in the center.
Once we accomplished that, with five minutes to spare, we rested on our backs.

"We're actually doing it. This is happening, oh my gosh," Colin giddily whispered.

"I know this is crazy, though maybe we should have brought a blanket; the grass is kinda damp. Are you scared at all?"

"No, surprisingly. This is exhilarating!" He, somehow, softly exclaimed.

His word choice made me sometimes laugh, "You're such a dork," giving him a playful nudge and returning my hands back to rest on my stomach.

"Wouldn't want it any other way, Lucy." I wasn't facing toward him, and the only light we got was the two seconds the rotating light flashed at us, but I could feel he had somewhat of a proud smile.

We stayed in electrifying silence until we heard a distant airplane; I could feel my stomach start to do summersaults, trying to make its way up and out. Colin grabbed my hand with a slight squeeze.

"Right on schedule!" He had to raise his voice so I could hear him. "This is going to be AWESOME!"

Both of us were laughing, but it was like we were on mute; I could see the outline of his mouth moving, but nothing was coming out that I could hear. Which made me laugh more. Colin checked his phone one last time, "This is it! Ready!?"

At his question, he gripped my hand tighter in his excitement.

Honestly, I still couldn't believe we were doing this. "Ready," my voice was too tight with anticipation to yell back to Colin.

With our hands wrapped around one another, side by side in our sneaky dark apparel, our heads up to the dark painted sky with a few scattered stars. About to be visited by the math person's private pilot father and his large toy, we were the happiest, proudest dorks in Virginia Beach.

It may sound stupid, but this was one of the most amazing feelings I've ever had. We could feel the rumbling underneath our bodies, shaking, making my heartbeat with suspense against my chest. The plane's engine was thunderous; earplugs probably would have been a smart idea.

At this moment, it felt like we were the only living souls in the world. A bit dramatic, but I swear what was only a few seconds of triumphant amazement felt like a lifetime surged through our bodies and then hitched a ride with the plane. And in a few more moments, the harsh winds from the roaring engines engulfed us momentarily. Rushing through our loose clothing and hair, and the aircraft flew over us with its lights reflecting in our eyes. I can't even put a word to the sensation that pumped through me, watching that plane fly over us. I don't even know why we really wanted to do this, but I don't regret it at all.

Then the plane was gone, and our ears rang for a few minutes before they popped, but after they did, we were fine. Our hands were clammy from the intense and odd experience we just had. We released them but still laid on our backs.

"That was amazing, oh my gosh, we are literally the coolest people alive right now," Colin expressed in the most wonder-filled tone.

"Math guy doesn't have shit on us." Both of us started laughing like little kids; the adrenaline was slowly beginning to wear off as we reverted to our comfortable stillness.

I was dreaming, recalling a memory, I know-

but I was finally dreaming about Colin and I being-

happy.

Perfectly happy,

I loved this moment.

After the reality started sinking in, though, so did the remaining feelings from what happened before I went to sleep.

Why did I do this? Why does this always happen?

It's almost like I feel guilty whenever I begin to be happy; because how can I be happy when Colin isn't there?

My throat felt lodged up, afraid to speak. I didn't want this moment to come to an end.

"Colin, I got into Seth's car tonight," but I needed to stop holding onto things I know are going to slip away.

A small pushed-out chuckle came from him as he sat up on his elbows. As he looked at me, every few seconds, we could see the expression on each other's faces from the obnoxious tower light.

He hopelessly protested. "No, no, you didn't. We've been together planning and preparing all night?" We didn't have eye contact for a second. Returning my attention to him and the courtesy of the light, his eyes opened to me. They were damp; the realization slipped into his mind.

"Oh, this, this isn't happening, is it?" I sat up with him. "This is a dream, again."

I scooted closer, both of us sitting up now.

“I’m getting a bit better at this” We looked at each other through the thick darkness. “Catching on, knowing when you’re just dreaming.”
The light came our way once again, his glossy eyes looking into mine for some sort of safety, as I searched through his hoping to find more time. The beam of illuminating whiteness pouring into my eyes, bringing me back to the morning light peeking in through my bedroom window and my body wrapped up in the quilts.
Ah, reality,
you fickle bitch.

Without a moment to compose myself, in came our drama queen we all know and love- “Heeellllloooooo, Goooodmoooooorning, messy-haired little woommannnn” -Carder.
Who swung the door open, kicked his leg up in a ballerina fashion, and sang the only way he knows how: overdramatically. This went on until he reached my bedside and the exaggerated performance stopped.
“You’re welcome, by the way. That performance was Tony Nominee worthy.” Giving me a sly wink, attempting to make me smile, which I won’t lie, I was smiling a little. But I was just still embarrassed from last night. And he could tell, “Lucy, come on,” he could always tell. “It was a mistake, it’s done, he’s gone, you’re here with me.” And that’s why he is my best friend.
“And you’re getting OUT of THIS BED!” I was caught off guard by his gracious speech after his oh-so-wonderful performance. With the surprising muscles he had, Carder threw the quilt off me and threw me over his shoulder in the next quick moment.
I’m not even gonna fight it.
At least I’m getting a free ride,
wherever we are going;
walking is overrated.
My no-walking-spree was sadly short-lived as he dropped me off at the bathroom. “So, I was thinking for today, if it sounds good to you, we could go to Sherlock’s to help him pick out an outfit for his sister’s wedding; he messaged this

morning and asked. And if you're feeling up to it, we could all come back here and hang out and, well, you know, talk."

I'd really have to take some time to think if I'm ready to have this kind of a vulnerable conversation with Jude, but with Carder there, I think I would feel all the support I need. And he went through a devastating loss as well; he and Colin were close.

After a nod and a playful salute to one another, Carder departed, and we both started to get ready for the day. My hair was going up in a ponytail, and my body will be clothed with the most comfortable casual wear I can find. Today was going to be a somewhat presentable lazy day. I could get dolled up all I wanted, but I don't think I can be fully ready for this day.

Talking about Colin.

Replaying everything in my head,

all over again,

pretending it doesn't bother me anymore,

acting like I'm strong,

not crying in front of Jude but telling him how much I cried when it all happened.

And the question, his question-

It was bound to come up today; it was inevitable.

Would I actually go outside the city?

Out of this state?

Would I feel a tear when I crossed the city limits?

Cause God knows this town has had its grip on me since the day I was born.

If I left the city, would Colin disappear from m-

"Lucy-Lou, let's get a move on, or I'm not buying your coffee!"

Goodness gracious, how does he get ready so fast. Running to my room and pulling a baseball tee on while stepping into some jeans, I called out,

"I'm almost-"

Woaahh, what the hell- I felt movement underneath me- discovering Carder, pulling up my pants. At the same time, I finally got my shirt all the way on. He met me in the front as I finished zipping and buttoning my pants. "Ready" sometimes his nonexistent boundary lines can come in handy.

After getting our coffee and a coffee for Jude, we hit the road to the adorable little house that already had a few uniquely odd memories in it. That's actually strange to think of; we've only known him for a short while. Usually, I'd say this is moving a bit fast, but he's never really had steady friendships, so I suppose this is normal for him.

Plus, Carder and I don't have friends.

Unless you count Alan,

which Carder wouldn't,

but I will.

We won't count my parents because that's just sad.

Carder's parents are assholes I've never met.

Oh! There's Tom!

And Julia, she's a character.

Upon walking into Mr. Johnson's humble abode and giving him his coffee, the house smelled like a mixture of sweet, warm vanilla and a campfire. Interesting, also makes me a little hungry.

"Aw, you guys! Thank you for the coffee, that's very nice, and thank you for coming over. I need some grand second opinions on my options here. Oh, and I'm sorry about the smell; I was baking a pie. Attempting to break gender roles. Alas, the patriarchy has won this time. I don't think it turned out very good."

Ah, alright, it's decided. I feel giddily amused by this. Imaging Jude baking for Carder and me, or just picturing him baking in general, was delightful.

"But make yourselves at home! Raid the fridge, watch some Netflix- whatever! I'll try something on and then come downstairs to show you guys, does that sound okay? Or weird? Too Weird?"

This time I had the reins of the conversation; hop down, Carder. "Not weird, it's our dream come true, we're like the judges on *America's Next Top Model*."

"Oh my Gosh, Virginia Beach's Next Top Bachelor." Well, we couldn't expect Carder to stay quiet for too long. "We won't judge too harshly, well she won't, I might." With a roll of my eyes and a grin from Jude, he strode upstairs as Carder, and I took a seat on the couch.
"Fo real though, what is up with this kid and the random placements of pistachios? I mean, come on, I've already seen like three and we've only been in one room."

Smiling to Carder's observations, I spotted the three pistachio stations:

1. A small goldfish bowl on the side table next to the door

2. The mason jar I gave him (a little over halfway gone) that we could see on the kitchen counter from the front door

3. And a fragile teacup chilling on the coffee table

Not long after, Carder and I guiltily devoured close to all the Pistachios in the teacup, hiding the evident shells in Carder's pockets. Jude walked to the front of the coffee table for us to view.
He was like a handsome mannequin in the window of a tailor shop, but with a face and not that far off dead stare.

Carder went from hungry hippo to Miss J Alexander with a twirl of his sassy finger. In return, Jude gave us a slow-motion turn to provide us with a full view of his outfit. Once his face was to us again, his hands went directly in his pockets, waiting for our critiques.

I was sincere, "I really like it. It's classic yet trendy, I give it a thumbs up." and trying to be Tyra Banks at the same time. I felt Carder's eyes on me, and as I slightly turned, there it was that judgmental glare. "What? I do. I like his outfit. What's wrong with it?"

This was the gist of his Getup:

Torso: Dark brown plaid long sleeve, covered with a charcoal knit cardigan, topped with an expensive-looking light brown blazer.

Torso Accessories: Red bow tie with golden vertical stripes, cute matching red pocket square.

Bottom Half: Dark brown pants to match the dark brown in his undershirt; I see what he did there.

Shoes: Classy black dress shoes.

Carder sighed, rolled his eyes back onto Jude, and started using his hands more than his words to speak. "The bow tie and the pocket square stay, it's going to be hot as hell at the ceremony and the reception, so I would suggest something more comfortable but still formal. You're dismissed."

Right as Carder removed his eyes from Jude, he gave us a slight bow and went back to the drawing board. And as soon as he was out of our view, I backhanded Carder's arm.

"Hey! Ow! You were too nice; besides, he would have died with all those layers on" Raising an eyebrow to him, reloading to backslap- "Okay, I was too harsh, I'm sorry, I'll be nicer." If it wasn't for that dazzling little smirk, he would have had it.

"I need something cold to wash down that hot coffee; I'm gonna get water. Do you want anything?"

Now that smile made me glare at him as he shoved all the pistachio shells in my pockets. What a saint I've got on my hands.

Luckily, I found his garbage can under his counter, without any embarrassment; I could live without that today. As I released the shells from my hands, I couldn't help looking at the few things on the countertop. I didn't look at his envelopes; that wasn't any of my business, but what caught my eye was a playing card. I couldn't really tell what it was at first; the design that was previously on the back was scratched off. This card has been through the wringer; goodness gracious, it was bent to hell. After the last of the shells made it into the can, I flipped the card over. Like the back, it was very bent and a bit faded; it was the king of hearts.
I heard Jude's footsteps on the stairs; in a panic, I raced back to the couch and landed almost on top of Carder's lap.

In my nervous manner, Carder, of course, took advantage of it in a whisper, "Someone was snooping, huh?"
Jude was entering the room, discreetly I kicked Carder's leg, and we both gave off the cheesiest smiles: acting natural.
"Yes! This is way better, I approve. Are those suspenders under that jacket?"
As Jude smiled and nodded, I observed his Carder stamp-of-approval outfit.

Torso: Classic white button-down dress shirt with a nicely form-fitting black blazer.

Torso Accessories: But of course, the red bow tie with golden stripes and red pocket square.

Bottom Half: Matching black slacks that also fit, might I say, nicely.

Shoes: Plain, but always a safe bet, black dress shoes.

We each gave him a thumbs-up as he thanked us again for our help and said he would be down quickly to head to the apartment. Once again, when he was out of sight, Carder's arm got the backhand.
We began to bicker in whispers.

"He could have heard you; you suck at whispering,"

"Oh, whatever, you're the one playing detective over there, pretending to get water; what did you find?"

"First off, I did want water. I got distracted from the chore you gave me, second off" my mind flashed again to the crumpled card, just peeking out from under the envelopes, "A playing card, it's all old looking and ruined."

A look of irritated disappointment portraited on his face. "I was hoping for a secret marriage certificate, or one of those notes psychos leave with all the cut-up magazine letters-"

"Oh, stop, but really what would that card be doing on his counter?"

"Lucy, he probably was cleaning and found it or something; this wasn't his house before, so he must have found it."

Taking that into consideration, I nodded. "Yea, you're right; it's just weird the back design was scraped off."
Before either of us could comment again, Jude came gliding down the stairs in a happy-go-lucky fashion. This time wearing shorts, red converse, and a plain white t-shirt, much like our first outing to the boardwalk.

The car ride back, I let Jude sit shotgun; I kinda wanted to be in the backseat. I was in desperate need of a car window session.
I loved car rides; often enough, I was a little disappointed when we got where we were driving. I loved the endless dead-end conversations Carder and I would have; somehow, we always found another pointless thing to talk about. Most of the time, it's memories or making fake plans for a pretend vacation we were on our way to. But what I loved most was looking out the car window. Looking out to all the objects flashing by, as my thoughts flash with each one, just as fast.

This car ride, while the background was the floating conversations of Carder and Jude, I don't even know what my mind was blasting. My thought's stereo volume turned to max, and the only emotions that stuck around for the dance were anxiety and worry. Gross, my heartbeat couldn't pick a pace, and I could practically hear it. I couldn't stop thinking and envisioning how this would play out; I didn't want Jude to think of Colin differently.

I know it sounds bizarre, but I just want Colin to be recalled for the dorky, loving, writer, little brother he is.

Was.

Ugh, I don't want him to look at me differently or think this was somehow somewhat my fault.

What if this mess wasn't Colin's; it was mine?

And I could have prevented it?

I could have waited another year, just one more fricken year, and we would both be off to California.

Why was I so eager to leave anyway?

I was so consumed in soaking in dreams and fantasies of San Francisco,

that I couldn't even tell that my own brother,

my best friend,

was drowning.

It hit me twice as hard when we walked into the apartment, and we all kicked off our shoes.

We all just naturally gravitated to the living room; Jude sat on the coffee table across from the couch where Carder and I took a seat. This seemed a bit rehearsed; this is probably what they were talking about in the car. I don't think Jude would just take a seat on someone's coffee table unless he was told. Well, I don't know. I might take that back; he's rather quirky.

Carder quietly cleared his throat. "So Luc, I was telling Jude in the car that you kind of wanted to possibly talk about something today."

I was right, point for Lucy.

"But listen, please." His knee drifted to mine, which knocked me out of the zoned-out zone I was in, and I looked into his eyes. "I know this isn't easy to talk about, and we haven't touched on it in a long time, and honestly, we don't need to talk about it if you don't want to, or if you don't feel ready to-"

Shaking my head slightly, I slid my hands under the back of my knees. "It's just hard, but I have to talk about it. I feel like I need to; I haven't really properly processed everything that happened, and maybe talking about it freely would help a little."

Looking to Jude, his gentle, comforting smile made my eyes a little less wet as I felt Carder scoot closer to me; this is it, Lucy. You can do this. This is going to be okay.

Moving my hands onto my lap, Carder slipped his hand in mine before I could fold them.

And so, I told them. I talked to both of them like this had happened last night, and neither of them was there. Carder's thumb lightly caressed my fingers, which gently held his. Holding his hand helped me to push on through the story, through the awful memory. I only looked to Jude one time, and that was the part where Seth didn't give me a ride home.

If I could have placed a bet before this talk that I was going to bawl my eyes out and barely get any words to spill from my mouth, I would have laid down all my money with a

'*Hell yea! No way she's keeping all her dignity after this conversation!*'

And I would have lost; I surprised myself by how collected I was. If I wasn't staring at the floor the whole time, though, I would have been rollin' in some pretty hefty winnings.

With all the bravery I could scrap up from inside me, I lifted my head. There was a glaze over Jude and Carder's eyes, "But," I pushed out. "There's something I didn't even tell you, Carder." His hand loosened from mine momentarily, then returned with a bit of a squeeze, our signal to continue. "He wrote mom, dad, and you, a letter remember that?"

"Of course, I still have it." I was taken for a second by how calm Carder was, I know Colin wasn't technically his brother, but they pretty much were. The three of us, best friends until the end; we were like *Harry*, *Ron*, and *Hermione*, just one of us got lost during the battle.
But oh, how our adventures would live on in our minds every day, always.

"He left me a letter and a small wooden rectangular box, but I've never opened it." Carder moved over, as did I, and Jude joined us on the couch; like we all had the same thought, we rested our feet on the coffee table. The quiet was comfortable for the moment, a break from the tension.
"I think I want to open it now."
They both looked at me; not knowing which side to turn to, I moved my feet off the table and sat across from them. Jude still had a thin layer of empathy over his grey-blue irises. Carder's face was relaxed, but he couldn't hide the flashes of memory in his eyes.

Jude softly spoke up for a moment, almost with slight hesitation. "If you do want to open it, would you like me to leave? It's completely okay if you do."

Carder's voice chimed in right after Jude's words cut off. "We can go for a drive, and you can have the place to yourself, however long you need."

Both their offers warmed me up, but I shook my head. "No, no, I don't want to be alone" Carder's eyes widened. "If it's okay with you guys, I mean, I don't know if that's awkward."
They looked to one another, confirmed with a nod, and turned back to me; Carder was always the spokesperson.

"We're here for ya, girly." And those were the words that got me to smile. Maybe this was going to be okay; perhaps it wouldn't be too painful if I had them with me.

I went to retrieve the last gift Colin had given me. I kept it under my bed, and to be honest, I hadn't thought about it for a long time. That's why I never brought it up to Carder; I never thought I would open it.
Kneeling down beside the bed, I gently lifted my quilt to reveal the small dark world beyond it. Its only inhabitants being my baseball bat, a few records from my grandpa's, and the letter and box which collected a thin layer of dust. As my hands were met with their corners, I felt this rush of familiarity I wasn't prepared for. I wanted it to last longer, but pulling the box out as the sunshine it had been deprived of for a year hit its smooth surface, the rush dissolved in the light. It was established as my hand glided across the letter and box; dust littered the air in my room to follow the rush into the light.

I thought my entrance to the living room was going to feel a lot more uncomfortable than it was. Carder and Jude had moved the coffee table to the side of the living room, making an open space for us to sit on the floor. Thank God they tried to make the situation brighter by giving me a smile and patting the floor for me to sit. Setting the mystery gift in the middle, we all took a long-concentrated stare, like we were about to paint the scene.

"I guess I should read the letter first," I said, more like a questionable statement than a direction. Carder gave my knee a slight squeeze and a nod while I took a deep breath.
The envelope was in good shape, turning it over to the front where it was signed.

'To My Companion'

'From Your Doctor'

Goodness gracious, this living room was going to turn into a community pool of tears soon. Here it goes, gently tearing the still crisp paper open.

"Hey Lucy, you don't have to read it out loud, okay?" Jude reassuringly shot out as I was starting to pull the folded notebook paper out.

Teasingly I cocked my eyebrow at him. "If I'm going through this, you two are too, don't try to get out of it, Johnson." I figured we all needed a little sass to ease the apprehension floating around us, to which it seemed he appreciated, as did Carder.

Clearing my throat as my hands unfolded the paper, I right there almost started to cry at the sight of his handwriting.

Who would have ever thought at a point in time we would ever miss someone's handwriting until we no longer get the pleasure of seeing it again? At least something we hadn't read of theirs before.

And so, after mentally embracing his perfectly missed penmanship, I began to read aloud.

'*My Dearest Lucy May MacArthur,*

Before I begin to unfold the directions for this high-tech fancy box's contents (bear with me; we both know I wasn't the funny one), I would like to say Hello.

Hello, as if this is our first Hello. It's kind of strange, isn't it? That we don't really get a free willing first Hello with our siblings? (This is most likely why I didn't have friends because I have bizarre thoughts like these.) But if I have to make my own wish happen, I will make do with achieving so through good 'ole fashion paper.

So, Hello.

Hello, my silly sister.

Hello, my beautiful relation.

Hello, my best friend.

Hello, my hero.

Hello, my muse.

Hello, my number one fan.

Hello, my two AM Netflix binging partner.

Hello, my Sherlock-obsessed pal.

Hello, my childhood friend.

Hello, my Companion.

Hello, my wonderful sister.

Hello.

Very Important Instructions:

I will list the items in the box (You will be surprised how much you can fit in a high-tech wooden box) with a specific purpose to follow. The other things are all for you.

• T-Shirt- Please put this on, you may do so over the clothes you already have on (I sure hope you are wearing a shirt or some sort of clothing)

• Tissue Box- Please place no more than an arm's length away (I'm not saying you're gonna cry, but I am predicting from the many movies we have watched you may)(They are extra soft, so they don't hurt your sensitive nose)(Your rants about tissues are legendary)

• DVD Labeled Allons-y- (Don't laugh, you know this is my favorite word) THIS IS THE LAST THING TO BE USED, PLEASE WATCH THIS LAST.

Love,
Colin Houston MacArthur

(P.S. My middle name is utterly ridiculous)

Damn him for making me laugh after his very last letter. After my surprised laugh was released, Carder and Jude let out a relief laugh as well.

"*That's* his middle name! He would never tell me!" Carder blurted amongst our short-lived laughter.

Jude turned his head in curiosity with a smiley gaze. "Is that really his middle name?"

With a soft giggle and a nod, I answered. "Yes, Colin wasn't exactly planned, and they couldn't think of a middle name, so they choose Houston. Like," putting on my best muffled sounding voice, "*Houston, we have a problem*" I shook my head and joined the giggling that soon came after that, "My parents are the biggest dorks."

While there was still a positive, somewhat happy feeling amongst us, I reached for the box, and with an anxious exhale, I opened the lid.

On the very top, covering up what was in the rest of the box, was Colin's favorite T-shirt, which he practically lived in. It was white, baggy, and in black print had the famous picture of John Lennon with his circular glasses on, staring off into nowhere. Taking it out, not looking at what was still left to explore, I slipped the shirt on over my clothes. For a second, it felt so weird. It felt almost normal until, again, reality told me otherwise. Before looking back into the box, I took a small sniff of Colin's shirt; and I wasn't disappointed. With a smile making its way to my face, it was like he was still here.

And as instructed, the tissue box was placed right next to me. I would later look at the other things in the box, but I didn't even know what to expect or think about this DVD.

Allons-y; ever since he first heard it, he would intersect it in any conversation he could. It's a French word; it was his favorite *Doctor*from *Doctor Who*catchphrase; it means '*Let's Go*'

Carder placed his hand on my back, looking at me as I lifted my head to him. "Do you want to watch it alone?"

I felt like I was pulling my throat from the outside in. Trying to restrain a cry from climbing up and out of my mouth. I shook my head. And then Carder politely asked if Jude could get my laptop out of my room. To which, of course, he said yes. Before he came back, Carder kissed my forehead and wrapped his arms around me for a quick, comforting embrace.

"You're so strong, Lucy-Lou" his whisper lingered in my ear as he drew back, Jude placing the laptop in front of me.

We all sat crisscross, our knees touching the other like we were linked; I was in the middle.

The computer finally booted up, clicking the button on the side for the DVD drive; the popping sound embarrassingly enough made me jump a little. Luckily, no comment from Carder.

In my mind, I wasn't ready for this; I wasn't prepared for whatever Colin had put on this DVD. But before my mind could make one last retreat, my hands had already surrendered to the inevitability that someday I would have to watch it. I'd rather watch it now with these guys than one day by myself with a cold cup of coffee in my hand and some sad sappy song playing in the background.

The computer took its time to recognize the CD, then without warning, the screen went black.

Showtime.

22. One Last Time

Placing both hands on each knee, Carder took one and Jude the other. I held Carder's a bit tighter.
I knew Carder wouldn't question it,
Jude, on the other hand-
no pun intended,
I'm embarrassed to say I just laughed at myself inside my mind,
anyway,
Jude would maybe get weirded out; I don't know.

The sound of the disc loading was nerve-racking, even more so when it stopped. I knew I would still have this precious mystery of Colin in one moment, one more thing I can hold onto, and in the next moment, I don't know what will happen; that's what scares me. I'm also afraid to confront this. In many ways, I haven't, and I probably haven't even appropriately grieved; maybe a part of me is still angry and confused by all of this. I just try to remember the Colin from my childhood. From our goofy moments, family memories; not so much the Colin that chose to leave this world for reasons I still can't completely wrap my mind around. That decided to leave me when I thought the world was more than ready for the both of us together.
My hands, both of them, clutched tighter as the screen flashed to white and then began to fade into an image of,
I can't tell what is that-
it's,
Colin's room.

The camera was propped up on his desk. I could see his bed he made every morning; he couldn't leave the house without doing so.
The posters that covered the majority of his walls, mostly Beatles posters, I know, shocker.

His color-coordinated closet; oh how I miss sneaking a red sweater in with the blues.
Notebooks stacked along random parts of the walls.
And catching me, well, all of us, off guard popped Colin from under the shot.
Releasing both of my hands, I quickly paused the video.
Colin, this is Colin; I had to pause it just to look at him and the room. And because I was shocked to see him, it's been so long since I've seen him, besides pictures.
Then I noticed his shirt, looking down to the shirt that was in the box that he asked me to wear; we were wearing the same shirt. I think we all gathered this at the same time, but I was too focused on the focused image of my little brother.
His dark brown hair that I would teasingly tussle from time to time. Sometimes he would gel it up, but most of the time, it just got pushed aside.
And the brown eyes I see each time I look in the mirror to my own. Sometimes for a pure split second, I mistake them for his, but that mostly happened when I worked early morning shifts at the nursing home.
Time to continue Lucy, you took a long enough timeout.

As I clicked resume, I slipped my hands back to Carder and Jude; they were already expecting my hand's company. They didn't say anything, but I could almost *feel* the words they would have said out loud through the pulse and warmth in their hands.

Colin chuckled a little from his own '*surprise*' attack. "Sorry Lucy, I know how easily you get scared. I won't mention all those horror film nights we tried to sit through but couldn't make it even halfway without either accidentally hitting ourselves from trying to cover our faces quickly. Which resulted in having to camp out in the living room and take shifts sleeping and being on the lookout. You were alllwwaayysss the one who got scared first-"

A slight snicker escaped from my exhaling of disbelieving. "Oh yea right, it was YOU-"

"I know I know, don't get all flustered like I *know* you are," on appeared that familiar Colin smirk I had so dearly missed. "I was the one who always got scared, but come on, who could blame me? How can people sleep at night knowing they came up with that demented stuff!"

I peeked at Carder; a glaze was beginning to layer his eyes. It was so comforting, I think for the both of us, to hear his voice. But this was also extremely difficult. To be honest, I didn't entirely know how to feel. Who on Earth thinks they'll ever have to go through something like this, especially with their little brother.

"I'm not sure when you'll watch this; if it's been a day, weeks, or months, whenever you did, it's all okay. I made this for you because I wanted you to always have clarity in case you need it. After all, you deserve it. If this video can bring you closure or even the slightest smile from reminiscing, that would be exactly what I wished for in creating it." He gave me a weak smile, and I couldn't help but reflect it; when he smiled, I smiled. It was a reflex I was so used to and haven't used in so long.

He sat criss-cross in his chair with his hands folded in his lap. While he adjusted, I wondered where I was at the time he made this, what was I doing then-

Colin took a deep breath, I could tell it was hard for him to continue without crying, but he pushed on through.

"I'm sorry, Lucy. I'm so sorry. And I know that you probably have the idea planted in your mind that this is all your fault, somehow or another, but this is the one rare case when you're actually wrong, big sister. My actions are my actions. They aren't a reflection on yours or anything like that because you are," he was trying not to choke up "you're the best big sister, the greatest best friend I could have ever been blessed with."

I was squeezing Carder's hand tighter. It hurt to hear those words, not because I didn't believe they were true but because if they were true, why did he leave me like this.

"When you found out you got accepted into practically your dream college, I really didn't want to see you go. I'll admit it I was upset and scared because I didn't know life without you, and you and Carder were my only friends, the reasons I would get through the day. But I knew you had to go because that's where you were going to truly find yourself. And you needed to have this journey, this self-exploration; I knew- I know you are the girl who has to get out of this town. You were born this cute, amazing sailboat ready to explore. But then unconsciously, I became an anchor, an unnecessary weight, holding you down when you needed to be free. Even though you enjoyed where you were harbored, that's not where you were meant to be. You would never see it that way, I didn't want you to see me that way, but I couldn't let you stay just because I wasn't ready. But Lucy, I just feel this weighted pain living in me, like it's always been in me. It's just getting heavier and harder, and when I think about the future, I just," His eyes looked so lost for a moment like he was searching the camera. "I don't see me there," Searching for his own clarity.

A gasp caught up with his voice that held his words down for a moment.

"This is so hard to say, I feel so detached, and it's awful. This thing, this dark ugly thing inside me that doesn't even feel like it belongs to me but I guess it does because it's inside of me; it echos these terrible words about me, this hopelessness, this despair. And I try to make it leave, I try to get it to stop because I don't want to feel this way anymore, but it won't leave me alone, it's clawed into me so sharp and tight-" He caught his frantic breath, and tried to replace it with a steady one.

"I've always been bad at trying to say how I feel. It comes out better when I put it in a story or I make an analogy. So here's one: Look at it as if life is a Merry-Go-Round. I'm on it, like everyone else. We're all hanging out, enjoying the rush, sometimes coming up on the turn, we feel a little anxious, but it doesn't last very long. I fell off the Merry-Go-Round. For some time, I hesitated as I was off the course everyone else was on. Watching them enjoying the ride while my body felt like it couldn't move. Throbbing still from the pain of falling. After being off it for a while, my mind started asking strange questions. Like if I even deserved to be on the Merry-Go-Round. And of course, the Merry-Go-Round didn't and can't stop just because I fell off. That wouldn't be fair to the other smiling people on the ride. It keeps spinning fast like nothing ever happened. I run alongside it, trying to catch up; sometimes, I'd get a grip on the bar but eventually, I trip, and I fall again. The Merry-Go-Round doesn't stop, and the reality is, some people just never get back on. I'm afraid I'll never be able to get back on and smiling with everyone else again, I'm afraid I'll be chasing after the bar my whole life until I trip once more in an attempt to reach it, but this time I don't get up. I guess that's the best way I can try and explain it."

He looked out of breath as he stared off onto the floor and took a deep breath before talking again; I took one with him, ready for anything and everything he has to say.

"Alright, okay," wiping his face, "Let's talk about our memories too because we really do have some of the best ones."
Just a little smile peeked on my face at the thought, and only a second later, his did as well; we really were connected, no matter the circumstances. It still wasn't the same, though, obviously; I'd give anything to have him sitting in front of me instead of my laptop.
"Goodness gracious, where can I begin, oh! Remember when we use to have family Fort Days; oh my gosh, they were the best. I think my favorite was when we built that big comfy fort and dad put the TV in there. Mom made, I don't even know how much popcorn, enough to feed guests at a small concert, and we watched movies all day and talked about them afterward like movie critics. Didn't we spend like almost an hour talking and quoting *The Princess Bride* even though we all have seen it probably a hundred times combined?"

"We did! I remember I laughed so hard I fell on my side and spilled the popcorn-" Carder rubbed his thumb across my hand. Gently bringing me back, but it felt like I was actually talking to him. Maybe that's what he wanted, though. To be honest, I wanted it too; I wanted to listen to him all day.

"I remember when you first showed me *Glee* and I pretended not to like it, but Dear God it was like crack, then that became our show to help us carry through until the next *BBC Sherlock* season came. We grew up on *Monk, Doctor Who,*

The Muppets, it's no wonder we were always the '*quiet kids who never talk*,' who would understand the greatness! The quotes! Look at me, getting all hyped up about how big of dorks we are. But, we did have our badass moments."

I felt Carder look at me from the corner of my eye with a little teasing grin as he nudged me.

"Who could ever forget the night of '*The Airport Scandal*,' but hey, just because I'm not there, you are *still* sworn to secrecy."
Colin's finger was pointed in a lecturing way, but as he put it down, that giddy smile took the scowling stare's place.
"In the box, I put the Polaroid pictures we took with grandpa when he found his old camera, and we used the film that was left in it. And, I don't know if you remember but, mom and dad use to leave us notes on paint swatches. They put them in our backpacks or tapped them on our doors; I remember waking up one morning to one on my ceiling right above my bed. I was actually impressed they got it up there without waking me up. Anywho, go ahead and pause this and take a look if you haven't already; I'll be here. There's no rush."
I reached for the box after I paused the video. Colin has his hands folded in his lap.

There they were, just as he said, pictures of grandpa, Colin, and I trying to squeeze in so we could all get in the picture.
Here's another one grandpa took of me and Colin on the dock with our feet hanging over and our backs faced to the camera, grandpa's thumb also made a small appearance.
There's the one we asked a tourist to take of Colin and me carrying grandpa as he laid on his side in our arms in front of the Farris Wheel at the Boardwalk. I remember how wide the tourist's eyes got when grandpa jumped up, and we caught him. Thank God for Colin and me that grandpa spent most of his time in a Hot Air Balloon and didn't eat much besides cashews and granola bars.

Our last one, we took with the three of us, mom, and dad in front of the old house. Dad held the camera up high with his long arms and managed to get us all in, looking up with squinting eyes and wide smiles.

After I was done silently reliving through each picture, I passed two to Carder and two to Jude. They could exchange when they were done. As Colin said, I did forget about the paint swatch notes. I don't know how I could, it was the strangest and purest thing. They started when I first began preschool. My dad always had paint swatches; the man just likes his quirks.
My gosh, there are so many, ones that bring back memories of specific days like before Choir Concerts or pumping us up for presentations we had to give that day. I know Colin said there wasn't a rush, and I wanted to eventually read all the forgotten notes, but my sole mission right now is to listen to what he has to say.
Without letting the boys in on this, I played the video.

"I hope those make you smile, Lucy. Those pictures with grandpa make me smile so much; man, he was one cool cat. Always had a joke, always had a story we hadn't heard before, and the way he talked about grandma was like seeing poetry in someone's eyes. The way he talked about her made me feel like we actually got to know her, you know? Spending time with him was like stepping out of your shoes and into the world of grandpa, barefoot, how he would have preferred it if it was socially acceptable. I never told you this, and if I never told you this, we both can automatically state I didn't tell anyone. A while after grandpa passed away, I would have dreams about him, like all the time."

My eyes widened. My heart felt like it was pounding in slow motion, intensifying each beat.

"It's like, the dream starts out as a memory, something I remember very well, and it plays out just as I remember. It's like I'm reliving it. The dream is in a first-person kind of view. But then as the memory ends, all of a sudden, something just clicks, and grandpa looks at me so sad and realizes it's just a dream. Sometimes the

dreams are scenarios that didn't even happen, but maybe somewhere in my mind, I had imagined it before. I don't know. I probably sound crazy."
He tried to laugh it off and dismiss the topic, but he stopped mid-laugh.
"I remember one dream, grandpa said something about you, but I can't remember what I'm trying to remember. Curse my horrible memory. Damn it, I'll keep working on that. I thought of another memory! Jumping off the pier, fully clothed, after I serenaded you with a *My Chemical Romance* classic. Ah, what a fine afternoon and what a fine cold we caught. I could honestly go on forever talking about all these stupid crazy moments we have together that would probably make no sense to anyone but us. Still, I want to tell you my favorite memory. Like of all time Lucy; here we go, we're about to take an awesome trip down memory lane."

Like the enormous dork he is, he pretended to strap on a seat belt and hang onto the sides of his chair like it was about to lift off for a galactic journey. After his metaphor had made me smile, he returned his hands in their folding position in his lap.

"We would play this continuous game all through our childhood, and admittedly sometimes even when we got bored in our teenage years. It didn't matter where we left off; we always picked up and went on with the adventure. My favorite memory isn't a specific day or moment; it's all the days and moments we played '*Doctor and Companion*.' Gosh, were we the coolest kids or what? I think at a point, mom and dad regretted bringing us into the fandom of *Doctor Who* because that's literally all we talked about. But the adventures we had, man, the adventures we came up with, in our minds, that made us escape from Virginia Beach for a small glimmer of time. Remember we painted on this huge cardboard box we got from some furniture set mom and dad had ordered, and we painted it like the *Tardis* and dragged it everywhere? Or how many times we saved the entire universe? The world should really thank us; we saved Earth so many times."

Everything was playing through my head like a slideshow, and Colin was clicking the button for the next slides.
I loved hearing him talk about our old times. Hearing him talk and get excited and smiley. As happy as it made me reminiscing with him, in some aspect, it equally hurt just as much to replay all those smiles and laughs. Once the first hot tear caressed its way down my face, there was no stopping the silent waterfall.

"Our expeditions were legendary in the Hall of Imagination, never to be forgotten and never to lose its touch of glistening enterprise!" He quickly hopped out of his chair with his arms up above his titled head, smiling to the ceiling as he looked back to the camera and sat down.
"Though I don't know if we can top our past ones, we have one more adventure."

All our heads,
all three of our heads,
perked up.
We stared at the screen in anticipation and puzzlement.

"One more adventure Lucy. I have something for you that I didn't put in the box because I want you to find it, one last adventure with my favorite Companion."
I choked up; my tears weren't so silent anymore.
"I can't tell you what the treasure is, that wouldn't be very fun, but! I can tell you that this expedition will be done in Note Style. I know you know what I'm talking about."
I nodded, even though it wouldn't have made a difference if I did or not. Colin was referring to when we found the notes in the old family house. Well, to him, it was still our house.
"You are a clever girl; I know you'll find it. You found most of the notes throughout the years, anywho." He gave me a slight smile. I wonder if he was wondering while making this how I would react to it.
"Always, always, always, always you will be my sister, my person, my companion, my best friend. And I wish for all the happiness in the world to find

its way to you and fill you up and touch every piece of your life. You are going places, kid, and those places better be outside of this town. I know Virginia Beach has its perks, but you have to explore- for the both of us."
I think the realization of his last words and their heavy meaning hit him and hit him hard. His half-smile was being overcome by the tears filling up in his eyes.
"I'm so sorry, Lucy," One escaped. "I'm so so sorry," Two came sliding down.
"I love you." As the third tear chased the others, he waved goodbye and covered the camera with his hand.

The screen went black.
The CD drive popped open.
He said goodbye.
But once again, I wasn't prepared to say it back.

The silence lingered for a few minutes, my hands were still being held, and tears were beginning to dry on my cheeks. Gently, I gave the boy's hands a small squeeze and let go, putting the disk back in the box and shutting off the computer.

"He probably never would have guessed we'd move out of that house." My voice was hoarse, pushing the words out as smoothly as possible. "I don't even know who lives there now, or if they did remodeling; whatever it is, it might not even be there anymore."

Carder's eyes met mine, his eyes that looked strained from holding back tears. "But the treasure might be there" he gave me a nod as if he heard the question in my head. "Yes, Lucy-Lou, it's okay to have a hope it's there, and yes, the three of us will go together."

Turning to Jude, he nodded in approval as I returned to Carder. "Okay," Taking a deep, we are flippin' crazy, sigh. "Let's do this."

The three of us got up.

I turned out the lights.
Jude held open the door.
Carder locked it.
When we heard the click of the lock, this adrenaline made its way into us. We ran down the apartment building stairs and booked it to Carder's car. This time I called shotgun.
As we buckled up, I turned to Jude, who was sitting in the middle seat in the back. "You get to see the old place after all," We both smiled. Before I turned around and Carder started the car, Jude mouthed the words thank you to me.
He didn't say it out loud, but I think he thanked me for letting him be a part of this, for including him in something so personal. But the strange thing is, it doesn't seem personal and exposing; I felt okay with him and Carder. I felt like they needed to be here with me through this.

I felt like we were taking part in a drive-by; Carder parked the car on the side of the road not directly in front of the house but a little ways from it.
Obviously, we are professionals.
There wasn't a car in the driveway, but they could have a car parked in the garage. I didn't see any lights on, but the shades were open, and it was still light outside. I could feel the both of them looking at me like I was their captain, and they were awaiting orders.

"This is a bad idea; I change my mind. We're not doing this."

If not all the amount of sass Carder has hoarded up inside of him, then a good portion of it came out as he whipped his seatbelt off, opened the door, and exited stage right. Clicking my seatbelt off and Jude following, I turned back to him as we both continued to watch Carder dramatically walk up to the front door.

"He better not"

Stopping mid-motion as he was about to ring the doorbell, he turned to the car, looking straight at me.

"Carder George Elizondo," I knew he could read my lips; we've had way too much practice from High School. "I swear," giving him a death glare. "Get. Back. Here. Now."
I had my hand on the door handle, ready to charge if need be,
"That little-"
Swinging open the car door and Jude playing follow the leader, we ran to Carder as I pinched the back of his arm.

"Ow ow ow ow!" he squirmed as I released after the third ow.

"Well, what the heck! I told you not to! We didn't even have a plan!"

Jude cleared his throat. "Hey, guys,"

"That doesn't give you the right to pinch my arm. You know that part is sensitive!"

"Guys, I think someone is coming to the door."

"Maybe if you didn't make everything so dramatic, we wouldn't be having this argument on someone's front step-"

As the door slowly opened, silencing our argument and Jude's attempt to get our attention, it reviled this adorable woman. She couldn't have been older than twenty-six; twenty-eight would be pushing it.
Her dark chocolate hair looked smooth as it draped down past her shoulders, tickling just above her elbow. The brown in her eyes was different than any brown I had seen before. There was this natural glow in them, this glossy-looking sparkle you couldn't help but stare into. And I'm pretty sure the three of us were staring into them. Though she is probably used to people being fascinated by her beauty, she was totally weirded out. Totally justified.

Elbowing Carder in his side, designating him as our speaker, he did his thing.

"Hi, I'm sorry to bother you. How are you doing today?"
She opened the door wider to get a better look at us. "Lo siento," pausing as she looked sympathetic, "no hablo Ingles."

My eyes unintentionally widened. Why couldn't I have retained any Spanish from school? Ugh, what should I do-
Wait, Carder knows Spanish!
Elbowing him again, immediately he turned to me in a whisper, "I only took like two years! I can barely ask her where the bathroom is! And maybe tell her I like her shoes!"
After nudging him once more, he dusted off the ole High School Spanish textbook in his mind and gave it a whirl. "Poco español"

She giggled a little, making the situation less tense. I'm guessing she found Carder's Spanish skills amusing. "Sí le puedo decir" she had tiny crinkles that appeared by her eyes when she laughed, but as quickly as they came, they faded away as her face lit up. "Puedo leer Inglés," she spoke in a hopeful tone as she mimed what looked like flipping pages of a book.

Carder politely smiled at her as he spoke to Jude and me, "I think she said she can read English."

She then smiled at me as I smiled back to her, and I told Carder to ask if she has a pen and paper. It's kind of weird but beautiful at the same time that a smile is a universal way of showing kindness. And at the response to Carder's valiant attempt at translating, she nodded and motioned us to come inside, shaking each of our hands as we came in and introducing herself to each of us.
"Mia" Her smile radiated into her name. She spoke so beautifully, and damn, her hands were soft.

As she gestured us to the table set for six, grabbing a pad of paper and a pen on her way, she accompanied us and gave the items to Carder, who pushed them to me.

I stared at the lined paper for a moment, not knowing where to start or even how to explain; Carder introduced all of us as I finally just went for it. I tried to keep it simple and to the point as much as I could. This was either going to result in a generous acceptance to let us search her house or a trip to the Virginia Beach jail. Gently I slid the paper to her with a hopeful smile on my face, and as it met her hands, she eagerly began to read.

'I used to live in this house. My little brother left something for me here after he died; can we please find it?'

Without hesitation or eye contact, she hurried to a room down the hall, which use to be my parents' room.

Panicked, I looked to Carder,

then to Jude,

gave Jude a reassuring smile,

and returned back to Carder with eyes that looked like we were in a hostage crisis.

After a few seconds of hearing a distant fumbling, Mia returned with a laptop in her hands, taking a seat next to me and pulling up Google Translate.

Okay, that's brilliant. Way to go, Mia!

Point for Mia.

As she typed each word in Spanish, the words appeared in a box beside it, in English.

"I am sorry for your loss."

We quickly developed a system; when I read her sentence, I would nod, and she would delete it and begin a new one.

"My house is your house."

Turning to her, I nodded, smiling. Actually feeling tears starting to develop in my eyes. This woman has known me for a total of maybe five minutes, and already she is treating me like we've known each other for years.

"My husband will be back from work soon."
Nodding to her, I looked back to the screen as she typed again.
"He lost his brother too. He would like to meet you."
My smile turned into a slant, I didn't even know the guy, and I felt terrible.
"It's okay. And he speaks English."
She giggled and smiled at me. I could tell she liked to laugh a lot. Just something about her emits that.
"I am making spaghetti stay for Lunch?"
Turning to the boys and then back to our new extremely kind friend, I graciously nodded, and this time I typed into the translator "Yes, thank you, we love spaghetti."

She was ecstatic from my response; closing the laptop, she practically hopped into my lap with the hug she gave me. It took me a moment to register, but hugging her back didn't really feel like hugging a stranger living in my old house. It felt like hugging a friend who took over the fort when I could hold it down anymore.

After our embrace, she made her way around the table, so everyone got a hug. She giggled after the hugging was over and then made her way to the kitchen. While not hearing us move, she turned around and shooed us to go off like we were her kids. And with that, it was time for the final adventure.
The three of us walked to the living room to come up with the plan.

"Okay," exhaling, pushing out all my anxiousness, "Can anyone else believe that just happened? What is even happening? I don't know where to begin."
I don't know what I was expecting them to say. It was a bit selfish; they hadn't even been there during the long-term Notes Expedition.

"Humanity still has its spark! Hmm, How many notes were there?" Jude spoke with a look of concentration on his face, like a man with a plan.

"Six"

"Okay, and do you remember where you found all of them?"

"Umm," Rewinding to the memories and then fast-forwarding through the search. "Yea, yea, I think I do."

"In order?"

Oh goodness, this was going to be a challenge. "I think so. I think I can remember."

"That's actually a pretty good idea, Sherlock" Carder gave Jude a bro slap on the back. "Are we in?"

I'm guessing from coordination observation that none of us have ever had experience being on a sports team. But all hands went in, and the spirit traveled through one hand to the next; now we had a team to call our own.

"Alright, the first place I remember" Looking around, trying to jog my memory, something dinged when my eyes landed on the hallway "Hallway! Hallway, living room hallway!"

My legs had a mind of their own as the rest of my body tried to keep up with them as I slid down on my knees to the middle of the hallway; the boys stood over me, watching. As if this hallway wasn't narrow enough.

"Colin and I were running through the house; I don't remember who, but one of us stepped on this floorboard, and it squeaked, so we checked it out."

Placing my palm on the board and wiggling it, the board moved enough for me to get my fingertips on the edges and lifted up.

"I can't believe it. It still feels the same," Setting the board aside, I could see the particles of dust that were trapped underneath. There it was, "Oh my gosh, it's there," a notecard with a thin layer of dust and Colin's handwriting.

I could feel my hand shaking as I reached for it, it wasn't noticeable, but it got worse once I had it in my hands and pulled from under the floor; I read it out loud.

'Didn't I tell you! You clever girl! You have the pattern; now, you just have to tap into the memory.
"The Game is On!" – Our BBC Sherlock'

My smirk was uncontrollable, the rush in those words; *the game is on.* It felt so good letting it spill from my mouth. Pocketing the note and standing up to see both Carder and Jude waiting for my facial expression to see what would be the appropriate one to display, instantly, they smiled.
My dorks.

"Sweet, we got the first one!" The excitement in Jude's eyes matched Carder's as well.

"Lucy-Lou, do you remember where the second place was?"

I could feel my smirk begin to droop, and a strain made its way to the crease in my forehead that made its appearance when I was trying to think. But I couldn't think. My mind is so preoccupied with this excitement by this, this last adventure. I needed to remember now.
"Wait," I could, I vaguely could. "We used to play hide-n-seek" Tapping, I tapped it; now just a little more to see the whole picture. "Colin was so tiny he could fit practically anywhere" Almost there. "One time I couldn't find him for almost thirty minutes, he found a new spot," Gotcha. "the pantry!"

Carder exchanged a glance with Jude. "The what?"

My eyes darted down the hall to the kitchen door that used to hold all our favorite snacks and mom's homemade bread. "The pantry, the kitchen pantry!" Gosh, that bread was good.

In a line: Me, Carder, and Jude ran through the dining room, past Mia, who wasn't even fazed by our heavy breathing and poor example of running, and to the pantry door.
With a swing of the door, I was on my knees. Crouching under the highly placed bottom shelf, feeling my way past the cobwebs and dust to find- yes, the comfortingly startling touch of a tiny gold knob.
Before opening it, though, I wanted the boys to get a chance to look at it. So, the three of us got pretty close in that tiny closet.
I certainly hope Mia was occupied by something during this time.

The cleverly hidden door swung out, but only a child could crawl their way through there. Placed neatly in the dark bunker, being able to catch just a bit of the light that was peaking in from beyond the pantry doors, was Colin's next note.

'Atta girl Lucy! Do you remember this? Granted, it wasn't the most comfortable hiding place, but I got you good for a while there! Like our Dear old Sherlock, in any adaptation, where does he spend most of his time? Hmmm... I wonder I wonder....'

"Any guesses, Sherlock fanatics?" As Carder looked at the two of us, we shrugged at one another.

"Wait," Jude, who was zoning out on the floor in thought, grabbed onto my arm. It's like the light bulb surged its way from his brain, through my arm, and to mine. Right as it clicked on, we looked at one another and nodded.
"Bedroom!" We blurted out, pushing to get out of the small space and sprinting our way up the stairs; I'm proud to say I skipped two at a time, three at one point.

It's been a while.
Point for Lucy.

I remembered this one. I remembered exactly where it is; my room. Well, my old room: up the stairs, to the left, down the hall, the second door on the right side. If Colin instructed me to do this blindfolded, I wouldn't have had a single problem. I could still see the rooms and all the memories captured in them.

As we walked in, Carder let out a sigh. "Gosh, this room has so many memories." He spun slowly around, taking in the view, as did I. Imagining everything as it used to be. Where my bed was, my mirror, the bookshelf, the pictures; I had so many photos on these walls. They were like four, very, large pages of a scrapbook.

The room was empty; there were different colored strokes of paint on the wall.
A nice house,
beautiful wife,
hardworking husband,
either this is going to be a lovely office space,
or they are expecting.

The third hidden place was found when I hung a frame on the wall and tiptoed onto the trim for an extra boost. I then, literally, stumbled upon the little compartment.
Kneeling down, I ran my finger along with the wooden trim until it was met with the discreet notch that gave you assistance to wiggling the small section of the edge out. Reveling a space just big enough for a rolled-up piece of paper.
Carder was still reminiscing as Jude came and kneeled next to me, marveling at the third hiding place.

"This has to be the most interesting adventure I have been on." His eyes were still fixed on the exposed note, my eyes fixed on his astonished expression.

Did I believe that this indeed was the most interesting adventure he had ever been on?

No, of course not; this guy has been all over the world. Kneeling on a floor and watching someone take out a chunk of wood from the bottom of a wall doesn't strike me as interesting—especially given the circumstances of how we even got on this adventure. The last adventure, to correctly state it.

Did I get a cage full of butterflies and pretty rainbows released into my stomach at the sound of his voice and the lovely view of his face?

Yes, of course, I did. Not staring aimlessly appealed at this guy would be like going to an Art Gallery and turning all the paintings around.

Did that analogy make any sense?

No, but what do you want from me? I can't concentrate with all these damn butterflies flying on through all my rational thoughts and rainbows shining in my eyes every time reality gleams back in.

"Lucy, are you okay?"

And like that, the butterflies took off. "Yea, sorry," the rainbows went off to find another sky, "I'm fine." and now I could focus.

As I peeled my eyes off of Jude, Carder joined us while I gently took the miniature scroll, unraveling it to read the following message.

'She strikes again! I can still remember hearing that thump when you tripped over that faulty piece of trim. I ran into the room, and moments later, we were cheering at the discovery of yet another secret note. Yes, your room was by far the winner of best decorated; but our rooms both had their secrets....'

Sliding the piece of trim back in its camouflaged place, I felt my eyebrows turn to one another as my mind blurted, *' What in the hell is he talking about?'*

"Ideas?" Jude softly asked.

Shaking my head while still concentrated on the bottom part of the wall, Carder struck me with the back of his hand on my arm from the sudden realization of something. As you can imagine, this is not the first time my arm has abruptly been attacked by the back of Carder's hand.

"Closet!"

"Carder, you already came out of that" My arm was once again struck, I deserved that one I'll give it to him, but he walked right into it-
Oh my gosh, I'm laughing again,
and I'm being hit again.
"Okay, I'm sorry, I'm sorry, what about the closet?"

"That square outlining we found on the ceiling of his closet when we were helping him pick an outfit out for something one time, do you remember that?"

My jaw involuntarily dipped down. "Yes! It opened up to the attic we didn't even know we had!"

Carder grabbed my shoulders in excitement. "Yes! That creepy ass attic!"

"This is too entertaining," Giggled Jude at the sight of us, though I probably would too. We looked ridiculous.

At the release of my shoulders, I smiled to Jude, "You're going to lift the opening." I wanted him to actually feel like he was a part of this, not just tagging along and being the encourager.

His eyes widened along with his mouth.

Carder stood up and nodded. "You've been given orders, you are the tree in this group, and this is your duty. Shine bright, star." Carder gave Jude a pat on the back as we went to Colin's room.

This room wasn't completely empty. There were a few boxes pushed in the corner, still waiting to be unpacked. It almost felt wrong to be in this room, especially from just watching Colin's video. It felt like my eyes had another lens over them for a few moments, being able to see everything back in its place until I reached the closet; the lens fell off.

Shake it off, MacArthur.

Carder took the honors of opening the closet door. I gracefully bent down on one knee with my arms extended out, giving a little more pizzazz to the entrance of the task Jude was about to tackle. All he could do was laugh as he walked in, and the two of us followed after I clicked on the light.

No, this closet is *not* very spacious.

We looked up to the square opening Carder had described; you could see where it was separate from the rest of the ceiling. All you had to do was push up and slide it over.

"Okay, guys, I'm tall, but I am not that tall."

"You're the tallest thing we've got. What do you suggest we do, Paul Bunyan" Goodness gracious Carder, just one sentence, one sentence without the sass.

"I have an idea," cutting off whatever conversation that was going to come out of Carder's remark, "Carder, get down on your hands and knees."

"Lucy, I'm flattered, but hell no, this floor is dirty."

Rolling my eyes, I pushed his shoulders down until he gave into my command, then it was time for Jude's instructions. "Alright, Jude, there's your stepping stool."

"Ww- I, I don't wanna just step-"

"Oh my gosh, just do it. She isn't going to change her mind."

I wasn't going to argue; that was pretty accurate.

Holding onto Jude's hand as he stepped onto Carder's back until he got his balance, I let go as he reached for the square opening.

"I know all you eat is pistachios, but holy f- man, you are heavy."

"Thank you, Carder," tiptoeing just a tad making Carder groan as Jude let out a sigh of relief, pushing the square aside onto the attic floor. "Love ya too"

"Alright, Jude, now grab both sides with your hands and lift yourself up into the attic" I felt like I was a coach, and this is the weirdest sport ever.
But my player was stellar as he lifted himself into the attic as my other player dramatically collapsed on the floor the moment Jude's feet were dangling above him.
Jude poked his head out. "This house has amazing ceiling support!"

Giggling while getting my Drama Queen off the floor, we both looked up to him. "Is there a note on the square?"
He disappeared for a moment, coming back with a proud smirk. Jude extended his arm down as far as he could without falling, meeting him halfway as he handed me the note.

"Take a look above you, discover the view.
If you haven't noticed, please do.
Please do. Please do."
-Kermit the Frog'"

"He, he didn't even say anything in this one, just the quote" Looking to Carder and then to Jude to see their reactions, which were identical to mine. "Okay, well, let's break it down."

"Take a look above you; I think it's safe to say he's referring to the attic," Carder pointed out as Jude was prepared with another thought.

"Discover the view- Lucy, have you ever found anything up here? Do you remember?"

Remember Lucy,

come on!
Remember,
remember it.
Please,
Please do,
Please do,
Plea-

"Jude!" Shooting my head up to the ceiling to the anxious look on his face. "Is there a window up there?"

Seeing him examine the area above within a second his face lit up. "Yea! Yea, it's over across the creepy-ass floor Carder was talking about."

"Creepy, ain't it?"

"Yea, just a whole lot"

"Are you guys finished?" Glancing at both of them like a teacher waiting for the class to be quiet. "The windowsill comes off, all you have to do is gently pull the wooden plank out, and there's a small rectangular space in there. I think that's what Colin is talking about; I know it is."

Damn, I sounded confident. I saw Carder look at me with his eyebrows raised from the corner of my eye as Jude nodded and made his way across the creepy-ass attic floor.

Carder and I stood with our arms crossed and our eyes pasted to the ceiling. Listening to the movement overhead like we were listening to one of those old soap opera radio shows. Perking up at the exact moment, we heard the climax of our show.

"You were right! I have it in my pocket; I didn't read it!" Jude's face now in the square opening. "Okay, so how are we going to do this?"

I saw Jude look at me,
and I could feel Carder's eyes on me as well.

"Well," damn it, Lucy, we never plan ahead. "I didn't think that part through"
Carder let out that stupid, sarcastically filled chuckle that instantly makes me want to hit him in the arm.
"Oh, stop, like you thought of anything!"
"I wasn't the one delivering orders!"

"Which is a shock to all of us seeing how much you *loovveee* to talk!"

"I didn't even do anything! You're overdramatic!"

"I'm overdramatic? You're the Drama Qu- HOLY-!" Amid our bickering, Jude had constructed his own exit plan. "Are you alright?!"
Jude jumped down from the attic like a pencil being dropped straight down from a desk.

After lifting himself up with the help of our Queen of not only Drama but Sass and me, he nodded. "Oh completely, I have jumped from trees far taller than that" those grey-blue eyes looked right into mine. "Thank you"
Oh my gosh, and the matching perfect smile.

Carder, irritated, dropped hold of Jude's arm and made his way out; embarrassingly enough, it took me until Carder was out and about in Colin's room to notice I was still holding Jude's arm.
Smooth move Lucy; let's make it through the rest of the day without any other awkward moments.
Let's be honest; that probably won't happen.

Once I clicked the light off and shut the closet door, we all looked at the note.

'I hope you are enjoying this adventure. I'm sorry it isn't the most organized and actually adventurous time we've had in the past. But I hope it is something you will at least remember with a smile. There's no clue for this last one; this one is all on you because I know you can do it. I don't know if you'll remember it right away, but I have a feeling it will- click.'

The rush, the excitement, the tiny lingering tingling in my fingers started to go away as the note went in my pocket. I didn't dare to look back up. I was having trouble remembering; I couldn't remember.
I felt a hand softly grasp my shoulder. I knew that comforting grip; it was Carder's hand.

"Don't beat yourself up; a lot has happened from then to now. Take your time."

"¡El almuerzo esta listo!" Mia's voice rang up the stairs, Jude and me turning to Carder for translation.

"Something about food, I think she's done making lunch" Carder gave Jude a look that somehow, maybe through their '*telepathic bromance*,' got him to go downstairs to Mia. Carder waited for Jude to be out of the room before turning to me, his hand still on my shoulder. "Alright, tell me."

Giving him a slightly confused look, "Tell you what?"

"Lucy, what's bothering you? Tell me what's going on up in that head of yours."

He knows me well. "I'm thinking of," I looked at his eyes, giving him a playful smirk he often throws to me when avoiding specific conversations. "Spaghetti." Along with the smirk, I took his famous forehead kiss trademark and hurried downstairs, hearing him sigh and, not as quickly, follow me.

The table was occupied already by Jude, Mia, and connecting the dots to assume the man holding Mia's hand across the table was her husband.

He had dark eyes like his beautiful wife, light brown hair, and a warm, friendly smile.
"Mia told me a bit of your story," His voice was just as friendly as his grin. "Go ahead and dig in; I know I'm going to, geez it was busy at the office today."
This guy is just friendly all around. I could see he was charismatic; he's a people person.

Carder took the seat next to Mia's husband as I took the seat next to Jude.
"Where are my manners? Excuse me, I'm Reed Russell, and you've met my awesome wife, Mia Russell."
Mia pointed to each of us, saying our names. These two were so cute together, so lovely, and always smiling.
"It's nice to meet you guys; now that we got that out of the way, let's eat." We all joined in for a laugh before our plates got filled with, I swear, the best tasting spaghetti I've had in my whole life.

My taste buds were groovin', having a party of their own. And I was staying engaged with the small table talk happening. My mind felt like it was slow dancing alone around the missing piece of the adventure.
Where in the world was the last note we found?
And why on Earth could I not remember.
With a friendly nudge from Jude's elbow, I was pulled back into the conversation.
"I'm sorry, I was spacing out."

"Oh no worries, it happens to me all the time at work" Oh great, the host was talking to me, and I was practically ignoring him. "I was just going to give my condolences; my brother got in a car accident two years ago. I know how heavy that loss can be." Giving him a sympathetic look, he turned to Mia with a smile of gratitude and brought his attention back to me. "Things get better. It doesn't feel like they will, but trust me, it does. And it's also okay to acknowledge that things *are* getting better."

I couldn't help but smile; she saved him. "Thank you, Reed. I appreciate that a lot." She saved him from grief. "I am sorry for your loss as well." My eyes drifted to Carder, the person who saved me from grief, and he was already looking at me with a slight smile.

"Thank you, some days are harder than others, but you find new reasons, or sometimes just one significant reason to get out of bed every morning. You're doin' just fine; seems you've got a great support system as well."
Reed slid his hand to Mia's and held it. "You know, I'd love to give you this book that helped me a lot after everything happened. I'll go run upstairs and get it-"

"Oh no, please," Pushing my chair out, "You and Mia have been really generous already."

"It's just going to collect dust; it would be a crime not to give it to someone who could benefit from it."
Holy Buckets, yea, this guy is definitely a people person; damn his persuasive charisma.

Surrendering with a sigh and a smile, "Thank you again, Reed, that's very kind. Can I at least get it for you? It would be a crime to make the guy who just had a long day at work go run up and then down the stairs."

He began laughing to the point where he gripped Mia's hand so tightly from the laughter she almost started laughing in pain. As it came to a rest, he turned to his wife, "Lo siento Amor," kissing her hand and then gently grazing his thumb over the skin he had kissed. "Son muy divertido" Mia smiled at me and nodded.

Discreetly I looked to Carder for a silent translation,
trying to read his lips quickly,
Carder, you silently talk too fast.
I think he was saying Reed said sorry for squeezing Mia's hand and that we were funny.

Made sense, good translation, Sass Master.

"If you insist." Reed brought my attention back to him, hoping he didn't notice what I was doing. "Upstairs down the right side of the hall, there's a bookshelf, it's called '*5 Dogs*'. I know the title sounds a little odd and irrelevant, but for some reason, the book really helped me escape during that dark time."

I chuckled, getting out of my chair and making my way up the stairs as I heard the small talk start up again.
Indeed, there it was, '*5 Dogs*' in bold blue letters with a yellow background. Holding the book in my hands, I couldn't believe a stranger was giving me this. This book obviously had a significant impact on him.

With the book cradled in my arms against my chest, I started making my way down the stairs. These stairs, I wonder how many times I've walked up and down them. Each of these steps-
I stopped.
I stopped moving.
What was that-
Lifting one foot back on the stair behind me, I heard it.
As I brought my other foot to the stair, I couldn't even imagine how big my smile was,
I heard it again.
Click.
Moving and kneeling down on the step below, placing the book next to me, I lifted the wooden plank posing as an ordinary step on a regular staircase.
Though this may be one of the most typical staircases on the market of staircases, in no way was this an ordinary step. This was the last hidden place. Removing the plank to uncover the slot underneath contained a large envelope with Colin's handwriting on the front.

'To My Companion'
'From Your Doctor'

I should be happy.
This would have made him smile.
This would have made him proud.
I remembered; it literally clicked.
Just as he cleverly said.
But having the treasure meant this was the end of our last *Doctor* and *Companion* adventure. Holding this envelope in my hand meant goodbye was right around the corner.

The three of us couldn't have thanked Mia and Reed enough for their incredible hospitality. And Mia and Reed couldn't have shown more gratitude for having company; I guess I should have gathered they were pretty new to the town with all the boxes.
As we walked out to the car, I heard Mia call my name, turning back to see them both standing in the doorway. I motioned Carder and Jude to go on ahead to the car, and I would be just a second, kindly approaching the couple once more.

Mia took my hand that wasn't carrying the book and envelope and held it so dearly with both hands. Looking into my eyes with such compassion, I felt like I was going to instantly cry.
"Hermosa niña" Her voice was so soft.

"Beautiful girl," Reed translated in the same tone, but I kept my eyes on Mia.

"Todo estará bien" She embraced my hands tighter.

"Everything will be okay."

Mia had a tear, just a single tear run down her cheek, but her smile was so genuine and filled with hope. "Todo estará bien."

Gently releasing my hands, she gave me one last hug and sent me on my way. I could softly hear her sniffle as they shuffled into the house, and I crawled into the car with glossy eyes.

Jude retook the backseat.

"They are the nicest people in Virginia Beach," Carder stated as he started the car and turned to me before going off into the road. "Do you want to wait to open it? It's okay if you do Lucy-Lou, don't feel like you have-"

"No," I intersected while refusing any tears to slide out of the corners of my eyes. "No, I want to open it now before we start driving."

Carder and Jude both nodded as I turned the envelope over and untangled the red string that has been closing it shut this whole time.

This is it,
here we go, Lucy;
this is it.

I slid my hand in and gripped the contents, spilling the treasure out. A cassette tape and a neatly bounded manuscript I've never seen. Flipping the decently sized document over to see the cover page, I read the title out loud.
"*Riding Shotgun with Cara Sohn*." Pausing as my eyes traveled down to the line below it, "By: C.H. Mac."
Letting out a chuckle of disbelief, I could feel my throat tighten. "He's, he's giving me his story. I read everything he wrote, except this story." I ran my fingertips over each printed letter of the title. "I guess I put it out of my mind because I thought I'd never get to read it." I ran my fingertips across his penname. "He's giving me his finished product; he worked so hard on this."

I held the manuscript in both my hands. I wanted to feel the engraving of the inked letters glide under my skin for so much longer than I had. Feeling a tear come on, I put the story back in the envelope; safe.

Now, for the last item, Colin has to give me. Holding the cassette in my hand, Carder turned his radio settings and turned the stereo up to a reasonable volume. Lifting my arm to put the tape in, my hand was shaking so much out of frustration I tossed the cassette in Carder's lap and hung my head down. My arms crossed over my pulled-up knees, my face hiding in the dark haven I had created for this time.

This time, it's going by too fast.
I heard Carder push the tape in.
This time that I wanted to stretch out forever.
White noise.
This time, more priceless than anything I've ever had.
Now fading out.
But I couldn't afford forever.

"Lucy!" I winced at the sound; Colin sounded so happy, which felt so out of place. "Congratulations, my *Companion*! You have found the treasure! You have successfully completed our adventure! Though I don't know if the story is much of a treasure, I bet you are at least a little relieved at the thought that you finally get to read what I've been hiding from you all these years. I wrote it for you, Lucy, for you to enjoy, for you to have someone you can maybe relate to, to have an escape."
His words reminded me of Reed's in comparison to the book he gave me; my stomach was squeezing into a knot.
"Lucy, you are by far the most amazing person I have the privilege of knowing. Honestly, you are so fricken awesome. I hate that you don't see it every time you look in the mirror, or when you hear yourself talk, or when you see yourself in a picture- there isn't any room or reason to make a change in you. You are my hero, Lucy."

My stomach was heaving, overwhelmed; I couldn't choke down my ugly cries.
"You hear me, you got that? You are a hero Lucy, you're my hero. Every time you look in the mirror, every single time you hear your voice, and appearing in every photo, you remember, that, that's a hero."
Even over my crying, I could hear Colin's voice beginning to crack.
"You're such a beautiful soul Lucy, an old soul trapped in a young body, trapped in a tourist box, trapped in this bubble of an idea that this is all your fault. Trapped in the idea that my choice was because of you. It wasn't because of you, Lucy, deep down, I know that you know- we both know that. You're the only light I have in this world, Lucy. I feel so deeply sad and scared all the time. And nothing is helping. Nothing is working. I feel like I am just draining life and light from you, and that's not fair and-" He gasped. "And I'm," gasping again, getting control of his breathing over his crying, "I'm setting you free, Lucy."
I sat up and looked at the radio like I was staring at him.
"I'm setting you free, off into the world, and out of the boat dock of Virginia Beach to a new adventure."
I felt my head ever so slightly shake in disagreement.
"I love you so much, Lucy, you'll always have me, you will always have me with you. I promise I will be with you. You won't be alone. You won't be alone, but you have to do this. Do this for me, plea- please Lucy, every time you do something new for the first time, every time you take a step in a new place; please remember that you are so much stronger than you realize you really are."
He was trying not to cry so much, I could tell. I was doing the same, but I couldn't help it. This was agonizing.
"You really really are. You are so strong."
A few seconds passed with just the noise of his reducing frantic breaths, cutting them off with a short laugh.
"I remember now what grandpa said in his dream about you."
I moved to the edge of the seat.
"He said, '*Watch her fly Colin, I swear watch that girl fly*.' Man, do I believe him. I believe him. I'm gonna."
I was starting to breathe slower; the tears ran out, hearing Colin clear his throat.
"*Blue skies, comin' your way*,"

He didn't completely lose the sadness in his voice as he started to sing.

"No," Shaking my head more.

"*Bluebirds*"

"No!" Feeling the nerves in my body tightening,
"*Singing your name*."

"No No No!" I slammed my fists on Carder's dashboard.

"*They sing*"

My tear ducts were reloaded,

"*Ll- Lucyy*"

Carder quickly grabbed both my hands and restrained them.

"*You're doin' just fiinee*."

Harshly landing my head where I had just pounded.

"*Blue skies Stayin' your way*,"

I felt a hand rub my upper back in small circles while my crying got louder.

"*Bluebirds Flyin' awaayy*"

I don't think I'll have enough tears to cry ever again.

"*They sing, Luucyy*"

After enduring this pain, I don't think I'll have a reason to.

" *You're doin' just fine.*"

How I wish I had the luxury to afford forever.

" *They sing, Lucy*"
Because I could feel our time coming to an end.

" *You'll be just finnee.*"

If only he knew, in my world, he already sang this goodbye to me.

"I love you, Lucy." Colin's last recorded words, my Colin's last recorded words.

I felt so broken,
so exposed,
so vulnerable.
Embarrassed,
and flooded with an emptiness.
I didn't have the strength Colin said I had; I didn't have the power to look up.

Carder had moved my hands, still in his now gently cupped embrace, to my lap. Jude, who I don't even want to know what he's thinking about me at this moment, was still rubbing my back in slow circles.
But Colin's words echoed through my mind as I finally opened my eyes.
Do this for me.
That's what he wanted, that's what he wants. And if I do it, maybe he really will be with me, but more peacefully, perhaps we can both be in peace.
As I lifted myself up, Jude pulled his hand away in surprise at my sudden movement; Carder gave my hands a squeeze before letting go. I wiped my eyes, and as hard as I could, I swallowed down whatever weeping I had left in me. I turned my body, so I was facing both Carder and Jude. I could feel my face was

red, and I could vividly picture the puffiness of my eyes and the glossy tint in them that would last for a while. But I pulled it together; I pulled whatever courage and strength in me that Colin was talking about and took in a breath, one deep, deep breath.

This is for you, Colin.

"Okay," I nodded, looking to Jude, answering his question. Then turning to Carder to confirm the news, "We're going to New York City."

Follow B.A. McRae's journey on
Facebook, Instagram, TikTok and Twitter
@b.a.mcrae

www.ingramcontent.com/pod-product-compliance
Lightning Source LLC
Chambersburg PA
CBHW020946310726
48980CB00001B/74

* 9 7 8 0 5 7 8 9 4 4 5 7 9 *